THE PROBLEM OF
THE
SURLY
SERVANT

Also by Roberta Rogow

The Problem of the Missing Miss
The Problem of the Spiteful Spiritualist
The Problem of the Evil Editor

THE PROBLEM OF
THE
SURLY
SERVANT

A
CHARLES DODGSON/ARTHUR CONAN DOYLE
MYSTERY

Roberta Rogow

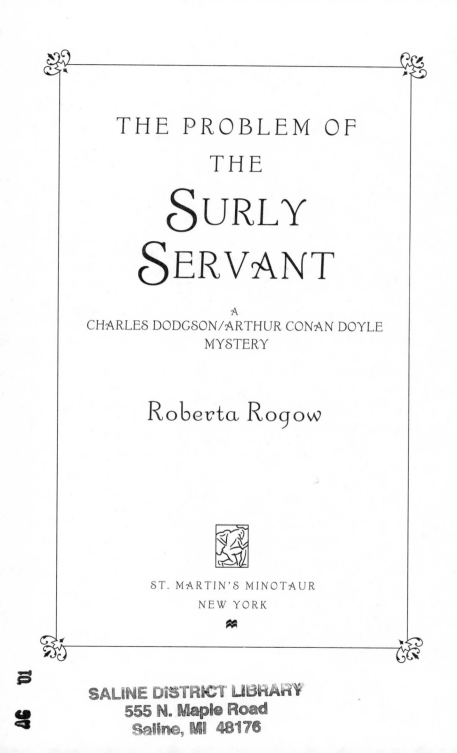

ST. MARTIN'S MINOTAUR
NEW YORK

www.minotaurbooks.com

Library of Congress Cataloging-in-Publication Data

Rogow, Roberta.
    The problem of the surly servant : a Charles Dodgson/
Arthur Conan Doyle Mystery / by Roberta Rogow.—1st ed.
        p. cm
    ISBN 0-312-26638-3
        1. Carroll, Lewis, 1832–1898—Fiction.   2. Doyle,
    Arthur Conan, Sir, 1859–1930—Fiction.   3. Corpus
    Christi College (University of Oxford)—Fiction.
        4. Oxford (England)—Fiction.   5. Authors—Fiction.
    I. Title.
    PS3568.O492 P75 2001
    813'.54—dc21
                                                    2001019583

First Edition: August 2001

10 9 8 7 6 5 4 3 2 1

This book is dedicated to
Miss Elizabeth Wordsworth
and
all those brave women who opened the doors
to higher education for the rest of us to walk through

THE PROBLEM OF
THE
SURLY
SERVANT

CHAPTER 1

M urder was not a part of the curriculum at any of the individual colleges that made up the University of Oxford.
It was not considered a fit subject for study, unless it had happened some centuries previously. Even prospective barristers were
not expected to discuss contemporary murders as reported by the
popular press. An undergraduate might write an essay on the fate
of the Little Princes in the Tower; a learned don might formulate
a theory as to the precise effects of hemlock on Socrates; but the
coarse act of murder was beneath the notice of the eminent scholars and noble students of the University. When it came to brutal
facts, those who wore the Gown preferred to look elsewhere.

While murder in the abstract could be discussed behind the
medieval stone walls and Jacobean bricks of Balliol, Trinity, or
Christ Church, murder in the more immediate sense was the business of the Town, which was made up of the citizens of Oxford
who served the noble youths and distinguished dons. They, on
this brilliant May morning, had other things on their collective
minds. After a brutal winter of agonizing snow and sleet, followed
by freezing winds that tore thatch off ancient cottages and shingles
from more modern edifices, the early spring had brought rains

1

that turned the usually placid stretches of the Cherwell and the Isis into raging torrents. On this beautiful May morning, the town of Oxford had to be refurbished in time for the influx of fond parents come to see their offspring attain that highest of achievements, a First in whatever they were reading. Roofs had to be slated, walls had to be painted, even the streets needed paving. Oxford hummed with activity as workmen plied their various trades, making the Town ready to receive its visitors before the Long Vac left the place vacant of all but the most determined of tourists. Up and down St. Aldgates, across the High, in the Broad and the Turl, tradesmen restocked their shelves while workmen made Oxford ready to live up to its reputation as the very hub of intellectual Britain.

Behind the stone walls, which dated to the days when Oxford had been a collection of churches and ramshackle halls, or the redbrick edifices only recently erected, flowering shrubs sent forth a perfume that attracted bees and butterflies intent on their task of propagating their species. Like everything else in Oxford on that May morning, the insects hummed with their own activities, relishing the warmth of spring after a furious winter. Birds nested in the ancient oaks and willows that hung over the banks of the Holywell Mill Stream and the Cherwell, the two channels that wound their way back to the main stream of the Thames (dubbed the Isis as long as it was within the boundaries of Oxford). Along the Oxford Canal, moles and water rats, toads and other small creatures scrabbled in the undergrowth, going about their business with all the intensity of humanity.

Of all the creatures in Oxford, the students were the most intense. With Trinity term nearly halfway through and the Long Vac looming ahead, those who had neglected their primary task of memorizing Latin verses or formulating elaborate responses to hypothetical questions realized that they had less than three weeks to make up what they should have been doing for the last nine months. Freshmen scrambled to complete their essays before their tutors could assess their work and make the all-important recommendations that would either permit the student to continue his academic career or condemn him to toil in some mediocre teaching position, forever labeled a failure. Second-year students crammed mercilessly, facing the examinations that would ensure them a place among the third-year men.

It was those who were about to graduate who uttered the words, "What do I do now?" with the most heartfelt emotion. What, indeed, would they do now that their studies were presumably completed? Would they venture forth into the Church, staunchly preaching the doctrine of the Church of England, slaving away as curates in country parishes until they could achieve the dignity of a living of their own? Would they become one of the many young men who scurried about in Whitehall or Westminster, doing the bidding of politicians and diplomats, learning the ins and outs of running the Empire? Would they "eat their terms" with the aim of claiming a place at the Bar, and the dignity of the initials Q.C. after their names in due course? Would they find posts in India or Africa, as yet another cog in the great wheel of the Foreign Service? Or would they simply do as so many decorative young men did and find a flat in London where they could while away the days and nights, waiting for someone to die and leave them lands and titles?

The Reverend Mr. Charles Lutwidge Dodgson was not among those worried about his future on this May morning. He stood in Tom Quad, a tall, spare figure in a long, black coat and high, black hat, secure in the knowledge that he would continue, as he had for thirty-four years, as a Senior Student (as the dons are called) at Christ Church. Since he had retired from active teaching and lecturing, he could pursue his eccentric hobbies, write quaint fairy tales or political pamphlets, and rule over the Senior Common Room as curator. His time was not circumscribed by college protocol, and he had the luxury of dining in his own rooms, instead of in Hall, whenever he chose to have a small party of his own.

It was such an impending dinner party that had led Mr. Dodgson to accost Mr. Telling, the Senior Common Room Steward in Tom Quad. Mr. Telling, as tall as Mr. Dodgson but considerably broader, nodded sympathetically and wished Mr. Dodgson had not decided to confront him in person but had used his usual means of communication—a long and detailed letter. It was much easier to deal with Mr. Dodgson's endless requests and constant menu changes in writing. Now Mr. Dodgson was going over the arrangements for his visitors again, a young doctor from Portsmouth and his wife. Telling had been in charge of the arrangements for the Senior Common Room for nearly twenty years. He could have done without Mr. Dodgson's constant nagging. However, like any good butler, he kept his face impassive as he listened to Mr. Dodgson's shrill orders.

"Telling, it is most important that the dinner be served quickly and quietly," Mr. Dodgson said. "Dr. Doyle was kind enough to be my host in Portsmouth, and I feel obliged to return the favor."

"Of course, Mr. Dodgson." Telling did not quite bow. "We must show them the best the House has to offer."

"Dr. Doyle and his wife will arrive this afternoon by train." Mr. Dodgson consulted the flimsy yellow paper in his hand, evidence of Dr. Doyle's fondness for sending telegrams at every opportunity. "Once they have established themselves at the White Hart across the road, they will present themselves at Tom Gate. I shall meet them myself and show them the grounds, and perhaps also the Cathedral. Dr. Doyle expressed a desire to see the chair where King Charles the First sat. We will have tea at four—"

"In the Senior Common Room?" Telling asked.

"Certainly not," Mr. Dodgson replied. "Mrs. Doyle will wish to refresh herself. We will have tea and cakes in my rooms. Then Dr. Doyle and Mrs. Doyle will return to their rooms at the White Hart and change for dinner. We will dine at seven. I have provided a menu . . ." He fished a folded piece of paper out of his coat pocket, together with a length of string, a bag of lemon drops, and a large red silk handkerchief.

Telling took the menu, scanned it, and nodded. "Very good, sir. We will be dining on fowl in Hall, so there will be no difficulty about that. I see you have listed several vegetables . . ."

"And do be more careful about the timing of the cookery," Mr. Dodgson complained. "The potatoes served in Hall have been inedible, either mealy or raw. And for a sweet, I think we shall have a cherry tart, if cherries are available."

"And the wine, sir?" Mr. Telling hinted.

"Sherry, I think, and port for myself and Dr. Doyle. Is there some difficulty, Telling?" Mr. Dodgson frowned as he bent to hear what Telling was trying to say.

"We seem to have some shortage of sherry, sir," Telling said.

Mr. Dodgson's frown deepened. "A shortage? Nonsense! I myself catalogued the entire wine cellar when I first took the position of curator. By my own calculations, we had enough sherry at that time to provide a bottle a day for every Fellow at the House for the next three hundred years."

"That may have been so then," Telling said, "but there are considerable gaps in the rows now."

"What?" Mr. Dodgson's voice, heavy with indignation, could be heard all over the quad.

"If you would care to examine the cellar yourself—," Telling began.

"I accept your word for the losses," Mr. Dodgson said. "Have you checked your findings against the wine list for the Senior Common Room?"

"I have, sir," Telling said grimly. "Unless we have a secret tippler among us, those bottles of sherry were not used by the Senior Students."

Mr. Dodgson looked around the quad. Windows had been raised to catch whatever fitful breeze might find its way past the walls erected by Cardinal Wolsey some three hundred years previously. He lowered his voice, suddenly aware that there might be listeners behind those open windows.

"Could some of the undergraduates have been pilfering?" he asked. "One does not like to think it, but young men can be quite ingenious, and there have always been unruly students."

Telling considered the possibility, then shook his head. "I don't see how," he said. "For one thing, they'd have to get by the stewards, and for another, they'd have to get rid of the bottles afterward. One of the scouts would have noticed, even if the scout on a particular staircase had been, ah—"

"Bribed," Mr. Dodgson said. "I am all too aware that scouts are as human as the next man, and that some of our undergrad-

5

uates are capable of playing on another person's weaknesses, but I would not like to think of the House as a hotbed of corruption. I shall look into the matter, Telling."

"And while you're at it, sir, could you look into another matter?" Telling pressed his advantage before Mr. Dodgson had time to move on.

"Eh?"

"There have been complaints," Telling said. "Certain small items have, er, gone missing."

"This is most distressing," Mr. Dodgson said. "What sort of small items? In which staircase?"

"Small things, sir. Watches, shirtstuds, a tiepin or two." Telling took a deep breath and carried on as Mr. Dodgson's frown creased his usually unlined face. "From Tom Quad principally. Mr. Duckworth mentioned the loss of a broach given to him by his dear mother, now deceased. I realize that this is not, strictly speaking, part of your commission as curator, but I thought you would wish to deal with this matter yourself."

"Quite so. One would not like to bring in the police," Mr. Dodgson said. "I shall look into this also, Telling. Thank you for bringing it to my attention."

"Better you than the Dean," Telling said, with a meaningful glance at the door to the deanery, at the far end of the quad.

"In this case, I agree that Dean Liddell should not be disturbed with so minor a matter." Mr. Dodgson settled his tall hat more firmly on his head.

Telling suddenly asked, "You haven't missed anything yourself, sir?"

"I don't think I have," Mr. Dodgson said. "I shall go to my rooms and make an inventory. If someone has been so thoughtless as to remove something, I shall track him down, and he will regret it." He strode off, across the quad, a tall figure in black, made taller by the old-fashioned high silk hat he insisted on wearing.

"And I wouldn't like to be the one who did it," Telling said to himself as he headed for the stewards' closet, where he would conduct a small investigation of his own. Undergraduates were

6

notoriously untidy, and it would be all too easy for a light-fingered servant to abstract a small piece of jewelry here and there, but not on his patch and not on his watch!

Mr. Dodgson headed toward the corner suite that he had held for the past fifteen years, four rooms that looked out on St. Aldgates from the northeast corner of Tom Quad, where he had settled into a comfortable sort of domesticity. His rooms, provided by Christ Church, were cleaned at regular intervals by one scout or another. He took his breakfast in his room, his meager luncheon wherever he found himself, his tea in the Senior Common Room, and his dinner in Hall, unless, as on this particular evening, he had arranged to give a private dinner party. His duties no longer included active instruction, although he occasionally obliged a colleague by lecturing on logic and mathematics. It could be said that the Reverend Mr. Charles Lutwidge Dodgson led an easy life, in good health and spirits, with few physical ailments and less mental stress than the average householder in England.

Nevertheless, Mr. Dodgson fretted over this meeting with the young man from Portsmouth. Their last encounter had been hectic, to say the least, involving a labor riot, a violent fall of snow, and several deaths. He had not had time to do much more than encourage the nephew of his old friend, Dicky Doyle, in his literary endeavors. Since then, Dr. Doyle had informed him that he had written something quite new, something that he wished to show Mr. Dodgson before sending it off to his usual publishers. Mr. Dodgson sincerely hoped that this time he would not be embroiled in some nasty police matter, as had happened every time he and Dr. Doyle had met since their first encounter the previous August. It would be pleasant to show the young man and his charming wife the glories of Oxford without the interference of murder and mayhem.

Meanwhile, there was the problem before him. Several solutions presented themselves, but only one would be the correct one. Mr. Dodgson loped across the quad, a tall black figure against the gray stones, yet another of the Great Monuments of Oxford.

At the same time, the object of his thoughts was moving toward Oxford on the afternoon train. The railway had come relatively late to Oxford, over the objections of those who preferred to keep the lure of the fleshpots of London out of the way of susceptible undergraduates and even more susceptible dons. Nevertheless, the Town would have its railway station, and the Town got it, albeit as far away as was legally possible from the colleges that clustered around High Street, Broad Street, and St. Giles.

Dr. Doyle, the muscular young doctor from Southsea, peered out the window of their compartment as the train slowed down at the Oxford railway station. His blue eyes sparkled; his red hair and mustache fairly crackled with delight. "I can't tell you how much I am looking forward to this," Dr. Doyle enthused.

Touie, his sweetly pretty wife, sensibly refrained from reminding her husband that he had been telling her exactly that ever since the decision had been made to break their journey north at Oxford for a day.

"It will give me the opportunity to see the scene at firsthand," he assured her. "I've already thought of several scenes to set in the Oxford country."

"I'm sure you will be inspired, Arthur. Do you have the portmanteau?" Touie took over, as her husband continued to wax rhapsodically about their destination.

"I'll be doing a bit of walking about, but you can shop for something for the Ma'am." Dr. Doyle made sure he had his portfolio, with its precious manuscript, tucked under his arm.

"Your mother is so self-sufficient, Arthur. It is difficult to buy something for her." Touie gathered up her shawl, a small reticule, and a larger net bag that held her husband's newspaper and two books they had brought with them to while away the time spent on the train. Her husband opened the door to their compartment.

Dr. Doyle continued to chatter as he handed his wife onto the platform. "Not to worry, Touie. She likes books, of course, and Oxford is full of quaint shops. And you will like the Cathedral." He looked about him. "Where is my hat?"

"On your head, Arthur."

8

"Where is my manuscript?"

"Under your arm," Touie pointed out. "And I do hope Mr. Dodgson will find the time to read your new story. I think it is quite the best thing you have ever done."

Dr. Doyle shifted the bulky portfolio from his right arm to his left, so that he might carry the portmanteau that held their modest wardrobes for the trip. "This is going to be wonderful!" Dr. Doyle crowed.

Touie sincerely hoped that Oxford would live up to her volatile husband's expectations and that all would go well. She was not particularly looking forward to their final destination. The Ma'am, as Arthur called his mother, could be prickly, and there had been some sort of distress about his father. Touie kept her fears to herself and followed her husband to the platform.

Dr. Doyle eyed the various vehicles lined up before them as they left the railway station. How should they approach their host? Should they take the omnibus? Should he hire one of the bath chairs for Touie, to be pushed along by one of the lugubrious chairmen, while he walked beside it?

"We shall go in style," he decided, imperiously beckoning a cab. "The White Hart," he ordered. He grinned happily at his wife. The Great Oxford Adventure had officially begun!

CHAPTER 2

W hat do we do now?"
    The Big Question hung almost visibly over the two
young men now lounging after an ample luncheon served in their
upper-story rooms on the west side of Tom Quad, overlooking
St. Aldgates.

Lord Nevil Farlow, the ostensible host, was a tall young man,
with biceps well developed from three years of rowing, long legs
that were needed on the cricket field, and a head hard enough to
sustain various knocks and falls from horses during hunting sea-
son. His fair hair was worn short, as if to announce to the world
that he was no Aesthete but a Hearty, one of those who achieved
more acclaim on the playing field than in his tutor's study. In the
course of time he would be the fifth Viscount Berwick, inheriting
whatever his eccentric father had left of a once sizeable fortune.
One would think that such a young man would have no cares,
but his blue eyes were troubled as he stared out the window that
faced St. Aldgates.

His guest sprawled on a well-sprung armchair and added to the
smoky atmosphere that wafted through the open windows into

the May air outside. Lord Herman Chatsworth, the youngest son of the Marquis of Digby (dubbed Minimum, or Minnie), was short, dark, and wiry, with a deceptively dim expression that was belied by the acute intelligence behind his eyes. He made an expansive gesture with his cigar, as if summing up their long friendship that had begun as schoolboys at Eton and carried on through three years at Christ Church.

"What's the good of all this Latin and Greek when it don't get you anywhere?" Chatsworth declaimed, with a wave of his cheroot. "I say, Nev, what are we supposed to do when we get our degrees and go forth into the world? I don't suppose you'd want to follow in your pater's footsteps and find a place at Court?"

Farlow emitted something between a snort and a laugh. "I'd only be in the way at Marlborough House. I'm a big enough embarrassment to the Mater as it is, a great lad like me, and she still playing the soubrette." He gloomily contemplated the photograph of his mother, dressed to the nines for a party or ball, propped up on the mantelpiece and sniffed his indignation. "As for Her Majesty, she wants no part of anyone or anything connected with HRH. I'd do better if I were a great hairy Highlander with a braw, braw kiltie. Or perhaps one of those Indians she's taken to carting about with her. What about you, Minnie? Thinking of standing for Parliament? That's where most younger sons wind up these days."

"I leave that to my brothers," Chatsworth said with a shrug. "Michael's got his seat in the Lords, and Minor's working with the Home Secretary. Can't have two of us in the House. Makes for confusion." He took another pull at his cheroot and blew a smoke ring. "Of course there's that ranch in America. I rather liked that last summer. You should have come with me, Nev."

"All the way to some godforsaken prairie to look at a lot of cows?" Farlow drew on his cigar and with an air of desperation let out a stream of smoke. "I was just thinking . . ."

"Don't do that, Nev. Bad for the brain." Young Mr. Chatsworth blew another perfect smoke ring. It was his greatest, and some thought his only, talent. "Of course, we could get a flat in London, find a man, and see some life. It's the least they'd expect of us after three years of slaving away here."

"That takes money," Farlow said pettishly. "At least you've got the cows."

"Only the income, Nev, and it's not all that much." Chatsworth tried to mollify his leader. "I can't help it if the Mater's brother emigrated. Not a bad chap, Uncle Badcock. Chip off the old block, I'm told. Went out with no more than a pocketful of dollars and wound up with the ranch and the cows. He told me I could come back anytime I liked." Chatsworth grinned and waved his cheroot gleefully. "You don't need Latin or Greek in Wyoming."

Farlow grimaced. "There you are, Minnie. He's made you the offer. All I've got is a pater who's thrown every penny we have over the card table, a mater who's no better than she should be, and a great pile of a house with leaks in every room. Last time I was home the Mater had drawn up a list of likely candidates for title of the future Lady Berwick, each one more ghastly than the next. There's a new crop of Americans coming over this summer, each with a doting papa and an ambitious mama, and a bucketful of dollars."

"Americans aren't all that bad," Chatsworth said. "They're rather nice, when you get to know them."

"Of course, you're a younger son," Farlow retorted. "You're not on the marriage market. I'm an heir, which makes me fair game for the matchmaking mamas. My revered parents have let Berwick Place for the summer to a party consisting of Mrs. Wilfred Whyte and her three daughters, her cousin, and some woman they hired to be their chaperon. Meanwhile, the Mater and Pater traipse off to Deauville in attendance to HRH. No thought for me, of course. I'm under orders to play host to this bevy of American beauties and pick one of them to refurbish the family fortunes." He swallowed the rest of his wine as if he had just taken the cup offered to Socrates.

"Steady on, Nev!" Chatsworth exclaimed.

12

"It's enough to make one take to crime!" Farlow exploded.

His follower was truly alarmed. "Nev, you can't! A gentleman can't be a criminal."

"Why not?" Farlow turned to his companion. "From what I can tell, the founder of my noble family tree got his fortune by piracy back in Good Queen Bess's time, which is simply robbery on the high seas."

"Well, you can't do it now," Chatsworth objected. "The navy's dead set against piracy, and highway robbery is not very profitable, not even in Wyoming. They hanged a chap while I was there. Very nasty, I assure you. Burglary? Ha! I can just see you creeping about in a jersey and mask. Besides, even if you did steal things, what would you do with the, um, loot? It's not as if you could pop things into pawn every day. Someone would rumble you, and there you are."

"Where are you?" Farlow asked, his attention turned once more to the activities in St. Aldgates, where a fellow in a plaid Balbriggan coat had just got off a cab and was handing a woman down, presumably to enter the White Hart.

"In prison," Chatsworth snapped back. "I don't think it's very pleasant."

"There are other crimes," Farlow said. "Blackmail, for instance."

Before Chatsworth could counter this, another student burst into the room.

"Has anyone seen my studs?" Gregory Martin demanded, his eyes blinking behind wire-rimmed spectacles, his sandy hair on end, and his round face red with the effort to keep his temper.

"What makes you think they're here, Greg?" Farlow asked.

"It would be just like you, Nev. You'd take them for a rag and think it was fun to watch me fuss." Young Mr. Martin gestured at his open collar, visible under his short student's gown. "I've got a tutorial in fifteen minutes, and old Duckworth is that particular about dress. I'm nearly finished, and I do want to come out ahead with the Duck."

"Don't see why you even bother," Chatsworth said, blowing

13

another smoke ring. "You're being ordained at the end of summer, with a nice living set up for you, whether you get a First or not."

"That isn't the point," Martin told his friend, as he fussed with his collar. "If one is going to do something, one should do it as well as one can."

Chatsworth made a rude noise. "You're not a parson yet, so don't preach at us. What did you do with your own studs?"

"I thought I left them in my shirt, but they're gone. They were rather nice, too, pearls from my mother's wedding necklace. Are you chaps sure you haven't seen them?" Martin peered through his spectacles at the assortment of oddities on Farlow's desk. His thick fingers poked through a wooden box that contained several stickpins, a gold watch fob, and various mismatched shirt studs.

"You could ask Ingram. He knows everything," Chatsworth put in.

"Ingram's not about, and I need those studs," Martin objected.

"Oh, take mine, and be off to your tutorial." Farlow rummaged in the box and found several round objects to be inserted into the shirtfront.

"And what's this about blackmail?" Mr. Martin struggled with the studs, until Chatsworth took pity on him and fastened the recalcitrant shirtfront into place.

"Oh, Nev here thought he might give it a go, although who he'd blackmail I don't know," Chatsworth said carelessly.

Martin's face grew stern. "Now see here, Nev, that's too much," he protested. "Blackmail's a rotter's game. Even if I weren't going into Orders, I'd have to cut you dead if I found out that you'd been doing that sort of thing."

"Oh, Nev didn't really mean it, did you?" Chatsworth finished his task and brushed Martin's shoulders off with a final pat.

Farlow smiled. It changed his whole face. Instead of looking like a sulky child, he looked like something Raphael might have painted. "Of course I didn't," he said. "Besides, as Minnie said, who would I blackmail? You have to know something that someone else doesn't want known, and everyone I know who might be blackmailed is unimpeachable."

"True," Chatsworth agreed. "You can't demand money for telling something that isn't really a secret, can you? I mean, everyone knows that your lovely mama was on the stage, so that's out. And as for your father's friends, well the Marlborough House set is—"

Martin cut him off. "That is neither here nor there. If I hear of any more such nonsense from you lot, I'll do worse than cut you. I . . . I won't row with you. Then where will you be, eh?" With that Parthian shot, the future clergyman clattered down the stairs, leaving his friends to their cigars once more.

"He's right, you know," Chatsworth said. "Blackmail's no game for a gentleman. What's more, you won't get anything by it. No one here's got enough of the ready to make blackmail pay. Although . . ."

"Yes?" Farlow glanced at him. "What do you know, Minnie?"

Chatsworth suddenly regretted having started something he might not be able to stop. "There's old Dodgson. He must have made something from those books of his."

"If you're going to trot out that old stuff about him making sheep's eyes at the Liddell girls, that's ancient history." Farlow sniffed. "He used to escort them about, take them on the river, that sort of thing; but that was when they were children."

"My brother Michael said that when he was a Fresher there was some sort of to-do about a squib someone wrote about Mrs. Liddell and poor old Dodgson," Chatsworth said. "The Dean didn't like it and everyone who wrote it was rusticated. But there's something better than that." His dark eyes gleamed with mischief.

Farlow's eyebrows rose. "What's the old boy been up to?"

"He's a jailbird," Chatsworth said, with a gleeful grin.

"What!" Farlow exclaimed.

"My brother Minor had to bail him out of Bow Street back in February when he went to London and didn't come back for three days." Chatsworth chortled happily. "According to my brother, he'd been caught up in all that fuss in Trafalgar Square, got picked up as a rioter, and had to be got out. Minor couldn't stop going on about it."

15

"And he wouldn't like Dean Liddell to know about that, would he?" Farlow said meditatively.

"But it would be a nasty thing to do to the poor old chap," Chatsworth said after a moment's thought. "And he was my brother Michael's tutor . . . no, we can't," he finished, stubbing out the remains of his cheroot. "I'm sorry, Nevil, but Greg's right. Blackmail's not the thing, and we can't do it. I tell you what, let's get the boat out and get a practice in before the river gets too crowded."

"You go on," Farlow said. "I've still got this Latin to finish. I say, as soon as Greg's finished with the Duck, get him and the others over to the boathouse, and we'll get in some time before dinner. And if you see Ingram, get him in here to take this stuff away."

He waved at the table, still strewn with the remains of luncheon. Chatsworth strolled out, leaving Farlow to his Latin dictionary.

Farlow's beautiful brow furrowed in thought as he considered his financial difficulties again. He sighed mightily.

His labors were interrupted by a tap at his door. "Come!"

A tall man in the black coat, white shirt, and bowler hat worn by the scouts and stewards of Christ Church hovered in the doorway. "I've done those errands of yours," he said gruffly. "I suppose you want me to clear away now."

"If you would be so kind," Farlow said, with biting sarcasm.

"And you may be interested in knowing that I have spoken to certain gentlemen regarding certain other matters." Ingram's long face grew longer. "I greatly fear, sir, that they are becoming insistent. The debt is owed and it must be paid."

"Yes, yes, I know all about it," Farlow fairly shrieked. "Tell them . . . tell them I shall see to it as soon as I can."

Ingram bowed, turned to leave, then turned back. "You know, there is a way to get around it, sir."

Farlow looked more cheerful. "They wouldn't take a *Post* obit, would they?"

"Not bloody likely," Ingram said coarsely, losing some of his polished facade. "Your pa is well known to be in perfect health.

16

He was seen at Deauville Races, in company with a 'certain royal person,' and no one's going to take anything on his leaving this earth in the near future. No, what the persons have suggested is something else. There is a certain boat race to be held here in a month's time—"

"Eights Week," Farlow interrupted him. "What about it?"

"It would be to a certain person's advantage if they could have advance information as to the fitness and, ah, willingness of the, ah, participants . . ." Ingram's voice trailed off, leaving the rest of the thought to Farlow's imagination.

It took a few minutes for the implications of the suggestion to sink in. Then Farlow exploded in wrath.

"Do you mean that I'm to go out and spy for you?" he exclaimed. "And all so that the chaps in London can get better odds?"

"If the information was correct, some adjustment could be made on your debt," Ingram said smoothly. "The persons to whom you owe a debt of honor—"

"No honor with those thieves," Farlow muttered fiercely.

"—they might put off payment of the debt completely." Ingram ignored the interruption.

Farlow closed his eyes in despair and ran his fingers over his head, while Ingram's eye was caught by the box on the desk. His quick fingers went through the various objects, lighted on one, and nipped it up while the younger man's back was turned to him.

Farlow stared out the window. There was no answer to his difficulties there. The street was full of passersby: students scurrying to tutorials or the library, dons strolling along contemplating the universe (or perhaps just the possibility of jam cakes for tea), cabs, drays, and private carriages, even two bath chairs trundling along with ladies on their way to or from paying the all-important calls that regulated the social world.

Ingram permitted himself a smug smile, which vanished as the younger man turned away from the window. "Don't blame me, Mr. Farlow. I'm only a messenger."

Farlow's mouth twitched in annoyance as he reached for his

cigar case. Ingram was there before him, offering the cigar and ready with a light.

"And did you deliver my message?" Farlow asked.

"I did, sir."

"Then all we have to do is wait, and as soon as I have the dibs, I can pay off everyone, including your bloodsuckers."

"Don't be too long about it, sir," Ingram warned him. "These people are not going to wait for someone to die."

"Oh, no one has to die," Farlow said, with a careless wave of his hand. "Just go about your business, Ingram, and tell your people that they'll get their damned money, one way or another."

Ingram bowed himself out, and Farlow turned back to his contemplation of St. Aldgates. This had to work! he told himself. The Old Boy would have to stump up, and then he could pay off these cursed leeches.

Ingram closed the door to the rooms behind him and opened his hand. The young fool hadn't even noticed that his diamond stickpin was missing. So much the better! This post had not been one that Ingram would have taken, given the choice, but it had opened previously untapped opportunities for a clever and resourceful man. Ingram considered himself both clever and resourceful, far worthier than the aristocratic youths whose soiled linen he picked up and whose dishes he cleared away. None of them would miss a trinket here and there.

He dodged into one of the open doorways to avoid Telling, who was on the prowl on the staircase leading to young Farlow's rooms. The chief scout was becoming suspicious. Perhaps he should be more careful, he thought, but there was a sure thing coming at Newmarket, and all he needed was a few pounds to put up for a truly spectacular win.

Ingram looked at the untidy sitting room. "Undergraduates!" he said to himself. "Always expecting someone else to clean up after them." Well, that was what scouts were for, weren't they? He had best get on with the job he was supposed to be doing before Telling came around to ask why he wasn't doing it.

Two miles north of Christ Church, three young women also asked the question: "What shall we do now?"

Miss Dianna Cahill and her two dearest friends, Mary Talbot and Gertrude Bell, sat at the long refectory table, which was the primary furnishing of the library at Lady Margaret Hall, a room lined with bookshelves but seriously devoid of books. They bent over a packet of papers at one end of the table, while Miss Daphne Laurel, the oldest student at Lady Margaret Hall, tried to concentrate on her own book a few chairs away from them.

"I don't understand what the great fuss is about," Gertrude said, with a toss of her auburn tresses. "It's just a photograph." She was a strongly built young woman, whose athletic prowess was evident in her slim figure and general air of determination.

"It's not just the picture," Dianna said. "It's what goes with it." Her plump cheeks reddened under her mop of fair curls, which were caught up in a blue ribbon in a knot at the top of her head, while her blue eyes filled with tears as she stared at the photograph before her.

Mary Talbot, a petite brunette whose gentle voice disguised a nature every bit as determined as Gertrude's, looked over the page and the photograph on the table before them. "I cannot believe that anyone could be so vile, so cruel, as to demand that you leave Oxford because of this!" She tapped the printed page before them.

"But why?" Dianna asked plaintively. "I don't know what these words mean, exactly, but it sounds horrid. And why does it have my picture with it?"

Gertrude looked over the printed page. "It's something about kissing," she pointed out. "And I know what that is." She indicated a very short word, and pointed to a portion of her own anatomy.

Dianna referred to the handwritten letter that accompanied the printed page and the photograph. "Leave this University at once, or this will go to every college and newspaper in Oxford," she read.

"Well, you can't do it." Gertrude pounded her fist on the table in righteous indignation. "I never heard such rot!"

"I beg your pardon, Miss Bell?" Miss Laurel turned from her book to stare at the younger woman. "Did you address me?"

"Of course not, Miss Laurel," Gertrude said. She turned back to her friends, who were hovering over the offensive pages.

"Unfortunately, some people will do anything to remove female students from Oxford." Mary sighed. "Although why they should pick on you, Dianna, is more than I can tell. No offense, dear, but you're hardly First material, and your family isn't particularly well-connected."

"I don't understand it either," Dianna said. "But this . . . this stuff . . . and the photograph . . ."

"How did it come to be taken?" Mary asked, dispassionately regarding the object before her. It showed a six-year-old girl, frontally nude, with one hand on a globe and the other hiding her crotch. The background was very dark, and the child's face was almost hidden in shadows, but there could be no mistaking the kinky curls that clustered about her face. This was Dianna Cahill, without a doubt.

Dianna looked helplessly at her two friends. "It was when my father had been appointed to his living in Northumberland. We broke our journey here in Oxford, and my parents went to tea with the Liddells at Christ Church."

"And they brought you along with them? How odd," Mary commented. "Why didn't they leave you with your nurse?"

"There was some commotion in the house," Dianna recalled. "We were staying with my aunt and uncle Roswell, and there was to be a visitor, and I was to be gotten out of the house so that I shouldn't see her. At least, that's what I think I heard."

"How perceptive of you," Miss Laurel commented, from her place at the table.

"I don't know about that, but I do remember being heartily bored at the tea party where everyone was older than I, even the other girls who thought me quite a baby. And then a gentleman came to deliver a book, I think, and he saw me and asked if he might take me to his rooms for tea. And we had the most delightful time . . . and he asked if I would like to be photographed. And so he took the pictures."

"Without your clothes on?" Gertrude's blue eyes fairly danced with the thought.

"I was six years old and thought nothing of it," Dianna said apologetically. "And he was quite respectful, and I felt so comfortable with him; and it was such great fun that I let him pose me with the book and the globe; and then we had jam cake, which I was never allowed at home. Not even at Aunt Roswell's, and she kept a very good table."

Dianna helped herself to the cake in front of her. Clearly, she had made up for lost time.

Mary frowned at the packet before them. "Who took the picture?" she asked.

Dianna frowned. "I can't remember!" she wailed.

"Try!" Gertrude ordered.

"Could it have been Mr. Dodgson?" Miss Laurel offered, laying aside her book and moving closer to the trio.

Dianna stared at the older woman. "That name does sound familiar. I suppose it could have been. Why do you think so?"

"I have lived in Oxford for some time," Miss Laurel explained. "Mr. Dodgson was well known as a photographer of children. It may well have been he who took the photograph."

"What I don't understand is why this person should single you out for this . . . this outrage!" Gertrude exploded.

Dianna's eyes filled with tears. "No more do I! Examinations are coming, and I don't know what to do! If I fail, I disappoint my dear aunt and uncle Roswell, who have spent so much time and money on my education. If I pass, this . . . thing . . . will be . . ."

"Will be what? Sold on the public market? I think not," Gertrude said staunchly. "I say, tell this blackguard to go about his business. 'Publish and be damned!' "

"Gertrude!" Miss Laurel corrected her wayward classmate. "Moderate your language!"

Mary covered the offending photograph with the even more offending letter. "The real question is, how did this blackmailer find this photograph? Once he found it, how did he find you?"

21

Dianna lifted her shoulders in a mute shrug of complete incomprehension.

"More to the point," Gertrude said, taking charge of her more reticent schoolmates, "what do we do about it?"

"We can't give in," Mary said firmly.

"Of course not," Gertrude agreed. She thought for a moment, then went on. "We have to find out where that photograph came from. Once we know that, we can find out who sent it; and once we know that, we can deal with him ourselves."

"But that means, I have to ask Mr. Dodgson," Dianna quavered. "I can't just call on him out of the blue! He doesn't remember me at all. I saw him when he called on Edith Rix, and he never even looked at me."

Gertrude's quick mind was already planning a strategy. "Weren't you going to the Cathedral today to look at the glass?" she asked Dianna.

"Yes, I was," Dianna admitted. "Miss Wordsworth gave permission, and Dean Liddell had no objections, so long as I was there within visiting hours and left before Evensong. Only," her blue eyes grew troubled, "we need a chaperon, and Miss Wordsworth has to go with Tessa to the lecture at Balliol—"

Miss Laurel coughed gently to remind the others of her presence. "Excuse me, Miss Cahill, but perhaps Miss Wordsworth will permit me to accompany you on this excursion. I am, after all, somewhat older than the rest of you, and I have been a governess."

Dianna considered this offer. "And what shall we do, once we get to Christ Church?"

"We must find Mr. Dodgson and ask him what happened to that photograph," Gertrude decided, with the air of a general who had devised the winning campaign.

"You can't think Mr. Dodgson had anything to do with this!" Mary protested. "Everyone knows he's the kindest, sweetest gentleman, and besides, he wrote *Alice in Wonderland*. He couldn't be a blackmailer!"

"But he might have left that photograph about, and someone

else might have found it," Gertrude said, the light of battle blazing in her eyes. "Miss Laurel, go ask Miss Wordsworth if you can come with us, and then let's get our hats and gowns. We're going to Church!"

CHAPTER 3

M r. Dodgson was waiting at the elaborately carved gateway that opened out onto St. Aldgates as the bell of Great Tom struck three. It mattered not that the time on the watches and clocks of Oxford stood at 3:05. Oxford was five degrees past the delineator set at the Greenwich Naval Academy, ergo Oxford University was exactly five minutes behind everyone else, and the school liked it that way.

The young man in the tweed suit bursting through the sea of black gowns was clearly five minutes ahead of everyone else. His mustache fairly bristled with excitement as he took in the medieval architecture about him; his blue eyes sparkled and he seemed to breathe in the scholarly atmosphere. Behind him trotted his wife, a young woman in a tartan traveling suit with a modest bustle, topped off with a straw hat trimmed with a matching tartan ribbon, the very image of the provincial doctor's wife ready to assist her husband in all things.

Dr. Arthur Conan Doyle spotted the tall figure in black at the gate and waved vigorously. "There he is, Touie!"

"Of course, Arthur," Touie answered breathlessly, trying to keep up with her husband's stride.

"Mr. Dodgson has promised to show us the Cathedral," Dr. Doyle reminded her. "I particularly want to see the chair that the king used before Naseby."

"I'm sure Mr. Dodgson will show it to you," Touie said, having caught up to her husband.

Mr. Dodgson lifted his hat and bowed ceremoniously to his guests. "Good afternoon, Dr. Doyle, Mrs. Doyle. I hope you are settled into your rooms?"

"Quite comfortably, thank you," Dr. Doyle said, with a glance across the street at the White Hart Inn. "An old coaching inn! Just the setting for my book!"

"That inn has been there since the reign of Richard the Second," Mr. Dodgson informed them, as he led the young couple into the quad. "Before the House was built, I might add." He gestured toward the pond in the center of the central grassy plot. "There was a statue of Mercury in that pool, and it is still called by that name. Some of the undergraduates find it amusing to duck each other in it, but it is strictly forbidden to do so."

The three adults stepped aside as two undergraduates hurried down the path, their gowns flapping behind them.

"Where are they off to?" Mrs. Doyle wondered.

"Lectures, possibly, or to the library," Mr. Dodgson replied. "At least, one hopes so. Many of the undergraduates seem to prefer sport to scholarship."

Dr. Doyle laughed heartily. "On such a day as this, I can only agree with them. I only wish my own student days had been so pleasant."

Mr. Dodgson recalled that Dr. Doyle had spent his time at the University of Edinburgh, where the prevailing cold and damp might well have encouraged his interest in the murkier side of life.

Mr. Dodgson continued his tour of the grounds, keeping to the south side of the quadrangle. "These buildings were designed by Sir Christopher Wren, although they were enlarged and, um, improved by our present dean." He paused, then decided not to tread on delicate ground. He detested the so-called improvements made by Dean Liddell and had written several biting pamphlets giving his opinion of the new belfrey (which he had likened to a tea caddy) and the passage into the gardens behind the walls of Tom Quad (which he had dubbed "the tunnel").

Instead, he pointed out the noble proportions of the buildings, and reminded his guests that the founder of Christ Church was none other than Cardinal Wolsey. "Of course, after his unfortunate dismissal by King Henry the Eighth, the House was expropriated, so to speak, by the king."

"Why do you keep calling it 'the House'?" Touie asked innocently.

"Why, because it is God's House, Mrs. Doyle," Mr. Dodgson explained. "And it is never referred to as Christ Church College. It is Christ Church or the House."

Touie made understanding noises. Dr. Doyle looked around him, mentally docketing the proportions of the quad for future reference. Mr. Dodgson quickly led his guest toward the Cathedral, keeping his back to the bell tower.

Dr. Doyle stopped at the entrance to the Cathedral to take in its medieval carving, much to the discomfort of two dons in caps and gowns who were trying to round the corner of the quad. Clearly, Mr. Dodgson was in full instructor mode, pointing out all salient features of Christ Church Cathedral.

"This is the smallest cathedral in Britain," he stated. "You do know why it is called a cathedral and not merely a church?" He looked expectantly at the Doyles, prepared to elucidate when ready.

"It's because of the Bishop, isn't it?" Touie smiled sweetly at Mr. Dodgson. "Is not the Dean of Christ Church also its Bishop?"

"I see you have informed yourself before coming here, Mrs. Doyle." Mr. Dodgson looked slightly put out. Some of his thunder had been stolen.

Touie glanced at her husband, who was by now entranced by the brass plates fastened to the walls of the church. "Arthur and I have been preparing for this excursion ever since you gave us the invitation," she told Mr. Dodgson. "It is something of a change for us."

"I understood that you were going north to visit Dr. Doyle's parents," Mr. Dodgson said, steering Touie around the small chairs that had been placed for the afternoon service.

"It's Arthur's father. He is not well." Touie's pretty face clouded. "And there is some difficulty about his mother as well. And there are his sisters . . ." She stopped, conscious of having said too much. "But this little excursion is just what Arthur needs. He is so enthusiastic about his historical novel, and he will find so much material here . . ."

"Eh?" Mr. Dodgson leaned closer to Touie.

Dr. Doyle had come up behind them. From the look on Mr. Dodgson's face, he could tell that she had just opened the one topic he had thought to broach himself. He cleared his throat, glanced at the older man, and blurted out, "Mr. Dodgson, while we are here, I wondered if . . . if you could perhaps get me into the Bodleian Library."

Mr. Dodgson turned his attention toward the younger man. "You did not mention the Bodleian in our correspondence," he said, a note of disapproval in his voice.

Dr. Doyle looked abashed. "I only thought that since you have been so kind as to encourage my literary ambitions, you might put in a word with the librarians. I don't want to make off with anything, I only want to see one or two letters . . ." His voice trailed off under the stony frown of the don.

"Dr. Doyle," Mr. Dodgson said frostily, "you are the nephew of an old acquaintance, and therefore I have continued to pursue this particular friendship. I have read your stories and found them quite interesting and well-written, which you may take as a compliment since I rarely read fiction of any sort. However, you must not think to take further advantage of my position. I have been sublibrarian here at the House, and I can make some of the collection here available to you, but I have no influence at the Bodleian."

Dr. Doyle's cheerful smile faded. Then he shrugged and said, "I apologize for thinking I could take advantage of the opportunity to look at the rare manuscripts, sir. Particularly accounts of the Bloody Assizes, which were held in the West Country and which figure largely in my new book."

"Can you not find such materials in London? I might suggest The Royal Archive." Mr. Dodgson ignored the party of students behind them to glare at Dr. Doyle.

"I know, but while we were here, I thought . . ." Dr. Doyle took one look at Mr. Dodgson's face and realized that he had made a massive error in judgment. Mr. Dodgson did not like to be surprised with impromptu requests. Dr. Doyle changed his tactics. "Of course, if the Bodleian Library is unavailable, I will have to find my research elsewhere. Perhaps I might use the library here at Christ Church. And I am particularly glad to see the Cathedral," he added, "and King Charles's chair, and the glass windows. The only one dedicated to Saint Thomas à Becket to survive the Dissolution, I understand?"

Mr. Dodgson unbent slightly. Dr. Doyle was young and bumptious and had to be put in his place. He was not so far removed in years from the undergraduates who were beginning to empty the Cathedral as they drifted back to their own rooms for tea. If Dr. Doyle wished to examine the Cathedral, Mr. Dodgson was perfectly willing to act as guide.

"The Cathedral is, of course, open to any of the public who wish to attend service," Mr. Dodgson said loftily. "However, the library is meant for the students only. I doubt that the materials at hand are those that you need. However," he added, "I can have a word with the librarian. Of course, you may not remove anything. If your time here is as short as your wife suggests, you may not be able to complete your researches before you have to continue your journey."

With that, Dr. Doyle had to be satisfied. Mr. Dodgson took over again. He would not let Dr. Doyle go off on his own but led his young guests to the altar.

There was no service in progress, but the Cathedral held a number of visitors. In the north transept three students in gowns were taking the measurements of the tomb of Saint Frideswide. Next to them a young man was proudly showing an older couple the windows, designed and executed by the fashionable artist Burne-Jones, that flanked the altar.

Mr. Dodgson pointed them out to Touie with the air of one who has done it so often that the recitation has been memorized.

"This window commemorates Frederic Vyner, who was slain by brigands in Greece in 1870. This window is dedicated to Saint Cecilia. And this—" he indicated the grandest of the three—"is the Life of Saint Frideswide. It was she, of course, who founded the abbey that became Oxford."

Touie gazed at the elaborate window and marveled at the complexity of the design. Each of the many panels depicted an incident in the life of what must have been an extraordinary woman. Here she was, repulsing an overeager suitor; there, dedicating her church. In one section of the window was the famous Well of Healing, and at the very end of the sequence, in the lower right-hand corner, the Death of Saint Frideswide.

Touie looked closer. Surely, that was not a . . . a "convenience"? In the background of a medieval death scene? Was the eminent artist having his little joke at the expense of his scholarly patrons? What should she say? Should she remark on it, showing that she had noticed it, or should she discreetly ignore it?

Her confusion was alleviated by a gleeful cry from her husband at the other side of the altar. Dr. Doyle had been drawn like a magnet to the tiny chapel at the right of the entrance. There, tucked away where it could remain almost unnoticed, was the celebrated window commemorating the martyrdom of Saint Thomas à Becket. There, too, were three young women in flowered spring dresses covered by the black fustian gowns used by Oxford undergraduates, accompanied by a fourth woman in a plain green dress and darker green mantle. The younger women wore spring straw hats, modestly trimmed with pink and green ribbons, while the older woman's hat was of black straw, trimmed to match her dark green dress.

Dr. Doyle ignored the ladies in his eagerness to share his discovery with his wife. "Touie, come and see this!"

Mr. Dodgson frowned slightly. Young women were not all that common in Christ Church, particularly young women unaccompanied by a male escort. The undergraduate gowns indicated those rare beings, female students. "I b-beg your p-pardon," he began. "Do you have permission . . ."

The three young women turned to face the men who had interrupted their contemplation of the window.

"Mr. Dodgson, I believe," the oldest of the four said, with a small dip that might have been a curtsey.

"Do I know you?" Mr. Dodgson peered at the trio.

"I am Miss Daphne Laurel," the older woman introduced herself. "We are from Lady Margaret Hall."

"Indeed." Mr. Dodgson bowed in return. "I have a young acquaintance there, Miss Edith Rix. I do not believe we have been introduced." He looked at the other three young ladies.

"I didn't suppose you would remember me," Dianna Cahill said as she giggled nervously. "It was only once, very many years ago, that we first met."

"Indeed?"

"In fact," Dianna went on, conscious of Gertrude and Mary behind her, silently urging her on, "I meant to send you a note. It is fortunate that we met this way." She paused. "I really don't know how to put this . . ."

"Someone's got hold of a photograph you took," Gertrude stated, taking charge of what was a rapidly deteriorating situation.

"And they're threatening to publish it if Dianna doesn't leave Oxford," Mary went on.

"Dear me!" It seemed inadequate to the occasion. Mr. Dodgson looked about for a seat, but the small chapel lacked such amenities.

"I apologize, Miss . . ."

"Cahill. Dianna Cahill. And these are my friends, Gertrude Bell and Mary Talbot." Dianna made the necessary introductions.

"We're all from Lady Margaret Hall," Mary explained, as Mr. Dodgson's confusion seemed to deepen. "Miss Cahill and I are second year, and Miss Bell just entered. And Miss Laurel came at Michaelmas term."

"I was working on my final paper," Dianna added, as they converged on the flustered don. "It's on the position of glassmaking in medieval England. I'm reading medieval history, and since my uncle Roswell is a manufacturer of colored glass, and he even provided some of the glass for Mr. Burne-Jones's windows, I thought that it would be appropriate—" She stopped, took a deep breath, and started again. "I meant to write to you, asking for an interview, but since you are here, and we are here—" She stopped again and looked helplessly at her two supporters.

"What's this about someone threatening to publish something?" Dr. Doyle was drawn into the discussion.

Dianna's plump cheeks reddened. "It's rather personal," she whispered.

Gertrude was more forthright. "It's a photograph that you took, Mr. Dodgson, when Dianna here was just a tot."

"Surely not the stuff of blackmail!" Dr. Doyle scoffed.

"It's not just the photograph," Dianna said. "It's the . . . the text. Whoever is doing this has written a dreadful poem. He sent me a page, already typeset, with the photograph, and a letter."

"And the subject of this poem?" Mr. Dodgson asked.

The three girls looked at one another. Gertrude took a deep breath. "I'm not sure of some of the words," she said, "but it seems to suggest that the purpose of Lady Margaret Hall is to corrupt children. And there is a photograph of a nude child to prove it. And Dianna says that you took it of her ages ago."

"How can this be?" Mr. Dodgson looked at the three young women and their older chaperon.

"I have no idea how this person got the photograph," Dianna said earnestly. "But he has it, and he's going to send it around to all the colleges and put it into the newspapers." She fumbled in her reticule for a handkerchief. Mary Talbot provided one.

"Dear me!" Mr. Dodgson looked at the four earnest young women before him. "Who is this person?"

"We don't know!" Dianna wailed.

"What does this blackguard want? Money?" Dr. Doyle's mustache bristled at the thought of someone trying to elicit money from helpless female undergraduates.

"Worse than that," Dianna said, close to tears. "The letter demands that I leave Oxford."

Mr. Dodgson's demeanor changed. He stood up, his face set in lines of outrage. "I have never been completely in favor of higher education for young women," he stated. "But to suggest that anyone, male or female, deliberately destroy a lifetime's work, is cowardly and despicable. Miss Cahill, if I was the unwitting cause of your distress, it is clearly up to me to set things right."

"Quite." Touie had joined the group. "Mr. Dodgson, you mentioned that you had tea laid on. Perhaps we could retire to your rooms and sort all this out. This place is somewhat public."

"An excellent suggestion," Dr. Doyle echoed his wife. "I've already thought of several points of this story that strike me as provocative."

"And I would like to hear more of this blackmail," Mr. Dodgson said. "Miss Cahill, would you and your friends join me for tea?"

Dianna looked at Miss Laurel. "I don't suppose it would break any of the rules?" she said hesitantly.

"Rules?" Dr. Doyle's eyebrows went up.

"We're not supposed to attend mixed parties," Gertrude stated. "Nor are we supposed to enter the rooms of any of the male students without our chaperon."

"But we have our chaperon," Mary pointed out. "Miss Laurel, you would be with us, wouldn't you? And you do see that we must speak with Mr. Dodgson and, um . . . ?"

"This is Dr. Doyle, and this is Mrs. Doyle. They are visiting me from Portsmouth." Mr. Dodgson made the necessary introductions.

"Oh, then it will be quite all right," Miss Laurel said. "If a married woman is present, as well as myself, there can be no difficulty."

"In that case, I suggest that we retire to my rooms for tea," Mr. Dodgson said. "Mrs. Grundy will be satisfied, and we can get to the bottom of this."

He led the group back into Tom Quad, brushing past Mr. Gregory Martin as they went. That earnest young man was hurrying back to his rooms after his tutorial with Mr. Duckworth, his hands full of papers, with a book tucked under one arm.

Mr. Martin stepped aside to let the young women go by. "Excuse me," he mumbled, as Dianna hurried by to keep up with the more athletic Gertrude Bell.

"Oh, no!" Dianna exclaimed, as she bumped into Martin. "Oh, I am so sorry!"

Papers were flying everywhere. The book fell to the stone pathway, as Martin scampered about, trying to catch his wayward essay.

The quad suddenly seemed full of students, chasing the flying papers. Gertrude looked behind her, saw Dianna, and called out, "Come on, Dianna! Stop playing with that man and come along!"

Dianna's blue eyes filled with tears of mortification as she trotted after her friends, holding her skirts with one hand against the ever-present draft.

Mr. Martin gazed after her, a look of total wonderment on his face. "Dianna!" he breathed.

Nevil Farlow stood in the doorway across Tom Quad and watched the paper chase that had enlivened the afternoon. He noted the student gowns over long skirts and Mr. Dodgson's tall, black hat as they marched toward the corner rooms that Mr. Dodgson had occupied for the last twenty years. Farlow frowned to himself. Trust Greg to bounce into the first female student he sees! With a sniff of disgust, Farlow turned out of the quad and proceeded along the lane to the boathouse. Ingram was right about one thing: the boat races were vitally important in the life of Christ Church. Farlow intended that Christ Church should retain the title of "Head of the River." To this end, he had donned white flannel trousers, a blazer with his Oxford Blue badge, and a straw hat. Thus clad, he sallied forth toward the river and his team.

From his station near the Porter's Desk, Ingram watched the five women and two men as they entered the corner door. On the board of the Porter's Lodge was a note: "Mr. Dodgson to have tea in his rooms." He'd better notify Telling; four more cups would be needed and more cakes, if the looks of the young ladies were any indication.

Ingram headed for the kitchens, where Telling was already organizing the tea urns and trays for those students who wanted tea sent to their rooms. The Senior Common Room had its tea at four; dinner in Hall would be served at seven-thirty.

Telling frowned as Ingram gave him the news that Mr. Dodgson had four more visitors, young lady students by the look of them, and their chaperon.

"Better help me with the trays then," Telling ordered, as he shifted cups and saucers, cakes and biscuits, and a massive urn of hot water. "And you're to serve Mr. Dodgson his dinner, Ingram, so look sharp! He's a particular gentleman."

"Seems a right naffy sort to me," Ingram grumbled, as he lifted the heavy urn.

Telling turned on his underling with raised eyebrows and biting scorn. "Mr. Dodgson is a very clever scholar," he told Ingram. "He is a great credit to this House. You will keep a civil tongue in your head when you serve him, Ingram!"

Ingram followed Telling across the quad. He thought there was something familiar about one of those bluestockings, something that would warrant a closer examination.

Ingram's long face gave no clue to the exultation he suddenly felt. If he was right, this would be the opportunity he had been waiting for all his life! For once he had stumbled onto a sure thing, something that would set him up for the rest of his days!

CHAPTER 4

M r. Dodgson had held the same suite of rooms on the northeast corner of Tom Quad since 1868: a spacious sitting
room and smaller dining room on the first story, a bathroom and
bedroom on the second, with a box room for his photographic
equipment between them. It was to the sitting room that he led
his visitors, and some time was spent in seeing that each of the
young women present had a seat. The two large armchairs were
appropriated by Gertrude and Mary, while Miss Laurel effaced
herself in the small chair behind the desk and Touie drew the
chair near the door closer to the central group. Dr. Doyle took up
a position near the fireplace, so that Mr. Dodgson could take center stage in the middle of the room.

This, unfortunately, was impossible. Dianna kept bouncing up
and down from the armchair assigned to her to exclaim over this
or that bit of bric-a-brac, evoking more and more from her memory of the brightest light in what appeared to have been an otherwise dreary childhood.

"I remember that screen," she cried out, "and there's the globe!
And you posed me over there, next to the window, with a book
on my lap."

A rap at the door put an end to her effusions. Telling and Ingram appeared with the tea tray and the urn on its little trolley.

The girls brightened up at the thought of food. Miss Laurel shrank back into the shadows, effectively withdrawing from the group.

Mr. Dodgson greeted Telling and Ingram with a wave of his hand as they marched in with the tea tray. "Put it on the table," he said absently.

"I took the liberty of ordering more cakes," Telling said, as Ingram set out the cups and plates on the small round table that had been set next to the armchairs, "seeing as how Ingram here told me you had extra visitors."

"That was most perceptive of Ingram," Mr. Dodgson commented.

"All part of the service," Ingram replied. He kept his face immobile as he laid the tray down on the table, masking his inward delight. He had been right!

Telling shot Ingram a look of dire warning. Scouts were not supposed to react in any way to dons. They were to be unheard and unseen, doing their work behind the scenes so that the learned men could get on with their studies without being bothered with mundane matters. Clearly, Telling thought, Ingram's glowing references had been sadly misleading. He would have to consider rehiring this scout after the summer hiatus. For now, however, Ingram was necessary, and a reprimand was in order . . . but not in front of Mr. Dodgson.

Mr. Dodgson ignored Ingram's gaffe. "You may come back to clear off the cups in an hour, Telling," he said. "And you may send up dinner for myself and Dr. Doyle and his wife at seven."

Telling bowed and nudged Ingram, who showed every inclination to remain in the sitting room. Once outside, Telling turned on his subordinate with righteous wrath.

"Mr. Ingram," he hissed, "do not ever address one of the Senior Common Room again, unless you are directly questioned."

"Just being cheerful," Ingram retorted.

"When cheerful commentary is needed, it will be requested," Telling told him loftily. "London manners will not do for the

House." Telling marched off, leaving Ingram to mutter a highly uncomplimentary phrase to himself.

Ingram thought furiously. What to do next? He had recognized her, but had she recognized him? How to get to her? He followed Telling down the stairs and headed for the Porter's Lodge at Tom Gate. She would hardly go back through the Meadows, along the Dead Man's Walk; she would have to pass through Tom Gate, and he could get to her there.

Back in Mr. Dodgson's rooms, Mrs. Doyle and Miss Laurel eyed each other and the tea urn, as if to determine who held precedence through age and/or social position. Then Mrs. Doyle asked, "Shall I pour out?"

"If you will be so kind," Mr. Dodgson said. "Miss Cahill, will you please sit down? We must sort out this problem, and you are making me quite giddy."

"It's just that . . . I don't know, I barely remembered being photographed, and now it's all coming back. Oh, you have jam cakes! I remember those jam cakes!" She accepted a cup of tea from Mrs. Doyle and a plate from Miss Laurel and perched on the arm of the nearest chair.

Mr. Dodgson took up a position in the center of the room. "Now then," he began, in his most professorial tone, "when did this outrage begin?"

"If you mean, when did I receive the first letter—?" Dianna began.

"The first letter?" Dr. Doyle put in sharply.

"Yes, the first. There were two before I got the photograph." Dianna took a sip of her tea.

"Were they delivered by hand or through the post?" Mr. Dodgson asked.

Dianna frowned. "I really don't know. You see, most of our correspondence passes through Miss Wordsworth's hands before we get it. Our letters are handed to us at breakfast."

"Miss Wordsworth reads your private correspondence?" Touie's pretty face crinkled in dismay. "That seems quite harsh. Doesn't she trust you?"

"Of course she does!" Dianna exclaimed.

"It's the other chaps she doesn't trust!" The irrepressible Gertrude gave a crack of laughter, echoed faintly by Mary, who glanced at Miss Laurel as if to ascertain that the chaperon was still there to preserve propriety.

"I take it that Miss Wordsworth is the dean or principal of this college for women," Dr. Doyle said.

"Miss Wordsworth is the Lady Principal of Lady Margaret Hall," Mr. Dodgson explained. "A most worthy and estimable woman, the grandniece of the great poet. She established Lady Margaret Hall seven years ago. I was one of those who attended the inaugural ceremonies, opening the college to young women; and my impression of Miss Wordsworth then, as now, is that she would have put a stop to any attempt to suborn one of her students immediately."

"In that case, we can safely assume that whoever is behind the extortion scheme must be resident here in Oxford, and that the letters must have been delivered by hand," Dr. Doyle stated. "Otherwise, the letters would have come in the post, and Miss Wordsworth would have found them."

"Very well," Mr. Dodgson said, taking the floor back from his prize pupil. "Did you save those letters, Miss Cahill?"

"I certainly did not," Dianna said firmly. "The first one called me all sorts of bad names and said that I was a disgrace to all women and that I had no right to attempt to gain academic honors. Well, I know better than that! I thought it was one of the cranky old dons, and I put the letter into the fire."

"We get them sometimes," Mary said with a sigh. "There are some old fogeys who simply will not understand that women deserve the chance to improve themselves, just as men do, and that we are fully capable of being good wives and mothers even though we have had the advantage of University education."

"In fact, Miss Wordsworth is of the opinion that an educated woman is a better wife and mother because she can fully enter into her husband's inner life and can impart knowledge to her children," Dianna added, as if quoting one of Miss Wordsworth's more impassioned speeches.

Mr. Dodgson nodded, partly in agreement with the sentiments

expressed, partly to indicate that the young women should continue their story.

"So, there was one letter expressing dislike for women undergraduates," Dr. Doyle summed up. "And you say there was a second letter?"

"Yes, but this one was directed specifically at me," Dianna said. Her cheeks turned bright pink as she said, "This time the letter said that there was a photograph that proved that the women of Lady Margaret Hall were . . ." She could not bring herself to say it.

Gertrude had no such compunction. "To put it as plainly as I may, that letter accused us all of being followers of Sappho, and that we indoctrinated the children of dons into our cult."

"Were those the exact words?" Mr. Dodgson asked.

Dianna looked at Mary and Gertrude, and the three young women nodded.

Mr. Dodgson frowned. Touie looked blankly at her husband, who was struggling not to laugh. Mr. Dodgson did not think this was a laughing matter.

"But who is this Sappho?" Touie asked innocently.

"She was a poet," Mr. Dodgson explained, "who had a group of, ah, young women about her."

"That doesn't sound all that dreadful," Touie said.

Before she could continue, Dianna produced the offensive package. "This came today, right before luncheon."

Mr. Dodgson examined the envelope carefully, then withdrew the contents: a page of typeset text, a handwritten letter, and a photograph.

His frown deepened as he scanned the letter, then looked at the typeset pages, and finally, recognized the photograph.

"Now I recall when I took this," Mr. Dodgson said slowly. "It was the last time that I saw Miss Alice Liddell before her marriage to Major Hargreaves. I had received a copy of *Alice's Adventures in Wonderland* in the Italian translation, and I thought that she might like to have it, since she had indicated that she was studying that language. When I arrived at the Deanery, there were already several people there—"

"My parents," Dianna put in. "And I think, some other people. I don't remember everything, only that there were too many grownups and no other children."

"And I left the book and was going to leave when I saw a child—"

"That was me!"

"—and I suggested that I might amuse her, since she seemed rather lonely."

"And we came up here," Dianna finished, "and you showed me all your pretty things, and we had a lovely time. I especially remember the jam cakes."

"But . . . the photograph . . ." Dr. Doyle prompted them.

"Oh, yes. The photograph." Mr. Dodgson looked at it, then went on. "At that time I was an avid photographer, using the wet-plate method. I rarely took a child who was not willing to be posed, and there was always someone about, and in this case, I suppose, I was overcome. You were a very pretty child."

Dianna blushed again. Miss Laurel echoed, "A very pretty child and quite clever, too."

"And so I suggested that you might like to remove your clothing, and I could take you in your favorite costume of nothing at all," Mr. Dodgson said. "Now it comes back to me. I believe I was experimenting with artificial light, which would account for the shadows in the background. At that time there was no electrical light," Mr. Dodgson reminded his audience. "I must have taken this by gaslight and with what little light was available through the windows."

Dr. Doyle examined the photograph with the eye of an expert. "An interesting effect. With the new electric lighting, I expect we shall see more indoor photography."

Touie didn't care about photography. "And what happened then?"

"We had jam cakes, and then Mr. Dodgson looked out into St. Aldgates and saw that my uncle Roswell's carriage had come for my parents; so I went back to the deanery, and that was the end of it," Dianna said with a shrug. "The next day we were off to my father's new living, which was in Northumberland on the

40

coast, quite remote, and many of the people were Chapel, so his congregation was quite small."

"And you told no one about your adventure with Mr. Dodgson?" Dr. Doyle was pursuing his own train of thought.

"There was no one to tell." Dianna looked blankly at her two friends. "It was a small, out-of-the-way parish, there were no children of my own age among the gentry, and the village children were considered beneath my touch. My mother educated me at home, with the help of my father, of course. I had almost forgotten that this photograph even existed until the letter came."

Dr. Doyle pulled at his mustache. "How many people knew about it then?"

Mr. Dodgson began to tick them off on his fingers. "Myself, of course, and the Reverend and Mrs. Cahill, for I asked their permission before taking Miss Dianna to tea, and I mentioned that I might wish to take her photograph. Mrs. Liddell and the Dean were present, and Mrs. Liddell encouraged Mrs. Cahill to permit the child to come to my rooms." The memory came back, and Mr. Dodgson frowned again. "Mrs. Liddell would not let her younger daughters come up, since they were becoming young ladies; but as I now recall, she took it upon herself to assure Mrs. Cahill that I was a noted photographer, who had taken the likenesses of several celebrated poets and artists, and that to have one's photograph taken by me was something of an honor."

"And so it was," Miss Laurel murmured.

"I felt that such reassurance was unnecessary," Mr. Dodgson said testily. "I would never take a photograph of a child who would not pose willingly or was in the least way uncomfortable." He closed his mouth over the unworthy thought that Mrs. Liddell had been puffing him off to her guests as a minor literary lion. The atmosphere between Mr. Dodgson and Mrs. Liddell had never been cordial, and in the early 1870s there was a distinct coolness between the Dean and his most persistent critic. For Mrs. Liddell to refuse to allow her daughters to accompany him to his rooms and then allow a stranger to be photographed was an implied insult to both the photographer and the subject.

Dr. Doyle was examining the photograph. "If I may say so, sir, this is an exceptionally fine photograph. The quality of the printing, the texture, so to speak, is unusual, and the lighting effect is superb. How many prints were made?"

"I think I made one for myself and one to send to the child," Mr. Dodgson said, after a moment's recollection. "I often sent my prints to be colored, but at the time I did not like the deep shadows that draw your attention, and I did not do so with this one." He felt the paper and frowned in puzzlement. "But this is not my print," he complained. "This is not the paper I used for my prints at all. It is coarser, and the definition is not as fine as I was used to getting."

"And what did you do with the prints?" Dr. Doyle asked.

"Eh?" Mr. Dodgson considered the question. "I usually sent a print to the child, but since your parents were only visiting, Miss Cahill, it is possible that I sent it to the relations—"

"My uncle and aunt Roswell," Dianna interrupted.

"But it was so long ago," Mr. Dodgson said apologetically, "that I really could not say."

"What about your own print?" Dr. Doyle asked. "Where would that have been kept?"

"In my albums," Mr. Dodgson said, turning to one of the bookcases. There were thirty small albums, marked with the dates, beginning with 1858 and ending in 1880. "It would be in, let me see . . . 1872, 1873?"

"I think 1873," Dianna said.

Mr. Dodgson frowned again. "Those albums have been disarranged," he said. "I cannot believe . . ." He pulled out the appropriate album, carried it to the desk, and laid it down reverently. The rest of the group crowded around him as he turned over the pages, careful not to tear the fragile paper.

"There is the last photograph I took of Miss Alice Liddell," he murmured. "And here is Miss Isa . . . and Miss Terry . . ."

"But where is Dianna?" Gertrude had to crane her neck to see over the heads of Mr. Dodgson and Dr. Doyle.

"Look here!" Touie pointed to a page with an obvious gap, where one square was darker than the rest of the page.

"Oh dear!" Mr. Dodgson moaned.

"And that explains where this photograph came from," Dr. Doyle said.

"But . . . that would mean that Mr. Dodgson sent the photograph, and we know that he did not," Dianna said.

Mr. Dodgson's face grew grim. "What may be deduced is that someone entered these rooms, looked into my albums, abstracted this particular photograph, and purloined it for the purpose of making a copy to send to you, Miss Cahill, so that you would be frightened into leaving Oxford. That is intolerable, and I will not rest until I have gotten to the bottom of it!"

"It seems a drastic step to take, to threaten to disgrace a whole school so that one student should leave it," Dr. Doyle said. "Miss Cahill, can you shed any light on this matter? Have you any enemies who would descend to this sort of crime?"

Dianna's eyes filled with tears of mortification. "I can't think of anyone who would want to hurt me," she sniffled.

Miss Laurel handed her a handkerchief from her reticule. "Miss Cahill is well-liked by everyone at Lady Margaret Hall," she said severely. "There's nothing behind this but spite."

Gertrude was also thinking. "Maybe not," she said. "What about that uncle of yours? The one who's paying your fees?"

"Uncle Roswell?" Dianna quavered, applying the handkerchief to her nose. "What has he to do with anything?"

"He's rich," Gertrude said succinctly.

"Yes, but he's not a blood relation, and he's quite healthy, so there's no question of an inheritance. . . . Oh!" Dianna stopped sniffling and sat up straight.

"What is it?" Dr. Doyle asked.

"When I came up there was a reporter who went to Uncle Roswell and asked his opinion of female scholars. Uncle Roswell allowed himself to be quoted as saying that he was in favor of University education, and that he would offer a large sum to any of his nieces or nephews who won honors at Oxford."

"Roswell . . . Roswell . . . ," Mr. Dodgson muttered to himself.

"The Roswell Glass Works," Dianna said helpfully. "His wife is my mother's sister. I believe he helped my father financially when he began his research into the trading cities of Northumbria.

My father is an expert on the Viking invasions of Britain," she added with pride.

"And Mr. Roswell is paying for your education?" Mr. Dodgson brought her back to the point.

"Oh, yes." Dianna smiled suddenly. "And if I do well, I shall have my own income, as Uncle Roswell promised."

Mr. Dodgson mulled this over. "Who else would benefit from this generous offer?"

Dianna concentrated. "I'm not at all sure," she said at last. "My uncle Roswell is the eldest in his family. There is one brother who went to America just after their Civil War, and I believe he is doing quite well. He has a son of age to be in college, but Mr. Roswell does not approve of the institution. It is some sort of school for chemists, called Cornell College."

"So you would be the sole beneficiary of this offer?" Mr. Dodgson pursued this line of thought.

"I suppose I would. Although . . ." Dianna paused. "There might be someone else; but every time I asked about her, I was told she was gone and not to ask any more questions."

"Oh?" Dr. Doyle's eyebrows went up.

"I think Mr. Roswell had a sister, but she must be dead. There is a very old photograph taken when Mr. Roswell was at the great exhibition at the Crystal Palace," Dianna explained. "I saw it once and asked about it. Mr. Roswell was with a boy, who is the American brother, and a girl, who must have been his sister, but Aunt Roswell said I was not to ask about her, not ever. She looked quite pretty."

The sounds of Great Tom ringing the hour of five reverberated through the rooms.

Miss Laurel made fussy noises, reminiscent of a mother hen calling to her chicks. "We must be back at Lady Margaret Hall for dinner," she reminded her charges. "It is nearly an hour's walk back to our college."

The three girls stood up and collected their assorted wraps. Mr. Dodgson escorted them down the stairs and along the path to the great carved gate that led into the busy street.

"I shall do everything in my power to discover this miserable blackguard," he promised Dianna. "There are several points of interest in your story that may lead to the unraveling of this mystery. In the meanwhile, I suggest that you concentrate your attention on passing your examinations and earning the bounty offered by your generous relation."

"Thank you, sir." Dianna curtsied and shook Mr. Dodgson's hand. Gertrude and Mary followed her, and Mr. Dodgson stood aside to let Miss Laurel take her place beside her charges. His eye was caught by a black coat and bowler hat.

"Here! You!" Mr. Dodgson accosted the owner of the black coat, who turned and faced him.

"Are you talking to me?" Ingram asked truculently.

"Yes, you! You are a scout, are you not?" Mr. Dodgson's shrill voice rang out over the hubbub of St. Aldgates, drawing the attention of the students as they flowed in and out of the gate. "You are the one who served us tea. What is your name?"

"Ingram. What is it to you?"

"Scouts are not to use Tom Gate but are to use the gate at the other end of the quad." Mr. Dodgson spoke as one who lays down the law and quotes from the Book of Regulations for Scouts.

"And what difference does it make which gate I use?" Ingram was becoming abusive. "A scout's as good as any don any day and better than some I could name. I don't photograph little girls, and I don't put on airs, pretending to be what I'm not." He glared at Mr. Dodgson, as if daring him to refute the charges and let his eyes drift toward the four women behind him.

"You have b-b-een in my rooms," Mr. Dodgson declared suddenly. "How d-dare you!" His voice grew loud and shrill, as the true infamy of Ingram's crime burst upon him.

"Mr. Dodgson . . ." Dr. Doyle was uncomfortably aware that they were drawing the attention of the entire crowd. "You cannot accuse a man without proof."

"For all I know you are the thief who has b-been abstracting small articles from Tom Quad," Mr. Dodgson sputtered. "You are d-discharged! You may collect whatever money is owed you, and you will be off by tomorrow! Without a character!"

"And good riddance!" Ingram shot back. "If you want to talk

to me, be at Magdalen Bridge at six o'clock, and we can have words there!"

Miss Laurel hustled the other girls northward toward the High, as Ingram turned back to the Porter's Lodge, and Mr. Dodgson seethed.

"Mr. Dodgson?" Dr. Doyle interposed himself between the don and the scout.

"Yes? What is it?" Mr. Dodgson snapped.

Dr. Doyle took a deep breath and tried to soothe the agitated don. "Why don't you come and have a small sherry with me at the White Hart, while Touie makes herself presentable for dinner. We can go over this blackmail business and see if we can make any sense of it. And besides," he added, as he helped the older man through the tangle of traffic, "I have something to show you. A new story I have written, something quite different from anything I've ever tried before."

Mr. Dodgson allowed himself to be removed from the crowd. "I shall be delighted to read it," he said. "And I, too, have noticed certain points in Miss Cahill's story. We shall discuss it over some sherry. And then we shall have dinner and discuss your new endeavor."

Ingram watched from the Porter's Lodge as the four ladies made their way along St. Aldgates and turned into High Street. He was sure his message had been received. Now all he had to do was decide how to use the tool that had been delivered into his hands.

CHAPTER 5

G reat Tom's sonorous tones boomed out over St. Aldgates. Tradesmen and workmen who had stopped for a four o'clock tea now went back to their labors, eager to take advantage of the extra hours of daylight. Street vendors enticed students with savory odors from baskets of hot potatoes or sausages to be carried back to their rooms for a late afternoon snack. Shopkeepers stayed open to make the last sales of the day.

The taverns and pubs were doing a brisk business. Tucked in and around the colleges, in the squalid lanes behind Christ Church and around Carfax, the worker bees of the Oxford hive found places to sit and have a quiet pint and some bread and cheese, while more sedate dons had their mid-afternoon refreshment in more gracious surroundings. In Senior Common Rooms around Oxford, tea, sherry, biscuits, and cakes were ingested along with weighty commentary and crisply enunciated witticisms. Undergraduates in their gowns and mortarboards hurried back to their respective colleges to devour hot pies and sandwiches that would stave off the pangs of hunger until the ceremonies of dinner in Hall at seven-thirty.

A few hardy souls could be seen on the river, bending over

their sculls. Boating practice was beginning in earnest, and each college wanted the title of Head of the River. As the final notes of the great bell hung in the air, the rowers pulled in their oars and grounded the boats. It was time to rest from their labors and dress for dinner.

Mr. Dodgson had not intended to accompany his young guests across the road, but the encounter with Ingram had shaken him more than he liked. He allowed Dr. Doyle to see him through the traffic and into the busy inn opposite Christ Church.

According to its prospectus, the White Hart served tea every afternoon in the lounge. Here Dr. Doyle commandeered three chairs and a small table.

Touie shook her head when her husband offered her a seat. "I must go up to our room," she explained. "I want to change for dinner, and I must make sure the maid has put our things out correctly. And besides, Mr. Dodgson, I know that Arthur wants to tell you about his new story." She merged with the crowd of visitors who filled the lounge, leaving Mr. Dodgson and Dr. Doyle together.

Mr. Dodgson nodded mutely. A waiter materialized out of the crowd and stood in front of them ready for instructions.

"Sherry," Dr. Doyle ordered, before Mr. Dodgson could protest. "It is medicinal, sir. You have had a shock."

"I certainly have!" Mr. Dodgson agreed. "To think that one of my photographs should be used for such a purpose! And the cheek of it! Removing it from my very rooms!"

"It was not the photograph itself," Dr. Doyle said. "It is the combination of the photograph and the text that makes the thing so vile. Who could have written such a thing?"

"Have you got the . . . the document?"

"Here it is. I picked it up after Miss Cahill laid it on your desk. I thought we might be able to go over the two items more carefully together." Dr. Doyle fished them out of his jacket pocket and handed them to the older man. "Although," Dr. Doyle added, "one can hardly call this room private."

"There is nothing more private than a public lounge," Mr.

Dodgson observed, with a glance at the crowd in the room. "Let us see this page."

Mr. Dodgson could barely bring himself to look at the galley-proof sheet that Dr. Doyle handed him. He held it at arms' length, as if to distance himself from the sentiments expressed.

"Most interesting," he said at last, laying down the galley proofs and taking up the letter. "The hand is copperplate, of the sort used by schoolboys when doing impositions. The paper may be found at any stationers in Oxford. The envelope is of the same grade as the notepaper."

"Well, you can't expect our blackmailer to be so generous as to leave clues to his identity," Dr. Doyle said, with an ironic twitch of his mustache.

"But he has," Mr. Dodgson pointed out. "Every writer has certain phrases, little expressions and tricks of syntax that mark him as an individual. Even you, Dr. Doyle, are beginning to show the elements of a particular style."

Dr. Doyle didn't know whether to be flattered by this enco-mium or not. He picked up the page and scanned it more closely than Mr. Dodgson, reminding himself that he was looking for style, not content.

"Whoever wrote this is an educated man," he finally pro-nounced. "The reference to the Greek poetess Sappho would not have been made by someone without a knowledge of the Classics. There is a French term in the text, as well as the more, um, Anglo-Saxon vulgarities."

"There are now schools in every parish," Mr. Dodgson pointed out.

"True," Dr. Doyle conceded. "But I can assure you, sir, that the poems of Sappho are not on the curriculum, nor is the French tongue. The national schools run more to the basics of reading, writing, and arithmetic, and whatever poetry is taught is of the staunch and moral variety. Mr. Tennyson, Mr. Southey, Mr. Pope . . . definitely not Madame Sappho!"

Mr. Dodgson tapped the paper before him. "And I can assure you, Dr. Doyle, that this is not a typeface commonly used by the

Oxford University Press. However, there are several printers who specialize in small press runs of pamphlets and tracts, and it is possible that one of those might have set these verses."

Dr. Doyle frowned and pulled at his mustache. "I suppose the next step is to visit each of these establishments and question the owner," he said at last.

"It may not be necessary to visit every printing shop in Oxford," Mr. Dodgson said. "We may be able to make certain assumptions, based on observations. For instance, this type has been used extensively. Observe the marks of wear on the t and the e, the most commonly used letters in the English alphabet. It is possible that this font was bought cheaply, or even acquired after a bankruptcy, at sale. Ergo, we are looking for a printing shop that is using old type, a shop that is probably only marginally successful, that will set any piece for a fee."

"If this is a sample of the product, I should think so!" Dr. Doyle said, with a brief laugh. "No reputable printer would have had anything to do with this sort of thing." He looked over the lines, scanning for typographical errors that might indicate an apprentice hand, someone in the shop who might have been bribed or coerced into setting the pages before them.

Mr. Dodgson frowned over the blackmail note as Dr. Doyle examined the printed page. "Let us consider all the facts, Dr. Doyle, before we make our conclusions. I can add one more assumption, however. The blackmailer must still be in possession of the original photograph."

"How do we know that?"

"I made two prints of every photograph I took," Mr. Dodgson explained. "One must have been sent to Miss Cahill's parents at their Oxford address, that is, the residence of Mr. Roswell. The other was the one I put into my album; the one that was taken. Now, why should the blackmailer go to all the trouble of stealing mine?" He looked at Dr. Doyle with the same expression he had bestowed on undergraduates at tutorials when waiting for the correct answer to a mathematical theorem.

"He knew of the existence of the photograph, but he did not have a print of his own," Dr. Doyle reasoned aloud. "You yourself pointed out that the print he sent to Miss Cahill was not the one you made. He must have made a copy of the one he stole. What I do not understand is, why he did not remove the negative while he was at it."

"Fifteen years ago, photography involved glass plates, chemicals, and a complex series of washes before one could obtain a good result," Mr. Dodgson explained. "Many of my own efforts were worthless. I discarded almost as many glass plates as I retained."

Dr. Doyle was still puzzled. "What about those glass plates, sir? Could not someone have removed one and made prints from it?"

Mr. Dodgson shook his head. "I think not, Dr. Doyle. My old plates are stored carefully, each glass plate carefully wrapped, since sunlight would destroy the image. It would be quite difficult for some intruder to find one plate in the locked case, unlike the albums, which are easily accessible. What is more, I do not know of many who could produce prints from them, since the method is now out of favor."

"Of course!" Dr. Doyle nodded, comprehension finally dawning. "In your day, photography was a delicate and costly business. Now, with the celluloid film, anyone can take a photograph."

"Indeed, anyone can," Mr. Dodgson echoed ironically. "What I do not understand, Dr. Doyle, is the motive behind this attempt to remove Miss Cahill from Oxford by using my photograph in this clumsy threat to bring disgrace on her school." Mr. Dodgson's ire began building again. "It seems quite pointless to deter a young woman from scholastic achievement simply because she will benefit financially from it."

"Unless there is someone who will lose by her gain," Dr. Doyle said. "Or someone who may claim the prize so generously offered by Mr. Roswell."

Their conversation was interrupted by the waiter, standing beside them with two glasses on a small tray. Dr. Doyle dismissed the waiter with a lordly, "Place it on my bill."

"You are my guest here," Dr. Doyle explained, as Mr. Dodgson experimentally sniffed his aperitif. "And my circumstances have improved slightly since we last met. In short, I have sold another story, and this little trip is being paid for by that sale."

Mr. Dodgson winced internally at the reference to money, yet another of Dr. Doyle's habits that indicated a lack of proper breeding. He decided to change the subject away from sordid blackmail and theft.

"You told me that you had written something new," Mr. Dodgson said, taking a small sip of his sherry.

"I had hoped you would have time to read it before I left. I took your suggestion after our last meeting and wrote . . . Well, I will let you decide if it meets with your approval." Dr. Doyle tossed off his drink and smiled expectantly.

Mr. Dodgson took a sip of his sherry, then another. He frowned, sipped again, and rose to his feet, his usually mild face distorted in anger. "Where did this sherry come from?" he demanded loudly, drawing the attention of the well-dressed crowd in the lounge.

Dr. Doyle stood up, conscious of being the object of disapproving glares from the tourists and commercial travelers around them. "I simply ordered a drink from the bar, sir. Is the sherry not good?"

"The sherry is very good. I should know! This sherry is that same sherry that my p-predecessor laid down at Christ Church! What is it d-doing here?" Mr. Dodgson was getting angrier by the minute, and his stammer was getting worse the angrier he got. He advanced toward the bar, with Dr. Doyle at his heels.

"Where is the p-person who p-purchases the sherry for this establishment?" Mr. Dodgson demanded.

The barman gulped at the vision of a tall and apparently demented man in clerical black bearing down upon him. "I only work here, sir. You must ask the proprietor." He pointed in the direction of the office of the White Hart, located in a cubbyhole behind the front desk.

"Is there some difficulty?" Mr. Jellicoe, the owner and manager of the White Hart, emerged from his sanctum at the sounds of the altercation.

"The sherry served at this b-bar. Where did you g-g-et it?"

Mr. Dodgson's voice grew louder and shriller, and his stammer more and more pronounced.

Mr. Jellicoe's face grew first pale, then red with the implications of the demand. "Are you accusing me of serving inferior wine, sir?"

"I am accusing someone of p-purchasing wine that was stolen from the Christ Church cellars," Mr. Dodgson countered. He took a deep breath, trying to conquer his stammer. "I am not one of those who insists he can tell the difference between wine from one field and another, but I do know my own sherry; and this, sir, is the same sherry I have been drinking for the last five years! Where did you get it?"

"Mr. Dodgson!" Dr. Doyle wished he had never ordered the sherry if it was going to have this effect on the older man. He briefly wondered if Mr. Dodgson might suffer from the same sad malady as Charles Doyle, his father, who was usually confined in a hospital where he could be kept away from all drink. Mr. Dodgson had seemed to be quite sane until he drank the sherry, but one never knew with drunkards. Only last year the elder Doyle had managed to escape his keepers and find some rum, and the results had been disastrous.

"I assure you, sir, that we purchase our supply of wine from Mr. Snow, who is the best wine merchant in Oxford," Mr. Jellicoe stated, with immense dignity, aware that the discussion had drawn the attention of every one of his guests. "It is possible that some of the sherry purchased for your college and the sherry purchased for my humble establishment came from the same source. I suggest you look there for the answer to your mystery. Good afternoon!" He deliberately turned to the next person in the queue in front of the desk, to welcome the gentleman in the top hat and traveling cloak and the lady in the dark purple velvet to the White Hart and to apologize for the unseemly behavior of one of the more eccentric dons.

"These scholarly gentlemen can sometimes get odd notions," Mr. Jellicoe explained, while Mr. Dodgson, still fuming, allowed himself to be led away by Dr. Doyle.

"This is our wine; I know it is," he muttered to himself.

Dr. Doyle maneuvered his host out into the street before they could attract any more attention. "It strikes me, sir, that I may be of use to you in this business," he said. "You cannot be seen in the sort of places where this stuff is printed, nor can you go about questioning wine merchants about their sales. I, on the other hand, am a stranger to Oxford, and no one knows me here. I can pursue these inquiries for you while you read my new manuscript. And perhaps, then, you can see your way clear to making some of the older papers in the library available for my researches." He looked eagerly at his mentor, like a puppy enticing his master to come out and play.

Mr. Dodgson took another deep breath to calm himself. "I fear you are as practiced a blackmailer as the one we are pursuing," he said with a rueful smile. "However, you are quite right on one point. I cannot be seen in the more questionable parts of the town. Very well, Dr. Doyle. I will read your manuscript, and you will discover what has happened to our sherry."

"I'll be back in a minute." Dr. Doyle darted back into the White Hart, leaving Mr. Dodgson to mutter to himself on St. Aldgates, while he galloped up the stairs and scrambled among his luggage for that all-important portfolio.

"He's going to read it," Dr. Doyle told his wife, as he picked up the folder containing his manuscript. "Only, I am going to have to leave you to look at the shops alone tomorrow. I have to find out where this hotel gets its sherry. What a strange man he is! He's convinced that someone's been pinching the college wine from its cellars and selling it off!"

Touie sat on the bed and watched her volatile husband as he dashed back down the stairs. She was certain that Mr. Dodgson, whatever his eccentricities, meant well; and if he thought that wine had been stolen, then he was very likely correct. She thought over the story the young ladies from Lady Margaret Hall had told and suddenly realized there was a missing piece to this puzzle, something that the men would never have thought of. She would bring it up when they met Mr. Dodgson for dinner.

Dr. Doyle, meanwhile, had thrust his manuscript upon his erstwhile mentor. "I suppose I could start with a visit to your usual wine merchant," he said. "They might still be open, and I could speak with the proprietors before dinner. Mr. Jellicoe may be quite correct when he says that the sherry at the White Hart and the sherry at Christ Church was simply part of a larger shipment."

"I shall discuss the matter with my colleague and predecessor in the Conservatorship, Vere Bayne," Mr. Dodgson said. "I am quite certain that he bought up a complete shipment of sherry, much to the dismay of the House. There are a number of Senior Students who do not care for sherry and prefer Madeira, of which I bought several cases myself."

"We shall have to taste it after dinner," Dr. Doyle said. "Now, sir, we must follow our respective leads, and Touie and I will be prompt for dinner, I assure you."

He loped back to the White Hart, while Mr. Dodgson made his way back to Christ Church.

Neither man was in a particularly good mood. Mr. Dodgson was more and more convinced that young Dr. Doyle was becoming far too assertive for someone in a modest station of life, while Dr. Doyle was wondering whether this friendship would ever lead to literary success. However, since both were now involved in solving the two problems of the missing wine and the insidious blackmailer, each decided to continue with the planned agenda for one more day.

Ingram had watched the two men enter the White Hart before he turned into the lane off St. Aldgates and sought the comfort of his own lodgings. He heard Mrs. Perkins, his redoubtable landlady, banging pots and pans in her kitchen, but Ingram had other matters on his mind besides food.

Ingram scowled in thought. He was used to people announcing that he was discharged, only to change their minds within the hour. He had been informed that he was to remain at Christ Church until otherwise notified. He would have to get back into the good graces of Mr. Telling and hope that the eccentric Mr. Dodgson would forget that he had been removed.

Ingram considered his next move carefully. He had been successfully juggling several masters, each with his own agenda. Now it was time to strike out on his own.

He bent down and pulled a small, square case out from under his bed and set it down on the table near the window. He opened it with the key on his watch chain and smiled down at the contents. He rummaged through the packets and papers and found one particular item, a daguerrotype of a young girl taken many years before. Oh yes, he thought. This little item will be the key that unlocks the door to a fortune.

The only question in Ingram's mind was whether his invitation had been understood. He smirked to himself and put the daguerrotype into the wardrobe drawer. He'd be at Magdalen Bridge at the appointed time. If no one came, then . . . He scowled to himself again. Oh, there would be someone there!

He placed his bowler hat on his head and headed out into St. Aldgates again. He had just enough time to stop by the Covered Market and have a bite to eat before his appointment.

CHAPTER 6

B etween six and eight o'clock Oxford's streets emptied. Black gowns and mortarboards vanished as if whisked away by some magical spell. Tradesmen and artisans alike shut their shops, packed up their tools, and retired to their domestic firesides, whether in the tangles of lanes behind the colleges or in the newly built suburbs like Jericho. Only the eating houses and taverns remained open for business, giving comfort to the transient population.

For the University, dinner was the major meal of the day, to be undertaken with the greatest of ceremony. All over Oxford, students of every stamp, from the lowliest undergraduate to the most revered and scholarly don, met for the evening meal, night after night, with great pomp. Particulars varied from college to college. The meal might be announced by trumpeters or by a stentorian steward; there might be a lengthy grace read in Latin or merely the perfunctory "For what we are about to receive, may we be truly grateful" in English. There might be distinctions made between those undergraduates of distinguished ancestry and those who were of more common clay, or there might be an egalitarian board, at which the students were divided according to their academic rather than their social class. Nevertheless, in colleges across the length of Oxford, dining in Hall was considered a requirement for all students; and all of them, at whatever level, had to be accounted for at that meal.

At Lady Margaret Hall, the table was set in the dining room of Talbot House, that brand-new edifice at the very end of Norham Gardens. There was no ancient grandeur here. Lady Margaret Hall was defiantly modern, and Mr. Morris's influence was paramount in the green and gold wallpaper and the curving lines of the draperies at the windows that looked out over the back gardens that led to the River Cherwell. Cut flowers graced the table and sideboards, giving the room the air of a fashionable dining room rather than a college refectory.

Miss Wordsworth herself presided at the head of the table, with two undergraduates at either side of her. It was Miss Wordsworth's contention that good conversation was a necessity in society and that keeping her entertained at dinner was as good a way as any to attain proficiency in this art.

The young ladies filed in, dressed in modest but fashionable dinner gowns. Miss Wordsworth watched approvingly as they marched into the dining room. Then she frowned. Someone was missing!

Miss Laurel burst breathlessly into the dining room, hastily buttoning her gloves, her lace cap slightly awry over her fair hair.

"Do forgive me," she babbled. "We were late getting back from Christ Church, and I spilled water all over my evening dress and had to find something else—"

"Quite all right, Miss Laurel," Miss Wordsworth said, as the latecomer slid into her place at the far end of the table. She nodded to her second-in-command. "Miss Johnson, will you read the grace?"

Grace was said slowly and meaningfully here. Lady Margaret Hall had been founded to educate the daughters of the clergy of the Church of England, and Church of England ritual prevailed. Once the ceremony was out of the way, the meal could be eaten.

Two scouts served the soup, fish, fowl, and roast, and the young ladies partook with hearty appetites.

Conversation at the students' table was brisk, and Miss Wordsworth allowed the girls the opportunity to chatter. Later she would direct the discourse toward a more scholarly theme, but for now, girls would be girls, and it was better so. Miss Wordsworth had no illusions about the superiority of female over male intellect. It was her intention to provide the Church of England with worthy helpmeets for its clergymen, and to that end she would encourage her students to participate in lectures, sports, and anything else that a young curate-to-be would do.

Miss Wordsworth frowned slightly as she regarded her oldest student; Miss Laurel was apparently perturbed. She was not eating her sweet. Perhaps Miss Wordsworth would have a word with Miss Laurel before they retired for the night. She had had some doubts about this student, who was so much older than the others; but Mrs. Toynbee herself had recommended her, and she had been a steadying influence on younger, giddier girls just out of the schoolroom.

Miss Wordsworth was so preoccupied with her thoughts that she did not hear the question addressed to her by Gertrude Bell, the young lady chosen by her to sit at her right hand.

"What do you think, Miss Wordsworth?" Gertrude asked again.

"I do beg your pardon, Miss Bell. I was thinking of something else. What did you say?" Miss Wordsworth put Miss Laurel in the back of her mind and concentrated on Miss Bell.

"We were talking about athletic and sporting activities," Gertrude reminded her. "When I was home, I went riding every day; but here, all we do is take walks, and that's not enough for me. Miss Pearson says that the river is too rough this year, but the Mill Stream looks calm enough for a punt." She glared at the diminutive bursar, who looked for guidance to the head of the table.

"There have been floods," Miss Pearson explained. "Even in our little canal, boats have capsized. Miss Bell and her friends wish to take out a punt, but I do not think it wise."

"Have you any objections, Miss Wordsworth?" Gertrude asked, with her most winning smile.

"Certainly not," Miss Wordsworth said. "If our students wish to take a boat out, they should be allowed to do so. Miss Bell is capable of holding her own, I am sure," Miss Wordsworth added, in tribute to her student's athletic prowess.

"But what of our rules?" Miss Pearson quoted from the sacred guidelines set down by Miss Wordsworth herself. "No student is to go out alone and never without a chaperon. I do not see how a chaperon will fit into a punt."

"I wasn't planning on going out alone," Gertrude protested. "Mary and Dianna would come with me."

Miss Wordsworth considered the matter, then gave her decision. "Miss Laurel, you will accompany Miss Bell and her team to the boathouse tomorrow. I trust you will use your good judgment and prevent them from taking unnecessary risks on the water."

Miss Laurel's cheeks seemed to grow pale as she contemplated her latest assignment. Gertrude and Mary grinned triumphantly at Dianna, who looked even more stricken than the chaperon.

"Boating?" she squeaked. "But I can't swim."

"We'll all be there, and the Mill Stream is not precisely the Amazon," Gertrude scoffed. "We need you for ballast. I'll take the rear pole, and Mary can take the paddle in the bow."

Miss Laurel took another bite of apple tart and smiled weakly at the other three girls. Clearly, she was going to be involved in the expedition, if only as spotter on the riverbank.

"And now we may have our tea in the sitting room." Miss Wordsworth rose majestically and led the ladies into the sitting room, where they could amuse themselves with music and conversation until ten o'clock, when the girls were supposed to retire to their individual rooms.

Two miles south of Lady Margaret Hall, the mighty walls of Christ Church's Hall looked down on quite a different scene. The nightly ritual here was more measured, sanctified by centuries of custom. The Senior Students and Fellows assembled in the Senior Common Room, hidden under the floor of the Hall, so that the older faculty members could gather, drink their sherry, and converse. The undergraduates assembled in Hall, under the gaze of painted images of deans and illustrious students long gone, in their subfusc best: gleaming white shirtfronts, black coats and trousers, student gowns, black mortarboards. Only when every undergraduate was in place could the High Table emerge from the door at the farthest end of the Hall, the door that some called the "Rabbit Hole," leading as it did down the winding stair to the Senior Common Room.

Dean Liddell led the parade, followed by the rest of the Senior Common Room members in strict order of seniority; the oldest faculty in the lead and the newest at the end, to be seated farthest from the seat of power. No one could speak until the grace had been read. Once that was done, the young men of Christ Church could fall upon their beef, bread, fowl, greens, and pudding with the vigor of all young men still in their teens or early twenties.

The students themselves preserved the social distinctions imposed by their parents. Sons of the aristocracy sat closer to the High Table, mere clergymen's offspring were seated toward the door, and those whose parents had to work for a living were social pariahs.

Lord Nevil Farlow was among those nearest the High Table, an accolade that had certain disadvantages. He slid into his seat just as the soup was being spooned out.

"Where have you been?" Chatsworth hissed. "The Dean's already noticed you were missing. Keep this up and you'll be gated!"

"I had to see someone," Farlow muttered.

"About a dog?" Chatsworth made a face. "This soup is half water! Why do they allow it?"

"Don't ask me, ask the cook." Farlow ingested his soup with the relish of a steam engine taking on water. "I say, Minnie, after dinner I want you to nip one of those bath chair things and bring it down to the boats under Magdalen Bridge."

"Whatever for?"

"I've got an idea that will shake up those dodos in the mortuary."

61

"I'm your man, always have been. What's afoot?"

"I'll tell you when you meet me." Farlow nudged the man on his other side, the stout Mr. Martin. "And, Greg, we'll need you, too."

Martin sighed. "I don't know why I let you talk me into these things, Nev. One of these days the bulldogs are going to nab you, and all your pater's influence won't get you off again."

"Greg, you are the greatest prig in nature!" Farlow chomped on the beef. "Where do they get this stuff, the tannery? I'd as soon eat an old boot."

"When we set up our flat in London, we'll get a man who can cook," Chatsworth assured him. "What do you want with a bath chair? You're not going to smuggle some female into the quad after hours, are you?"

"Of course not!" Conversation stopped as the scout dished out vegetables. Farlow, Chatsworth, and Martin regarded the soggy mess on their plates with despair before digging in.

"Well, then, what do you want with a chair?" Chatsworth repeated.

"You'll find out when you meet me. It's one of the best rags we've ever pulled." Farlow grinned at his two comrades-in-arms.

Martin shook his head in disapproval. "This is the last time, Nev. I really cannot get involved in any more of your antics! Not when I'm to be ordained! I can't get rusticated now!"

"Nothing will happen, Greg, I promise. Just meet me at Magdalen Bridge with the chair, and we'll have some fun, I promise you!" Farlow decided to change the subject. "There's an empty chair up at the High Table," he observed. "I wonder where old Dodgson is? It's not like him to miss a meal."

"He was leading a bevy of beauties into his rooms at tea time," Chatsworth chuckled. "I saw him when we were coming back from the river."

Martin looked up from his plate to frown at his frivolous friends. "Those beauties, as you call them, were undergraduates from one of the ladies' colleges. I heard one of them mention Lady Margaret Hall. I bumped into one of them on my way back from my tutorial in Duckworth's rooms."

Chatsworth grinned. "I saw it all. There was a nice little brunette, but the red-haired one looked quite the Tartar, and the fat blond . . ."

"She was not fat," Martin demurred. "She was rather pretty, pleasingly plump. Her name is Dianna." He gazed soulfully into the distance.

Farlow frowned at his friend. "Gregory Martin, I'm shocked. A nice, clean parson like you, getting misty-eyed over a female undergraduate. They're all man haters anyway."

"I thought she looked rather sweet," Martin said, more to his meal than to his friend.

The dinner concluded with the sweet and the savory, and the High Table stood up and reversed the procession down the winding stairs back to the Senior Common Room, where the Dean would partake of after-dinner drinks and conversation, while the undergraduates were allowed to disperse to their own rooms or to wander about the town until the urgent tones of Great Tom sounded the magic hour of nine.

Farlow, Chatsworth, and Martin strolled around the quad. They ducked around the passage through the Cathedral and into the side street that led to the High.

"You find a chair, Minnie. Greg, you come with me, and we'll all meet at the bridge. Now . . . Go!"

The three undergraduates headed back toward the town bent on mischief.

Mr. Dodgson was not at the High Table on this May evening. He was in his own rooms, preparing his table for the dinner party so much anticipated by Dr. and Mrs. Doyle. Mr. Dodgson had decided not to invite any other guests but to keep this party a private one. Dean Liddell had uttered the gravest reservations about young Dr. Doyle when Mr. Dodgson had arrived late from his summer holidays, after having been detained in Portsmouth during a visit to the young couple; and although the recent difficulties in returning from London had been laid down to the weather, the Dean had hinted to Mr. Dodgson that perhaps his young friend had shown too much of a tendency to become involved with matters that did not directly concern him, to wit, murder, kidnapping, and similar criminal activities.

Mr. Dodgson agreed that his young friend did seem to attract crime; but on the other hand, he was a personable young man with a definite literary talent, and after all, he was Dicky Doyle's nephew. On either or both of those accounts, Mr. Dodgson had decided to continue the friendship.

Dr. Doyle's youth and energy were assets that the more retiring Mr. Dodgson could put to good use in solving this current problem of the missing wine and the thefts. The young man could approach pawnbrokers and wine merchants; and if indeed the thief was Ingram, he would be dealt with by the college proctors, who insisted on their authority to punish minor crimes and misdemeanors committed on University grounds. Mr. Dodgson would then allow Dr. Doyle access to the library, where the eager young writer could examine some of the fragile relics of more turbulent times.

Mr. Dodgson turned his attention to the table setting. He laid down the cardboard squares he preferred to pretentious lace placemats, and wondered what was keeping Telling. He had specifically told the Senior Steward to have wine and biscuits ready; and here it was, nearly fifteen minutes after the hour and no wine and no biscuits!

His misgivings increased when Dr. Doyle and Touie presented themselves at the door to his rooms.

Mr. Dodgson looked down the staircase. "Why did you not ask to be announced?"

"No one seemed to be about," Dr. Doyle said cheerfully, as he greeted his host. "Everyone's at dinner."

"You understand, Dr. Doyle, that Mrs. Doyle could not dine in Hall," Mr. Dodgson explained. "And since she cannot be excluded from our conversation, I have arranged that our dinner should be served here. At least, I think I did." Mr. Dodgson's usually unwrinkled brow furrowed in confusion.

"It is quite all right," Touie said. "You have such an interesting room. We were so caught up in our conversation earlier, we did not get a good look at your decorations. And what a view you have! Right into the street. Why, you can see everything from here!"

"Doesn't the noise bother you?" Dr. Doyle asked.

Mr. Dodgson flushed slightly. "I do not notice it," he said. He hated to refer to his deafness.

Touie was examining the pictures on the walls, most of which depicted young girls. "Do you know any of these children?" she asked.

"A few," Mr. Dodgson admitted. "Dr. Doyle, here is my new microscope. I have read some interesting monographs regarding the use of microscopic evidence in criminal cases. I believe that in the future such evidence will become more and more acceptable to the Court and may lead to more criminal convictions."

"I agree, sir. Why, a man may live or die by the evidence of a thread or a hair or a fragment of a leaf," Dr. Doyle replied. "A magnificent instrument, sir! I intend to get one as soon as I can afford it."

"And my photograph albums are kept here in this bookcase. As I told you, I used the wet-plate method, until 1880, when I turned to drawing instead of photography."

"And have you many photographs?" Touie asked unnecessarily. There were the albums, a whole shelf of them.

The two young people looked at each other, and Mr. Dodgson began to worry in earnest. Where, oh where, was dinner? He could not continue to chatter with these people for much longer. He could not entertain them with conundrums or magic tricks, as he did his child friends, and Bob the Bat was hardly a fitting companion for Dr. and Mrs. Doyle of Southsea.

In desperation, he pulled out the photograph albums. He had been something of a lion hunter when he was younger; now he could point with pride to portraits of such notables as Alfred Lord Tennyson and the Rosetti family.

Dr. Doyle and Touie made appropriate noises. The photographs were interesting, and some were quite beautiful; but one little girl looked much like another, and they had been promised a meal. Where was it?

In the vast kitchens Telling was directing the last of the scouts to bring up the hot puddings. He noticed a small table in a corner with a selection of covered dishes on it.

"What's this?" he demanded.

"Dinner for Mr. Dodgson." The harried scout dashed up the stone stairs with a jug of beer.

"Mr. Dodgson!" Telling suddenly remembered. Mr. Dodgson was giving a dinner party! "I thought Ingram was supposed to take that up."

"Ingram's gone," one of the cooks informed him.

"Gone? Gone where?" Telling's confusion grew.

"Dunno." The cook wiped his brow with one meaty hand.

"Then who's to take Mr. Dodgson and his friends their dinner?" Mr. Telling asked the world at large.

"Dunno," the cook said, with a shrug.

"I'd better do it," Telling decided. "It'll be cold, of course. And late. And he's not going to be in a good temper."

"When is 'e ever?" The cook gave a bark of laughter.

Telling thought about reproving the underling, then decided that it was too late for recriminations. The meal would have to be served, and he would have a word with Ingram when and if he saw him again.

Telling arrived at Mr. Dodgson's rooms with the tray at eight o'clock. Mr. Dodgson had exhausted the photograph albums, the paintings, the microscopes, and the globe as topics of conversation. He was reduced to asking after the Doyle's circle of friends with whom he had become acquainted during his brief stay in Portsmouth the previous autumn. Telling's arrival was providential.

Mr. Dodgson greeted Telling testily. "Where have you been?" he demanded.

"There was a small difficulty in the kitchens," Telling said apologetically. "Ingram was to have served you tonight, but he seems to have taken himself off somewhere and has not been seen since teatime."

"Ingram? That insolent scout who served us tea?" Mr. Dodgson frowned. "I met him coming out of Tom Gate. I discharged him for rudeness and insubordination."

Telling stifled a sigh. "I wish you would inform me when making changes to the staff," he said, setting up the small folding table. "Now he has taken the liberty of removing himself without completing his day's work."

"That was most improper of him," Mr. Dodgson said.

"But not unexpected," Dr. Doyle added. "He seemed to be a most surly and disrespectful person. Not at all the sort one would find in service of any kind, let alone in a college like this."

"Well, now that dinner is here, we may as well eat it," Touie said, pragmatic as always.

Dinner there was, but eating it was something else. Mr. Telling did his best in the small kitchen used to heat up food for Mr. Dodgson's parties, but the stove had not been lit, and the water not laid on. The soup was cold, with gobbets of fat riding on top of the broth like little dumplings. The fowls were tough, with burned patches of skin that had not been removed when the spits were not properly turned. The new asparagus was stringy, the carrots still had bits of dirt that had not been scrubbed off, and even the sweet was sour, since the only form of tart was dried cherry.

Mr. Dodgson endured the meal in silence feeling more and more mortified with every bite. Touie bravely ate what was put before her, but Mr. Dodgson could read dismay on her usually cheerful face. Touie's redoubtable mother had set a veritable banquet before him in Southsea, and this was hardly a way to repay the social obligation.

For his part, Dr. Doyle decided to treat the whole matter as a joke. "Touie, my dear, did I ever tell you about the time my mother's old cook decided to serve us a haggis?"

"No, Arthur, I do not think you did."

Dr. Doyle turned to his taciturn host. "It's a Scottish country dish, you see, of oatmeal and vegetables and the, ah, odds and ends of a sheep, all baked in a sheep's stomach. Robert Burns wrote a poem on the subject, but it's clear he never actually ate one."

Mr. Dodgson swallowed a piece of cold chicken.

"Of course, there were worse meals than this one on the whaler

I sailed in the Arctic," Dr. Doyle went on, apparently oblivious to his host's displeasure. "There was one time I was persuaded to try seal blubber."

"How odd!" Touie glanced at Mr. Dodgson. The older man's face was becoming more and more set in lines of rigid disapproval.

Dr. Doyle continued to chatter. The more he talked, the more silent Mr. Dodgson became. Touie looked from one man to the other with a sinking feeling. They were so different, these two: the dry, pedantic scholar in his literal ivory tower, and the vibrant young doctor, with his zest for adventure and endless curiousity. Was there any possibility that they could be friends?

Finally, Telling cleared the dishes and set out a small decanter and two glasses. Touie smiled sweetly at the two of them. "I am the only lady present, but I suppose I must now take my leave and permit you to have your port." Dr. Doyle produced his postprandial cigar from his breast pocket.

Mr. Dodgson had had enough. "Dr. Doyle," he said, in his most disapproving tones, "if I had known you wished to indulge in tobacco, I would have had the smoking room opened for you. You may leave these rooms now. I will have Telling see you to the gate. Good night!"

Dr. Doyle looked at his host. This was more than just rudeness; this was a positive dismissal. What could he do? He looked helplessly at Touie, put his cigar back into his breast pocket, and rose.

"This has indeed been a memorable evening, sir," Dr. Doyle said formally, with an ironic bow. "I trust we will see you tomorrow when you are in a better humor. Good night."

Touie smiled helplessly and took her husband's arm. They followed Telling out the door, where they stood in confusion. Two gentlemen in evening suits and scholars' gowns bowed as they passed on the stairs.

"Good evening," the taller of the two greeted them. "I take it you have been dining with Dodgson."

"If you can call it that," Dr. Doyle said ruefully. "He just threw us out."

The shorter, stouter man with the mutton-chop whiskers gave a sudden crack of laughter. "I daresay you wanted to smoke," he commented. "You should have been warned. Dodgson loathes to-bacco in any form."

"But . . . he never said . . ." Dr. Doyle remembered the occasions when he had lit his pipe in the presence of the sensitive don.

"He wouldn't," the taller man said. "Don't worry, young man. He'll get over his fuss. He always does." The scholar patted the young doctor on the shoulder, leaving the two guests to Telling's care.

"I have never been more disappointed in a man," fumed Dr. Doyle, as Telling led them back to Tom Gate. "Of all the cranky, testy, unpleasant old fogeys! Serving us a cold meal, late, and then denying me a cigar! We would have done better at the White Hart!"

"It was not his fault, Arthur," Touie tried to soothe her husband. "Mr. Dodgson could not know that the very man he discharged so publicly would be the one assigned to serve his dinner. It was very bad, to be sure, but you cannot blame Mr. Dodgson for the food."

"I can blame him for not telling me that he dislikes smoking," Dr. Doyle said. "And dismissing us like that! We go on tomorrow, Touie, wine theft or no wine theft. Let him find his own thieves and blackmailers!" Dr. Doyle defiantly stuck his cigar into his mouth and lit it with a flourish as they marched through the gate and back into St. Aldgates.

Behind them, Mr. Dodgson slunk back into the shadows. He was chagrined that the dinner party had turned out so badly. He had wanted to demonstrate his superiority as a host and instead had revealed himself to be a foolish and proud old man. He would have to apologize to young Dr. Doyle, but not now. Perhaps he would take a walk and clear his mind. Then he could sleep on his anger and make it up to the young man in the morning. He would allow Dr. Doyle to read the proceedings of the so-called Bloody Assizes of 1685. It was the least he could do for Dicky Doyle's nephew.

Dr. Doyle led his wife across the street, back to the White Hart. At the very least he could buy her a small sweet and a cup of tea, if the inn's dining room was still open.

Mr. Dodgson crossed the quad and followed the lane into Christ Church Meadows. Perhaps the murmur of the river would soothe his troubled soul. He strode into the deepening mist that wreathed the grassy swath between the river and the town.

CHAPTER 7

The dinner hour was nearly over, but the twilight lingered. Students who had spent the day in a library or lecture hall now sought the comforts of nature in the college gardens or along the banks of the rivers, before the sounds of Great Tom should drive them behind the college walls for the rest of the night. The shops were closed, but eating places, taverns, and pubs were full of diners and drinkers, debaters and defenders of whatever the topic of debate was at the moment.

The transient guests staying at the White Hart had their choice of entertainment for the evening. According to the knowledgeable porter at the front door, the Apollo Music Hall had the usual bill of singers, dancers, comic recitations, and trained animals. For those lucky enough to receive passes from their offspring, the Oxford Union was debating Home Rule for Ireland. The Oxford University Dramatic Society was presenting *Coriolanus*. Two churches were presenting concerts, and the well-known preacher, Mr. Henry Liddon, was holding a lecture at St. Margaret's Church, where he was vociferously defending the Church against Mr. Darwin's heretical theory of evolution.

Dr. Doyle considered his options. He had thought to spend the evening in consultation with Mr. Dodgson, discussing his new story and possibly getting some more insights into the events of 1685, which were to be the focus of his historical novel. Instead he had been unceremoniously ousted from Christ Church, still hungry, and without even a cigar to console him.

"It's too early for bed," he complained to Touie, as they crossed the road to the White Hart. "And it's too late to get tickets for the theater."

"I should like to see some of the town, Arthur," Touie said. "There is still light, and it is quite warm. I shall get my mantle and perhaps we can stroll along High Street."

"Capital idea!" Dr. Doyle agreed. "It's not as if this were London, where we·might be in some danger. Just run up and get your wrap, and we can take our after-dinner walk."

With Touie safely wrapped up against the rising mist, the two of them joined the steady stream of passersby who strolled northward on St. Aldgates to High Street.

"Over here is where the Bishops Latimer and Cranmer were burned at the stake," Dr. Doyle announced, consulting his guidebook. "And that is Magdalen Bridge." He waved toward the end of High Street.

Touie smiled and nodded. Her thoughts were far from Oxford. She had truly hoped that this brief break in their journey would provide some solace for her husband's troubled conscience. Dr. Waller, the owner of the cottage now used by the elder Mrs. Doyle, had taken Mr. Charles Doyle from his sanctuary and brought him back to grace the family hearth. This, as far as she could tell, was not a good idea. Poor Arthur would have to discuss the matter with the well-meaning landlord and get his father back into custody. In Touie's opinion, this dispute between Mr. Dodgson and Arthur was most unfortunate, destroying the peace of mind so necessary when dealing with persons as difficult as the elder Doyles. Touie sighed and wondered whether she could make peace between her husband and his elderly mentor before she and Arthur had to face the inevitable family unpleasantness waiting for them.

Dr. Doyle, on his part, was already regretting his hasty words.

The old duffer had tried to give them a good dinner. It wasn't his fault that the staff didn't live up to expectations. The young man's natural good spirits took hold, as he found a small bakeshop still open. He and Touie could have a small supper of meat pies and cider, and he would write a little note of reconciliation when he got back to the hotel.

He looked fondly at Touie. At least she had not behaved as many women would, pouting and scowling at the dreadful food and service. He tucked her hand under his arm and led her back down the High to the bakeshop. Tomorrow he would have to get back on the train and face the Ma'am. Tonight, he would enjoy himself.

Their putative host was not among the black-clad students in the High, nor was he among the strollers in St. Aldgates. He had turned east, toward the river and away from the street. Mr. Dodgson had been mortified by the failure of his attempt at sociability. His own college had let him down. He had wanted to show off before the provincial doctor, and instead he had been shown up, to use his students' sporting phrase. What must this young man think of him? A dreadful old crosspatch, a fuddy-duddy of the worst sort! What made the situation even worse was that he had come to respect Dr. Doyle, not only as the nephew of an old friend, but as an up and coming literary figure. He must walk and think of how to make up this ridiculous quarrel.

Mr. Dodgson followed the Dead Man's Walk toward the Botanic Gardens. Perhaps a look at the shrubbery would soothe his harried soul before the evening mist grew to the density of a fog.

Dead Man's Walk, the gruesomely named passage behind Merton and Corpus Christi, held a few passersby on their way toward Christ Church. Mr. Dodgson strode on, around the playing fields, where a squad of Hearties had organized a rugby game. He turned at Rose Lane, where the iron gates of the Botanic Gardens blocked his path, and headed for the High, where he could gather his thoughts on Magdalen Bridge.

The bridge across the Holywell Mill Stream was a focal point for both Town and Gown. Here young women of dubious reputations could find customers for their wares, in spite of the frowns of the college proctors and the urging of the town constables to "Move on, there!" Here chairmen gathered to put their ungainly vehicles away for the night. On a fine spring evening like this, students could gather on the bridge to rehash their debates or join in waggish conversation.

The night was closing in. The gas lamps had been lit on the bridge, sending eerie shadows across the water and making the punts under the bridge look like so many coffins.

Mr. Dodgson stared down at the punts and considered the two problems set before him that afternoon. He was convinced that the scout, Ingram, was responsible for the thefts. He had discharged Ingram out of hand, but that would only send the man elsewhere. Tomorrow, Mr. Dodgson decided, he would send Dr. Doyle out to find evidence that Ingram had pawned the small items that had been stolen. With this in hand, the thief could be turned over to the proper authorities.

That done, Mr. Dodgson turned to the second of the two problems. That a photograph he had taken should be used out of its proper context revolted him more than the meal he had just forced onto his unsuspecting guests. What was more heinous in Mr. Dodgson's eyes was that the page of text that accompanied it smacked of scholarship. Mr. Dodgson was all too aware of the tendency to levity of most of the undergraduates at Christ Church, who were there primarily because it was expected of them rather than for any love of scholarship. Still, there were limits beyond which levity turned into something far more sinister and not humorous at all. Terrorizing female undergraduates came under that heading.

"Why?" Mr. Dodgson said aloud, as he reached the bridge. Why single out Miss Cahill, the daughter of an undistinguished clergyman, for such an attack? Why simply demand that she leave Oxford? The more logical approach would be to threaten to send the photograph to the notoriously straitlaced glass manufacturer unless a certain sum was paid, but no such request had been made. Could it be that the blackmailer's intent was that Miss Cahill should forfeit the legacy offered by her wealthy relation, as reported in the *Oxford Mail*? If so, how did the blackmailer hope to gain by removing Miss Cahill from her school?

Mr. Dodgson stared down into the misty water. The only way that the blackmailer could gain, he decided, was if he belonged to the family or to the household. Clearly, some deeper investigation of Miss Cahill's family circumstances was necessary, but Mr. Dodgson hesitated at using Dr. Doyle's services for so delicate a matter.

Mr. Dodgson frowned into the deepening twilight. He had promised to read Dr. Doyle's new story. He really should return to Christ Church and do it. At least he could give the young writer the benefit of his opinion, and perhaps that would make up for the wretched meal he had served him. Mr. Dodgson's frown relaxed into a rueful smile. He rather liked the energetic Dr. Doyle, and after all, he was Dicky Doyle's nephew.

By this time, Mr. Dodgson had reached the end of the bridge. Now he turned to go back to the High Street side. His attention was drawn to an agitation under the bridge near the stairs that led from the punts docked on the water to the street above. Two figures were struggling with something large and heavy, while a third voice was urging them onward.

The boats under the bridge bobbled and splashed. There was a hollow booming noise, as if someone were stamping on the wooden punts.

"Shh! You're making too much noise! You'll have the bulldogs down on us if you're not careful!" one of the men under the bridge hissed.

"I wish you'd never got me involved in this!" A second whisper echoed under the bridge.

"Just give us a hand, and you can get back to the House."

There was more agitated splashing and the boats joggled again under the bridge.

Mr. Dodgson was now thoroughly alarmed. He looked around for assistance, but the constables and the proctors had done their duty and chased the young women away down the High. The bridge was deserted.

"What's going on down there?" Mr. Dodgson shouted down to the three black-gowned figures he could see in the mist.

The lines of boats jiggled and joggled, as someone clambered about in the darkness. Mr. Dodgson could hear muffled grunts and moans, as if someone under the bridge was carrying a heavy burden.

He tried to make out what was going on. Even the hardiest sportsmen had beached their boats and were making their way back to college by this time of night. Clearly, anyone under Magdalen Bridge must be up to no good.

"Who is there?" Mr. Dodgson called out sharply. "Come out, you two. I can see you!"

There was another grunt, and a creak, and steps echoed on the stone stairs leading up to the street. Mr. Dodgson peered through the rising mist. He could just make out the flapping gowns of undergraduates surrounding one of the bath chairs used to wheel the ladies of Oxford about on their social rounds.

"Stop!" Mr. Dodgson called out. The undergraduates gave the chair a shove that sent it down the High, past the iron gates and carved masonry of the Botanic Gardens.

Mr. Dodgson forgot about his guest, the terrible meal, even the matter of the blackmail. This was far more important and immediate. He was all too aware that undergraduates had deplorably low tastes and were very likely to introduce such unpleasant items as dead fish and live pigs into their college rooms. It was highly probable that these undergraduates had put something undesirable in that bath chair and were conveying it to their college; and it was up to Mr. Dodgson, as a senior member of the University, to prevent them from embarrassing themselves and their college, especially if that college happened to be Christ Church.

The undergraduates wheeled the chair along the High, around the gate that led to Rose Lane, and back toward Christ Church Meadows. They passed the stately elms planted by Dean Liddell and turned into the Broad Walk that led back around the playing fields to Christ Church and the tumbledown slums across the lane.

Mr. Dodgson loped after them, his long coat flapping around

his legs, his high hat apparently held on through sheer magic. The students redoubled their efforts, pushing the chair ahead of them. The chair bounced over stones on the rough gravel path, swaying back and forth on its tiny wheels, while the students pulled, pushed, and guided it around the curved path.

Suddenly, through the mist, the sounds of the bell of Great Tom rang out. It was the hour of nine! There would be one hundred and one strokes of the bell, one for each of the original Fellows of Christ Church. All students must be within the walls of Christ Church before the sound of the last stroke died or face dreadful consequences!

The rugby players ceased their efforts and joined the strollers along Dead Man's Walk or Merton Walk, who gathered their gowns about them and headed back to their colleges. Mr. Dodgson lost sight of the bath chair in a sea of black gowns and mist, as the last stroke of Great Tom left almost visible reverberations in the misty air.

He looked about him. He was in the lane behind the Hall, with the Cathedral doors in front of him and the grubby lodging houses and tumbledown shacks of the Oxford poor behind him.

There was silence, unnerving after the clamor of the bells. Mr. Dodgson stood in the lane at the end of the Broad Walk peering down at his feet. The bath chair had been abandoned by its abductors, who had vanished into Tom Quad. A black form lay across the lane.

"What on earth?" Mr. Dodgson knelt to turn the man over. "Help! Someone help me! There is a man injured here!" He peered more closely at the man who had been dumped at his feet, a sprawling figure in a long black coat.

Heads popped out of windows as dons and undergraduates looked to see what was happening in the lane.

Mr. Dodgson waved urgently. "Someone summon the police! This man is dead!"

CHAPTER 8

T he scholars of Christ Church were faced with a dilemma. The college rules clearly stated that all students had to be within college walls by the time Great Tom finished striking. Nevertheless, the news that there was a dead man in the lane was startling enough to evoke the curiosity of every student in the House. Undergraduates hung out the windows to see what was happening in the lane. Dons peered out from behind the gate that divided the college from the meadows. Scouts ventured into the lane, impelled by the all-too-human failing of curiosity.

In the kitchens, Telling had just finished his evening chores. The information that there was a dead man in the lane came from one of the undercooks, who was setting out the dustbins for the collectors.

"What shall we do about it?" the scullion asked.

"We must inform Dean Liddell," Telling decided and went to the deanery to do so.

On the other side of the lane, the inhabitants of the twisted alleys were just as curious as the learned scholars within the walls of Christ Church to learn what was happening. Lights flickered in the windows of the houses on the Town side of the lane. Men in laborers' corduroy trousers; women in full skirts, checked aprons, and shawls; even children in clean hand-me-downs filtered into the lane from St. Aldgates. More passersby from the road filled the lane, including the patrons of the White Hart and students from Pembroke College, across St. Aldgates from Christ Church. From one person to another the news was carried through the lane to St. Aldgates: There's a dead man in the lane behind Christ Church!

The noise had reached the White Hart, where Constable Effingham had stopped on his evening rounds. A grimy urchin bounced with excitement as he reported, "There's a dead 'un in the lane be'ind Christ Church!"

Constable Effingham frowned. This was serious! He sent the boy to Constabulary Headquarters in Blue Boar Lane and proceeded to the scene of the crime, followed by the entire population of the White Hart.

Dr. Doyle and Touie had just arrived at the White Hart when the procession down St. Aldgates and toward the lane began.

"What's going on?" Dr. Doyle asked.

"Dead man found behind Christ Church," someone reported.

"I may be needed," Dr. Doyle told Touie.

"Surely, not if he's already dead," Touie pointed out.

"Someone may fall into a faint," Dr. Doyle said hopefully.

Touie followed her husband down St. Aldgates and through the crowd into the lane. Nothing she said or did would ever dissuade him from doing what he wanted to do, and she would prefer to be with him rather than be left alone among strangers.

Mr. Dodgson found himself in the unenviable position of being the center of attention. He stood beside the body as the crowd grew larger. Lanterns shed some light on the black-clad form at his feet, while more light streamed out of the windows of the college.

Constable Effingham thrust his way through the crowd, pushing aside the curious onlookers with his baton.

"Wot's all this, then?" the constable demanded, fixing his gaze on Mr. Dodgson and the inert figure at his feet.

"This man is . . . ," Mr. Dodgson began.

Dean Liddell marched into the lane from behind the small mortuary that backed the mews where the college horses had been stabled, followed by the proctor, Mr. Seward, and the ever-present Telling.

"Mr. Dodgson," he began, somewhat breathlessly, "what is this about a body?"

"Good lord! Mr. Dodgson? Have you found another one?" Dr. Doyle's unmistakable Scottish burr rang over the buzz of the crowd. The young man had wriggled his way to the fore, dragging Touie with him.

" 'Oo is it, then?" Constable Effingham demanded.

"It ap-pears to be one of our scouts. I b-believe his name was Ingram," Mr. Dodgson began.

"Ingram!" That was Telling, frowning grimly at the defunct scout. "What does he think he's playing at?"

"He is not p-playing." Mr. Dodgson struggled to control his stammer. "He is very d-dead."

Dr. Doyle squatted to examine the body. "Here, let's have a look." He motioned one of the townsmen to bring his lantern closer. "This is quite interesting."

" 'Ow did 'e die?" Constable Effingham asked.

"I can't say without an autopsy, but he appears to have been in the river." Dr. Doyle pointed to the man's soaking-wet jacket and trousers. "Here's waterweed, and there's more on his hands and ground under his nails."

"Dear me," Mr. Dodgson said, in distress. "I spoke very sharply to him just this afternoon. In p-point of fact, I had to discharge him. For insolence," he added, with an apologetic look at Dean Liddell.

"Did you now?" Constable Effingham had his notebook out and was carefully inscribing this information.

"Not a suicide, surely!" Dean Liddell exclaimed.

"He did not strike me as the sort of man who would jump into the river because he had been sacked from his job," Dr. Doyle said. "Quite the opposite, I think."

Telling agreed. "He did not return to Christ Church this evening," he told the constable.

"Then 'oo was the last to see 'im?" Constable Effingham looked about, in case some witness should come forward. None did. He turned back to Mr. Dodgson with a ferocious scowl. "Wot did you think you was doing, out 'ere in the fog?"

"I was walking," Mr. Dodgson said testily. "I was near Magdalen Bridge, and I thought I saw some students pushing a bath chair. I could only assume that they were bent on some mischief, so I followed them to stop them if I could."

Doyle pointed to the ground near the body. "Tracks," he said crisply. "At least three men and the wheels of the chair. They stop there." He pointed to the chair, still canted over on its side.

"No other footprints?" Mr. Dodgson peered at the ground.

"Effaced by this crowd." Dr. Doyle grimaced, frustrated by the lack of evidence.

Constable Effingham looked over the crowd and saw reinforcements arriving. "Everybody clear away," he ordered.

The crowd took two paces back then parted so that a second group of policemen could advance into the lane, led by Inspector Truscott of the Oxford Constabulary.

"Constable, what have we here?" Inspector Truscott, a tall man in the pepper-and-salt sack suit worn by every office worker from Plymouth to Glasgow took over the investigation with quiet authority.

Effingham saluted and reverted to the official formula he had memorized. "Body of college scout, name of Ingram, as identified by this gentleman," he stated, in his most official tones.

Inspector Truscott eyed the man squatting down beside the body. "And who are you?" he demanded.

"Dr. Doyle. Arthur Conan Doyle, of Portsmouth," Dr. Doyle stood up and introduced himself.

"Indeed." Inspector Truscott knelt and gave the late Ingram a cursory look. "And what can you tell us, Dr. Doyle?"

"Without a proper autopsy, I can't tell much," Dr. Doyle admitted. "However, I don't think he fell into the river accidentally, and I'm sure he was held under for some time."

"And what makes you think that?" Inspector Truscott regarded the visitor with a quizzical air.

"Look here," Dr. Doyle squatted down again. "Look at the hands." He picked up one of the limp arms to exhibit them. "Under the nails. Dirt is ground in, and there are pieces of grass and weed, also ground in, as if the victim had been clutching at the bank of the river." Dr. Doyle whipped out his trusty magnifying glass from his waistcoat pocket to demonstrate. "He'd hardly try to get out if he'd just pitched himself in."

"Quite so." Inspector Truscott took a better look at the young man in the dress suit and deerstalker cap.

"Dr. Doyle has had a good deal of experience in forensic examinations." Mr. Dodgson put in a good word for his protégé. "He has assisted the police in Portsmouth and Brighton on several occasions."

"In that case," Dean Liddell announced, as he decided to make his presence felt, "perhaps this young man might give us the benefit of his expertise. Inspector . . . ah . . . ?"

"Truscott. Oxford Constabulary." He stood up, eye to eye with the stately Dean of Christ Church. "And this is a matter for the police, sir. We will remove the body."

"I beg your pardon, Inspector, but this man was an employee of Christ Church, which makes it a University matter," the Dean demurred. "And we have our own mortuary right here where we may perform the autopsy tomorrow morning under the direction of our own pathologist. Naturally, we shall report our findings to the police."

Inspector Truscott's expression hardened. Constable Effingham glanced at the uniformed sergeant who had accompanied the Inspector. Clearly, the Oxford Constabulary had its rights and privileges, and the old Town versus Gown battle was about to be joined again.

"Dean, Inspector," Mr. Dodgson put in, "may I suggest that this unfortunate man be removed from this place as soon as possible? It is getting late and nothing can be gained by wrangling over who has the honor of the autopsy."

"And what do you propose?" Dean Liddell asked, annoyed at being interrupted by a mere don, and one with whom he had had many disputes on college matters.

"That our own Dr. Kitchin should conduct the autopsy, as he would in any case, but that Dr. Doyle should assist and that a police surgeon should also be present," Mr. Dodgson said. "I shall be glad to give my statement to Inspector Truscott. As I told this constable, I saw some students near Magdalen Bridge. I suspect it is they who found this unfortunate man. I would not like to think it of our undergraduates, but one of them might have felt it necessary to convey the man here. Perhaps they did not know the gravity of their offense."

"You had words with the man," Constable Effingham referred to his notes.

"That 'e did!" A woman in a checked shirt and flowered skirt corroborated it. "Right in the street! Nice way for a gentleman to carry on, I says."

"I was upset," Mr. Dodgson tried to defend himself.

"This fellow had been extremely rude," Dr. Doyle defended his mentor. "And there was a possibility that he might have been behind certain thefts that were reported to Mr. Dodgson earlier in the day."

"Doesn't seem to be a good reason to sack a man in the middle of the street," Truscott commented. "I'll have to speak with anyone who knew this man. What were his duties? Where did he live?"

Before he could continue, Dean Liddell took over. "This outrage took place on University grounds, and it was perpetrated on a University employee," he pronounced loftily. "We will conduct the investigation, Inspector, although you and your men may inform us of anything you find outside the college grounds."

Inspector Truscott's face began to redden as he listened to Dean Liddell's measured tones. In a voice trembling with supressed rage, he replied, "Sir, this body may be that of a University employee, but it was not found on University property. This lane divides the University from the town, and this body is lying upon it. Therefore, sir, I respectfully suggest that you leave the detecting to those who are trained to do it and return to your own bailiwick. I would not venture to instruct you in Greek, sir; do not try to tell me how to do my job."

Dean Liddell's tone was frosty. "Inspector Truscott, I will have you know that we have among us a master of logic, who has taken part in at least one major criminal investigation." He gazed on Mr. Dodgson, who blinked back in some confusion. "Apparently he has also taken it upon himself to conduct a small investigation of his own." He glared at Mr. Dodgson. "Telling has informed me of your conversation this morning regarding the thefts in Tom Quad."

"What investigation?" Inspector Truscott broke in. "What thefts?"

"Small objects were reported missing," Mr. Dodgson confessed. "We did not feel this was a matter for the police."

"Or, apparently, for me!" Dean Liddell snapped. "Well, Mr. Dodgson, I am inclined to let Mr. Seward take over from you in this matter. He is our proctor," the Dean explained to Truscott, "and as such is responsible for the behavior of our students, whether in the town or the University."

Inspector Truscott and Mr. Seward scowled at each other. Proctors had been known to usurp the authority of the town police, arresting prostitutes and pickpockets and removing drunken students from the custody of the constables.

"This isn't a student rag," Truscott reminded the crowd. "This is murder, if this Dr. Doyle is right. And for all I know, one of you might have done it." He looked around the crowd. The students drew back into the shadow of the college walls. The townspeople stepped to their side of the lane. Only the sprawling body of Ingram stayed in its place.

Telling took over. At his signal, three large men in the soiled aprons worn by the college cooks came forward to remove the late Ingram from the road, while Inspector Truscott's men pulled the official ambulance out of the lane.

Inspector Truscott gave in. "Take him to your mortuary," he ordered. "And don't do a thing to him until I can get the police surgeon in to give him a proper autopsy!"

Ingram was borne off, to be laid on a wooden table in the small stone building that had been the site of anatomy classes for the past three hundred years.

"And now, Mr. Dodgson, perhaps you can tell me some more about this Ingram," Truscott said.

"I will be glad to give you my statement, sir, but not in this lane. If you wish, you may come to my rooms and we shall have some hot tea. Dr. Doyle, if you would care for something more stimulating, I have some sherry. Good sherry," he added.

Dean Liddell stepped back into the discussion. "If Inspector Truscott is to conduct any investigation, it should not be done in your rooms, Mr. Dodgson, but in Hall, where the students may be summoned by our own proctor."

Dr. Doyle tried to find Touie, who had worked her way through the crowd. He now looked questioningly at Mr. Dodgson, as if to ask, "What about my wife?"

"Perhaps you should see your wife back to her rooms and then come back to the Hall," Mr. Dodgson answered the unspoken question. It was as much of an apology as he could give, and Dr. Doyle accepted it as such.

"I would like to speak to the inspector myself," he said.

The townspeople drifted back to the other side of the lane and dispersed into their own hovels. The undergraduates and Senior Students moved back to Tom and Peckwater Quads, behind the walls of Christ Church. Once again silence reigned in the college.

One man remained in the shadows, a burly figure with a military air about him. "Damned greedy bastard," he swore. "Now it's all to do over again. The gentlemen are not going to like this, not one bit."

CHAPTER 9

Inspector Truscott followed Dean Liddell and his entourage through the back gate behind the mews into Tom Quad, while the body of the late James Ingram was deposited in the mortuary.

Sergeant Everett approached his superior officer with a deferential cough.

"We've interviewed everyone in the lane, sir. No one saw anything until this gentleman here"—he indicated Mr. Dodgson—"gave the alarm."

Inspector Truscott turned to Dean Liddell. "In that case, I will want to interview everyone who knew the deceased," he said. "It would be convenient if I could do so on the college premises. Otherwise, the interviews would have to take place at Headquarters in Blue Boar Lane."

Dean Liddell's expression made it clear that neither of these choices was a good one. "Can this not wait until morning?" he asked.

"The sooner the better," Inspector Truscott replied. "The usual procedure in these cases is to conduct the interviews in the home of the deceased, but in this case, the deceased had no proper home."

Telling glanced at Dean Liddell and said, "Ingram had rooms in the lodging house across the lane." He pointed to a window directly opposite the walls of Christ Church. "Several of our scouts who do not live in the college have rooms there. Mrs. Perkins is the widow of one of our old scouts, and we often send customers her way."

"No family?" Inspector Truscott had his notebook out and was jotting cryptic notes. "Did he never tell you of any kin hereabouts?"

"We did not converse," Telling said loftily. "But when he applied for the position, he mentioned that he had once been in private service near Oxford."

"Indeed." Inspector Truscott's voice was noncommittal.

Dean Liddell had conferred with Seward. Now he turned to Inspector Truscott and said, "You may conduct your interviews in Hall. Mr. Seward and I will be present, of course."

Truscott's face betrayed no hint of emotion at the news that he would be merely tolerated on the college grounds.

"Sergeant Everett," he said crisply, "there is a bath chair here. Find out where it came from, who owns it, and who brought it here."

"Yes, sir." Sergeant Everett leaned over the chair and noted the number on the brass plate on the overhanging hood. Each chair would be registered to one or another chairman, just as the cabs were registered. It would be easy to find out whose this chair was.

"B-but I was certain there were undergraduates . . ." Mr. Dodgson tried to explain.

Truscott ignored him and turned to the rest of the scholars of Christ Church. The quad was filled with men, young and old, in subfusc and tweeds, all chattering among themselves. Undergraduates, drawn by the noise, filled the quad, buzzing with excitement. Senior Students were more circumspect, although just as curious. They clustered around Dean Liddell as he and Inspector Truscott rounded the corner of the morgue and stepped onto the stone-flagged path around the grassy lawn in the middle of the quad.

"Is it true that one of our students is accused of murder?" That was Vere Bayne, the former curator of the Senior Common Room.

"We shall all be killed in our beds!" Mr. Duckworth declared, in a voice quavering with fear.

"Nonsense!" Dean Liddell's forthright tone cut through the hubbub. "Gentlemen, this is Inspector Truscott. He is the policeman in charge of this unfortunate business. It seems that one of our scouts had a fatal accident and drowned in the river. According to Mr. Dodgson, some students must have thought it a lark to transport the body and drop it in our lane. This is most serious. The removal of a body from the scene of the crime is itself a crime. It is also irreligious, a desecration of human dignity, and hardly a matter for levity." The Dean stared at some very young men who were tittering among themselves. "If there is anyone here who has any information about this man"—he turned to Seward who gave him the name—"Ingram . . ."

"Wasn't he the scout on the west side of Tom Quad?" someone piped up.

"Tall chap? Po-faced? Nasty tongue in his head?" The descriptions came from various directions.

"So it would appear." Inspector Truscott was taking notes in the small notebook carried by all members of the Oxford Constabulary.

Telling had overseen the depositing of the body in the mortuary. Now he approached Inspector Truscott deferentially but with a certain dignity.

"If I may have a word, Inspector . . ."

"Yes? What is it?"

"In private?" Telling hinted. Inspector Truscott nodded gravely. He turned his attention to the gathering before him.

"I must ask that anyone with any information about this man Ingram come forward now. I will be in this Hall. . . . ?" He turned to Seward, who nodded back. "Very well. Gentlemen, I will be taking your statements in Hall. Dean Liddell will also be present, as will your own proctor." He did not mention Mr. Dodgson, who edged through the crowd with a worried frown.

Dr. Doyle was torn between his duty to his wife and his desire to continue with his investigations. Touie came to his rescue.

"Go along, Arthur," she whispered. "Mrs. Gelbart has been telling me about her son and his new living." She smiled at a stout woman in a ribbon-trimmed bonnet and paisley shawl with whom she had apparently struck up a friendship. "She and her husband are staying at the White Hart, and they can see me back there."

"You're sure?" Dr. Doyle asked.

"You must help Mr. Dodgson," Touie said, with a smile. "But you must tell me all about it when you come back to our rooms."

Dr. Doyle gave in and followed the crowd back into Tom Quad and to the shallow steps that led up to the Hall, the oldest and largest single area in Christ Church. Telling and Seward stood at the doors, as if to say, Enter and be awed!

Inspector Truscott refused to be awed. The stained-glass windows were dark by now; the polished tables lay bare, without their usual quota of napery and tableware; the painted portraits of notable graduates of Christ Church were nearly invisible in the shadows cast by the oil lamps that hung from the famous hammer beams of the ceiling.

Dean Liddell and Mr. Seward arranged themselves behind Telling and regarded Inspector Truscott with the look one gives an unwanted door-to-door salesman. Mr. Dodgson and Dr. Doyle edged into the Hall and lurked in the shadows behind the Dean and the proctor. Inspector Truscott ignored them all. Instead, the Inspector sat down on one of the long benches and indicated that Telling should do the same. Telling remained standing, his face impassive, as any good butler's would be under similar circumstances.

"Now," he said firmly. "Who was this Ingram, and how did he get into the lane?"

"He was a scout," Telling said. "One of our servants," he added, condescendingly.

"Who hired him?" Truscott shot out.

"I did," Mr. Dodgson said, stepping out of the shadowy nook

where he had effaced himself. "I am in charge of hiring all the college scouts in my capacity as curator of the Senior Common Room."

Inspector Truscott noticed someone lurking behind Mr. Dodgson. "Isn't that the doctor? What's he doing here?"

"Dr. Doyle thought he might be able to add more to what is known." Mr. Dodgson stepped aside to let Dr. Doyle touch his hat to the police and the two senior servants.

"I don't see how, considering he never clapped eyes on Ingram until today," Telling said snidely, allowing himself one moment of human emotion. He instantly regretted it, and the impassive expression of the butler took over once again.

"But there were certain indications that led me to conclusions," Dr. Doyle defended himself.

Inspector Truscott sighed. "Very well, Doctor, what did you notice, aside from the fact that the man was dead and that he had dirt under his nails?"

Dr. Doyle tugged at his mustache. "I know very little of college protocol," he admitted. "My days as an undergraduate were spent in Edinburgh, and I did not live in college but in digs. But I was struck by Ingram's manner toward his superiors. He was surly and rude."

Telling shrugged. "Some of our scouts have been with us for so long that they take a fatherly interest in undergraduates."

"Did Ingram?" Inspector Truscott wanted to know. He took out his notebook again.

"Ingram was new," Mr. Dodgson said, looking at Telling for reassurance. "I believe he was taken on after Christmas, for Hilary term. We were rather short of staff, due to the dreadful weather. Several of our scouts had been given permission to go home for the holidays, and two did not return, having contracted pleuresy and catarrh. They had to be replaced quickly, and Ingram was hired to take the place of, um . . ." He looked at Telling again.

"Jackson," Telling supplied.

"And I suppose this Jackson will confirm that he really was ill." Inspector Truscott's tone implied that the unknown Jackson might have been malingering.

Telling looked at Inspector Truscott with great pity. "As to that I could not say, but it was a very hard winter, as you may recall. In fact"—he turned to Mr. Dodgson—"Jackson has written to ask if he may take up his duties here again. He was with us for some time, sir, and I was sorry to have to replace him; but Hilary term was upon us, and Ingram's references were in order."

"I don't suppose you'd have them handy?" Inspector Truscott eyed Telling with misgiving. Clearly this man would do anything to uphold the honor of Christ Church.

"I could not say." Telling's face was that of the perfect butler, betraying nothing.

"So you hired this man on the strength of his references," Truscott summed it up. "Where had he worked before?"

"He came with a letter from White's in London. He was recommended to apply here after he had looked for a position at Vincent's, where there were no openings. Vincent's is a club for the sporting gentlemen in Oxford," Telling added.

"I've heard of it," Inspector Truscott admitted.

Telling went on, "If I had had any doubts about Ingram, I would never have taken him on. He knew his work, and he did it."

"What, exactly, did he do?" Inspector Truscott looked about the Hall.

Telling smiled smugly. "Scouts are expected to keep the students' rooms in order. They make up the beds, do the dusting, perform all the services expected of a gentleman's attendant. Young gentlemen can be untidy."

Inspector Truscott allowed himself a small smile. His own sons kept their room in the small detached house in Jericho in a constant turmoil.

"Is that all that Ingram was supposed to do? Keep the rooms tidy?"

"Our scouts also serve meals in Hall and in rooms, should any student care to dine privately," Telling explained.

"And they occasionally run errands for students, should they be called on to do so," Seward added.

"Errands that take them out of the college grounds?" Inspector

Truscott was on the trail of something. "What was Ingram doing by the river?"

"That, Inspector, is the question!" Everyone turned to look at Mr. Dodgson, who tapped the table with one gray-gloved finger. "I last saw Ingram alive as the clock was striking five in St. Aldgates, as Dr. Doyle here will confirm. He was supposed to serve my dinner at seven. Mr. Telling will tell you that he was not in the kitchens, for my dinner was not served until nearly eight o'clock."

Telling and Doyle both nodded in agreement.

"Therefore," Mr. Dodgson continued, "we can place the probable time of death between five o'clock and eight forty-five, which is when I saw the body being removed from Magdalen Bridge."

"That's very interesting, but what was he doing?" Inspector Truscott asked. "Aside from being drowned, of course."

Mr. Dodgson frowned slightly. "Before he took leave of us, he said something quite odd. Do you recall, Dr. Doyle? He said, 'If you wish to speak to me, be at Magdalen Bridge at six o'clock.' At the time I was quite annoyed with him, and there was no reason for me to go all the way to Magdalen Bridge to speak with him, assuming that I wished to do so."

"He must have meant that invitation for someone else," Dr. Doyle pointed out.

"Any idea who?" Inspector Truscott asked sarcastically.

Dr. Doyle looked at Mr. Dodgson, then back at the Inspector. "It was going on five o'clock. The street was quite full of all sorts of people. I suppose Ingram might have seen someone, or recognized someone, and made the appointment for them to meet at six."

"There would be few persons out at that time," Mr. Dodgson put in. "Most of the citizens go home to their suppers by then, and there are no colleges whose dining halls have a view of the bridge. The trees and shrubs are in full leaf, and the shrubbery conceals the steps down to the boats under the bridge."

"And Ingram could meet someone for a nice, quiet chat," Truscott finished. "Now, if one of you could tell me just who the someone was, we could all go home."

Mr. Dodgson shook his head with a puzzled frown. "I cannot tell you more," he said. "Perhaps Dr. Doyle's autopsy will give more information tomorrow."

Inspector Truscott's face wrinkled into a grimace that passed as a smile. "Thank you, gentlemen. You have been most helpful." His tone implied otherwise. "Sergeant!" Truscott shouted. Everett appeared at the door. "Sergeant, I want to speak with everyone who had rooms where this Ingram worked."

"That would include me," Mr. Dodgson said. "Ingram was posted at the west side of Tom Quad where I have my rooms."

"And you've given me your statement, sir," Truscott assured him. "Now, if you will let me do my job, you can go back to those rooms, and a good night to you, too, Dr. Doyle."

Mr. Dodgson and Dr. Doyle were firmly shown out by Sergeant Everett, who looked over the sea of black-gowned scholars and undergraduates.

One young man shoved to the front of the crowd, while the dons muttered behind him.

"I have important evidence," he announced.

"And who are you, sir?" Sergeant Everett inquired.

"Martin, Gregory Martin," the young man explained. "Ingram was the scout on my staircase. He was always poking about where he wasn't expected or wanted. I'm sure he took things . . ."

Mr. Dodgson interrupted the impassioned undergraduate. "What is this? I was informed that there had been reports of thefts on Ingram's staircase."

Martin turned to the older man. "Yes, I told Telling about it. Things were missing, like my studs." He took a deep breath and went on. "And it occurred to me that if Ingram was pinching things, then maybe one of his, er, mob, found out that he'd been, er, copping out on him, and, ah, grassed on him." He looked from Sergeant Everett to Mr. Dodgson, waiting for applause at this example of logic, his blue eyes bright behind his spectacles.

"Where on earth did you learn thieve's slang?" Dr. Doyle exclaimed.

Martin's face grew pink with embarrassment. "I'm going into Orders soon, and my living includes some rather unsavory areas near Birmingham," he confessed. "And I thought I should learn some of the, er, lingo. In order to be able to speak with my parishioners, you see," he explained earnestly.

"And just how did you acquire this linguistic knowledge?" Mr. Dodgson queried.

Mr. Martin grew even pinker. "There are certain, ah, books," he said. "Crime stories, and so forth."

"Indeed." Mr. Dodgson considered Mr. Martin for a moment. "I think you should tell the good Inspector what you suspect about Ingram," he decided. "It is possible that the police will discover that this is a very ordinary, sordid misunderstanding between villains." Young Mr. Martin looked eagerly at Sergeant Everett.

"If you please, young man, I'll have a word with the Inspector." Sergeant Everett ducked back into the Hall, leaving Martin to wilt under the glares directed at him by Senior Students and classmates alike.

"Do you think this is the result of a quarrel between villains?" Dr. Doyle followed Mr. Dodgson across Tom Quad and back to the gate.

"I think there is more to it than that," Mr. Dodgson said firmly. "When I accused Ingram of the thefts, I may have been overwrought; but I am more and more convinced that I was right, and he was the thief. He may well have been behind the theft of the wine, although I do not understand why he should remove the bottles, only to sell them where they would be likely to be recognized. And then there is the matter of Miss Cahill . . ." Mr. Dodgson's voice drifted off as he mumbled to himself.

"What does Ingram have to do with Miss Cahill and her difficulties?" Dr. Doyle asked.

"I do not know that Ingram's death has anything to do with either the thefts or Miss Cahill. I suspect that one or the other might be at the bottom of the matter, but there is as yet no proof of anything. If Inspector Truscott and his men find a pawnshop ticket in Ingram's possessions, then they will find proof of something . . . but what, I could not say. Good night, Dr. Doyle. We shall meet tomorrow morning, when we will discuss these matters further."

"Will you breakfast with Touie and me at the White Hart?" Dr. Doyle offered.

"Perhaps you should come to me," Mr. Dodgson countered. "I do owe you a meal, and this time, Telling will serve it himself."

Dr. Doyle nodded. "Very well, sir. I will not continue my journey until we have solved this mystery, one way or another!"

Mr. Dodgson smiled suddenly in the darkness. "Dr. Doyle," he said, "I have been a dreadful host to you and your good wife. You must not let me hold you from your family obligations any longer."

"Nonsense!" Dr. Doyle said forcefully. "You know me, sir. I am like the sleuthhound when the game is afoot. I shall meet you here for breakfast, sir, and we will decide on a course of action that will uncover the truth of Ingram's crimes."

"Indeed, I believe we will," Mr. Dodgson said. "And I shall read your newest manuscript tonight, Dr. Doyle. It is the least I can do for Dicky Doyle's nephew."

CHAPTER 10

The May evening turned into a chilly night, as Oxford, both Town and Gown, settled into its usual routines. Behind the stone walls and redbrick edifices, students pored over their essays and dons disputed their theories until well after midnight. The unfortunate demise of a college servant was not so important as the declension of Latin verbs or the inner meaning of the verses of Dante in the eyes of those undergraduates who might be asked to discourse on these in the very near future. To the learned scholars, scouts were part of the furniture, the wheels that kept the college going. The death of one scout was an inconvenience, not so important as the state of the Flemish economy during the Wars of the Roses, or the origin of the Hungarian language, or the underlying meaning in the poems of William Blake.

Not everyone connected with the University was engaged in scholarship. The proctors knew just which billiard halls, taverns, and houses of pleasure catered to the sprigs of the aristocracy who came to Oxford, not for learning, but for sport of one kind or another. On this night as every night, they made their rounds, scooping up young men engaged in cards or dice, or dallying with young women. If any of these young men knew or cared that a servant had been taken out of the river and transported to Christ Church, they did not say so. They were sent back to their colleges to be fined, gated, or rusticated, as their preceptors saw fit.

None of the young ladies at Lady Margaret Hall were among those engaged in sport or dalliance. Miss Wordsworth's charges were safely indoors by nine o'clock, chattering away in the Junior Common Room as if they were debutantes and not the standard-bearers of the New Woman, blazing a path for the next generation of female scholars. Several of the undergraduates were clustered around the piano, singing. Others were engaged in fancywork, embroidery and crochet. While none could be called beauties, the ladies of Lady Margaret Hall would eventually be able to grace any dinner table in any corner of the Empire, holding their own with the Empire builders around them. Miss Wordsworth smiled fondly on the scene, mentally checking over the roster of young ladies, as she sat and dispensed both tea and advice from her post at the table where tea and cakes were made available to the ever-hungry students.

"Miss Laurel." Miss Wordsworth beckoned the oldest of her students over to the table.

"Yes, Miss Wordsworth?" Miss Laurel looked up from her book.

"You accompanied Miss Cahill, Miss Bell, and Miss Talbot to the Cathedral this afternoon," Miss Wordsworth noted. "Did they have a good afternoon at Christ Church?"

"It was most interesting," Miss Laurel said. "We examined the stained glass in the Cathedral, and we met Mr. Dodgson. It seems Miss Cahill had a previous acquaintance with Mr. Dodgson, and he kindly invited Miss Cahill to tea."

"Mr. Dodgson?" Miss Wordsworth's eyebrows rose and the very ribbons on her cap rustled in curiosity. "I had no idea that Miss Cahill had acquaintance with Mr. Dodgson. He has never mentioned such a thing to me."

Miss Laurel looked blankly at her mentor. "Miss Cahill's acquaintance, if such you may call it, was quite brief. Mr. Dodgson photographed her when she was small, during a visit her parents paid to Oxford. He was entertaining guests, a Dr. Doyle and his wife; and I assumed that under those circumstances, I could allow the young ladies to go to his rooms for tea. I hope I did the correct thing."

Miss Wordsworth smiled graciously. "Of course, Miss Laurel. Mr. Dodgson is well known to us, and since there was another woman present, our rules could be relaxed. I see no harm in Miss Cahill's recalling the occasion of their meeting."

Miss Laurel smiled gratefully at Miss Wordsworth. "Nor did I. It was a most pleasant afternoon."

"And the conversation . . . ?" Miss Wordsworth's eyebrows raised in inquiry.

Miss Laurel wetted her suddenly dry lips. "Miss Cahill recalled how Mr. Dodgson had taken her photograph on the occasion of her parents' visit to Oxford when she was a child," Miss Laurel repeated. She briefly considered relating the rest of the afternoon's disclosures but decided against it. Miss Wordsworth was not to know that one of her students had placed herself in a position to be blackmailed, and the nature of the blackmail was such that it would only bring pain to Miss Wordsworth and dishonor upon the school. Better to be silent and let Mr. Dodgson and his redoubtable ally, Dr. Doyle, handle the situation.

"I see." Miss Wordsworth saw that there was more to it, but that she would get nothing out of Miss Laurel by direct questioning. She tried another approach. "I could not help but notice that you were upset at dinner, Miss Laurel," Miss Wordsworth said, lowering her voice so that they would not be overheard by the girls. "Surely, nothing occurred during this tea party that would shock or offend our students! Mr. Dodgson has the habit of striking up friendships with young children, but I have never heard of him taking any liberties with our undergraduates. You know that Miss Rix is a particular favorite of his, and that she may prevail upon him to lecture here on logic and mathematics."

Miss Laurel looked at Miss Wordsworth in astonishment. "Mr. Dodgson was quite kind," she said. "Oh, my, Miss Wordsworth! You must not think . . . that is, nothing was said . . ." She lost herself in a series of half sentences. "No, ma'am. Nothing like that! Only I have had something of a shock."

"Not bad news, I hope." Miss Wordsworth's concern was evident.

"It is not something I care to speak of," Miss Laurel demurred. "I saw someone that I had not seen in some time. I had never expected to see him again."

Him? Miss Wordsworth's eyebrows went up another notch. Here was a mystery, but not one that would be solved easily. Probably the old story: a false lover who had jilted the girl and left for greener pastures. According to her informants at the Women's Educational Alliance, Miss Laurel had been employed as a governess, a situation well known to leave young women prey to the male relations of their little charges.

Miss Wordsworth's eyes hardened. If some blackguard came around Lady Margaret Hall, he would be sent packing! Miss Laurel had been seriously applying herself, with the announced intention of returning to teaching, hopefully in a school where she would continue the work of Lady Margaret Hall by preparing young women for higher studies.

Miss Wordsworth poured out a cup of tea and handed it to Miss Laurel, who accepted it gratefully.

"Thank you, Miss Wordsworth," Miss Laurel whispered. "If I may, I think I shall retire to my room. I wish to go over some notes for tomorrow's tutorial."

Miss Wordsworth listened to the girls at the piano. Gertrude Bell was holding forth, while Dianna Cahill played the piano with more enthusiasm than accuracy.

" 'They intend to send a wire to the moon' " Gertrude caroled, her powerful alto ringing out over the chatter of her friends.

" 'To the moon,' " Mary echoed.

" 'And they'll set the Thames on fire very soon . . .' "

" 'Very soon.' "

Miss Wordsworth frowned. The girls' choice was not to her liking. *Princess Ida* had not been a great success as an opera. Mr. Gilbert's satire on women's education was far too pointed to be humorous, although Sir Arthur Sullivan's melodies were pleasing to the ear. She would have to find more suitable music for the piano; perhaps some of Sir Arthur Sullivan's other compositions.

Miss Wordsworth considered Misses Bell, Cahill, and Talbot, and decided to have a word with each of them before the lights were turned out for the night. They were being too cheerful. Miss Bell sang defiantly, Miss Talbot answered with vigor, but Miss Cahill seemed to be worried about something that had nothing to do with the music. There was definitely something going on, and Miss Wordsworth was going to ferret it out lest it reflect badly on Lady Margaret Hall.

Two miles south of Lady Margaret Hall, Dean Henry Liddell braced himself to deal with his most difficult Senior Student. Mr. Dodgson and Dean Liddell had had a stormy relationship since the Dean had taken charge in 1855. Mr. Dodgson had been tutor to the Dean's oldest son and a willing playmate for his three eldest daughters. The excursion that had led to the story of *Alice's Adventures Underground* had been one of many that Mr. Dodgson took with the Liddell children, and that particular story had been expanded and embellished, printed and illustrated, and was now part of the national consciousness. Little Alice Liddell herself had grown up and was now Mrs. Reginald Hargreaves, with two strapping sons to her credit.

In the intervening years since that summer day on the river, Mr. Dodgson had opposed many of the Dean's reforms. He had been particularly vicious about the ambitious building program that had embellished the old quad with a new tower, in Dean Liddell's eyes a most necessary improvement since the original tower was unsafe. Mr. Dodgson had been officious in his management of the Senior Common Room, making endless lists of wine and supplies, and constantly complaining about the quality of the food, the delivery of his letters, and the presence of workmen at his windows.

Now Mr. Dodgson had taken up a new hobbyhorse, and one that Dean Liddell could only think unsuitable for a scholar of Mr. Dodgson's caliber. It was bad enough when he had been involved in the abduction and rescue of Lord Marbury's daughter, but Mr. Dodgson's explanation of his late arrival from his summer holidays the previous October seemed to have had something to do with another criminal case, and Dean Liddell suspected that there was more than just the bad weather and blockage of snow on the railroad tracks that had kept him in London two months before.

The problem before Dean Liddell was that he needed Mr. Dodgson's advice, as much as he deplored this interest in criminal investigation. The police were unwelcome within University walls, but the death by drowning of one of the college servants could not go unnoticed. Mr. Dodgson's medical companion might be useful in the investigation. On the other hand, Dean Liddell thought, as he watched Mr. Dodgson confer with the young man before sending him back to his inn, the young doctor was not an Oxford man but a jumped-up nobody from Edinburgh. It was all very difficult.

Dean Liddell waited until Mr. Dodgson had made his good-byes to his guest and turned back into Tom Quad. Then he called to the scholar from the Hall steps.

"Mr. Dodgson, may I have a word?" Dean Liddell tried to keep his voice neutral, but Mr. Dodgson could sense the under-tone of urgency. He diverted his steps and proceeded back around Tom Quad to the Hall, where Dean Liddell was waiting patiently for him.

"Dean, it is quite late . . . ," Mr. Dodgson began.

"I am all too aware of the hour," Dean Liddell said testily. As if to answer him, Great Tom boomed out eleven strokes.

"It is also getting quite chilly," Mr. Dodgson noted.

"This will only take a moment." Dean Liddell led the way into the opening of the connecting passage to the cloister garden, which Mr. Dodgson had once labeled "the tunnel."

Mr. Dodgson could only follow his leader, and the two of them stood on the path between the garden and the Cathedral, with one lantern flickering over the passage.

Dean Liddell took a deep breath. This was not going to be easy. "I noticed that you were somewhat forthcoming with the police," he began.

Mr. Dodgson nodded gravely. "I had information pertinent to the case at hand," he stated.

"And you brought forward that protégé of yours, the doctor from Portsmouth."

"Dr. Doyle. Yes, I did. Dr. Doyle is an astute observer, who has had some experience as a police surgeon." Mr. Dodgson's voice took on a defensive edge.

Dean Liddell's voice took on a magisterial tone. "I think, Mr. Dodgson, that you might leave this matter to those best suited to deal with it," he pronounced.

"Meaning the police and the proctors?" Mr. Dodgson's shrill tone rebounded off the walls of the passage.

"Precisely. They have been trained in criminal investigation, whereas you, sir, are a scholar and mathematician. Dabbling in crime is unworthy of your talents, Mr. Dodgson."

Mr. Dodgon's face could not be seen in the shadows, but his voice grew sharper as he replied. "Dean Liddell, I have been involved in this crime already. I saw the undergraduates push the bath chair from Magdalen Bridge, which apparently contained the body of that scout, Ingram. Inspector Truscott seems to suspect that I may have caused this unfortunate man to destroy himself by discharging him without cause. I cannot sit idly by and let my fate be decided by persons unknown to me. If Dr. Doyle can assist in clearing my name, as I am assured he can, then I feel obligated to let him try to do it. Besides," he added, in a softer tone, "thanks to that wretched man's defection, I fed Dr. Doyle an inferior dinner. He and his good wife entertained me quite lavishly when I was detained in Portsmouth last autumn, and I deeply regret that I was not able to reciprocate."

Dean Liddell listened sympathetically to the last part of Mr. Dodgson's speech. He might not be in favor of criminal investigation as a pastime, but he certainly understood social niceties.

"I must insist that you remain on University grounds until this matter is cleared up," the Dean said at last. "However, I see your point about clearing your reputation. It would never do to have one of our dons accused of driving a scout to his death!"

"I never said that I . . ." Mr. Dodgson protested.

Dean Liddell ignored the interruption. "As for your social dilemma, we can have the young man to dine with us in Hall to-morrow."

"That is quite handsome of you, Dean," Mr. Dodgson said. "I shall inform Dr. Doyle of the invitation. I assume, sir, that Dr. Doyle has your permission to investigate the matter of the thefts from the west wing of Tom Quad."

Dean Liddell let out an exasperated sigh. "If your Scottish friend finds anything pertinent to the death of this unhappy man, of course he must lay it before the proper authorities," he told Mr. Dodgson, as he led the way back to Tom Quad. "But I cannot like your indulgence in this sort of thing, Dodgson. You should leave criminal investigation to the police and the proctors, and be content to write your lovely tales and mathematical puzzles."

Mr. Dodgson watched with seething resentment as Dean Liddell marched down to the door of the deanery, where Mrs. Liddell waited to find out what had drawn her husband out at this hour of the night. The Dean, however, smiled to himself in the darkness. He had handled Mr. Dodgson quite well, he thought. Mr. Dodgson would undoubtedly take action now that he had been told to refrain from investigating Ingram's death. The Dean greeted his wife with the news that there had been an unpleasant incident, but the unfortunate matter was in good hands.

Mr. Dodgson took all of two minutes to decide on his next course of action. He had never been one to shirk his duty. It was clearly his duty to remove the taint from his good name. He had deliberately avoided mentioning the matter of Miss Cahill and her photograph to the Dean. "Sufficient unto the day is the evil thereof!"

Now it was late, and Mr. Dodgson had had a strenuous day. He hoped that Telling had removed the remains of the disastrous dinner from his rooms, and that the next day would bring enlightenment.

He climbed the stairs to his own rooms and looked about him. His eye fell on the manuscript left by Dr. Doyle in its marbled portfolio. Mr. Dodgson opened the folder, his heart sinking. The

103

last time he had tried to read one of Dr. Doyle's longer effusions, it had nearly put him to sleep.

This one seemed even less promising. The opening sentence read: "In the year 1878 I took my degree of Doctor of Medicine at the University of London and proceeded to Netley to go through the course prescribed for surgeons in the army." The next two pages detailed the career of this unpromising surgeon.

Mr. Dodgson closed his eyes for a moment and wondered what he should do. Dr. Doyle clearly expected him to read this manuscript, and he had given his word that he would do so, but unbidden thoughts came tumbling through his head. Why had Miss Cahill been singled out from the other women students at Oxford for calumny? What part did the photograph play in the sinister plot? If Ingram was behind it, who had killed Ingram?

With all this running through his brain, Mr. Dodgson gave up on the manuscript. He could not deal with this John Watson, M.D., and his search for lodgings right now. He laid the manuscript aside, promising himself that he would read it before Dr. Doyle left Oxford.

Dr. Doyle and his wife could see the lights in Mr. Dodgson's windows across the road from their rooms at the White Hart as they prepared for bed.

"I'll have to send a telegram tomorrow," Dr. Doyle decided, as he struggled into his nightshirt. "I only hope the Ma'am will understand that I must give whatever assistance I can to the police."

"And to Miss Cahill," Touie added, braiding up her hair as she did every night before retiring. "You know, Arthur, I've been thinking about that photograph."

"Rather murky, wasn't it?" Dr. Doyle folded his jacket and laid it across the rack provided by the White Hart.

"Yes, but I wondered . . . where was the nursemaid?"

"What nursemaid?"

"Why, the one who dressed the child, of course." Touie snuggled under the bedclothes, as her husband proceeded to disrobe. "You wouldn't think of such things, but I remember the dresses

I had to wear when I was a child, and I wasn't a vicar's daughter, either, but the child of a moderately well-to-do gentleman. I remember being laced and buttoned, and I could get out of the dress easily enough, but I couldn't do the buttons and laces myself to get in."

Dr. Doyle blew out the bedside lamp. "Well, do you think you could get out of your dress now?"

Touie's answer was a giggle in the darkness.

There was no such diversion at the headquarters of the Oxford Constabulary, a small apartment just off Blue Boar Lane, conveniently next to one of the best pubs in town. Here Chief Inspector Wheeler listened as Inspector Truscott presented the facts.

"And that's where it stands, sir," he concluded. "Body of one James Ingram, drowned in the river, now in the mortuary at Christ Church awaiting autopsy. Carried into the lane via bath chair, as evidenced by dampness of the seat of the chair and straws from the chair found on the body. Corroboration by Mr. Charles Lutwidge Dodgson, Senior Student of Christ Church, who claims that he saw undergraduates pushing said chair from Magdalen Bridge to the lane behind the college." Truscott shut his notebook with a decided slap of disgust.

Inspector Wheeler frowned. "Transporting a body is interfering with evidence," he stated flatly. "It's not a student lark or a rag. And what's this about some doctor putting his oar in?"

"Visiting from Portsmouth." Truscott consulted his notes again. "Friend of this Dodgson."

"What else?" Wheeler growled.

"Statements taken from undergraduates seem to indicate that this Ingram might have been behind a series of thefts in the students' rooms."

"Thefts?" Wheeler echoed. "Why weren't we called in?"

Truscott's said gravely, "It's the University, sir. They won't call in the police until they have to. I'll have one of the constables go around the pawnshops tomorrow and see where that leads us."

"Up the garden path, more likely than not." Chief Inspector Wheeler shifted uneasily in his chair. "What do you say, Truscott? Is this Dodgson involved in this or not?"

"He's known for writing little puzzles, sir. I'd say, if anyone were to be called in on this thieving business, it would be him and not the proctors."

"Proctors!" Wheeler snorted his disdain. "Fat lot of good they've been. Students grabbing bodies up out of the river, hauling them here and there, and where are the proctors? Chasing whores, that's where!" It was a sore point, as it was with all good citizens of Oxford, that the proctors had the right to enter any residence in search of miscreants and haul them away to be jailed, fined, or stand before a magistrate.

Truscott put his notebook away in his pocket. "Do we call in Scotland Yard, sir?"

Wheeler's face contorted in fury. "We do not! This is the sort of thing we can handle by ourselves, without some jack-a-dandy from London telling us how to run our own cases. Truscott, you take as many men as we can spare and look into this Ingram fellow. I want this cleared up, and quickly!" He pounded the table for emphasis.

"Yes, Chief Inspector." Truscott let himself out of the room, to find Sergeant Everett gazing at him in sympathy.

"What do we do now, sir?"

"We sleep on it," Truscott said. "Things always look better in the morning."

In their rooms in Tom Quad, three undergraduates held a council of war.

"What business was it of yours to go blabbing to the police?" Farlow turned on his least reliable companion in crime and grabbed him by the front of his gown. Chatsworth wriggled between them to separate the former friends.

Martin smoothed out his shirtfront with an air of martyrdom. "I had information pertinent to the inquiry," he said, with wounded dignity. "Ingram was a thief. It is perfectly possible that someone found out about it . . ."

106

"And threw him into the river? For a few trumpery trinkets?" Farlow laughed mirthlessly.

"And how did you know he was there in the first place?" Martin asked.

"What does that matter? I was walking along, and there he was; and I thought it would be a good rag, that's all." Farlow shrugged apologetically at his old schoolmate.

Martin was not to be cajoled. "I still think you might have told me that the body we were supposedly inserting into the job lot for the medical students to have a go at was someone we knew. I don't think that's at all funny, even if you do."

"Couldn't you just see it? Old Kitchin, nattering away, and someone says, 'This is Ingram!' " Farlow fairly beamed with joy at the discomforture of the earnest medical students, most of whom were far below him on the social ladder.

"I just wish you'd left me out of it, Nev, cousin or no cousin. You'll go too far one of these days." The prospective vicar sat back in a fit of sulks.

"He's upset because he's afraid his new inamorata will find out," Chatsworth commented, lighting one of his long, thin cheroots. "The one he bumped into in quad this afternoon." Chatsworth blew a smoke ring. "You know, I do believe we saw them at the Balliol lectures last term perched up on the dais with Briggs. They're from Lady Margaret Hall. The blond's all right, I suppose, if you like them well-stuffed."

"Her name is Dianna," Martin breathed.

"Bother girls!" Farlow dismissed the entire sex with one wave of his arms. "More to the point, Greg, are you rowing with us tomorrow? We need you!"

Young Mr. Martin considered his situation. Which was more important, personal integrity or the honor of the college?

"All right," he said reluctantly. "I'll be at the boathouse tomorrow. But don't think for one moment that you can bamboozle me into taking part in another rag like this one."

He slammed out of the room, leaving Farlow and Chatsworth to their brandy, their cigars, and their thoughts.

CHAPTER 11

The next day brought clear skies and rising temperatures. For the town, this meant another profitable day. Drapers and men's furnishers in Turl Street looked over their stocks and anticipated sales of summer suiting, linen shirts, and lightweight accessories for the coming summer. Farmers brought their fresh produce to the Covered Market early so that the housekeepers serving the married professors in North Oxford could select the choicest bits for the day's meals. Hedgers, thatchers, and other outside workers took up their tools before the heat of midday could overtake them.

The *Oxford Mail* had a brief paragraph stating that the body of one James Ingram had been found in the lane behind Christ Church, and that the police were investigating the circumstance; but word-of-mouth was more powerful than the press. Throughout the town the gossip chain hummed with the news that the body of one of the Christ Church scouts had been found dead in the lane behind the college, and that the likelihood was that obstreperous undergraduates had, for some reason, removed it from the river. The stableman in the college mews had told his friend at the White Hart, who had informed the dustman, who had spread the information along with the more fragrant of his offerings on his rounds. Scouts, maids, outside and inside servants, all knew before their masters and mistresses did that there had been a tragedy at Christ Church, and that the eccentric Mr. Dodgson was mixed up in it.

The passing of a mere scout was not particularly interesting to the scholars behind their college walls. For them, mornings in Oxford began with chapel. All students, of whatever religious persuasion, were expected to file into the space designated by their particular college for the Church of England service, a reminder of those days when the University was run by and for the Church. From Christ Church at the southernmost end of St. Aldgates to Keble at the north end of Park Road, young men flocked into churches, chapels, and small book-lined rooms, their tweed Norfolk suits covered with black fustian gowns, ready to receive religious instruction from their elders.

Morning service in Christ Church filled the Cathedral with dons, undergraduates, and those scouts and cooks who cared to crowd into the limited space made for them at the rear of the building. Nevil Farlow, Minnie Chatsworth, and Gregory Martin were among the late-coming undergraduates, squeezing into the end of their row of wooden chairs.

Usually, the service was conducted by one of Dean Liddell's many substitutes. There was no shortage of clergymen at Christ Church, where most of the dons were ordained into the Church of England. However, this morning was different. A mutter ran through the crowd as Dean Liddell himself mounted the pulpit.

"What's he up to?" murmured Nevil Farlow.

"You don't think he's on to us?" Chatsworth squeaked.

"I knew something like this would happen," Martin said gloomily.

The Dean adjusted his gown and frowned down at his congregation. He had thought long and hard over what he had to impart, and when would be the best time to do it. He had come to the conclusion that the best time to address all of the population of

109

his little kingdom was at this morning's service, ergo, he would do his duty and inform those who did not already know of the tragedy in their midst.

"Gentlemen," Dean Liddell began. The hubbub ceased, as the men of Christ Church listened to their leader.

"As some of you are aware, a most unpleasant incident occurred last night."

Another hubbub indicated that some of the congregation had no idea what the Dean was talking about. He held up a hand for silence.

"The body of one of our scouts was left in the lane behind Tom Quad," the Dean went on. "One of our own dons witnessed the event. He is certain that the perpetrators of this outrage were undergraduates."

Another hubbub, with an undertone of incredulity and outrage, filled the small Cathedral.

Dean Liddell continued his announcements: "Naturally, we will give the police our fullest cooperation in this matter. The death of any of our little family here at the House is always difficult, and although Ingram was but a scout, he was nevertheless one of our own."

"Our own what?" Chatsworth said, just loud enough for his friends to hear.

Dean Liddell's voice drowned out any further irreverent remarks. "Inspector Truscott has been put in charge of the investigation. If anyone has any information pertinent to this matter, I strongly advise him to come forward as soon as possible so that this unpleasant business may be concluded and we can all get on with our studies."

Dean Liddell gazed around the nave. One or more of those men had moved the body of the late Ingram, but to what purpose? Probably some undergraduate with a misplaced sense of humor, he thought, as he descended to more mundane levels. Three decades of guiding lads just going through the last stages of adolescence had left him with a tolerance for youthful mischief that might have driven a lesser man to drink or rage or worse. The Dean was certain that whoever had moved the body had had no

110

idea of the serious implications of the act. He would have to remind them.

"I must bring to your attention the fact that interfering with evidence of a crime is also a crime, and that although some students may consider themselves beyond the reach of the law, this is not so in the case of a wrongful death. I repeat, anyone with knowledge of last night's activities must come forward. Mr. Seward will be in his office, and I shall be in my study should anyone wish to consult us." Dean Liddell looked over the congregation once more, his penetrating glance aimed at driving home the implied warning.

"Let us pray." Dean Liddell opened his prayer book. There was a general rustle of pages, as the men of Christ Church prepared for the morning service.

In his usual place, Mr. Dodgson considered the repercussions of Ingram's death as he went through the service almost automatically as he had for nearly forty years. "It is not logical," he said aloud, causing his friend Duckworth to give him a sharp look and a poke in the side.

"Eh?" Mr. Dodgson tried to keep his mind on the service, but stray thoughts kept creeping in between the canticles of the psalms. Assuming that Ingram had been stealing small items from Tom Quad, what had he done with them? Had he also been stealing the wine? If so, how had he disposed of it, and how had the suspect bottle gotten into the stock at the White Hart? And what, if anything, did this have to do with Miss Cahill's photograph and the feeble attempt to blackmail her through it?

Dean Liddell finished the service. The choir sang their last hymn and the recessional boomed through the small Cathedral as the students burst into the morning sunshine.

Most of them headed for the Hall, where breakfast had been laid out for those who did not take it in their own rooms. Farlow, Chatsworth, and Martin stepped out of the way of the thundering herd and huddled together in the doorway.

"That tears it!" Martin said, turning on the other two. "Why did you have to drag me into this mess, Nev? I'm supposed to be ordained in three months!"

"We needed your brawny arms, Greg," Chatsworth soothed him. "And besides, how were we supposed to know the fellow had been murdered?"

"You bally well did know," Martin retorted. "For all I know, you did it yourselves."

"What?" Farlow grabbed his friend by the front of his gown. "What sort of fellow do you think I am, Greg?"

"The sort who'd move a body for a rag and drag your cousin into it," Martin retorted. He pulled himself away and adjusted his fustian gown. "Well, hear me out, Nev. I won't be party to any more of your rags!"

Chatsworth stood between the two young men, as Mr. Dodgson passed them on the path. All conversation stopped as the don strode by, his eyes on Tom Gate.

"I say we go to Inspector Truscott and tell him we moved the body," Martin insisted, once he was certain that Mr. Dodgson was out of earshot. "He's sure to find out sooner or later anyway, and it will go better with us if we come forward now."

"And lay ourselves open to charges of tampering with evidence? Don't be absurd!" Farlow sniffed.

"It was a rag, that's all," Chatsworth said. "We can say I thought it was funny. We can say we were squiffed."

"And that would be even worse!" Martin clutched his head with both hands, pulling his sandy hair up into spikes. "Oh, why do I let you chaps talk me into these things?"

"Because we make your dull life a little brighter," Chatsworth said, patting his distraught friend on the shoulder.

The budding clergyman shrugged the soothing hand off, straightened his cap, and rearranged his gown. "I still think we should do the right thing and come forward."

Farlow threw his hands up in a gesture of defeat. "Very well, Greg, if you insist. After breakfast you go along to the Bulldog and explain how you were talked into Conduct Unbecoming a Curate by your dreadful cousin Nevil. As for Minnie and me, we're going to the river, and you can meet us there at the boathouse. You need some exercise! You're getting fat!" He aimed a punch at Mr. Martin's substantial midsection. Martin blocked it neatly, sidestepped his companions, and the three of them cheerfully walked around the quad to their breakfasts.

Dr. Doyle and his wife had made their morning ablutions and had drunk an early cup of tea before crossing the road to Tom Gate, where they waited expectantly until Mr. Dodgson hurried over to greet them.

"I see you have deferred your journey," Mr. Dodgson said, as Dr. Doyle and Touie were let into the quad. "After our difficulties last night, I feared you would prefer to continue north to your family."

"I can't rest until I get to the bottom of this mystery," Dr. Doyle admitted. "And Touie has some notions of her own."

"Indeed? We shall discuss them in my rooms," Mr. Dodgson said, as he led the way up the stairs.

Telling himself had seen to the catering this time. A small table had been set up with chafing dishes for eggs, bacon, and sausage, and a rack of toast with a plate of butter pats and a jar of marmalade had been placed on Mr. Dodgson's dining table. Coffee was hot in the pot, and a tea urn was boiling so that Touie could procure her morning beverage.

"Telling," Mr. Dodgson said, before the chief scout could leave, "I would like a word with you when you come to clear the plates."

"On the subject of the late Ingram, sir?" Telling was already ahead of him.

"I wondered that you had taken on such a surly fellow," Dr. Doyle said. "I had heard about the independent ways of Oxford scouts, but he seemed to go beyond what was properly eccentric."

Telling glanced at Mr. Dodgson, as if asking for permission to tell tales out of school.

"Dr. Doyle has offered to assist the police in their inquiries," Mr. Dodgson explained. "He has acted as a consultant to the Portsmouth Constabulary."

Telling's disapproving expression softened slightly. "Ingram was a temporary," he said. "I was going to hand him his notice after we broke up for the summer. I did not consider him suitable for the House." Telling's raised eyebrows spoke louder than his carefully chosen words.

"But surely," Touie put in, "he came with references." Even a lowly kitchen maid had references, that all-important "character" that would follow her throughout her career in service.

"There was a letter from a club in London," Telling said finally. "It stated that Ingram had been with them for some time and had given satisfaction. And, as I told Inspector Truscott last night, he had been sent over from Vincent's, where he had first applied."

"That should have been good enough." Dr. Doyle looked at his wife, who shook her head.

"Nothing said about his honesty?" Touie asked delicately.

"Not in so many words," Telling replied.

"And nothing said about previous employment? Before the London club, I mean?"

Telling frowned. "As I told Inspector Truscott last night, Ingram was not particularly forthcoming on that subject," he said. "However, from some things he said, I would think he had been in private service for a time. He stooped, but when he stood straight he would have been six foot tall. Tall enough for a footman."

"Indeed." Mr. Dodgson nodded. "That might explain his attitude. Footmen are said to be rather haughty, particularly those from distinguished households."

"I know very little about servants," Touie said meekly, "but I do wonder how you get so many of them here. I mean, how do they know there is a position open? I should think it a great honor to be in service at one of these grand colleges, with all this history behind them."

Telling's forbidding look softened at this feminine dithering. "We do not advertise," he told her. "But from time to time there are places, and they are usually filled by persons recommended by other servants. Family members and such."

Mr. Dodgson frowned. "We must have been quite short of staff to take on a person otherwise unknown to us."

"Quite so, sir." Telling was back to the official face again.

"However, considering the references he carried, and the good word put in for him by my colleague at Vincent's, I made an exception. I shall not do so again."

"Have his rooms been examined?" Mr. Dodgson asked.

"Ingram did not have rooms in the college," Telling reminded him. "He lodged in the street opposite us, at Mrs. Perkins's establishment."

"I daresay the police will have been through the place by now," Dr. Doyle said, buttering a muffin.

"Perhaps you will be able to get into his rooms on some pretext," Touie said brightly. "I'm sure you will find a way."

"I should like to know whether any of the small objects removed from Tom Quad might have been found in those rooms," Mr. Dodgson said. "Unfortunately, Dean Liddell has requested that I not leave University grounds until this dreadful business has been cleared up to everyone's satisfaction."

"That seems quite unfair," Touie commented. "How can you clear your name if you are not allowed to leave the grounds?"

Mr. Dodgson slathered marmelade on toast. "I have been gated! Like an unruly undergraduate!" he burst out.

Dr. Doyle set his cup down and had a last bite of his muffin. "In that case, sir, I am at your disposal," he announced, as Telling collected the cups and saucers. "Where do we begin?"

"I believe you should attend the autopsy on Ingram," Mr. Dodgson decided. "After which, you might find out whether the White Hart purchases their wine from our wine merchant. It is possible that I overreacted yesterday and that a natural mistake was made. If necessary, you could consult Snow, who has a stand in the Covered Market. We order most of our wine from him."

Touie cleared her throat. "Mr. Dodgson?"

Mr. Dodgson turned to see who had interrupted his train of thought.

"Mr. Dodgson, I think I may be of some use in this business," Touie said. "It occurred to me last night that I am much the same age as the young ladies of Lady Margaret Hall, and they might be able to speak to me of matters that they would never discuss with a gentleman."

"Excellent idea, Touie!" Dr. Doyle applauded. "But you will be careful, won't you? I don't want you running into any danger. If there's a murderer on the loose, I don't want you anywhere near him."

Touie laughed and patted her husband's hand. "I won't be in any danger at all, Arthur. Who would want to hurt me?"

"Dr. Doyle is quite right," Mr. Dodgson said severely. "Someone is desperate enough to have killed once. We must be on our guard, Mrs. Doyle."

"And what will you be doing while Arthur and I are running about finding things for you, sir?" Touie asked Mr. Dodgson, as her husband helped her on with her jacket.

"I think I shall have a word with one or two of my colleagues regarding the authorship of this piece of, ahem, literature." Mr. Dodgson picked up the loathsome page and read it again, his face screwed into an expression of the utmost repulsion. "Last night's adventure indicated to me that undergraduates of Christ Church are involved in this escapade, and perhaps some of my colleagues here at the House may recognize either the hand or the style. Well, Dr. Doyle, Mrs. Doyle, shall we get on with it?"

Dr. Doyle adjusted his tweed deerstalker cap. "The game is afoot!" he proclaimed, and left his wife with Mr. Dodgson, while he descended into Tom Quad, eager to be the first one at the mortuary to observe the autopsy.

The news of the tragedy at Christ Church reached Lady Margaret Hall with the delivery of the milk. Miss Wordsworth frowned as the scouts whispered behind the door to the dining room, where the students were gathered for breakfast.

"What is the matter?" she asked, as the maid allowed the toast to spill off the platter and onto the table.

"Oh, ma'am, there is such news! One of the scouts at Christ Church found in the lane behind the college! Discharged in the middle of the street, they say, and took his own life!" the girl blurted out.

"Nonsense!" Miss Wordsworth snapped. "Where did you ever hear such a thing?"

116

"Milkman says he got it from the dustman, and he got it from the stableman at the White Hart, who saw it all," the maid sniveled.

"I agree it is a dreadful thing but not the sort of news one expects to get at breakfast," Miss Wordsworth said severely. "Besides, it has nothing to do with us. None of you stands in any danger of such a fate," she added, with an eye on the door to the lower regions of the house.

"But suppose there's some murderer out there . . . ," the maid began.

Miss Wordsworth held up her hand for silence. "I am going to Christ Church myself for luncheon with Dean Liddell and his wife," she said. "I shall find out all there is to know about this dreadful affair. Will that suffice?"

"Yes, ma'am." The maid bobbed a curtsey and darted back to the sanctuary of the kitchens. The girls continued to eat their porridge and drink their coffee, pretending they had not heard the news.

Miss Wordsworth tapped her cup for attention. "I regret that you had to hear that exchange," she said. "However, as I told Betty, it is nothing to do with any of us. You will study this morning as you always do. Who is to go to tutorials?"

Two hands were raised. "Miss Johnson will accompany you. The rest of you may walk in the gardens, but remember to wear your hats and gloves."

Gertrude spoke up: "Miss Wordsworth, last night you said that I might take out a punt with Mary and Dianna. Will we need a chaperon?"

"Of course you will," Miss Wordsworth declared. "Miss Laurel, you will act as spotter on the bank for Miss Bell and her crew. Do not go into the Cherwell, but stay in the Holywell Mill Stream. How far do you intend to go?"

"We want to get to Christ Church Meadows," Gertrude said, before Miss Laurel could object to the program set before her.

"Do be careful, Miss Bell. The men are practicing for Eights Week," Miss Wordsworth reminded her.

Gertrude's eyes flashed with anger. "Why should they take over the river?" she muttered to her friends. "Why may we not row instead of poking along in a punt?"

"Miss Laurel, are you well?" Miss Wordsworth noticed the older woman at the foot of the table. "You have not eaten your porridge. I do hope this tragedy has not affected your appetite."

Miss Laurel managed a weak smile. "I am a little unwell this morning, but it will pass, Miss Wordsworth. I shall study my mathematics in the library until Miss Bell and her friends are ready to leave."

"There will be two hours of study," Miss Wordsworth decreed. "After which Miss Bell and her friends may take out the punt. I shall be at luncheon with Dean Liddell and some others at Christ Church if I am needed. Good morning, ladies!"

Miss Wordsworth rose, and the students of Lady Margaret Hall rose with her. No matter how delightfully the gardens beckoned, they must never forget why they had come to Oxford in the first place. The undergraduates of Lady Margaret Hall dispersed to their tasks.

CHAPTER 12

D r. Doyle was waiting at the door to the mortuary when the police arrived at Tom Gate, to be let in by a disapproving porter. Five prospective doctors had already assembled, ready for their lesson in human anatomy. A scrawny man in a much-worn checked suit and dingy gray shirt carefully opened the door to the mortuary.

Inspector Truscott was brushed aside by Dr. Kitchin, the tall bearded don who was Christ Church's leading scientific expert.

"Are we ready?" Dr. Kitchin asked of his assistant.

"Here's the specimen brought in last night. Body of one James Ingram," the attendant reported. "For official autopsy."

"We don't usually name the subjects," Dr. Kitchin pointed out. "Who are all these people?" He glared at the crowd behind him.

Inspector Truscott stepped forward. "Truscott, Oxford Constabulary," he said curtly. "Dean Liddell insisted that you do this autopsy, sir, but we've got our own man along." He indicated the short, stout man in striped trousers and frock coat who had followed the police into the mortuary.

"Gentlemen!" Mr. Colfax trotted in with his bag of instruments. "I see we're all here." He looked about and nodded familiarly to the two policemen and bowed to Dr. Kitchin, acknowledging the superiority of a physician over a mere surgeon. For his part, Dr. Kitchin looked down his nose at Mr. Colfax and glared at the interloper in the tweed suit and deerstalker cap.

"And who is this?" Dr. Kitchin demanded.

"Dr. Doyle of Portsmouth," Inspector Truscott said, with an air of annoyance. "He was present when the body was discovered and has evidence that he will give at the inquest."

"Then he should give it there," Dr. Kitchin huffed. "He's no business being present. Go away, young man!"

"Dean Liddell told me that I should be here," Dr. Doyle said firmly. "Besides, you might have difficulty about this body. It's one of your own, after all."

"I understand this is the body of one of our scouts," Dr. Kitchin said, peering at the body. "I do not know the scouts. The particulars?" He turned to the policemen with a vague wave of the hand.

"James Ingram. Age, thirty-five. Height, six feet, one inch. Weight, ten stone or thereabouts," Sergeant Everett reported.

"Time of death?" Mr. Colfax asked.

"That's for you to say, isn't it?" Inspector Truscott retorted.

"I had hoped for a more definite answer," Mr. Colfax admitted. "Let's see . . . Has anything been removed from the body?"

"Nothing touched," Sergeant Everett stated, as if reciting from the official forms. "He was brought here at nine-fifty last night by the college clock and hasn't been removed. Pockets still as found. No personal possessions removed."

"He should have been brought to the official mortuary," Colfax fussed.

"That would have been most improper, considering that he was found on University grounds," Dr. Kitchin said pompously.

"Ahem!" Dr. Doyle coughed sharply, ending the argument before it deteriorated into a genteel brawl. "Perhaps I can narrow the window of opportunity here. I saw and spoke with the deceased at five o'clock yesterday. Mr. Dodgson saw his body being transported from Magdalen Bridge as the clock was striking nine.

It would appear that the deceased met his end between five and nine o'clock yesterday."

"Close enough," Colfax said with a shrug. "All right, let's have his pockets out."

Ingram's belongings were arranged on the stone slab that was the only furnishing in the room. A pocket watch and chain, a pen-knife, and some coins were all that could be found.

"Not much to show," Sergeant Everett commented, as he regarded the meager collection of oddments.

"What is interesting to me is what isn't there," Dr. Doyle said. "Where are his keys?"

"Eh?" Inspector Truscott looked about sharply to see who had spoken.

The young doctor pointed to the slab. "Mr. Telling said that Ingram had lodgings across the way. He must have had a latchkey or a key to his own rooms. Where is it?"

Inspector Truscott looked at Sergeant Everett, who shook his head in negation.

"No keys were found near the body," Everett answered the unspoken question.

"If the body had been moved, they might have fallen out of his pocket where he was killed," Dr. Doyle pointed out.

"Have the constables been out along the riverbank?" Truscott asked his sergeant.

"Aye, they're out," Everett said, gloomily. "Not that there's all that much to see. The bank's been trampled, and all sorts of animals were out last night."

"And another point," Dr. Doyle went on, in full cry now. "These wounds on the head"—he pointed to several large gashes on Ingram's scalp—"they seem to have been inflicted before death, but none of them is really deep enough to have caused the death itself."

"Could be that someone bashed him, then left him to drown," one of the medical students piped up.

"In that case," Dr. Doyle said, "what are these marks on his back and shoulders?"

121

"First he was bashed, and then he was held under?" The medical student offered his solution.

Dr. Kitchin tried to ascertain which of his lowly students had had the temerity to pronounce an opinion.

"Anything else, young man?" Mr. Colfax asked with awful politeness.

"Not at the moment. Proceed, sir." Dr. Doyle stepped back to let Mr. Colfax do his work. Ingram's black coat, white shirt, and dark waistcoat were removed, revealing his woolen combination underwear. When that was peeled away, he was laid out on the slab, a taller man than had been supposed, his cheeks covered with stubble, his chest ready for the scalpel.

"Observe!" Dr. Kitchin ordered as Mr. Colfax made the incision, and the undergraduates paled and wished they had not eaten eggs for breakfast.

Ingram's thorax was laid open. "There!" Dr. Doyle pointed to the lungs. Mr. Colfax and Dr. Kitchin glared at the young man who had dared to inject himself into their proceedings.

"We shall continue methodically," Mr. Colfax said firmly. "Examining the mouth of the victim, I find remains of plants, possibly waterweed. There is water in the lungs, also traces of the same waterweed." A stroke of the scalpel confirmed the diagnosis. "It is my opinion that this man died of drowning, in a natural body of water, as opposed to a bath."

"I agree," Dr. Kitchin stated.

"No one says he didn't drown," Inspector Truscott said. "And that Dodgson chap says he heard someone take him out of the water at Magdalen Bridge. What I want to know is, was it an accident or suicide?"

Dr. Doyle was peering at Ingram's back and neck. The scout's thinning hair had been pushed aside when he was deposited on the slab. Now Dr. Doyle asked, "Would someone turn him over? If you please?" he added.

The scrawny attendant obligingly lifted the body for Dr. Doyle. "Aha!" He pointed to the marks on the man's back. "I noticed the indentations on the coat and the dark marks on the shirt collar.

This man did not simply fall into the river, gentlemen. He was most certainly assisted and held down forcibly."

"Most observant of you," Mr. Colfax said dryly.

"I am sure we would have discovered this ourselves," Dr. Kitchin added. "This confirms the diagnosis. The man was held under the water, presumably while unconscious."

"But if he was unconscious, he wouldn't have dirt under his fingernails," Dr. Doyle reminded them. "He was bashed with something, fell into the water, revived, and was then held under until he drowned."

"Have you any more information for us?" Inspector Truscott asked sarcastically.

Dr. Doyle was examining the watch with his magnifying glass. "Well," he began, "I would say this is a most unusual item for a man in Ingram's circumstances to own. Wouldn't you agree, Inspector?" He held out the watch to Truscott, who took it and turned it over in his hands.

"A gold watch, engraved on the back . . ."

"With a crest?" Dr. Doyle pointed to the design on the watch. "A bear, erect. Whose arms, do you suppose? Not at all the sort of thing to be owned by a servant."

"Unless the servant had been given it by his master," Dr. Kitchin put in.

"Or unless it was stolen," Truscott said.

"Or he could have come by it quite innocently in a pawnbroker's shop," Dr. Doyle said. "The question is, which explanation is the right one?" He snapped the case open and stepped closer to the windows that let in the spring sunlight, his magnifying glass at the ready. "Aha! An inscription: 'To James Ingram. Well Done Thou Good and Trusty Servant.' The watch was his."

"And the penknife?" Inspector Truscott asked, as he took Ingram's watch into custody.

Dr. Doyle frowned over the object. "This is an elegant object, made of mother-of-pearl, with a folding blade. Not the sort of thing one would expect a servant to own. Inspector, have you searched Ingram's rooms yet?"

"That I have not," Inspector Truscott said. "I suppose you want to come along to that, too."

"Thank you very much, Inspector," Dr. Doyle said cheerfully, apparently oblivious to sarcasm on any side.

Dr. Kitchin harumphed and drew his students' attention to the pertinent portions of Ingram's anatomy, while Mr. Colfax continued to cut.

Dr. Doyle peered at Ingram once again. "What sort of water-weeds were found on the man's fingers and in his mouth?" he asked suddenly.

Mr. Colfax shrugged. "I'm not a botanist," he said.

"I suggest you find one and check to see if the weeds under Magdalen Bridge match the ones in Mr. Ingram's mouth. If not, he might have been drowned somewhere else and taken to the bridge."

The stolid policeman nodded. "Everett, find someone who knows plants and find out where this fellow was when he went in. It shouldn't be hard to find a botanist in a University."

"And look for something long, with something flat at one end . . . ," Dr. Doyle added.

"An oar," Everett stated. "Plenty of those about, but not along the bank. Could be this chap went in under Magdalen Bridge, among the boats. If that's so, there'll be someone to see."

"Get on it," Truscott ordered. He looked at Dr. Doyle and gave it up as a lost cause. There was no way short of incarceration to keep this eager amateur sleuth away from Ingram's rooms. "If you must come along, then do it, but stay out of our way." Truscott glanced at the late Ingram. "Anything else we should know, Mr. Colfax?"

"Nothing in particular, sir. The man had a pork pie for his tea, which gives us another clue as to the time of his death. I would put it between six and seven o'clock yesterday." Mr. Colfax stepped back to allow Dr. Kitchin to point out the internal organs to his students while the assistant did the actual cutting.

"Is that all?" Inspector Truscott glanced at what was left of Ingram and shook his head. Then he beckoned to his own squad, glared at Dr. Doyle, and proceeded out the door, across the lane, and around the corner to the door of the grubby lodging house that the late Ingram had called home. Their arrival was noted by the many children who scampered about, regardless of the laws that provided national education for all children under the age of twelve.

"Who's knocking?" A rough female voice bellowed from within.

"Police!" That sent the neighborhood into a frenzy of speculation and the landlady to the door. Mrs. Perkins was a tall and bony woman of indeterminate age, who exclaimed loudly that she had never had the police in her house, that she was an honest woman who had never broken the law, and that she knew nothing of James Ingram save that he paid his rent and kept to himself.

"Not that I'm one to complain," she said, leading Inspector Truscott and Dr. Doyle up a rickety stair, "and I've been letting these rooms to the college scouts since I lost my husband, which is twenty years this March." She produced a large key from a ring jangling at her waist to open the door to Ingram's room.

"Did Mr. Ingram have his own keys?" Inspector Truscott asked, glancing at Dr. Doyle.

"A latchkey? Yes, he had one. He would sometimes be out late, attending to the students he said, and he didn't like to wake the house. And he insisted on a key for his own rooms, but I kept one myself so that I could get in to clean."

Ingram had occupied one room, overlooking the lane and the walls of Christ Church. A narrow bed in one corner, a washstand in another, a wooden chair, and a large wardrobe were the principal furnishings. A wooden table had been dragged over to the window, and two kerosene lanterns added to the amount of light shed on the table's surface.

"What do you make of that?" Inspector Truscott asked, pointing to the table.

Dr. Doyle examined the tabletop with his magnifying glass. "Most interesting," he commented. "Inspector, I suggest you search for a camera. One of the newest models that uses celluloid films not the old glass plates so cherished by Mr. Dodgson. I think you will find that Mr. Ingram was photographing something that needed a great deal of light. He placed the object upon this table, fixed it into place with pins, and photographed it by both natural and artificial light. See, here are the holes made by the pins." He indicated four minute blemishes on, the table's wooden top.

"What sort of object?" Inspector Truscott was examining the clothes in the wardrobe.

"By the size of the space, I should say, a photograph," Dr. Doyle said slowly. How much should he tell the police? he wondered to himself. Mr. Dodgson would be extremely distressed if the information about the nude photograph were to be given to the police, yet here was evidence that Ingram had been able to copy that photograph. In that case, where was the original?

"Photograph? Why should he photograph a photograph?" Inspector Truscott asked.

Dr. Doyle was already off on another search, down on his knees, peering under the bed. "Aha!" He withdrew a flat wooden box. "Here is your camera, Inspector. A most expensive one, too. I wonder how a servant could have afforded such a fine instrument? He could not have bought such a thing on a servant's pay. And what have we here?" He pulled out the heavy suitcase with its expensive lock that fairly shrieked "secrets within."

"What do you mean . . . Ah!" Light dawned on Inspector Truscott. "This Ingram was putting the black on someone, is that it?" Truscott regarded the locked box with intense suspicion.

"With a camera of this sort, one may take pictures without the model even noticing that they are being captured on celluloid," Dr. Doyle said. "Quite unlike the very bulky equipment of Mr. Dodgson's day. If Ingram made a practice of following his noble masters about and catching them in unguarded moments, he might very well have attempted to blackmail them, using the photographs as bait. And I strongly suspect, Inspector, that the originals of those photographs are inside this suitcase."

"So this here Ingram takes photographs and uses them to blackmail folks, which might lead one of 'em to bash him with an oar and dump him into the river," Truscott finished the thought. "It bears looking into."

"And what of his wardrobe?" Dr. Doyle glanced into the cavernous interior of the piece, which contained Ingram's winter coat, a second black coat and pair of trousers, and a striped dressing-gown. The drawers of the wardrobe held white shirts of the accepted sort for scouts and the usual undergarments. Dr. Doyle rummaged in the drawers and found another small packet of personal items, which he examined before handing them to the perplexed Truscott. Then he wandered over to the washstand, where he examined Ingram's razor and shaving brush. Finally he looked over the pile of newspapers and magazines next to the bed.

"I see Ingram was a follower of the Turf," Dr. Doyle commented, pointing to the *Sporting News*. "And here we have his calculations." Dr. Doyle pointed to several loose sheets of paper, with penciled notations, addition problems, and names of racehorses with the appropriate odds. He frowned as he scanned the other side of the papers, and put one page into his coat pocket, even as he handed the others to Inspector Truscott, who accepted them with a grunt, looked at them, and put them back onto the table again.

"My, my," Dr. Doyle commented. He held up a copy of the *Illustrated London News*. "Mr. Ingram seems to have taken an interest in the fashionable life." He frowned as he read scrawled comments over some of the well-bred and well-connected personages depicted therein.

"Checking up on his old employers?" Inspector Truscott's eyebrows went up as he scanned the newspaper.

"More likely targeting new victims," Dr. Doyle said. "He's got some nasty things to say. This chap's labeled *bugger*, and this lady's got *whore* written over her pretty face. And here's Lord Berwick, disfigured with the word *hypocrite*."

Inspector Truscott turned to his faithful sergeant. "Everett, take these papers over to Headquarters. Anything else I should know about?" Truscott glared at Dr. Doyle.

"You might consider the possibility that Ingram was a habitual gambler, who financed his addiction with petty thefts, as witnessed by these pawn tickets in his wardrobe drawers. He used scraps from the students' wastebaskets for his calculations. A thrifty man, our Mr. Ingram, except for his betting, of course."

"It's something to think of," Inspector Truscott said slowly. "Now, young man, I suggest that you and your lovely lady take yourself off and leave the detective work to those who know it best. If, as you say, Ingram was mixed up with gambling, I know exactly who to talk to. I'll just have a word with the sergeant-major, and we'll settle this right and proper, with no fuss."

"No fuss?" Dr. Doyle was indignant. "Whether or not Ingram was a thief and a blackmailer is not important. He was a human being and as such had the right to life, however vile that life might seem to me and you, and whatever misery he might have inflicted on others."

"That's a fine speech, young man," Truscott said, "but we're not in court, and you're no barrister. Leave this business to the professionals, sir."

Dr. Doyle's mustache began to bristle in indignation. "Inspector, I have been asked by the Dean of Christ Church to assist you in this matter," he said. "I have given you the benefit of my expertise. If you do not choose to take what I offer, then I can only say good morning and leave you to your fruitless search for Ingram's murderer."

"And you think you can find out who knocked this scout on the head and dragged him into the river?" Truscott asked with awful sarcasm.

"I think between us, Mr. Dodgson and I can discover what happened to Ingram," Dr. Doyle amended. "I suggest you open that box very carefully, Inspector, and use its contents wisely. There may be a bomb inside."

Inspector Truscott regarded the suitcase with suspicious eyes as Dr. Doyle made his way down the stairs, out into the lane, and from there back to St. Aldgates.

The young Scot stood in the sunlight for a few moments, gathering his thoughts. Where to now? he asked himself. Should he pursue the errant wine or go after the missing jewelry?

Mr. Dodgson had mentioned Snow and the Covered Market. The White Hart lay on his way to High Street. Dr. Doyle decided to continue his search at the White Hart.

Nevil Farlow and Minnie Chatsworth had partaken of an ample breakfast in Hall and were proceeding to their rooms to change into their boating clothes. Now they stood at the corner of Tom Quad and watched Dr. Doyle as he stood on St. Aldgates.

"What did I tell you?" Chatsworth said, in gloomy triumph. "I can see Ingram's rooms from my window. He was up to something; I know he was."

"We can't go up there now," Farlow told him. "Not with the police all over the place. Look, Minnie, there's that Scotsman, the one who's tagging along after old Dodgson. I wonder what he's up to?"

"He's heading for the White Hart," Chatsworth observed.

"Wants a drink, I suppose, after being with that policeman all morning. Look, there goes Ingram!" Farlow and Chatsworth shrank back against the wall of the mortuary and shuddered as the remains of James Ingram were carried out of the mortuary and back into the lane, where a police wagon waited to take the body to the Oxford morgue until the Coroner's Inquest, after which he could be decently interred.

Chatsworth looked away from the wagon in the lane. "I wonder if that Scottish chap knows something we don't," he mused.

Farlow scowled. "We'd better follow him," he decided.

"I thought we were going out on the river," Chatsworth reminded his friend.

"Not until we find out what that Scotsman knows about Ingram," Farlow decided. "We'll wait outside the White Hart."

"And then what?"

Farlow looked at his follower in exasperation. "And then, when we find out what he knows, we stop him from finding out any more, of course. He's not a gentleman; he's only a doctor. He'll do as he's told!"

With the supreme arrogance of one who had never been thwarted in anything, Nevil Farlow led his friend across St. Aldgates to wait for Dr. Doyle to finish whatever business had taken him to the White Hart.

CHAPTER 13

I t was now midmorning, and the population of St. Aldgates had increased considerably. Students from Pembroke and Christ Church strode along the narrow pavement on their way toward High Street and their lectures. Stout housewives emerged from the squalid lanes south of Christ Church to eke out a few coins with a day's work scrubbing out the kitchens of more prosperous neighbors. Men in corduroy trousers and velveteen waistcoats toiled on the roofs or walls or pavements, repairing the ravages of the previous winter. Oxford was humming, and Dr. Doyle had to thread his way through the crowd. Behind him, Farlow and Chatsworth strolled, trying to look innocent and succeeding only in looking furtive.

Dr. Doyle's attention was on the White Hart. He ignored the tiny shop opposite Christ Church, where an old woman stood guard over her supply of barley sugar and other sweets. He fended off the importuning children, who offered him everything from pen wipers to peppermints. His goal was the bar of the White Hart, which was relatively empty at that hour of the morning. Only one man sat in a corner, nursing a glass of something brown.

The barman stood at his post, however, busily polishing glassware so as to be ready for the luncheon patrons.

Dr. Doyle regarded the day bartender with care. This was not the harried night man, but a stout, jovial fellow, whose rotund figure and reddened nose led the doctor to believe that he had sampled some of the inn's wares fairly recently.

"Good morning," Dr. Doyle greeted the barman.

"And what may I give you today, sir?" The barman stopped polishing his glassware long enough to nod to this potential customer.

"I'll have a pint of your best bitter, if you please." Dr. Doyle watched as the barman operated the taps and produced the required beverage. He tried a sip, nodded, and pronounced it acceptable. "Not that I would be able to judge," Dr. Doyle said modestly. "Now there are some, I daresay, who could tell whether that beer came from near Oxford or elsewhere. I've even heard that some fellows can distinguish one field of hops from another."

The barman nodded sagely. "That's a fact, sir. There are those with such a palate that they can tell if the beer's been drawn today or leftover. And some of them will complain if they get bottled, saying that it's none so good as what's in the wood. There's a rhyme for you!" He punctuated his joke with a flourish of his dishcloth.

"Ah." Dr. Doyle sipped his beer carefully. "And then there are the wine fanciers. Don't get many of those here, I daresay." He looked about the room as if to say, Wine drinkers stay behind the college walls.

"Now there you are mistaken, sir." The barman put down his cloth ready to do battle for the reputation of his establishment. "Many of the Fellows of the University bring their friends here, and if I may say so, sir, we can usually supply what is wanted. Mr. Jellicoe, our proprietor, has laid down a fine cellar, sir. Sherry, port, Madiera, all you have to do is ask, and we can provide it."

"Sherry, you say?" Dr. Doyle frowned. "I heard there was a bit of bother last night about the sherry."

"One of the old chaps across the way said it was pinched from his cellars!" The day barman had clearly been briefed by the night man. "As if Mr. Jellicoe would stoop to buying wine from any but our own man!"

"Really?" Dr. Doyle looked skeptical. "But wouldn't it be a temptation for a barman to buy a bottle or two, if it were offered by someone you knew, if the price were right? You could charge the same for a drink as for the usual stock and pocket the difference yourself." Dr. Doyle watched the bartender over the rim of his glass.

The barman drew himself up, the picture of outraged professional pride. "Mr. Jellicoe would never purchase stolen goods, not poached game nor pinched wine! You may ask at Mr. Snow's, in the Covered Market, which is where Mr. Jellicoe has done his business these ten years past, if you like. And none of us what works for him would do so either!" He glared fiercely at Dr. Doyle, daring him to say otherwise.

Dr. Doyle looked properly abashed. "I only wondered because I thought it might be a dreadful temptation," he said. "All those dons sitting behind the walls across the road, swilling down the port . . ." He stopped before the barman's disapproving frown.

"The gentlemen of Christ Church," the barman said with withering scorn, "are known as great scholars, and the White Hart is proud to be of service to them. Good morning, sir!" Clearly the barman wanted nothing to do with such a Philistine as Dr. Doyle, who paid for his drink and left the White Hart still puzzled. His first thought had been that the barman at the White Hart had purchased the wine, thinking to make an easy few shillings' profit. Clearly, this was not the case. The next step, he decided, would be to go to the source of the wine. To this end, Dr. Doyle headed north on St. Aldgates to the High Street and turned right. The gates of the Covered Market were open to all, and apparently, the entire town was heading there this morning. Dr. Doyle joined the throng, with Farlow and Chatsworth close behind him.

The good citizens of Oxford relied on the market for their daily shopping. Beneath the iron roof with its glass panes were stalls where the local farmers hawked their produce, butchers proclaimed the virtues of their meats, and wine merchants praised their vintages. Dairymen extolled the flavor of their cheeses; bakers produced loaves for consumption on the premises or to be taken back to digs. Poor scholars could buy their meager meals ready cooked; and more affluent citizens could send housekeepers, cooks, and butlers to order their provisions. On this day, with graduation parties near at hand and an influx of guests in the offing, both Town and Gown wanted to top up their supplies. The market was correspondingly packed with humanity.

Dr. Doyle threaded his way between stout housewives and superior servants carrying wicker baskets loaded with the day's supply of vegetables, meats, and whatever else their households might require. College scouts, in their distinctive long black coats and black bowler hats, argued with butchers and grocers to get the most for the least amount of their college's funds. Representatives from the White Hart, the Mitre, and the Randolph Hotel were making their latest purchases, to be sent directly to the kitchens of those establishments before the luncheon crowd descended upon them.

Dr. Doyle's ears were assaulted by the sound of voices rebounding off the iron-and-glass roof. He looked about him, trying to get his bearings. He spotted his destination along one wall. Mr. Snow had taken a large stand in the Covered Market, where his stock of bottles and crates could be easily seen. Mr. Snow himself, correctly attired in cutaway coat and striped trousers, stood ready to greet anyone who wished to purchase wine, while his lanky assistant, a sly-looking youth who had discarded the jacket of his checked suit of dittoes, the better to display well-muscled arms under rolled-up shirtsleeves, lurked in the background.

Dr. Doyle edged around a well-upholstered woman arguing over some fowls with a butcher and very nearly bumped into Mr. Snow. "Good morning," he said politely.

"And a fine spring day it is," Mr. Snow agreed. "And what may I do for you, sir?"

Dr. Doyle smiled cheerily. "I am visiting a friend here in Oxford, and he recommended your selection of wines. I thought I

133

might buy a bottle of port, to present to a relation of mine in the north of England." Dr. Doyle looked over the stock, as if he knew everything there was to know about wine.

"Indeed, I may be able to accommodate you. May I ask which of my customers it was who suggested that you visit my stand?" Mr. Snow scanned his rack for a likely bottle to offer.

"It was Mr. Dodgson, of Christ Church . . . ," Dr. Doyle said casually. Mr. Snow reacted as if someone had handed him a cup of vinegar and told him it was champagne. His face contracted, his eyes narrowed, and his mouth pursed into a round bow of distaste.

"I have had dealings with Mr. Dodgson since his taking the curatorship," Mr. Snow said finally. "He has ordered from me many times. But he can be extremely trying."

"Mr. Dodgson is, um, exacting," Dr. Doyle said diplomatically.

"Mr. Dodgson is a persnickety old codger," Mr. Snow declared. "My dealings with Mr. Vere Bayne were of a different sort altogether. Mr. Vere Bayne ordered the wine, which I then delivered. Mr. Vere Bayne accepted my decisions as to vintage and price. Mr. Vere Bayne then paid the amounts I charged without complaint."

"Mr. Dodgson is more precise," Dr. Doyle murmured.

Mr. Snow's jowls quivered in exasperation. "Is Mr. Dodgson a good friend of yours, sir?"

"An acquaintance of sorts," Dr. Doyle said, with a depreciating grin. "I am all too aware of his, um, mannerisms."

Mr. Snow lowered his voice. "Let me tell you, sir, I have never had so exacting a customer as Mr. Dodgson. Mr. Dodgson must question every order, must taste every vintage, before he will pronounce it good enough for his cellars." Clearly Mr. Snow felt affronted that he should be questioned as to the quality of his wares. "As for the charges, he must add every bill himself, not once, but three times, before paying it."

"Mr. Dodgson is a mathematician," Dr. Doyle reminded the enraged merchant.

"That does not entitle him to question my addition," Mr. Snow said indignantly. "As for his claim that we have sent double the order, that is ridiculous, and so I told him."

"Mr. Snow!" A stout man in the black coat and bowler hat worn by scouts called for attention.

"If you will care to make your selection, my boy here will assist you." Mr. Snow hurried to attend to the next customer. "Find the gentleman a nice bottle of port, Fred."

Behind him, Dr. Doyle thought he heard a stifled snort from Mr. Snow's shop assistant. "Do you know something about Mr. Dodgson's wine?" Dr. Doyle asked, assessing the smirking Fred as being one who would go along with Ingram's schemes.

"Only that Mr. Snow don't know all that passes at Christ Church," Fred said with a wink.

Dr. Doyle put on a knowing grin. "Aha! Let me guess . . . one of the scouts came to you with a little proposition, eh? That he could get you the Christ Church wine, which you could then sell on your own, and the pair of you would split the proceeds?"

"Oh, you are a sharp one, you are," the assistant said. "You're that sharp, you'll be cut one of these days."

"Not so badly as you," Dr. Doyle retorted. "What's more, I'll bet you anything you like that I can name the scout."

"And how would you know that, what's never been here before?" The assistant summed up Dr. Doyle with one sharp look.

"Haven't you heard that Ingram was found dead behind Christ Church last night?" Dr. Doyle watched as incredulity, then horror, then guilt chased each other across the assistant's face.

"I didn't know it was him!" the assistant burst out. "I heard there was a man found in the lane behind Christ Church, but no name was mentioned. I didn't have nothing to do with that!"

"No one is saying that you did," Dr. Doyle said. "Ingram seems to have had a finger in a number of pies. Just how long did you expect to get away with this little scheme? Mr. Snow must keep the accounts. Sooner or later he would realize that the tally of bottles sold did not match the inventory."

"That was Ingram's idea," the assistant said hurriedly. "See, he'd bring me the bottles, then he'd have me furnish the same wine to the undergraduates, for their parties and suchlike. He'd had a word with some of the scouts from other colleges, and they'd pay me on the sly. Then Ingram and me, we'd split the coin, and we'd both be the richer for it; and Mr. Snow none the wiser since the transaction never appeared on his books. It was all Ingram's idea," he repeated.

"He seems to have had a remarkable ability to work out criminal schemes," Dr. Doyle observed. "I wonder why he needed you since he could just as easily have handed the wine over himself."

"But you see, the wine had to come from Mr. Snow," Fred pointed out. "Otherwise the scouts would have twigged it wasn't prime stock, and that wouldn't have done at all. Mr. Snow's got a good reputation, and wine from Mr. Snow is always of the best."

"Which would be well-known to everyone in Oxford," Dr. Doyle said, with a nod of appreciation for the plan. "Very clever."

"Aye, quite the lad he was, was Ingram," the assistant agreed. "But I didn't have anything to do with him being dead. Ask Mr. Snow! I was here until we close, which is seven in the evening, and then I went straight home, which is with my mum, behind Pembroke."

"I did not mention when Ingram was found," Dr. Doyle remarked. "I don't suppose you happened to see him yesterday?"

Fred made a show of handing Dr. Doyle one of the bottles standing on a crate. "Now this here is a nice little bottle, a good year; our dons find it very palatable," he said loudly, conscious of Mr. Snow's eye on him. Mr. Snow's attention wandered again. Fred lowered his voice. "Ingram came to the market just after five to fetch a meat pie for his tea. He come over to this stand in a right temper, growling about how he'd been given the sack and how he'd make someone pay dearly. And then he went off, and I never saw him again."

"Perhaps you had best come forward with the information," Dr. Doyle suggested.

"I don't want nothing to do with the police," the assistant protested.

"Better for you to come forward than for them to find you."

Dr. Doyle turned to leave, then turned back. "These undergraduates, the ones who asked Ingram to provide their wine. Did he ever mention their names? It might be useful to know who they are."

The assistant dug into his trousers pocket and produced a folded piece of paper and the stub of a pencil. "This is a list, what Ingram gave me last time he was here, not yesterday, but the day before." He handed it to Dr. Doyle, who scanned it on both sides and returned it to its owner.

"Most interesting. One more point: How did the wine get to the White Hart?"

The assistant reddened. "That was my mistake. I put a basket with two bottles of sherry that was supposed to go to Merton next to the one meant for the White Hart, and their boy took 'em both before I could stop him."

Dr. Doyle smiled to himself. "Mr. Dodgson will be pleased to know that University wine usually stayed in the University," he said. "But I don't think you'd better try anything like that again. This time all's well, but next time . . . ?"

The assistant nodded. "Mr. Snow's all right," he agreed. "And the shilling or two I got out of it weren't enough to make the difference to my conscience."

Dr. Doyle turned to go again. He frowned to himself. Had he imagined it or was someone lurking behind him? He turned back to Mr. Snow, who had taken the order of the portly man in the black jacket and trousers and bowler hat worn by the custodians of the University colleges.

"And have you made your selection, sir?" he asked Dr. Doyle.

"I believe I shall take this." Dr. Doyle pointed to the bottle Fred had offered. "I would be much obliged if you would send it to my rooms at the White Hart." He handed Mr. Snow his visiting card and paid for the wine. "I only hope the management will not think that I disdain their selection," he said with a smile. "I would have presented it to Mr. Dodgson, but he probably has a sample of this wine already."

Mr. Snow nodded. "This is a vintage much favored by the gentlemen of Christ Church. We are honored by the custom of many of the colleges," he said expansively. "In addition, several Fellows and their clubs also purchase their wine from my stock."

"Really? I had no idea there were private clubs in Oxford," Dr. Doyle said. "I was of the opinion that all the activities here centered around the colleges."

Mr. Snow gazed condescendingly upon the stranger, anxious to enlighten him as to the glories of Oxford. "There are several clubs not directly connected with the University," he said. "For instance, there is Vincent's, where certain gentlemen meet to discuss sporting events."

"My, my," Dr. Doyle said. "I hadn't thought of Oxford as a sporting place."

"Shows how much you know," the assistant put in, to Mr. Snow's evident displeasure. "We've got rugger, we've got cricket, we've got the boats and Eights Week . . ."

"And for those who believe in keeping physically fit, there is the Oxford Gentleman's Athletic Club," Mr. Snow added, glaring at his assistant. "Sergeant-Major Howard is the proprietor. He has often ordered wine for young gentlemen to be served at private parties after their athletic exhibitions."

Dr. Doyle smiled under his mustache, and nodded affably. He had solved the problem of Mr. Dodgson's missing wine. Now all he needed was to find the pawnbroker patronized by Ingram, and he would have solved two of the three problems set before him. He still had no idea who had murdered Ingram, or why, but he was sure the answer would come out as he delved into the unsavory servant's past life.

He stopped suddenly. Someone had just turned around to examine the contents of the next stall. Two undergraduates, notable for their dark students' gowns, seemed preoccupied with the dead birds arranged neatly in a row, feathers and all, waiting for someone to take them home for dinner.

Dr. Doyle frowned. What were undergraduates doing in the Covered Market? Surely young men would not be purchasing their own supplies when they had scouts to do it for them. As for the baked goods, pork pies, and hot potatoes, they could be had from vendors on the streets if youthful appetites had to be slaked with snacks in the middle of the morning. In the crowd in the market, black fustian gowns and tasseled caps were conspicuously absent. It was perfectly clear to Dr. Doyle that these two had to be following him!

Dr. Doyle continued his trek through the Covered Market, dodging around stout farmwomen in old-fashioned full skirts and bonnets, until he found another stand, this one filled with fresh spring vegetables. Once more Dr. Doyle stopped and peered around.

There they were again! The same two undergraduates, he was sure of it! One was taller than he, very fair, with a particularly classic profile. The other was shorter and darker than his friend. Dr. Doyle was now certain that he had seen them before. They had been among the undergraduates in Tom Quad when Inspector Truscott had conducted his preliminary investigation, and they had been hanging about the mortuary this morning.

The market was laid out in a pattern of stands, around a central aisle. Dr. Doyle ducked into one stall and out the other side. From there he dodged around a pair of men haggling over a brace of rabbits, slipped around another stall holding jars of home-bottled preserves, and edged through a party of country folk come to gawk at the big town and sell their produce at the same time.

By now he was behind the two undergraduates, who were looking for him in the growing crowds.

"This won't do, Nev," the shorter one said. "We've lost him."

"Damn him!" the taller man spat out. "What's he want at Snow's anyway?"

"I daresay he's following the trail of our sherry. I could have told you it was pinched from the Senior Common Room stock." Chatsworth shrugged philosophically. "Ingram's price was far too low."

"What?" Farlow gasped.

"Of course it would be," Chatsworth told him. "Trouble with you, Nev, is that you don't know what things cost until the bill comes due, and then you don't like it."

"Just because my mother's a cit doesn't make me one, Minnie. I'm not a blasted merchant!"

Chatsworth regarded his friend sympathetically. "Can't get around it, Nev," he said. "You've told me often enough about your mater's brother, the one who manufactures glass. Now I'm quite reconciled to my mater's fortune, even if it did come from cotton mills. If it don't bother my pater, why should it bother me? You really ought to be kinder to your uncle. Glass is a very necessary commodity. Look at this market . . ."

"Blast my uncle and his blasted glass!" Farlow's exploded. "Where's that blasted Scotsman?"

"Can't find him in this scrum," Chatsworth said. "I say, Nev, let's get out of here and go to Vincent's. We can pick up the news and find out if anyone knows anything abut Ingram. Maybe Burlingame will be in, and we can quiz him about Eights Week."

"Is that all you can think of, Minnie?" Farlow regarded his faithful friend with exasperated amusement.

"Well, we can't do anyone any good here, and we've lost the Scotsman, so we might as well go somewhere else," Chatsworth decided.

Dr. Doyle listened to this conversation from his position behind one of the iron pillars next to the pair. He thought quickly. Vincent's was the club that had recommended Ingram to Christ Church in the first place. Vincent's was a sporting club, and Ingram had been empoyed by a club in London. There might be a connection, and if there was, Dr. Doyle was determined to find it.

He caught a glimpse of himself, reflected in the glass case of the cheesemonger's stall. His hand flew to the mustache that adorned his upper lip. No disguising that, he thought. But there were other ways to change one's appearance. He stuffed his deerstalker into the pocket of his jacket and beckoned a youth who was hawking cloth caps. A few pennies got him a dashing black and white houndstooth check object, which he adjusted to a rakish tilt over his red hair. He opened his shirt and removed his collar, so that he looked slightly disheveled. Thus disguised, he followed the two undergraduates out of the Covered Market and back to the High. The prey had become the pursuer, and he could not be satisfied until he found out just what they were doing.

140

CHAPTER 14

D r. Doyle followed the two undergraduates as they made their way through the Covered Market back to High Street. Who are they? he wondered. And what do they want with me?

He frowned in thought. His surly expression, combined with his scruffy and disheveled clothing, made the assorted shoppers in the Covered Market edge away from him. Someone who stalked through the market in a cloth cap, without a collar, scowling, was clearly up to no good. The uniformed constable on duty near the door stepped forward, ready to act if this uncouth stranger should decide to help himself to someone else's pocketbook.

Dr. Doyle's attention was entirely focused on the two gowned undergraduates ahead of him. They, in turn, strolled out of the market and onto the High, feeling frustrated.

"Do you really think we should go to Vincent's at this hour?" Farlow complained. "No one will be there."

"Burlingame will," Chatsworth said, with a knowing look and a decided nod of the head. "And Bob will be at the bar. He knows everything that goes on in town. He'll know what the police are up to before they even know it themselves."

Farlow shrugged. "At least we can get a decent drink," he said.

"And then," Chatsworth told him, "we can go to the sergeant-major, and you can work off some of that steam. You're ready to blow up like a volcano, Nev!"

Farlow patted his classmate on the shoulder. "Minnie, what would I do without you?"

Chatsworth grinned. "You'd have to write your own essays for one thing," he countered. The two headed toward the bridge but turned off into a small street of shops. Dr. Doyle followed at a discreet distance as they entered a door marked only by a brass plate that announced that the premises was Vincent's. There the two undergraduates were let in by a porter, who scanned the street carefully and glared at the interloper.

"This is a private club," the porter informed Dr. Doyle, who backed away, looking properly disappointed.

"So that is Vincent's," Dr. Doyle said to himself. His eye was drawn to the shop on the ground floor of the building. A large sign proclaimed that the establishment was owned by one H. Vincent, who would provide *cartes de visite,* advertising circulars, tracts, newsletters, or any other printed matter on request. Samples of Mr. Vincent's handiwork were displayed in the window of the shop, so that the prospective customer could see for himself the quality of the product.

Dr. Doyle pulled the much-folded sheet of paper out of his pocket. Ingram had used one side to make his abstruse calculations. On the other was a copy of the verses that were being used to threaten Miss Cahill.

Dr. Doyle compared the type on the paper to the sample in the window. The typeface matched, and there was more . . . There it was! A telltale nick in one of the serifs of a t. It appeared on every page of the samples hung out by Mr. Vincent, and it was on the page from Ingram's room. Dr. Doyle was now convinced that this shop was the one that had printed the offensive material that had been sent to Lady Margaret Hall.

Dr. Doyle considered how to proceed. Surely, no reputable printer would have allowed material of this sort to come under his presses, if for no other reason than that there might be repercussions if it became known that he would provide such stuff . . . unless he had a clientele that already knew of his products and would shield him from any embarrassment. If, as Dr. Doyle suspected, the premises upstairs was being used as a private club by noble persons connected with the University, then the printer downstairs would have virtual immunity. The events of the previous summer had shown Dr. Doyle how far the gentry would go to preserve their right to indulge in the vices they denied the lower orders.

In that case, Dr. Doyle decided, I might try to persuade this fellow to print something of mine. He used the window as a mirror. Do I look sufficiently furtive, he wondered. How does a pornographic writer look anyway? Mr. Wilde's writing has been condemned as pornography, and he looks quite dashing and not at all criminal.

Dr. Doyle gave his hair another ruffle and decided that he looked sufficiently outrageous. He opened the door and entered the shop.

The tinkle of a bell over the door announced his arrival. A large, ink-stained man, whose fair hair was covered with a paper cap and whose striped shirt and corduroy trousers were protected from flying ink by a canvas apron, emerged from the back of the shop. From the sounds of the machinery clanking away, and the strong odor of ink, the presses were running at Vincent's.

"Mr. Vincent, I presume?" Dr. Doyle asked.

"Yes, that is my name, and this is my shop." The printer regarded his potential customer with the look of one who has summed up the customer and found him wanting. "May I help you?"

"I was wondering . . . ," Dr. Doyle began. He took a deep breath and tried to organize his thoughts.

Vincent tried to help him out. "Did you want something printed?" he asked, with a scornful twist of his lips that seemed to deny that anyone who looked like that could read, let alone write something worth setting into type.

"Ah . . . yes, that is it. I wanted you to print something for me." Dr. Doyle put on what he hoped was a lascivious leer. "I've written a little piece, you know, with, ah . . . illustrations."

"Have you now." Vincent didn't seem too surprised. Oxford was full of people who had written little pieces, with or without illustrations. Some of them might even come to H. Vincent to set a small run of their poems, to be distributed to doting relatives or admiring friends.

"Yes, with illustrations," Dr. Doyle repeated. "And I was told you would print my little, um, piece, at a reasonable rate." He leaned against the high counter and winked.

Vincent was not impressed. "That depends, sir, on the nature of the writing, and the nature of the illustrations," he said. "I know a very good man who can do your zinc facsimile, as it is called, for drawings, but that will cost you an extra sixpence the hundred."

"But these are photographs," Dr. Doyle protested. "Of the highest quality, I assure you."

Vincent frowned. "I don't suppose you could provide the negative, could you?"

Dr. Doyle shook his head. "These are very, ah, special photographs, you understand. The, ah, persons in them are, ah, very . . ." He left the sentence dangling, daring the printer to provide the appropriate adjectives.

Vincent's expression changed from scornful to disapproving. "Now that sort of printing may cost extra," Vincent said slowly. "I wonder that you came here, seeing as how I never laid eyes on you before, and I daresay I know most of the literary gentlemen in Oxford." He crossed his brawny arms over his broad chest with the air of one who has had his share of brawls and come out the winner.

"I'm just passing through, you might say," Dr. Doyle told him. "Visiting a literary gentleman connected with Christ Church, in fact. Do you know Mr. Dodgson?"

"Mr. Dodgson does not use this shop," Vincent said grudgingly, "but he is known in Oxford. He writes mathematical books, does he not?"

"And fairy tales for children," Dr. Doyle reminded him.

"Does he now?" Vincent looked Dr. Doyle up and down. "And where did you hear that I might print the sort of thing that you have in mind?" He glowered in righteous wrath, leaving no doubt as to his opinion of the putative work in question.

"I must have been mistaken then because I felt sure that this page came from this shop." Dr. Doyle produced the page he had removed from Ingram's rooms. "As you can see, sir, there is a t with a small nick in the serif. It appears somewhere on every page you have set in your samples, and here it is again on this page. It is not uncommon for one letter in the font to be damaged, and it is hardly noticeable without a magnifying glass, but it is there nonetheless." Dr. Doyle fumbled for his ever-present lens and beckoned the printer over to examine the offending letter.

Vincent's truculence ebbed as he studied the evidence. "Very well," he admitted. "I did print up that piece. I had my doubts when I read it over, but the man who ordered it was from the University, and he told me it was for one of the gentlemen at Christ Church. All about some Greek lady poet of bygone years, he said. Sounded odd to me, but I printed it up as it stood."

"How many copies?" Dr. Doyle asked.

"Fifty, and I charged him well for 'em," Vincent replied. "Rum order, I thought, for a piece like that."

Dr. Doyle shrugged. "I suppose there is not much of a market for this sort of thing here in Oxford," he said.

Vincent grinned suddenly. "I don't say there is and I don't say there ain't," he commented. "But the po-faced chap who placed the order swore it was for one of the students." Vincent shook his head. "Were it not for the fancy French and Latin in it, I'd have swore it was the sort of thing I do not print as a rule, but being as how the order was from one of the members upstairs . . ." He gestured at the ceiling.

"French and Latin?" Dr. Doyle's eyebrows went up. "Are you familiar with those languages?"

The printer's affability vanished again in outraged dignity. "I may not know those tongues, sir, but I know some words and the look of 'em. And it being but one page, I thought it was for a joke, like, some student rag. The young gentlemen will have their jokes; and if they want to put 'em into print, who am I to deny 'em?" Vincent shrugged eloquently, expressing his opinion of the wealthy young men who could afford to spend several pounds to have only a few copies made of salacious material.

"Indeed." Dr. Doyle smiled ruefully. "I suppose I had better look for another printer to provide my little, um, piece."

"It might be well, sir, to go to London," Vincent said, at his most forbidding. "I understand there are printers there who will provide that sort of thing at cost, and then give you a royalty should you permit them to reproduce it. I'm an honest man, sir, and I do not print offensive matter. Good day to you!" With a final sniff of disapproval, Vincent returned to his presses.

Dr. Doyle considered what he had learned. The "po-faced chap from Christ Church" must have been Ingram. The offensive pamphlet originated at Christ Church, but Ingram certainly did not write it. In all of this, Ingram had acted as an intermediary, a go-between . . . but between whom and whom?

Dr. Doyle glanced at his watch and wondered how to proceed. Should he wait for the two undergraduates, or should he go down the lane and try to find Mr. Dodgson to report what he had learned?

The sonorous tones of Great Tom were tolling eleven. Lord Nevil Farlow clattered down the stairs and out into the lane, followed by his faithful shadow, Minnie Chatsworth. Dr. Doyle had been standing in the doorway of the printing shop, considering his options, and now started toward Christ Church.

"Watch where you are going!" Farlow thrust Dr. Doyle out of his way with one powerful arm and continued down High Street toward St. Aldgates without a backward glance. Chatsworth followed his leader down the street. From the whiff that he got, Dr. Doyle realized that both young men had been sampling the stock at the club bar.

What shall I do next? Dr. Doyle wondered. I've found the man who printed the verses. I've found out what happened to the college wine. I still have no idea who killed Ingram or why. Should

I try the pawnshops next or. . . . He watched the two young men wander down the street back toward the walls of Christ Church.

Dr. Doyle thought it over then decided to leave the pawnshops to Inspector Truscott and his men. They would know which of Oxford's pawnbrokers was most likely to be a receiver of stolen goods, and which ones would be most likely to grass on a customer, particularly if said customer had just turned up dead under suspicious circumstances.

"However," Dr. Doyle said to himself, as he started after Farlow and Chatsworth, "these two young man have been following me all morning. They must know about the print shop downstairs from their club. For all I know, they may even have been the undergraduates under Ingram's care. I shall have to see where they are going."

Dr. Doyle fumbled for his collar and adjusted it as he hurried after Farlow and Chatsworth. They ducked through Peckwater and out into Tom Quad then skirted the quad and headed for the mews. Dr. Doyle trotted after them.

He caught sight of Touie and Mr. Dodgson as he continued across the quad and waved at them as they entered the Hall.

"Picnic in the Meadows!" Touie shouted, as her husband dashed past, hot on the heels of the two young men, who had vanished through the gap between the mortuary and the mews.

"I've lost them!" Dr. Doyle fumed, as he found himself back in the lane where Ingram's body had been so unceremoniously dumped the evening before.

He looked about. Aha! There was a flash of a black gown in the gap between two buildings. Dr. Doyle hurried through the noisome alley and found himself in another street of a sort far removed from the commercial bustle of the High or the tree-lined quiet of St. Giles. This was a slum, with no mincing of words. Careworn women stood in the doorways of tumbledown houses, watching their grubby offspring at play. A few men with weathered features and toothless grins were enjoying the spring sunshine in their golden years, while a trio of tough-looking characters lounged in front of a tavern.

Dr. Doyle was no stranger to the seedier parts of Portsmouth; but this was not his home, and he would have to go carefully here. He looked about him, trying to match the truculence of the loungers with an equally fierce stare of his own.

At the end of the street was a large structure with a swinging sign that announced that it was the Oxford Gentleman's Athletic Club. Dr. Doyle looked up and down the street. Ingram's lodgings were at one end of the passageway, the Oxford Gentleman's Athletic Club marked the other, with the greensward of Christ Church Meadows just visible in the gap between the houses behind the buildings.

Very well, Dr. Doyle thought. Since our young gentlemen are not in the tavern, and it is highly unlikely that they would be visiting any of these estimable women, I will proceed on the assumption that they have gone to the Oxford Gentleman's Athletic Club. I will, therefore, follow them and find out why they have chosen to follow me!

CHAPTER 15

The Oxford Gentleman's Athletic Club stood at the intersection of three lanes that converged into the one cobbled street that led eventually to the Broad Walk and Christ Church Meadows, the well-kept swath of grass between the college and the river. The building had once been a barn, and the fragrance of its previous inhabitants still hung over it like a visible miasma. There did not seem to be much business at this hour of the morning. Presumably those young men who wished to indulge in physical activities were out of doors on such a fine spring day. A large, shaven-headed individual stood beside the door under the sign, observing the passing scene. Dr. Doyle straightened his collar, smoothed back his hair, replaced the recently purchased cloth cap with his deerstalker, and stepped forward with an imbecilic grin plastered over his face.

"Good morning!" He nodded to the doorkeeper. He hoped he looked like one of the idle fellows he had seen ogling young women on the esplanade in Brighton or dancing attendance on elderly relatives in Southsea.

The doorkeeper grunted something that might have been a greeting. Dr. Doyle grinned cheerfully at him.

"Is this the Oxford Gentleman's Athletic Club?" he asked, assuming the affected drawl of the London loafer.

"Yer see it is." The doorkeeper jerked a thumb at the sign.

Dr. Doyle nodded. "Of course it is. The chap at the White Hart sent me over. Said a chap could get a good workout here, what?"

"Wot chap?" the doorkeeper asked suspiciously.

"The name escapes me at the moment; but there was a chap at the bar, and I said I wished I could find a bit of action, don't y'know, and he said to come here. I do hope I'm not too early. Nearly dawn, ain't it?" Dr. Doyle tried to look as if he rarely got out of bed until noon and jingled the coins in his pocket meaningfully.

The doorkeeper assessed the stranger. Good clothes but not expensive; odd cap he was wearing; but he was staying at the White Hart; and if the barman at the White Hart had sent him, he couldn't be a copper. Besides, the man had a half crown in his hand, ready to slip into a waiting palm.

"Step in," the doorkeeper said, moving aside. "If the sergeant-major has time for yer, yer might be able to put on the gloves wif' 'im."

Dr. Doyle nodded graciously and stepped into the Oxford Gentleman's Athletic Club.

The door led to a small anteroom, where sporting prints covered the walls and posters announcing boxing matches and horse races filled whatever space was left. The anteroom, in turn, led to the large, open space that had once held stalls for horses. The aroma still clung to the place, augmented by the smells of male sweat, cheap tobacco, and liniment. Here, obviously, was where the main business of the Oxford Gentleman's Athletic Club took place, i.e., the preparation of young men for the rigors of London life.

Here a young man could learn the fine art of fisticuffs and the finer art of fencing. Hooks on the bare wooden walls held boxing gloves and fencing foils, masks, and chest protectors. Mats covered the wooden floorboards, and a boxing ring had been set up in the middle of the room, with ropes on stanchions marking the space demanded by the rules laid down by the Marquis of Queensbery. Dr. Doyle looked about for his missing undergraduates and frowned as he heard loud voices coming from the farthest corner of the room, where a cubicle had been walled off to make a private office, presumably for the proprietor of the Oxford Gentleman's Athletic Club.

Whatever was going on in the office was noisy, but Dr. Doyle could not make out the words. Only the emotion came through, and that was clear enough. Someone was very, very angry!

The two undergraduates emerged from the office followed by the sergeant-major himself, a man of middle height, balding, with a mighty military mustache and steel gray side-whiskers.

"I don't know what you're talking about!" he repeated to the two young men who had bullied their way into his office.

"Don't come the old soldier with me!" Nevil Farlow shouted furiously. "I've just been talking with Burlingame of Merton. He says his scout tried the same trick on him that Ingram tried on me! Trying to get inside information about Eights Week!"

"And why would I care about that?"

"Because you've been taking the bets on Eights Week for as long as you've been set up here," Chatsworth said calmly. "My brothers both told me that if I wanted to do any wagering, I should place my bets with you because at least you ran an honest shop."

"And I do," the sergeant-major blustered. "Now run along, lads. Who's this?" He turned on Dr. Doyle with a sudden frown. "Who are you?" he demanded. "Who let you in? I don't know you, do I?"

Dr. Doyle rocked back and forth on his heels, grinning fatuously. "Just visitin', don't y'know? Thought I might take a turn with the old gloves, what?"

"You were following me!" Farlow interrupted him. "You were in the High, and you were in the Covered Market . . ."

"I beg your pardon!" Dr. Doyle lost the fatuous look and the fashionable drawl and reverted to his customary Edinburgh burr.

151

"It is you who were following me, sir. You were in the mews this morning, and you have no business in the Covered Market that I know of."

"You don't know anything about my business," the younger man sneered. "But I know yours. You're that interfering Scotchman . . ."

"Scotsman," Dr. Doyle corrected him automatically.

"I say! Aren't you the chap who found old Ingram in the lane? I saw you from my rooms." Chatsworth tried to interpose himself between his argumentative friend and the doctor. "I'm Chatsworth, Chatsworth Minim. This is Lord Nevil Farlow."

"How do you do?" Dr. Doyle found his hand being pumped by the enthusiastic undergraduate, whose friend extended two fingers languidly.

"We're awfully sorry about the mix-up," Chatsworth babbled, moving Dr. Doyle away from the sergeant-major and toward the exit door. "I mean to say, who's following who, what?"

Dr. Doyle pulled away from the well-meaning young man. "While I have the two of you here, I'd like a word with you." He pulled out the much-folded paper. "Did one of you write this piece of trash?"

"How dare you question me, you miserable cur?" Farlow snarled. "Don't you know who I am?"

Dr. Doyle's temper was rising, but he kept his voice level as he replied, "I don't care who you are, sir. You are behaving like an arrogant puppy who is hiding behind a student's gown and is using his scholarship to terrify a young woman into leaving her college."

"What!" Chatsworth regarded his friend with sorrow. "Nev, I told you that wouldn't do." He turned back to Dr. Doyle. "It was all a rag, you know. A joke. One writes them, you know."

"Then you admit that you are the author of that . . . that rubbish?" Dr. Doyle's temper began to rise.

"That is no business of yours, sir! You are offensive! Let me go!" Farlow drew back his fist, only to find it caught in the firm grip of Sergeant-Major Howard.

"There's no fighting in this establishment unless I say so," he decreed.

"Then bring out your gloves, Sergeant-Major, and we'll see if this Scotch upstart can fight as well as he can talk." Farlow was already pulling off his gown and unbuttoning his waistcoat.

"Nev, you can't fight him! He's a doctor!" Chatsworth wailed.

"Are you telling me that I am not worthy of bloodying the nose of this arrogant youngster?" Dr. Doyle's temper was truly gone now. He removed his own jacket and opened his collar again. If young Farlow wanted a thrashing, he was going to get one!

The sergeant-major had removed two sets of padded mitts from the hooks on the walls. Now he held them out to the combatants.

"It's the gloves or the door, and I'll not have you here again if you refuse. We fight fair here, sir."

Dr. Doyle nodded as the doorkeeper laced him into the mitts and assisted him into the ring. Chatsworth acted as second for his friend, helping him up onto the raised platform and tying his mitts securely. Dr. Doyle faced his opponent in the ring, while the sergeant-major ponderously clambered through the ropes and stood between them.

"I will act as referee," the sergeant-major decided. "All this is totally irregular; but if you will have it so, Lord Farlow, you will abide by the rules. No gouging, no punching on the neck, no blows below the belt. First blood wins."

Farlow advanced fiercely, secure in the knowledge that he was younger and taller than his opponent. Dr. Doyle, on the other hand, sidestepped Farlow's wild swing and landed a quick jab to the younger man's ribs. Farlow aimed again and was sidestepped again. Dr. Doyle aimed at his midsection, while Farlow was out for blood and a knockout punch that would destroy his opponent.

The fight continued. Farlow landed a glancing blow on Dr. Doyle's cheek that scraped some skin off but did not deter his opponent. Dr. Doyle watched carefully, then lashed out, a right and a left, connecting with Farlow's jaw. The undergraduate sagged, and the sergeant-major held up Dr. Doyle's hand.

"I declare a winner!" The sergeant-major unlaced the gloves, while Chatsworth climbed into the ring to revive his friend with

153

smelling salts and a wet towel provided by the burly doorkeeper.

Dr. Doyle knelt down beside the young man, all animosity forgotten. "He'll be all right," he announced. "He's only stunned. I didn't hit him all that hard, you know. An ice pack and a day's rest will do wonders for him."

Chatsworth shook his head ruefully. "He won't do it," he said. "We're supposed to be down at the river. Eights practice," he added, as Farlow groaned and lifted his head to glare at Dr. Doyle.

"Take him back to his rooms," Dr. Doyle suggested.

"And don't you come 'round again until you're in a better temper," the sergeant-major added.

Farlow struggled to his knees, then let Chatsworth help him to his feet. "I could have taken you bare-knuckled," he mumbled.

"Perhaps," Dr. Doyle said, accepting his waistcoat and collar from the hands of the admiring doorkeeper. "But we shall never know that, shall we? Good morning, Lord Farlow."

"I haven't told you a thing!" Farlow spat out. "And you have no proof that I did anything! Stop fussing, Minnie! You're worse than my mother!"

He shook off his faithful follower and strode out the door, with Chatsworth trailing after him. The sergeant-major watched them leave with a grim look on his face.

"That there is a young man I'd like to have had the training of," the sergeant-major declared. "Not that I'd have had the chance, of course. I knew his father."

"He's not half bad," Dr. Doyle admitted, feeling his jaw, "but he's got no discipline."

"Unlike you, sir," the sergeant-major said, matching Dr. Doyle's rueful grin. "You've trained, I believe."

Dr. Doyle shrugged himself back into his coat. "I've done some boxing," he said. He stroked his mustache back into place and considered himself properly dressed. "I wanted to have a word with you in any case," he said.

"With me?" The sergeant-major looked astonished.

"About the late and unlamented James Ingram," Dr. Doyle said. "You must have known him."

"Oh? And what makes you think that?"

"Ingram's lodgings are at the end of the street. He had several betting slips in his rooms as well as pawnbrokers' tickets. Young Farlow intimated that you might have been involved in some scheme to fix the odds of the boat races, and for that you would have needed the assistance of servants inside the various competing colleges. What better way to do that than to place your own people in such posts, especially when there were so many vacancies after the hard winter?"

Sergeant-Major Howard led Dr. Doyle back to his tiny office, where he took his own chair and lit up a cigar.

"Why should I talk to you, Dr. Whoever-you-are . . . ?"

"Doyle. My name is Arthur Conan Doyle."

"As you say, sir. Why should I talk to you at all?"

"Because if you wanted to come forward, Sergeant-Major, you would have done so last night. I don't have to tell the police anything about Ingram that they don't already know. In fact, I strongly suspect that Inspector Truscott will be paying you a visit quite shortly. He's no fool, and he knows far more than I do about the ins and outs of the sporting crowd here in Oxford. If I could find you out, it won't take him much longer to get around to you."

The sergeant-major stroked his mustache and frowned. "What do you want to know?"

"How well did you know Ingram?"

"I knew him as well as anyone, which is to say, not at all. The gentlemen in London sent a few chaps down that they thought would be able to suss out information as to the fitness of the rowing teams," the sergeant-major said dryly.

"Nothing illegal about that," Dr. Doyle said, after a moment's thought. "Of course, there are those who would say it is not ethical, but there's no law against having inside info, as they say in racing circles. And so Ingram was taken on at Christ Church, having been provided with a reference from the gentleman in London."

"But they didn't tell me he was a light-fingered rogue who couldn't keep a civil tongue in his head," the sergeant-major sputtered. "I don't know how he got his position in London, or how he expected to keep this one the way he went on, dropping hints

155

of what he'd seen and heard in grand houses and clubs! No one in good service ever does that, not even when he's a drop taken!"

"Indeed?" Dr. Doyle raised an eyebrow.

"Aye, my mother, bless her soul, was in service. Willy, she told me, always remember your place. Pity is that she never saw me in my uniform. She was a grand woman, my mother." The sergeant-major coughed, then eyed Dr. Doyle. "What's your part in all this?"

Dr. Doyle touched his cheek. At least one of Farlow's wild jabs had left its mark. He would have a dandy bruise to explain to Touie.

"Mr. Dodgson is a friend of mine," he said. "He's been accused of driving Ingram to his death."

The sergeant-major gave a crack of laughter. "Driving Ingram to jump into the river? Haw! The shoe'd be on the other foot, I'd say. It would be Ingram who did the driving, were I asked my opinion, which I am not."

"Indeed?" Dr. Doyle cocked his head expectantly.

"From the hints he dropped, I'd say he wouldn't be above putting the black on someone," the sergeant-major said, with a knowing look. "He seemed to have it in for his betters. Hypocrites, he'd call 'em."

"If our friend Ingram had a line in blackmail," Dr. Doyle said slowly, "he might have had enemies. What do you say to that, Sergeant-Major?"

The sergeant-major stood up to dismiss his unwanted caller. "I say that if, as you say, Ingram was playing that game, he got what he deserved. I don't know who killed him, and I can tell you straight out that I didn't nor did I ask anyone else to. In point of fact, I'm now going to have to tell some gentlemen in London that their scheme's been rumbled, and they'll have to find another way of setting their odds. And if this Inspector Truscott comes along, I'll tell him the same. Good day, Dr. Doyle."

"Good day, Sergeant-Major." Dr. Doyle did not quite salute, but he turned smartly on his heels and reached for the door.

"And you take care, Dr. Doyle," the sergeant-major called after him. "Lord Farlow don't always play by the Marquis of Queensberry rules."

"I will bear that in mind, sir." Dr. Doyle touched his cheek again. I'd best put some plaster on this before Touie sees me, he thought. What was it she'd called out? Something about a picnic on the Meadows? He turned to the sergeant-major.

"One more thing, sir. If someone told you they were having a picnic in the Meadows, where would you go?"

"Why, Christ Church Meadows, of course!" The sergeant-major shrugged at the ignorance of strangers to Oxford, and Dr. Doyle decided on his next course of action. He would go back to the White Hart, change his shirt, and make some notes for Mr. Dodgson. Then he could go to Christ Church Meadows and meet his wife and Mr. Dodgson on the green, where they could exchange information.

I only hope Touie is not too bored with the old gentleman, Dr. Doyle thought. I wonder what sort of a day she's having with him?

CHAPTER 16

✧❀✧

After Dr. Doyle had left for his autopsy appointment, Touie and Mr. Dodgson stared blankly at each other for a few moments.

"Arthur can be enthusiastic," Touie said finally, in explanation of her husband's abrupt departure.

"Quite." Mr. Dodgson fussed about rearranging books and papers on his writing table and setting out his pen and inkwell. "Now, Mrs. Doyle, let us be methodical in this matter of Miss Cahill's photograph." He took a sheet of paper out of the appropriate pile and drew it toward him, ready to take notes.

Touie sat up straight, strongly reminded of her brief school-days, when she was brought before the headmistress of her day school for examinations.

"What do we know as fact?" Mr. Dodgson asked.

"Well," Touie said, "we know that there was a photograph, because we have seen it. And we know there were at least two prints made, yours and the one you sent to Miss Cahill. How did you know where to send it?"

"Eh?" Mr. Dodgson looked at his guest.

Touie blushed prettily. "What I mean to say is, if Miss Cahill's parents were not resident here in Oxford but were only passing through, as it were, where did you send the print that you made of Miss Cahill's photograph?"

Mr. Dodgson considered the question. "Of course, Mrs. Doyle, the photographic process at that time was more complex than it is now. Today one may buy dry plates ready to expose or purchase a camera with the celluloid film already inserted. At that time one had to make the negative as soon as the plates were exposed, and the prints were made from that negative. I would have made the negative first, then taken a print from it and presented it to the child at the time of my making it."

Touie shook her head. "But you didn't do that," she objected. "Miss Cahill would certainly have recalled whether or not you presented her with the photograph. She remembered everything else about the visit, even if you didn't."

Mr. Dodgson nodded. "I could consult my diaries," he suggested. He turned to a large bookcase in one corner filled with leather-bound notebooks. "It would have been 1872 or thereabouts . . ." He found the volume and started to flip over pages. "February, Miss Cahill said. Dear me, how long ago that was!" He sighed, then frowned. "I have a notation here that I visited the Deanery and left a copy of the Italian translation of *Alice* for Miss Liddell, but that there were other persons present for tea and I was not to have conversation with Miss Liddell. Ah, here it is . . . 'Took photographs of a very pretty child under artificial light.' It was something I rarely did, artificial lighting for photography. I much preferred natural light, but Miss Cahill remarked that the day was inclement."

"And that is all?" Touie sounded disappointed, as Mr. Dodgson carefully put the notebook back in its place on the shelf.

Mr. Dodgson sighed again. "One never realizes the effect one's actions may have in the future. My only reason for visiting the Deanery was to present Miss Liddell with the book. She was otherwise occupied, and I did not have any conversation with her."

"So you amused little Dianna instead," Touie said. "And you took the photograph, but for some reason you did not present it to the child at that time."

159

Mr. Dodgson closed his eyes in concentration, then opened them. "Now I remember," he said. "It was February, quite a blustery day. After I had taken my photographs, the child was dressed, and her parents came to call for her to return to their lodgings."

"Surely not lodgings," Touie exclaimed. "Didn't Dianna mention something about their being on a family visit? They would have returned to the house where they were staying with Miss Cahill's relations, whoever they were."

"Roswell," Mr. Dodgson said. "I know that name. Of course, the Roswell Glass Works provided some of the glass used by Mr. Burne-Jones for the windows in the Cathedral. He is also contracted to provide window glass for the rooms, should it be needed. I have had some dealings with the firm. Mr. Roswell has the reputation for scrupulous honesty in all his business affairs, although I have heard there was some sort of scandal in his family. That was many years ago," he added hurriedly, "and I know nothing about it."

Touie considered the Roswell connection. "Miss Cahill seems quite fond of her relations," she said. "Mr. Roswell, having no children of his own, appears to have been quite generous to Miss Cahill, who is not a blood relative but a connection through marriage. Do you know anything else about him?"

Mr. Dodgson frowned. "He sits on several town committees," he said finally. "And I have heard it said that he is so strict a Methodist that he will not enter a theater. Of course, that is true of some of my friends as well," he added.

"And so you never presented the child with her photograph," Touie got back to the original point, "because she had been taken away before you had a chance to make the print from the negative. In that case, who dressed the child?"

Mr. Dodgson looked blank. "I have no idea," he said at last. "There must have been a maidservant at hand, because I never took a child who was unwilling or the least bit uncomfortable, and there was always a mama or a nurse present."

"That's what I told Arthur," Touie said. "It had occurred to me that while Miss Cahill was chattering yesterday, she never

160

mentioned her nanny. Now most young ladies in Miss Cahill's position would have a nurse in attendance. We shall have to ask whether she did, and who this woman was." Mr. Dodgson's eyebrows went up. Touie went on, "Because, you see, the question is, who knew there was a photograph taken and of what nature? Miss Cahill was a child who would not know or care whether or not the photograph could be construed as irregular in any way."

"Quite so," Mr. Dodgson agreed. "Children are innocent of any pretense. And while her parents knew that I had taken her photograph, they may not have known that I would ask her to pose without the restraints of clothing. I, myself, may not have known, until I made the request; and if the child had shown any reluctance, I would never have proceeded."

"Therefore," Touie concluded, "we must assume that you made the print after the child had left and sent it on. And that, sir, brings us back to the first point. How did you know where to send the print?"

Mr. Dodgson thought for a moment. "I would have asked Dean Liddell," he said at last. "After all, the Reverend Mr. Cahill had come to tea at the deanery, and I would have assumed that Dean Liddell would know where they were staying in Oxford."

"And you would have sent the print to that direction." Touie nodded, sending the flowers bouncing on her straw hat.

"I see where this is leading," Mr. Dodgson said. "I sent the photograph to the residence of Mr. Roswell, but by that time Mr. and Mrs. Cahill and their daughter must have left for Mr. Cahill's new living in Northumberland."

"And it is possible that they never received the photograph at all," Touie finished triumphantly.

Mr. Dodgson shook his head. "If Mr. or Mrs. Roswell had received it, they would have sent it on, I am sure."

"Perhaps they never saw it," Touie offered. "That is, suppose one of the servants took it upon himself or herself to open the packet you sent from Christ Church to see what had been sent to Mr. and Mrs. Cahill, saw the photograph, and placed the wrong interpretation upon it?"

Mr. Dodgson gave an indignant squawk. "What sort of interpretation could there be? The child is innocent; the photograph was pure!"

Touie tried to soothe the agitated don. "Well, as you have seen, someone has already used the photograph in a way you did not intend. Perhaps the servants thought they were protecting Miss Cahill from embarrassment or the necessity for explanations as to how the photograph came to be taken. Or perhaps, with Mr. Roswell being such a strict Methodist, as you have told me, they might have thought he would be offended by the photograph and so kept it from him."

Mr. Dodgson was not to be mollified. "That is interference of the highest order," he sputtered. "How dare they?"

"Well, they must have," Touie said pragmatically. "Otherwise, Miss Cahill or her parents would have received their copy of the photograph, and we wouldn't be in this pickle, would we?"

Mr. Dodgson nodded solemnly. "Mrs. Doyle, you are a most remarkable young woman. Let us continue along this line of reasoning. The photograph was sent to the Roswell establishment. One of the servants—"

"The butler, if they had one, or the parlor maid if they didn't," Touie interrupted. Mr. Dodgson silenced her with a look.

"A servant opened the packet, saw the photograph, and decided not to send it on but to . . . to do what with it?" He looked at Touie, who shrugged.

"If such a thing were to come into my possession, I might very well try to discard it," Touie said frankly. "It is a lovely photograph, Mr. Dodgson, but it is somewhat, um . . ." She searched for a diplomatic word.

Mr. Dodgson sighed. "There are many persons in this world who will put the worst possible interpretation on the purest of intentions," he stated. "This child was simply posing in the most natural and charming manner. I regarded her as an object to be lighted, nothing more."

"Well, someone did not discard this photograph," Touie said. "Instead, they kept it."

"Why?" Mr. Dodgson asked. He looked at Touie and repeated

the question. "Why would a servant keep this photograph in his possession all these years?"

"Or her," Touie reminded him. "I have been considering this problem, and do you know, I may have an answer. We know that Miss Cahill had traveled with her parents and was staying with Mr. and Mrs. Roswell, who had no children of their own. The Reverend Mr. Cahill and his wife were going to a distant living and may not have been traveling with servants, expecting to hire someone locally, particularly if, as Miss Cahill has so carefully avoided telling us, they were not circumstanced well enough to have personal servants with them.

"It is possible that one of the maids in the Roswell household might have been impressed into the nursery, so to speak, and that this young person would have become attached to Miss Dianna Cahill. She would not wish the photograph to become the subject of ill-natured gossip for the sake of the child. She might have decided not to send the photograph on but to keep it as a memento instead." Touie looked at Mr. Dodgson. "Does that sound reasonable, sir?"

Mr. Dodgson considered all aspects of the proposed solution and nodded. "It is difficult to say what did or did not happen in a household some fifteen years ago," he added. "However, what you propose is quite logical. The question before us now is, how did this photograph get into the hands of whoever sent it to Miss Cahill? You cannot have it both ways," he said sternly, before Touie could speak again. "If a person abstracted the photograph out of regard for a child's sensibilities fifteen years ago, why should that same person use it to such devastating effect now?"

"There must have been two people involved," Touie said firmly. "There was the one who kept the photograph in the first place, and there was someone else who learned of the existence of a second copy from her."

"Her?" Mr. Dodgson's eyebrows raised in inquiry.

"Of course, her," Touie said. "It must have been the nursemaid, the girl who was here when the photograph was taken, the one who helped Miss Dianna on with her clothes and took her down to her parents while you were fussing with the negatives, and all that so that you never got the chance to give her the original print you made." She looked triumphantly at Mr. Dodgson, waiting for applause.

Mr. Dodgson obliged with a brief nod and a smile. "Mrs. Doyle, you may have found the answer to a part of our problem. Now all we have to do is find the nursemaid, and then find out who, if anyone, she told about the second copy."

Touie's smile of triumph faded. "Oh dear. I hadn't thought of that. It's been fifteen years. She might be anywhere by now, and she may have told any number of people about it. Maids do tend to chatter." She frowned in thought. "It might be useful," she said slowly, "to find out if this man Ingram, who was in your rooms, ever worked for Mr. Roswell."

Mr. Dodgson nodded. "I see where you are going with this. Servants talk among themselves. Ingram might have heard about this photograph from someone in a household in which he was in service."

"Only that still doesn't explain why he put the photograph together with that dreadful poem to try to get poor Miss Cahill out of Oxford." Touie sighed. "It is all so confusing."

"True," Mr. Dodgson said. "It is a pity that we cannot take this information to Inspector Truscott. He might be able to send one of his men around to Mr. Roswell's house to chat with the servants. Policemen are supposed to be good at doing that."

"It would do Miss Cahill no good to have the police involved in her problem," Touie agreed. "Well, Mr. Dodgson, what shall we do now?" She looked at her elderly host expectantly.

Mr. Dodgson suddenly realized that he had been chatting with a young woman on terms of near equality. He was overcome with a bout of shyness that brought on his stammer again.

He came up with a plan. "Would you c-care to insp-pect the k-kitchens? They were designed by no less a p-personage than Cardinal Wolsey himself and are c-considered worthy of examination."

Touie covered her smile with one gloved hand. "I should very much like to see the famous kitchens," she said politely. "And perhaps we could walk in Christ Church Meadows and look at the boats on the river. And we could send a note to the White Hart to ask Arthur to join us, and we can all compare notes."

"An excellent plan, Mrs. Doyle." Mr. Dodgson found his tall hat, put on his gray cotton gloves, and prepared to descend to Tom Quad, while Touie prepared to be instructed. She wondered how her husband was getting on with his assignment and hoped that he would have the time to join them for their picnic luncheon.

"Shall we go, Mrs. Doyle?" Mr. Dodgson led his guest down the stairs into the May sunshine.

CHAPTER 17

The sun had cleared the top of the hated bell tower, and Tom Quad was filled with students in caps and gowns when Mr. Dodgson and Touie came down the stairs. The grassy lawn surrounding the famous pool seemed to sparkle in the spring sunlight. Mr. Dodgson fussed with his gloves, while Touie drank in the scene. She was all too aware that she was the only female in sight.

"But I'm not the only female," she amended to herself. A well-dressed woman was emerging from one of the doors opposite Mr. Dodgson's tower.

Mr. Dodgson looked up as the woman approached the two of them.

"Good morning, Mr. Dodgson." The woman addressed him in the well-bred tones used by the upper segments of society toward those who were one step lower on the social ladder and held out her hand.

"Mrs. Hargreaves! What a surprise!" Mr. Dodgson bowed slightly and accepted the three fingers held out to him. Touie coughed expectantly. Mr. Dodgson turned and made the introductions: "Mrs. Hargreaves, may I present Mrs. Doyle. Her husband is Dr. Arthur Conan Doyle. Dicky Doyle's nephew, you know."

"We are visiting Oxford, on our way north," Touie explained, as Mrs. Hargreaves subjected her to a searching examination that took in her modest flowered-print dress, straw bonnet, and youthful appearance.

"I am so glad to have seen you, Mr. Dodgson," Mrs. Hargreaves said, turning her attention away from the young woman to the older man. "You wrote to me asking if I could find the little book you made for me so long ago."

"The original story of *Alice's Adventures Underground*,"Mr. Dodgson recalled. "Have you found it?"

"I have found it. Here it is." Mrs. Hargreaves handed him a small package wrapped in brown paper. "I was going to send it by post; but since I wanted to visit Mama today, I thought I would bring it myself."

Mr. Dodgson took the package reverently and undid the string. A small, vellum-bound notebook was revealed.

Touie suddenly realized to whom she was talking. This imposing lady, dressed in the height of fashion, with a tight velvet basque, grand bustle, and draped skirt, topped off with a grand hat dripping with feathers, had once been little Alice Liddell, the darling of Christ Church.

Mr. Dodgson stroked the book lovingly. "Thank you for permitting me to borrow it," he said. "Some persons have requested that I make a facsimile copy by photographing the pages and having them reproduced. I would not do so if you do not wish it, of course," he added.

Mrs. Hargreaves smiled indulgently at her old playfellow. "I have no particular use for the book now," she said. "My boys are rather inclined to their father's sporting interests and would not be interested in it. If you wish, you may keep it."

"Oh, no," Mr. Dodgson demurred. "I would never demand the return of a gift. The story was told at your request and was written down at your demand. I shall return this book to you when it has been duplicated." He bowed again and turned to Touie. "Mrs. Doyle, would you excuse me? I must place this book where it will be safe. I shall be back directly." He bustled back up the stairs, leaving Touie to face the intimidating Mrs. Hargreaves.

There was an awkward moment of silence, as the two women gazed at each other. Then Touie blurted out, "Were you really Alice?"

Mrs. Hargreaves laughed at the younger woman's naïve remark. "That was over twenty years ago," she said, with a sigh. "I was a child. Mr. Dodgson was a dear, dear playmate to my sisters and myself, but we grew up." She shrugged. "Apparently, Mr. Dodgson never did."

"But surely you kept up the acquaintance," Touie said.

Mrs. Hargreaves shook her head. "My mother did not think it appropriate, once my sisters and I were above a certain age, to continue to go about with Mr. Dodgson. And there were other reasons for the estrangement." She closed her lips firmly, as if locking family secrets tightly behind them.

"Mr. Dodgson mentioned that there had been a . . ." Touie searched for a diplomatic way to put it. "A break of some sort," she said finally.

Mrs. Hargreaves sighed. "It was partially Mama's fault. She had certain ambitions for my sisters and myself."

Touie nodded, slightly mystified. "I suppose every mother wishes the best for her children," she said.

"I suppose it was for the best," Mrs. Hargreaves agreed. "I went for an extended visit to Wales one summer to my grandmother; and while I was away, my mother took it upon herself to remove all my childish toys and books. She even burned the correspondence I had had from Mr. Dodgson and would not let me write to him. She told me that it was because I was no longer a child but a young lady, and I suppose she was right; but at the time, I did not understand."

"It does seem somewhat hard-hearted of her," Touie remarked. "I wonder that your little book survived such a sweeping, um, holocaust."

"Oh, that was because I had taken the book with me on my

holiday," Mrs. Hargreaves explained. "It was something of a talisman of mine."

"Mr. Dodgson must have been pleased with that. After all, he had written the story for you."

Mrs. Hargreaves smiled slightly. "Yes, and that was another matter that Mama disliked intensely. She felt it was an impertinence, that he had no right to do so; and when it was actually published, she thought it quite dreadful, an imposition on our privacy."

Touie frowned slightly. "But Mr. Dodgson used a nom de plume," she observed. "The book was published under the name of Lewis Carroll."

Mrs. Hargreaves sighed. "It made no difference to Mama. She was affronted at the mere mention of it. And then, when it turned out to be such a success, she was even more upset."

Touie suppressed a desire to laugh and said, "Didn't you feel at all impressed?" Mrs. Hargreaves stared haughtily, and Touie amended her statement. "What I mean to say is, Mr. Dodgson's little story is quite famous all over the world. There are translations into several languages, I understand."

Mrs. Hargreaves shook her head. "That only made it worse! Especially when Mr. Dodson and my father were at odds about the improvements to the buildings on Tom Quad." She gestured toward the bell tower. "Mr. Dodgson wrote a pamphlet about it. It was quite witty, but dreadfully inappropriate of him to do so."

"So you never spoke with Mr. Dodgson after *Alice's Adventures in Wonderland* came out?" Touie asked.

"Only the merest commonplaces," Mrs. Hargreaves admitted. "In fact, I do believe the last time we spoke at all was . . ." She concentrated, then went on. "Dear me, it must have been nearly fifteen years ago. He came to the Deanery with the copy of *Alice* in Italian, thinking that I should like to have it because I was studying Italian at the time."

"But you didn't really want it?" Touie hinted.

"I was far too old for fairy stories by then, and I had already had quite enough of Alice and her adventures. Of course, I could not tell Mr. Dodgson so," Mrs. Hargreaves said, with a smile of complicity, as one woman to another.

Touie nodded, in womanly understanding. "One does hate to snub an old acquaintance," she said. "Mr. Dodgson mentioned that he had left the Italian translation for you at the Deanery, but he didn't tell us that he had actually spoken with you about it."

Mrs. Hargreaves shrugged, setting the feathers on her hat a-flutter. "I really don't recall . . . there were people to tea, I think, and we couldn't say very much." She frowned, then said, "Now I remember. There was a little girl with the guests, and Mr. Dodgson asked if he could borrow her, as he put it, for tea. So off they went, and that was the last I saw of him, except for a brief glimpse in the quad, until today."

"But surely Mr. Dodgson saw you married?"

"Why on earth should he?" Mrs. Hargreaves asked in astonishment. "It was not a college affair. Once I married Major Hargreaves, I had my own establishment to run. I only came today to pay a call on my mother and to leave off this book. Mr. Dodgson seems to feel that it should be reproduced by this new method. I have no objections to its being done, and my mother has nothing to say in the matter."

"How lucky, then, that your little book was preserved!" Touie exclaimed. "How fortunate for all the children who will be able to read the story as it was first told."

"Yes, I suppose it is." Mrs. Hargreaves smiled wistfully. Somewhere, under the velvet and the feathers, might be the ghost of that little girl who was such an inspiration to the shy Mr. Dodgson, Touie thought.

"Well, I must be off," Mrs. Hargreaves said, offering Touie two gloved fingers to shake. "My carriage will be here shortly, and it never does to keep the servants waiting."

Touie trotted after the other woman. "Mrs. Hargreaves, a moment of your time, if you please."

"I beg your pardon?" Mrs. Hargreaves was not used to being accosted after she had dismissed someone.

"I express myself badly . . . and I do hope you don't think it forward of me . . ." Touie sputtered. "But . . . I wondered if you could advise me on a domestic matter."

Mrs. Hargreaves regarded the younger woman with astonishment. "Whatever do you mean?"

Touie began again. "You see, Arthur, my husband, and I have a very modest establishment at present, but we have certain expectations." Touie had no intention of elaborating on this information. The household at Southsea consisted of herself, her husband, her mother, and a slavey in the kitchen; and the expectations would come when Arthur's literary genius was made manifest to the world, as Touie had every reason to believe it would.

"But what has this to do with me?" Mrs. Hargreaves asked haughtily.

"Servants," Touie blurted out. "If we are to have them, I should know how to get on with them, and I don't."

Mrs. Hargreaves laughed indulgently. "My dear child, I do understand your dilemma. When I married Major Hargreaves, I was put in charge of quite a large establishment, and I had no idea how to go on."

"Arthur says that one should always be prepared," Touie said, as if reciting a piece of ancient wisdom from an unimpeachable source. "And so I wondered if you could give me some advice."

Mrs. Hargreaves stopped in midstride. "What sort of advice?"

Touie took a deep breath. "Well, there is the matter of maids. There are ladies of my acquaintance in Portsmouth who have a housemaid and a parlor maid . . ."

Mrs. Hargreaves shook her head. "A parlor maid is a poor excuse for a butler," she stated. "Better to have a manservant, if you can afford one. A parlor maid simply advertises that one cannot keep a manservant in the house."

Touie nodded meekly, as befitted one being instructed. "I see. And if, in the course of time, we should set up a nursery, I don't suppose we could ask one of the housemaids to—"

"Certainly not!" Mrs. Hargreaves cut in indignantly. "The care of children should not be left to the housemaids. One must hire a reputable nanny, with a nursemaid to assist her. The housemaids have their own work to do. And a parlor maid, should you have one, is far too smart for the nursery. The nursemaid should be quite young and innocent."

"But suppose," Touie continued, "that a child were to be brought into a household where there is no nursery."

"As a visitor, do you mean?" Mrs. Hargreaves considered the idea briefly then dismissed it. "Quite unlikely, Mrs. Doyle. Any respectable parents will bring someone with them to care for the child."

"I see." Touie frowned. "Then one must not ask a housemaid, or a between maid to care for a small child even for a short time?"

"Well, I suppose, if someone came to stay for an extended visit with a small child and did not bring a nurse for the child, one might do that," Mrs. Hargreaves conceded. "But it is not done in the best circles." Which I move in, was the unspoken coda.

"Thank you so much for your advice," Touie said, as Mrs. Hargreaves proceeded majestically through Tom Gate and into her carriage, just as Mr. Dodgson emerged once more into the sunlit quad.

"Mr. Dodgson!" Touie greeted him with a wave.

The don peered about, then found Touie at the gate, staring after the Hargreaves carriage.

"Did you really write the story for her?" Touie asked.

"Oh, yes." Mr. Dodgson smiled, as he recalled that day, so many years ago, when he and Mr. Duckworth had taken the three Liddell girls on a boating picnic down the river, and he had told a long and fantastic story about a little girl named Alice who had fallen down a rabbit hole into a Wonderland.

"She is very different now," Touie commented.

Mr. Dodgson's smile faded. "Quite different," he said. "Well, Mrs. Doyle, I have considered our little problem and have come to some conclusions."

"As have I, Mr. Dodgson." Touie nodded decisively. "What shall we do now?"

"I offered to show you the kitchens," Mr. Dodgson reminded her. "They are considered quite extraordinary."

Touie smiled sweetly. "I should very much like to see the

famous Christ Church kitchens," she said. "And then we can bespeak a hamper and cloth for a picnic on Christ Church Meadows. It is getting quite warm, and we shall have a lovely day. We can leave a note with the porter for Arthur to meet us there, and we can all compare our notes."

"I do not usually take luncheon," Mr. Dodgson demurred.

"Arthur does," Touie reminded him. "And I think I shall be rather hungry by the time we all meet. Would you be so kind as to speak to Telling about a hamper?" She smiled winningly up at Mr. Dodgson.

"Very well, Mrs. Doyle, I shall speak to Telling." Mr. Dodgson conceded defeat. He led the way around the quad to the vaulted entrance to the Hall, ignoring the surprised stares of the students who gawked at the female intrusion into their domains.

"The Hall was erected in 1529," Mr. Dodgson lectured his guest, pointing to the architectural features of the building, "at the bequest of Cardinal Wolsey. King Henry the Eighth took over construction after the cardinal's misfortunes halted the expansion of the college. You may see the rose of the Tudors incised into the stonework." Touie noted the decorations, then turned to see her husband running around the pathway.

"Picnic in the Meadows!" she called out. She was answered with a frantic wave, and then Arthur was gone, running through the gap in the walls and back into the lane. Touie only hoped that he had gotten her message. Perhaps she should send a note to the White Hart anyway, just in case he had not understood her.

"Ahem!" Mr. Dodgson coughed sharply to bring her attention back to the architecture. He led her into the Hall, down a set of stone steps, and into a vast, vaulted room, where fires burned in two huge fireplaces set along the farther wall. Cooks were already preparing chickens for the spit, to be roasted for dinner, while underlings were shredding vegetables for the steaming pots on the stoves in the center of the room.

Touie took it all in and marveled at the chaos that went into preparation of meals for so many people at once. Mr. Dodgson, on the other hand, was more interested in finding Telling.

The Chief Scout was looking harried. "I have a few minutes,

Mr. Dodgson, but as you can see, we are shorthanded this morning, and the Dean is entertaining Miss Wordsworth, of Lady Margaret Hall, and Mr. Talbot, of Keble, with an al fresco luncheon to be set up on the Meadows. The police have been here," he added ominously. "They wanted to know more about Ingram."

"Dear me." Mr. Dodgson made unhappy noises. "This is dreadful. Telling, do you have Ingram's letter of reference to hand?"

"Just what that Inspector Truscott asked," Telling said. "I have not had the opportunity to find it, things being so confused at present, but I shall do so as soon as I can find the time. Will you be dining in Hall tonight, sir, or are you planning another dinner party?"

Mr. Dogson looked blankly at Touie, then said, "I am not sure at this moment of my plans for dinner. However, I shall certainly inform you as soon as I know."

Touie coughed expectantly. Mr. Dodgson looked startled, then said, "Telling, would it be possible to have some sandwiches cut and put into a basket for a picnic? Mrs. Doyle would very much like to have her luncheon on the grass."

"I can have a hamper made up directly." Telling waved at one of the cooks, who dropped his chopper and came over. "Walton, make up a basket for Mr. Dodgson and his guest. And, er," he glanced at Touie's modest bustle, "find a camp stool for the lady."

"That looks delicious," Touie said, as the cook sliced bread, inserted the meat, and looked expectantly at her with a mustard pot in his hand. "No, no mustard," Touie instructed the cook. "Arthur dislikes mustard. Butter only and perhaps some of the apple tart I see in that corner, if there is any extra?" The cook shrugged and cut several wedges of pie, wrapping each one into a napkin, and fitting the whole into a marketing basket from a pile under the central table.

Touie watched the proceeding carefully, thinking of Arthur and his assignment. What could he have been doing, running about in Tom Quad? "I saw Arthur just now," she said aloud. "I only hope he has not gotten himself into some sort of difficulty. He is so impetuous!"

"Quite unlike the stolid Inspector Truscott. I wonder how the good Inspector is getting on?" Mr. Dodgson commented.

"He seems quite competent," Touie observed, as the basket was delivered to her, and a folding stool was handed to her companion. "Shall we go, Mr. Dodgson?"

"I shall be delighted to show you our little piece of the river, Mrs. Doyle." Mr. Dodgson led Touie through the back door of the kitchens, across the lane, and through the turnstile to the grassy fields known as Christ Church Meadows.

CHAPTER 18

Inspector Truscott had had a busy morning.

He had been up at dawn to direct the constables at Magdalen Bridge in their search for clues to Ingram's murderer. He had attended the autopsy on the scout and searched his rooms, with the interfering Dr. Doyle peering over his shoulder. Once the young doctor had taken himself off, Truscott metaphorically rolled up his sleeves and set to work, feeling that now he could conduct the investigation into the death of James Ingram by the rules, as decreed by the instructions laid down by Sir Robert Peel himself. He would question everyone connected with the deceased, examine the circumstances of the death, and fix the blame on the most likely suspect. This was the so-called System, and it usually worked.

The difficulty here, Truscott said to himself, as he prepared to follow Sergeant Everett down the stairs and back to the Oxford Constabulary Headquarters in Blue Boar Lane, is that there are no likely suspects. He said as much to the sergeant, who was overseeing the handling of the locked chest.

"Depends on what's in this chest, don't it?" Everett said. "Yon

Dr. Doyle seems to think Ingram was trying the black on someone."

"Blackmailer, eh?" Truscott grunted. "We'll see what secrets he ferreted out."

"Strange that he should have that old daguerrotype out in the open," Everett observed. "I shouldn't think he'd have kept something like that where anyone could find it."

"He might have had a soft spot for the girl," Truscott ventured.

"Lost sweetheart?" Everett thought it over. "Don't seem likely somehow."

"Oh? Did you know the man?" Truscott shot his underling a searching glance.

"Not to do more than speak to," Everett confessed. "Now I think on it, I may have seen him at the sergeant-major's."

"And just what were you doing there, Sergeant?" Truscott asked sharply.

"I was there in the pursuit of my duties," Everett stated stolidly. "We had had a tip that there was to be an illegal boxing match on the premises, and that wouldn't do; so I felt it my duty to inform the sergeant-major that we was on to him, and that he might be in difficulties if he persisted in staging such a bout of fisticuffs."

"And Ingram was present?" Truscott mulled this over.

"I couldn't say for certain. There were several other persons present as well," Everett said defensively.

"And you had no way of knowing the fellow would be thrown into the river and drowned," Truscott finished for him. "When was this warning delivered?"

Everett frowned. "Maybe two weeks ago."

Truscott nodded sagely. "So, Sergeant-Major Willy Howard is up to his stiff neck in something," he said knowingly.

"The sergeant-major's establishment is something of an institution," Everett reminded his superior. "Young gentlemen of the University have been going there ever since the sergeant-major put up his shingle. There's some as says he's been financed by certain toffs in London as want to keep their eyes on things, so to speak. I've also heard that a few of the older chaps, dons and suchlike, may be seen there, keeping fit, so to speak."

Inspector Truscott drew in his considerable stomach. "I'm not saying there's anything amiss with the sergeant-major's establishment," he said. "But I strongly suggest that we have a word with the sergeant-major before the day's out."

"Indeed, sir." Sergeant Everett agreed.

The heavy suitcase was carried down the rickety stairs by one of Everett's constables and placed into a wheelbarrow. Sergeant Everett and Inspector Truscott followed at a measured pace, threading their way along St. Aldgates between carts, carriages, and passersby. They did not notice Dr. Doyle and the two undergraduates as they passed on their way to the Covered Market, so intent were they on their own conversation.

"Have you heard from the men at Magdalen Bridge?" Truscott demanded.

"They've found a good deal of mud and not much else," Everett confessed. "The landing's stone, with no tracks we could see. I've had them collect all the trash they could find; but apart from the usual cigar ends, there was nothing that you could call a clue."

Truscott made a noise of exasperation. "Tchah! What about those waterweeds that Scottish chap was going on about? The stuff in Ingram's insides?"

"Nothing out of the ordinary, sir," Everett reported.

Truscott made another impatient noise. "What about the bath chair? Whose is that?"

Everett consulted his notebook. "By its number plate, we traced it back to one particular chairman, to wit, Henry Jones. He stated that he put it in its rightful spot at Magdalen Bridge, where he puts all his chairs at the end of the working day. He was most annoyed to find out that it had been used and for what purpose. He didn't like having dead corpses carried about in one of his chairs."

Truscott stifled a laugh. "Tell him he can use the chair again, but he don't have to tell anyone what went in it."

Everett scowled. "Mr. Dodgson stated that he saw students

pushing the chair. They must have brought it to Christ Church for a reason. If they was from Magdalen or Merton, they'd have kept to the High and not bothered to run the chair all the way to the Broad Walk."

"Meaning, I take it, that the students in question must have been from Christ Church," Truscott finished for him. "The thought had occurred to me, Everett."

"It beats me what they thought they were playing at," Everett complained.

"Students have been known to play practical jokes," Truscott said sagely. "Perhaps one of these young sprigs came across Ingram, just floating there in the water, and thought it would be funny to transport the body and place it somewhere else."

"Strange sense of humor," Everett said, his nose wrinkling with distaste.

"But typical," Truscott added.

By now they had reached Blue Boar Lane, a narrow street off St. Aldgates, where the headquarters of the Oxford Constabulary occupied a suite of three small rooms. The largest of these was for the processing of such prisoners as had to be detained for the city magistrate. Inspector Truscott had to share the second room with the rest of the Oxford Constabulary. Only Chief Inspector Wheeler had the dignity of his own room, and it was there that the suspicious suitcase was brought for inspection.

Chief Inspector Wheeler regarded the box with the expression of one who expects to be blown up at any moment. "No keys?" he asked.

"No keys were found on the person of the deceased," Truscott reported. "No keys were found in the room used by the deceased."

"Then the keys were stolen by someone else," Chief Inspector Wheeler concluded.

"So it would seem, sir."

"We'll have to get it open," Wheeler said, "one way or another."

"I'd advise a locksmith, sir," Inspector Truscott said. "That way, there would be less chance of damaging any evidence inside it."

"Easier to break the lock," Chief Inspector Wheeler countered. "We'll do it as soon as Effingham gets here." He looked sharply at Truscott and Everett. "Has a watch been set on the rooms previously used by this Ingram?"

"I've got a constable watching the street," Truscott assured him. "If anyone approaches, we'll nab him."

"Hmmm. I should hope so." Wheeler eyed the chest again. "You say this fellow Ingram was a blackmailer?"

"According to Dr. Doyle." Truscott cleared his throat. "I have taken the liberty of contacting the Portsmouth Constabulary through the telephone, sir."

"Telephone, eh?" Wheeler raised his sandy brows. "Useful thing, the telephone. What do they have to say about the inquisitive Dr. Doyle?"

Truscott shrugged. "He's acted as police surgeon on several cases. He's well-known in Portsmouth. He fancies himself a detective of sorts."

"Not my sort!" Wheeler growled. "Look here, Truscott, we don't want outsiders mixing into our affairs. Get this solved quickly, before the Chief Constable sends for Scotland Yard over my head."

"In that case, sir, I may have to consult with this Doyle," Truscott said. "He's onto something. What do you make of this?" He handed the printed sheet with Ingram's scrawled notations on the blank side to the Chief Inspector, who scowled back.

"Notes. Additions. What of it?"

"Look at the printing on the reverse side, sir."

Chief Inspector Wheeler's scowl deepened, and the man's complexion turned brick red as the full import of what he was reading took hold. "This is disgusting!" he pronounced.

"I didn't understand some of the words," Inspector Truscott said innocently, "but from the context, I'd say it's about corrupting young girls."

Everett took the paper from Chief Inspector Wheeler's trembling fingers. " 'Observe Miss Dye,' " he read aloud, " 'the little honey, opening her hairless . . .' "

"This is totally disgusting!" Chief Inspector Wheeler broke in. "If that's the sort of thing Ingram has in that chest . . ." He took a deep breath and eyed the suitcase as if it were about to explode.

"We don't know that it's his," Truscott corrected him. "For all we know, it might well have been in some undergraduate's rooms, and he could have simply taken the paper to write on the blank side. Here are his calculations, as you see." Truscott turned the paper over to the scrawled numbers.

"Fine thing for young gentlemen to be reading," fumed Wheeler.

"Or writing," Everett added, with a censorious frown.

Truscott looked thoughtfully at the printed sheet before them. "This seems to refer to an illustration of some kind," he said. "Dr. Doyle found a camera, and there are indications that Ingram had set up some sort of way of copying a photograph on a table near his window. May we suppose that there was a photograph that would accompany this writing?"

Wheeler nodded. "Or some other kind of drawing," he amended. "In that case, the subject of the illustration might have a very good reason to kill Ingram."

Truscott shook his head. "The text refers to a female," he objected. "Ingram was a good six feet tall. Not many women would be able to drown an able-bodied man that tall . . ."

"Not without some help," Everett put in. "But there were marks on the body . . . she could have whacked him over the noggin and held him down with the oar."

"Or he," Truscott reminded him. "Young ladies have brothers, fathers, and even husbands. Any of them could have taken his revenge on the man who was trying to blackmail their near and dear one."

"All this is based on assumptions," Wheeler said. "What we need are facts!" He scrabbled about in the papers on his desk. "What about this business of the thefts at Christ Church?" He read over one of the carefully written reports. "Was this Ingram stealing, do you think?"

Everett looked smugly at his superiors. "I've got Oakley out this morning, checking our usual sources. James Ingram was known to two of them, and we've got a little list of his recent loot. I think we've got our thief, sir."

"People don't knock a man on the head and drown him for the sake of a few trinkets," Wheeler snarled. He looked at the list of Ingram's personal belongings again.

"Unless the trinkets had deep and personal meaning," Truscott put in. "He was wearing an unusually fine watch."

"With a crest," Everett added. "Which crest, if you don't mind the interruption, I have taken the liberty of identifying."

Chief Inspector Wheeler and Inspector Truscott looked sharply at the sergeant. "I thought I knew the crest, sir," Sergeant Everett said staunchly. "My dad was a carrier in these parts, and he let me come along with him on his rounds to help with the bundles and crates. I learned most of the crests hereabouts from the gates and suchlike, and it came to me that I'd seen that crest before. It's the Berwick crest, which is a bear, standing up, carrying a spear."

"Berwick?" Inspector Truscott frowned. "I've heard that name before."

Sergeant Everett consulted his notebook. "Lord Nevil Farlow, son of Lord Berwick. He's got rooms on the staircase served by the late Ingram."

"What's he got to say about all this?" Wheeler growled.

"Nothing," Truscott said. "He wasn't available for questioning last night."

Wheeler's frown deepened. "Anything known about him? Has he been up before the proctors or the magistrate? Youthful high spirits, that sort of thing?"

Truscott paused before speaking. "He's known as a sportsman," he said at last. "Well thought of, but a nasty temper when crossed. He's a Blue on the cricket team, and Christ Church is heavily favored to win Head of the River again this year thanks to him."

Everett cleared his throat. "Ahem! On the occasion I spoke of, when I visited the sergeant-major's establishment during a prize-fight, I noticed a number of young men present. Lord Nevil Farlow was one of them. He's hard to miss."

"Then perhaps you'd best have a word with the sergeant-major," Truscott decided. "If this Ingram was connected with gambling, he'd be sure to know about it."

Everett nodded gravely. "The sergeant-major's closemouthed, but he'll talk to me. I'll see him after I check on the men at Magdalen Bridge. They may have come up with something by now."

"And what about this young fellow, Farlow?" Chief Inspector Wheeler asked.

"I shall have to deal with him myself," Truscott said, adjusting his bowler hat and shrugging himself into better adjustment with his coat. "I shall go to Christ Church, find young Farlow, and ask him a few questions."

"And what if he decides not to answer?" Sergeant Everett asked.

"Then I will know he has something to hide," the Inspector said grimly. "And I will find out what it is."

He settled his hat firmly on his head and marched back to St. Aldgates. He would have to take the long way around, back through Tom Gate, and he would have to run the gauntlet of scouts; but he would question this young man, and he would get his answers, lord's son or no lord's son!

It took Inspector Truscott nearly an hour before he could find anyone with the authority to allow him to question Lord Nevil Farlow. By that time the young man had taken himself and his grievances to the boathouse, where he and his crew assembled to row down the River Cherwell.

Inspector Truscott gave it up as a bad job. He would have to question young Farlow later when he came off the river. Instead, he decided to join Everett and his men at Magdalen Bridge. There may have been some small piece of evidence they had overlooked.

At the same time, in the library at Lady Margaret Hall, Gertrude Bell yawned and stretched and drew the attention of the other girls.

"Miss Bell," Miss Laurel chided her, "the rest of us are trying to study."

"It's too hot," Gertrude complained. "I've been swotting away at Charles the First all morning. I simply cannot agree with Professor Soames's assessment of him. He wasn't a martyr to anything. He was a very silly little man with an absolute shrew of a wife, and I can certainly understand why Oliver Cromwell thought he had to be executed."

"Gertrude!" Dianna exclaimed.

"Miss Bell!" Miss Laurel was thoroughly outraged. "Dr. Soames is the leading expert on the reign of King Charles the First."

"He may well be, but he's wrong for all of that," Gertrude said stoutly. "Mary, Dianna, I have got to get out of here. Come on, let's get the punt out now."

"Now?" Dianna squeaked.

"Now," Gertrude said firmly. "Dianna, you must conquer your fear of water. Mary and I will be with you, and Miss Laurel will be on the bank. It's not as if we're going to be in deep water, after all."

"But . . ." Dianna allowed herself to be swept away by her more dashing classmate.

"And I shall wear my bloomer suit," Gertrude announced.

"Gertrude!" Mary gasped. "You can't!"

"Why not? It's perfectly proper for sporting activities. We'll be in the boat, so no one will be able to see my legs . . . all right, limbs," she amended, before Miss Laurel could correct her.

"Are you sure you can manage a punt by yourself?" Miss Laurel asked.

Gertrude's green eyes fairly flashed as she retorted, "I can do anything I set my mind to!"

"But have you ever been out in a punt?" Mary persisted.

"It's easy enough to do," Gertrude said. "There's the pole, and there's the paddle. I'll use the pole in the back, and you steer with the paddle, Mary."

"And what do I do?" Dianna asked.

"You act as ballast," Gertrude said with a laugh. "Come on, girls. We're not going to let those men get the better of us, are we?"

"Certainly not!" Dianna took a deep breath, straining the laces of her corset.

"But you must not go beyond Magdalen Bridge," Miss Laurel warned them. "The men are out practicing for Eights Week, and they will be very cross if you disturb them."

"Pooh!" Gertrude waved a hand at an imaginary rower. "Let them watch out for us. Come along, Mary, Dianna. It's too nice a day to stay indoors. Let's go on the river!"

CHAPTER 19

G reat Tom boomed out the hour of noon, and all across Oxford undergraduates and dons, tradesmen and manual workers, market women and ladies of higher standing stopped whatever they were doing and considered the noonday meal.

For the students luncheon might consist of a hurried sandwich taken in quick bites between lectures and tutorials. The dons were more apt to regard luncheon as a social occasion, not quite so formal as dining in Hall, when they might pay a call on a colleague in another college and chat over a well-turned omelet or a cold bird. The wives of respectable tradesmen entertained one another at luncheon parties that displayed the hostess's fine china and silver without the onerous presence of the male of the species, who might take his midday meal at the back of the shop rather than coming home.

The men who had spent the morning toiling on the streets, walls, and roofs of Oxford had no illusions of gentility. For them a piece of cold meat pie, a slab of bread and cheese, and a draught of local ale served to keep body and soul together until they could get back to the cottages, shacks, and hovels that lurked in the corners of the great colleges.

For those who could afford the luxury of an afternoon not burdened by physical or mental labor, the river beckoned. The sun had warmed the cold stones of Oxford to the point where youthful undergraduates tended to open their collars and gowns, and elderly dons wished that they could do the same without loss to their dignity. Even the stately Dean Liddell had decided to hold his luncheon meeting with the heads of Keble and Lady Margaret Hall al fresco on such a fine day and had ordered that a table should be set for them out of doors in the shade of the elms that he himself had planted.

The broad green lawns of Christ Church Meadows were dotted with clumps of students, their gowns thrown open to reveal tweed waistcoats or hand-knitted pullovers in startling combinations of colors, munching on bread and cheese and swilling beer and cider from bottles. Youthful voices were raised in dispute, whether on some academic point or on the merits of one cricket team over another. It was spring, and the young men of Oxford were sowing their wild oats.

There were few bonnets or flowered straw hats on Christ Church Meadows that afternoon. The serious young ladies of Somerville and Lady Margaret Hall were not to be lured out even on this glorious day. They were safely behind the walls of their colleges, enjoying the sunshine in cloistered gardens. The only females present on Christ Church Meadows that afternoon were Mrs. Doyle and two or three stout, provincial-looking matrons, clearly visitors being entertained by their long-suffering sons. They sat stiffly in folding chairs, while their menfolk sprawled at their feet. Christ Church scouts were very much in evidence, scurrying between the kitchens and the meadows with baskets and canvas folding stools.

Mr. Dodgson paid no attention to the crowd of picnickers. He found a clear spot and folded himself down onto the grass, leaving Touie to deal with the tablecloth, the basket, and the folding camp stool thoughtfully provided by Telling.

187

Touie set the basket down and spread out the cloth. She was glad she did not have a very large bustle to cope with, but her small nod to fashion was awkward to sit on. Instead, she stood and watched the boats on the water.

"How very many people are out on the river today," Touie remarked, as she observed the scene. "What are they doing?"

Mr. Dodgson rose to his feet to point out the various types of craft with a gray-gloved hand. "This is the Holywell Mill Stream," he lectured his guest, "named for a well that was renowned for its healing powers. You saw the reference in the stained-glass window in the Cathedral."

Touie nodded. "And what is that little canoe?" She pointed to the small object erratically making its way down the stream toward the southernmost point of the meadow, where the narrow channel met the wider, more turbulent Cherwell.

"It is not a canoe," Mr. Dodgson corrected her. "It is a punt. Canoes are propelled by means of paddles. A punt is pushed forward by means of the pole."

"I see." Touie shaded her eyes with one hand. "They seem to be in some difficulty," she observed.

Mr. Dodgson frowned. "They should not be so close to the Cherwell," he said. "Punts are more difficult to control than would be thought."

Touie pointed at the long, narrow sculls that could be seen over the grassy island that separated the Holywell Mill Stream from the river proper. "What are those other boats, the long ones?" Touie asked,

"Those are shells," Mr. Dodgson explained. "Each college has a team of rowers, who compete against one another for the title of Head of the River."

"How exciting!" Touie shaded her eyes against the glare of the sun. "I know about the races against Cambridge, of course, but I didn't realize how many competitors there were. They quite fill the water!"

"This is practice," Mr. Dodgson said. "The channel here is quite narrow, so that only one or two boats can get through at a time. The object of the contest is to bump the lead boat and so gain the advantage. The college that can do that and hold off all comers is named Head of the River for the year."

Touie watched the young men as they bent over their oars. Between the heat and the intense physical activity, they had been obliged to lay aside their academic garb. Most were in shirtsleeves, their collars opened and their sleeves rolled up to display well-muscled arms. Tousled fair or dark heads bent and stretched, while the coxswain in the stern acted as guide and shouted directions to the rowers.

"That is the Christ Church team," Mr. Dodgson announced with satisfaction. "We have every reason to believe that we will maintain our position as Head of the River."

"Oh, my!" Touie watched the progress of the punt. "There are ladies in that boat!"

There certainly were three women in white shirtwaists, bloomer skirts, and straw hats. Gertrude Bell, Mary Talbot, and Dianna Cahill had taken their punt out, as they had said, but they had gone far beyond their appointed destination.

The watchers on the banks realized that something was in the offing. Conversation died and all disputation ceased as the drama unfolded before the shocked and amused eyes of the picnickers on Christ Church Meadow.

The punters were clearly out of their depth. The Holywell Mill Stream, usually a placid channel, was deeper this year by at least six inches thanks to the snows of the previous winter. The pole, which should have been long enough to reach the bottom of the channel, was too short, so that the girl in the stern found herself without anything to push. This left the paddler in the bows with the responsibility of guiding the craft, a task totally beyond her capability given the strength of the current.

On the other side of the grassy island that separated the Holy-well Mill Stream from the main flow of the Cherwell the Christ Church rowers bent their backs, unaware of the tragedy ahead of them. The coxswain, Minnie Chatsworth, spotted the punt, but by then the sweeps of the oars had already caught the little craft in their wake. Collision was inevitable.

The shell and the punt met at the point where the stream joined the Cherwell. The men roared their disapproval as the girls struggled to keep their little craft afloat.

"You stupid cow! Get off our river!" Lord Farlow, the lead rower, vigorously plied an oar to shove the offending craft out of the way.

"Your river! Who gave it to you?" Gertrude was not to be run off. "Mary, pull! Dianna, what are you thinking of? Now is no time to design a bonnet!"

"I can't keep it steady!" Dianna howled.

"The current's too strong!" Mary struggled with the front paddle.

"Who the devil are you, and who told you you could punt?" Farlow yelled, as he tried to push the punt out of the way of the shell. The teams from Corpus Christi and Merton shot past them, while the Christ Church men did battle with the punt.

"We're from Lady Margaret Hall," Gertrude proudly proclaimed. "Miss Gertrude Bell, at your service." She managed a bow from her place at the pole and swept an arm toward her crew. "And this is Miss Dianna Cahill and Miss Mary Talbot."

Farlow's face paled, then reddened. He suddenly thrust his oar at the side of the women's boat, causing it to rock dangerously.

This seemed to be the signal for an all-out attack on the punt. Oars were plied vigorously, thumping against the boat, while the three girls clung to the sides.

Amid the splashing and shouting, the punt tipped over and the three girls went into the river with a soggy splash. A cheer of triumph went up from the Christ Church rowers. The crowd on the shore was more alarmed.

"Are they all right?"

"They are swimming!"

"The water should not be so deep as to be a danger to them," the shrill voice of Mr. Dodgson seemed to cut through the babble, as he strode through the crowd with Touie right behind him.

Gertrude and Mary made for the shore, weighted down by the water that filled the heavy serge of their bloomer suits. Hands were extended to get them up, while the rowers pulled their boat to the shore, furious that they had been deprived of their chance to shine by a senseless and humiliating collision with a pack of silly females.

Farlow strode over to where Gertrude and Mary were being fussed over by two of the motherly visitors, each of whom had sacrificed a shawl to dry off the intrepid female boaters. Minnie Chatsworth and Gregory Martin followed in his wake, ready to intervene if their volatile comrade should attack once again.

Touie drew nearer to see who had caused the accident. "It is Miss Bell and Miss Talbot," Touie said, recognizing them. Gertrude waved cheerfully then suddenly realized that someone was missing.

"Where is Dianna?" Gertrude scanned the water's surface. "Dianna?"

"How deep is it?" Touie asked anxiously, as she scanned the murky stream, made murkier by the mud brought up by Gertrude and Mary's efforts.

Mr. Dodgson's voice reflected his concern. "The rivers have been quite high this spring," he admitted. "And there is a strong current."

"She's there! I see her!" Gregory Martin took off his spectacles and carefully put them into his jacket pocket. He handed the blazer to Minnie Chatsworth before he jumped into the water and made his way to a clump of weeds, where the billowing bloomers were just visible under the surface. "She's caught in the rushes," he announced, "Here, Nevil, Minnie, give us a hand."

"Let the silly bitch drown!" Farlow muttered, his words drowned in a torrent of helpful advice shouted by the rest of the crew.

"Her hair is caught in the weeds," Martin reported, coming up for air. He took in a huge gulp of air and ducked underwater again. With a massive effort, he heaved the girl out of the mud and pulled her over to the bank, where her former attackers grabbed her and dragged her out. The assembled dons and students crowded around the prostrate form, giving advice and arguing over it.

"Give her air!"

"Who is she?"

"What can she have been thinking of?"

"Is she dead?" Gertrude asked, her face drawn and anxious.

"Let me through! I am a doctor!" Touie was never so glad to hear her husband's Scottish burr.

"Arthur!" Touie cried out. "This poor girl is nearly drowned."

Dr. Doyle took charge. "Lay her flat on her, um, front," he ordered. "Touie, you'll have to help here. Bend her arms, and put her hands under her head. Ladies, if you will screen your friend from the curious, my wife will undo her stays, and we can get her breathing again."

Touie came forward with a tablecloth, supposedly for their picnic. Gertrude and Mary held it up, while Touie unbuttoned Dianna's shirtwaist and pulled at her corset-strings.

"This won't do at all," Dr. Doyle fumed. "Here, Touie, just cut them. She can't breathe in that thing anyway!"

"Yes, Arthur." Touie took the pocketknife that was handed to her and ruthlessly cut open the constricting garment, which flew apart as Dianna's tortured lungs took in air.

"What can I do?" Gregory Martin knelt down beside his damsel in distress.

Dr. Doyle placed Dianna's hands under her head, in the approved manner. He put his hands on her ribcage and pressed down, counted to ten, then released his pressure, lifted her elbows and dropped them again. "Just keep that up, young man," he directed.

Young Martin bent to his task, aware that only a thin layer of linen separated his hands from the flesh of his goddess.

Dianna gasped suddenly and choked. She spat out mud and weeds and coughed again.

"She's alive!" Gertrude announced.

"Well done, young man!" Dean Liddell had observed the entire episode from his luncheon table. Now he joined the crowd, with Miss Wordsworth and Dr. Talbot close behind him, and advanced to congratulate the heroes of the hour. He patted Dr. Doyle on the shoulder and nodded approvingly at Mr. Martin. "You are Mr. Martin, are you not?"

"Yes, sir." Mr. Martin fumbled for his spectacles and managed a bow.

"That was quite brave of you, if a little rash," Dean Liddel pronounced. He then turned to the rowers. "Who began this outrage?" Dean Liddell asked.

"They did," Lord Farlow said, pointing to the dripping girls. "What right had they to take out a punt when we were out?"

Gertrude stood her ground, green eyes flashing. "We have every right to be out," she declared. "If Lady Margaret Hall is to be accepted on equal terms with every other college, we must be able to compete in athletics as well as academic subjects."

"And are you planning on playing cricket, too?" Farlow demanded, advancing on the slender redhead.

"Steady on, Nev!" Minnie Chatsworth was at his side, pulling him away before he could strike the girl.

Miss Wordsworth stepped into the dispute. "Miss Bell," she said, "I thought you were supposed to confine your activity to the Mill Stream above Magdalen Bridge."

"We did, but the current took us," Gertrude explained.

"And we got around the boats, but the paddle didn't work," Mary added.

Dianna coughed again. Gregory carefully lifted her up and patted her on the back. She suddenly realized that her corsets were no longer in place, and crossed her arms over her chest.

Touie covered the distraught girl with the tablecloth, while the argument continued over their heads.

Dean Liddell shook his head sadly. "The actions of these young men are reprehensible and very nearly led to a tragedy. However, in order to prevent a recurrence of this event, I strongly suggest that the young ladies should take their exercise at a time more convenient to the gentlemen."

"And where is Miss Laurel?" Miss Wordsworth suddenly noticed the lack of a chaperon.

"We lost her at Magdalen Bridge," Gertrude giggled.

Miss Laurel herself struggled through the crowd, her bonnet awry and her shawl flying behind her. "What were you girls thinking of?" she scolded her wayward charges.

Miss Wordsworth considered what should be done next, while Gregory helped Dianna to her feet.

"We haven't been formally introduced, but I'm Gregory Martin," he explained.

"I'm Dianna Cahill," she said, choking again. "Someone cut my stays!"

"I'm afraid that was necessary," Touie said.

"Oh, my goodness!" Dianna clutched the tablecloth and pulled it tighter under her chin. "You're the doctor's wife, aren't you? The one who's visiting Mr. Dodgson?"

"Yes, I am," Touie admitted. "Arthur, what's to be done with Miss Cahill?"

"I strongly suggest that she should be taken back to her college as quickly as possible," Dr. Doyle said firmly. "She has suffered a severe shock to her nerves, and all of you are quite wet. Is there a cart or carriage available to get Miss Cahill back to her school?"

"We were going to punt back," Gertrude said.

"If you can keep to the Mill Stream, I suggest you do that," Dean Liddell told her. "As for Miss Cahill . . ."

"Miss Cahill is in no condition to walk," Dr. Doyle decreed. "And under the circumstances, she should not go back onto the river."

Touie broke into the discussion. "Arthur, why don't I accompany Miss Cahill back to Lady Margaret Hall with a bath chair, while these two young ladies do as this lady suggests."

Miss Wordsworth looked at Mr. Dodgson for enlightenment. Mr. Dodgson explained, "Miss Wordsworth, may I present my guests, Dr. Doyle and his wife. Dr. Doyle has been most efficacious in reviving your student, Miss Cahill."

Miss Wordsworth looked Touie over and decided that she was a sensible young woman who would see that Dianna got back to her college safely.

While Dianna's fate was being decided, Gertrude and Mary found their craft floating in the weeds. The pole and the paddle had caught in the rushes beside them.

"Is the boat all right?" Mary asked anxiously.

"Not a scratch," Gertrude said gaily. "Mary, we'll go the other way, against the current."

"Won't that be difficult?" Mary demurred.

"Of course, but that's the fun of it! Come on, we'll be dry by the time we get back to LMH!" Gertrude wiped the mud off her face and settled back into her boat. Mary joined her with a rueful shrug.

The crowd began to disperse since the dramatic scene was over. Miss Laurel called out from the Broad Walk. A bath chair had been pushed onto the grass by one of Oxford's characteristic chairmen, a wizened individual in corduroy trousers and jacket, with a cloth cap tipped over one eye.

"Arthur, this is an excellent opportunity for me to question the girls at Lady Margaret Hall," Touie whispered to her husband, as Miss Laurel tenderly assisted Dianna into the bath chair.

"I do hope I can find out something useful."

"I depend on you," Dr. Doyle said.

"Then I must do my best," Touie told him, kissing him quickly on the cheek. She followed the chair along the gravel walk, back toward St. Aldgates and the center of town.

Dean Liddell turned his attention to the undergraduates, who had formed a shamefaced clump, with Farlow as their spokesman. "I hope this has been a lesson to you," he scolded them. "There could have been a tragedy here. You are all gated. . . ."

A cry of protest went up from the group.

"Gated, I say," Dean Liddell's voice carried over the protest. "Lord Farlow, you were the instigator of this dastardly attack on helpless females?"

Farlow nodded, speechless.

"But they had it coming to them," Chatsworth put in. "They shot out in front of us, just as we were gaining . . ."

"Enough!" Dean Liddell frowned at his students. "You will each compose an essay, in your least execrable hand, in Latin, on the subject of proper behavior toward female undergraduates."

"How were we supposed to know they were bluestockings?" Chatsworth asked innocently.

"They were wearing bloomers!" Someone from the back of the crowd cracked a joke.

Dean Liddell turned to Miss Wordsworth. "I must apologize

195

for the rudeness of my students," he said. "I sincerely hope that the young lady will suffer no ill effects from her experience. And I strongly suggest," he added, as they made their way back to the luncheon table, "that you tell the young woman with the red hair . . ."

"Gertrude Bell. She is very young, Dean, only seventeen, and you know how silly they can be," Miss Wordsworth said.

"Nevertheless, she should temper her enthusiasm for athletics with some caution."

Miss Wordsworth smiled ruefully. "Caution, I fear, is not Miss Bell's strong suit."

Dean Liddell escorted Miss Wordsworth back to their luncheon table, leaving Mr. Dodgson to deal with the exuberant Dr. Doyle.

Great Tom boomed out again. It was two o'clock. Undergraduates and scholars, workers and tradesmen, all had to return to their appointed tasks. Christ Church Meadows were empty of all but the few who could spend the afternoon in idle contemplation of nature.

CHAPTER 20

❦

W hile Dean Liddell had been lecturing the undergraduates, Dr. Doyle had taken the opportunity to explore the basket thrust upon him by his wife before she left on her mission of mercy. Now he munched on a sandwich as he walked along the bank of the Holywell Mill Stream with Mr. Dodgson.

"And what have you been doing, Dr. Doyle?" Mr. Dodgson asked.

"I spent a very active morning tracing the activities of the deceased," Dr. Doyle told his mentor. "Apparently, the late James Ingram was a remarkably ingenious individual. He had fingers in several pies. Thieving was the least of his crimes."

"Then it was he who stole the wine." Mr. Dodgson nodded, satisfied that he had been correct, and that he had done the right thing by discharging the dishonest scout.

"It was," Dr. Doyle confirmed. "He took the bottles to the very place where they had been bought. Snow's man then sold them to undergraduates from other colleges, who paid well for drinking Christ Church wine."

"Other colleges? Outrageous!" Mr. Dodgson exclaimed.

"What's more, I followed a pair of undergraduates to an establishment called the Oxford Gentleman's Athletic Club."

"Oh, that place." Mr. Dodgson's tone was distinctly chilly.

"You know it?"

"It is not a place that I frequent, but I have heard that some of the younger Fellows of other colleges use the facilities. I take my exercise by walking," Mr. Dodgson explained. "What business did Ingram have there?"

"I suspect he was deliberately placed in Christ Church by the proprietor to ferret out information about Oxford sporting events, such as Eights Week, which would then be passed on to certain members of the sporting and gambling fraternity in London."

"And the bookmakers would use the information to set the odds for the wagering on the event," Mr. Dodgson finished for him, "in the manner of horse racing. Not illegal, precisely, but certainly not done in the best houses."

"Quite," Dr. Doyle agreed. "What's more, I found evidence that Ingram was also involved in the plot to oust Miss Cahill from Oxford."

Mr. Dodgson's eyebrows rose in silent interrogation.

"I found typeset copies of the verses that defamed Lady Margaret Hall and its students in Ingram's rooms, and I found the very shop in which the, um, material had been printed," Dr. Doyle said, taking a swig from the jug of cider. "Mmm, this is good!" He offered the jug to Mr. Dodgson, who refused it with a shudder and a shake of his head.

"Did you discover who had brought it into the shop?"

"The printer described Ingram," Dr. Doyle said. "Proof positive, in my opinion. He was up to his neck in it."

"But he could not have written the, um, verses himself," Mr. Dodgson pointed out, "the reference to Sappho, for instance, and the Latin terms."

"I am not all that familiar with vulgar language," Dr. Doyle said, with a glance at his prim companion, "but I don't think the French word is used by too many servants either. The spelling and grammar were correct, which would indicate that whoever wrote it had some education."

"Do you know, I have a thought about that, um, screed," Mr. Dodgson said slowly. "If the writer is, as we suspect, one of our undergraduates, his tutor would certainly be able to identify the writer."

They had reached the Broad Walk, and the table that had been set up for Dean Liddell and his guests. Miss Wordsworth had insisted that Miss Laurel should sit down and have a cup of tea before she went back to Lady Margaret Hall to care for Dianna. The former governess had recovered her usual composure and now sat at the farthest end of the table, consuming her meager luncheon, while the scouts hovered in the background eager to remove the table and chairs.

The Dean stopped Mr. Dodgson as he was about to continue his stroll along the path that led from Christ Church Meadows to Magdalen Bridge.

"Mr. Dodgson, where do you think you are going?" Dean Liddell asked, his long face registering his disapproval.

"I have business on Magdalen Bridge," Mr. Dodgson began.

"Need I remind you that I requested that you remain on University grounds until this business of the dead servant is settled to the satisfaction of all parties?" Dean Liddell scowled at Dr. Doyle, as if the young man had lured the older one off the straight and narrow path of Virtue into the byways of Vice.

Spots of color flamed on Mr. Dodgson's cheeks. Once again Dean Liddell was reminding him of his position. He was no longer teaching; he was a Senior Student of the college, but he had never taken any but Minor Orders, and he rated below those who were fully ordained in the Church of England in the college hierarchy.

"I beg your pardon, Dean, but I felt it necessary to examine the site of that unfortunate man's demise myself," Mr. Dodgson explained.

"I suggest you let the police do that," Dean Liddell told him. "Dr. Doyle, I trust the autopsy this morning was satisfactory?"

"There's no question that the man went into the river and drowned," Dr. Doyle answered cheerfully. "However, there are indications that he was forcibly held down."

199

Miss Laurel uttered a small cry of horror. "How dreadful!"

"Not a pleasant death," Dr. Doyle agreed.

"But who would do such a thing?" Dean Liddell asked. "And why?"

Mr. Dodgson glanced at Dr. Doyle. "Ingram may have been connected with certain unsavory persons, who, in turn, may have had an interest in corrupting our young people," Mr. Dodgson said slowly. "Dr. Doyle has uncovered evidence that links Ingram to a scheme to set odds on Eights Week, encouraging wagering on the chances of success."

"Then it may be a case of thieves falling out," Dean Liddell said sharply. "If that is so, we may leave it in the hands of In-spector Truscott and his men. They are most likely to know of such ruffians and will arrest them in due course. I must remind you, Mr. Dodgson, that you are a scholar and not a policeman. You may inform the good Inspector of your findings and let him carry on from there."

Mr. Dodgson's back stiffened. "I beg you pardon, Dean," he said, "but I cannot let this situation continue for another day. I will not be accused of driving a man to take his own life, nor will I allow any further damage to the reputation of the House." He turned to Dr. Doyle. "Since I am confined to college grounds, I must ask that you act for me. Will you now go to Magdalen Bridge and look very carefully around the stairs and at the base of the bridge?"

"But . . . what should I look for?" Dr. Doyle looked puzzled.

"You will know when you see it."

"How may I best get to this bridge?" Dr. Doyle looked vaguely about him.

"You may continue along this path, then turn at the iron fence and go through Rose Lane," Mr. Dodgson instructed him. "Mag-dalen Bridge is at the end of the High." He pointed in the ap-propriate direction.

Dr. Doyle settled his deerstalker cap firmly on his head, bowed to the Dean and Miss Wordsworth, and strode off in the direction of the iron gate at the end of the Broad Walk, where Merton and Magdalen students were congregating.

Once Dr. Doyle was out of earshot, Mr. Dodgson looked from Dean Liddell to Miss Wordsworth. "I did not wish to discuss this matter before Dr. Doyle," he said. "He is an enthusiastic investigator into mysteries, and he will not stop until he is satisfied. However, part of this puzzle concerns one of Miss Wordsworth's young charges. The man, Ingram, may have been in possession of an object that would have damaged a young lady's reputation. One does not wish to air one's linen in public, as the saying goes."

Miss Wordsworth rose to do battle on behalf of her students. "I cannot imagine . . ."

"The young lady who had the accident in the punt," Mr. Dodgson explained. "She approached me yesterday with a most distressing tale. She claimed to be an acquaintance, one of my child friends, and I, alas, could not recall her at all!"

"Dianna Cahill?" Miss Wordsworth frowned. "She never mentioned to anyone that she had ever met you, sir, and you are hardly a stranger at Lady Margaret Hall. You have called on Miss Rix several times."

"Cahill . . . Cahill . . ." Dean Liddell mused. "Of course! He is the Vicar of Whitby in Northumberland. One of the Christ Church livings," he added.

"I had no idea we had anything so far north as Northumberland," Mr. Dodgson said.

Dean Liddell looked embarrassed. "It is a very small living and not much sought after," he said. "Mr. Cahill was one of my Old Boys from my Westminster days."

"Not a Christ Church man then," Mr. Dodgson said. "I had wondered that I had not heard of him. If his daughter is now twenty, then he must have married, oh, back in the sixties."

"Oh, he was not at the House," Dean Liddell said. "Wadham, I do believe. Inclined to be Low Church in his doctrine, but otherwise quite sound. He made a rather odd marriage, but there was nothing against him otherwise. I like to maintain contact with my Old Boys; and when the living in Northumberland came vacant, I thought of him. I did not go so far as to read him in, but I did have him and his wife to tea when he came here to be presented to his living."

"That was the occasion on which Miss Cahill claims I made her acquaintance," Mr. Dodgson said. "I wondered that a child should be present when there was no particular need."

"They didn't want her in the house," came a voice from the end of the table.

"Miss Laurel?" Dean Liddell and Miss Wordsworth turned to stare at the former governess.

"Miss Cahill said something about it," Miss Laurel explained, "something about a difficult situation." She seemed to shrink under the scrutiny of so many eyes.

"Difficult?" Mr. Dodgson echoed. "I was given to understand that Miss Cahill's maternal relations were quite worthy, if somewhat vulgar persons. A Mr. Roswell, connected with the manufacture of glass."

"Quite so," Miss Wordsworth said. "Mr. Roswell is known for his philanthropy. He has served as selectman in the town, and his wife is on the committee of the Women's Educational Alliance, which supports our efforts at Lady Margaret Hall. Miss Cahill's expenses are paid directly by Mr. Roswell. However," she cleared her throat and glanced at Dean Liddell again, "there is the unfortunate matter of his religious affiliation."

"A Catholic?" Mr. Dodgson whispered.

"A Methodist," Miss Wordsworth corrected him primly. "Quite strict, and very sincere. He has the greatest respect for serious studies. He offers a prize of twenty-five pounds every year for the Oxford Grammar School student who achieves the highest academic honors."

"A most worthy gentleman," Mr. Dodgson murmured.

"Well, I would not quite call him a gentleman," Dean Liddell said, "something of a rough diamond or a glass one." He laughed at his own wit.

"And one cannot hold his other connections against him," Miss Wordsworth added.

Mr. Dodgson's eyebrows rose in silent inquiry.

"One should not gossip," Miss Wordsworth went on, determined to do just that. "And in the end, all worked out well for the girl."

Mr. Dodgson nodded. "I was told there was a sister."

"Quite a charming young person," Miss Wordsworth said. "Well, she must have been, Dean, to capture the heart of Berwick's heir. And she on the stage!"

Dean Liddell's eyebrows raised and his aquiline nose seemed to elevate at the thought of the theater and its practitioners. "Lady Berwick's theatrical past is quite forgotten. She is now much courted by fashionable society. I have had the privilege of meeting Lord and Lady Berwick when they attended the Oxford and Cambridge regatta last year with His Royal Highness. That very violent young man, Farlow, is her son. I suppose he inherits his dramatic nature from his mother."

Mr. Dodgson had been thinking furiously. "Dean, Miss Wordsworth, are you telling me that Mr. Farlow and Miss Cahill are, in fact, cousins?"

"One might say that," Miss Wordsworth conceded. "Although they are not related by blood but through marriage. Farlow's mother is the sister of Miss Cahill's mother's sister's husband." She smiled at the working out of this complex family tree.

"How very odd that both of them should be up at the same time!" Miss Laurel exclaimed from her place at the table.

Miss Wordsworth ignored her. "Miss Cahill has said nothing to me about her relations, except for Mr. Roswell. I believe her father's people are all gone, and her mother is equally alone, except for her sister. The living in Northumberland must have been seen as a godsend."

"Yes," Dean Liddell said, "Mr. Cahill has been most grateful. He is something of an antiquarian, with an interest in Viking ruins, and there are a number of sites worthy of examination in his living. He has read papers before the Royal Society on the subject of archaeological exploration in the north of England."

"Then I met Miss Cahill on the occasion of her father's accepting his living," Mr. Dodgson said, glad to have clarified that knotty point. "I had completely forgotten. She, on the other hand, remembered every detail of the event."

"Odd, what one recalls and what one does not," Dean Liddell said. "Do you know, I begin to remember the occasion. Mrs.

Cahill explained that Lady Berwick had sent a note, announcing her intention of paying a call upon her brother, who had informed the household that she was not to be admitted under any circumstances. Mrs. Cahill seemed to be afraid that the ensuing scene would terrify the child. They were most protective of her."

"And so she was got out of the house," Mr. Dodgson said. "And I happened to see her and took her to my rooms to tea. What an odd tale it is, to be sure."

"But what has all this to do with that unfortunate scout?" Dean Liddell asked.

"The photograph that I took on that occasion," Mr. Dodgson said. He swallowed, then plunged ahead. "It could have led to a misunderstanding. I have reason to believe it was removed from my rooms by that man."

Dean Liddell's long face grew longer. "That might lead to the conclusion that you had a motive for removing him," he said.

"Oh, no!" Miss Laurel squeaked out. "Ingram was a dreadful rogue, meant for a bad end!"

Mr. Dodgson faced the Dean. "I did not kill that man. Clearly, the only way that I can prove that I did not is to uncover the one who did. I have a hypothesis, but it is tenuous at best, and I must have more evidence. Miss Wordsworth, you must get back to Lady Margaret Hall. Tell Mrs. Doyle that we shall meet in my rooms and then go to dinner at the White Hart. I shall send Telling to bespeak . . ."

"You cannot leave Tom Quad," Dean Liddell reminded him.

"I cannot give Dr. Doyle another inferior dinner," Mr. Dodgson retorted.

"Dr. Doyle may dine in Hall," Dean Liddell decided, "but Mrs. Doyle is quite another matter. We cannot have women dining in Hall at the House."

Miss Wordsworth rolled her eyes at Miss Laurel as if to say, "What fools men are!" Then she said, "If you are so punctilious, then Mrs. Doyle may dine with us, and you can have Dr. Doyle with you to dine in Hall. And now, Miss Laurel and I must get back, and I must give those silly girls a strong lecture. They could all have been killed!" Miss Wordsworth strode majestically

204

down the Broad Walk. Miss Laurel followed her leader to St Ald-gates, where they could find a cab to take them back to Lady Margaret Hall.

Dean Liddell turned to Mr. Dodgson. "I strongly suggest that you return to your own rooms, sir, and permit the police to do their job."

"I want a word with young Farlow," Mr. Dodgson said. "And then I shall take your advice, Dean. I must think. There is some-thing missing, a piece of the puzzle that I have not uncovered . . ."

Dean Liddell watched as Mr. Dodgson ambled away. Then he gave a nod to summon Telling and the scouts.

"There will be one extra at the High Table tonight," he in-formed Telling. "Mr. Dodgson's guest will be dining in Hall. I trust we have a better dinner than was served last night?"

Telling realized the honor of Christ Church was at stake. Never let it be said that the House provided an inferior meal to its guests!

"I shall see to it, sir."

Dean Liddell proceeded back to Tom Quad. He would deal with Farlow, Chatsworth, and Martin in due course. He only hoped that the brash young Scot would behave with proper de-corum when admitted to the Senior Common Room. As for Mr. Dodgson, it was Dean Liddell's sincere wish that the old scholar would devote himself to mathematical puzzles and photographing little girls and leave the criminals to the police.

Both Dean Liddell and Inspector Truscott would have been horrified to know that their thoughts on this matter were identical.

CHAPTER 21

D r. Doyle followed the path around the iron fence of the Botanic Gardens and emerged onto High Street. The afternoon traffic had increased to the point where it was nearly impossible to see across the road. Large drays, movers' vans, farmers' wagons, and donkey carts all tried to get over the narrow bridge that spanned the Cherwell. The drivers cracked their whips and swore at the blue-coated constables who swarmed up and down the stairs that led to a flotilla of rowboats anchored under the bridge.

He darted across the road, under the nose of a surprised Percheron team pulling a load of furniture. The driver struggled to control his horses as Dr. Doyle waved at the policemen who had congregated on the steps leading to the boat landing under the bridge.

"Inspector Truscott!" He hailed the stolid policeman, who greeted him with muted enthusiasm.

"Dr. Doyle, how are you getting on?" Inspector Truscott turned back to his own men. "Look sharp there!"

"I've found out a few things about Ingram," Dr. Doyle began.

Inspector Truscott cut him off. "You needn't tell me that he'd been hand in glove with Sergeant-Major Howard and his lot," he said, before Dr. Doyle could continue. "He's been identified as having been present at two illegal prizefights that we know of, and a few we're not supposed to know of, but we do anyway."

"If they are illegal—" Dr. Doyle began indignantly.

"Why don't we shut 'em down?" Inspector Truscott shrugged. "Young gentlemen will have their fun, sir, and the sergeant-major's straight. He's been of assistance to us in other matters, and we don't bother him."

"I see." Dr. Doyle realized that in this case, rank did indeed have its privileges, and nobly born undergraduates seeking harmless entertainment would not be threatened by the Oxford Constabulary, particularly when the University proctors were so vigilant. He looked over the parapet of the bridge. "Have your men found anything?"

"Naught but rubbish!" Sergeant Everett's face showed what he thought of careless people who threw trash over Magdalen Bridge. "Look at that! Beer bottles, ginger-beer bottles, wine bottles. Chicken bones, a marrow bone, chop bones. Cigar ends without number." The sergeant indicated a pile of remains.

"Cigar ends?" Dr. Doyle's face lit up. "I've made something of a study of cigars."

"Nothing out of the ordinary in these," Truscott said. "No telling how long they've been there."

"Actually," Dr. Doyle said, peering at the collection of butts in front of him, "we can. Cigars are merely leaves, leaves rot at a given rate, and there has been no rain for at least a day. Ergo, we can assume that these were thrown here in the last two days. Can you tell me exactly where these cigars came from?"

"Do you mean which shop?" Sergeant Everett asked incredulously.

"Of course not. Can your men tell me where each of these was found?" Dr. Doyle eyed the mess and looked for something to separate it out into component parts.

Truscott and Everett stared at each other. Then Everett said, "I can ask the men, but I don't see how this will help us."

Dr. Doyle separated the cigars into several piles, using a handy twig. "These are nearly disintegrated," he said, indicating a pile of soggy leaves. "They have clearly been here for some time. Whereas these," he pointed to the line of well-formed ends he had sorted out of the general mess, "were deposited here no later than last night."

"And now all we have to do is find the ones who smoked 'em?" Inspector Truscott was not looking forward to interviewing the entire population of Oxford on its smoking habits

"That might be easier than you think," Dr. Doyle said. "Look here, Inspector. I don't think you'll find this in every humidor in Oxford." He rolled one long, thin cigar aside. "The rest of these are common enough, but this is an American cigar, what they call a cheroot. Not at all the sort of thing you'd expect a don to smoke."

"Not even the sort of thing an Oxford tobacconist would have in stock," Truscott admitted. "Now, who'd smoke a thing like that?"

"An American," Sergeant Everett replied.

"Or someone who'd formed a taste for them in America," Dr. Doyle amended. "Where, exactly, did this object come to light?"

Everett repeated the question to his men under the bridge. Constable Effingham shouted up from below the arch.

"Hoy! I've found another one!"

Dr. Doyle followed Inspector Truscott and Sergeant Everett down the stairs to the boat landing, and under the bridge itself, where Constable Effingham stood guard over his prize.

"Long, thin American cigar," he announced, pointing to it.

Dr. Doyle squatted to examine the cigar stub. "Right here," he mumbled. "And here's a footprint, too. How convenient!"

"Too convenient," Truscott grumbled.

"Someone stood here, smoking this long cheroot," Dr. Doyle said. He peered about. "What was he doing here?"

"Waiting for someone?" Sergeant Everett offered.

"Waiting for who?" Inspector Truscott countered.

"Waiting for Ingram," Dr. Doyle pronounced. "Ingram had uttered a challenge, in the middle of St. Aldgates, that he'd be under Magdalen Bridge at six o'clock. Clearly, he meant that challenge for someone in St. Aldgates that afternoon."

"Which might be anyone," Inspector Truscott objected, "including your Mr. Dodgson."

"This cigar end clearly exonerates Mr. Dodgson," Dr. Doyle stated firmly. "Mr. Dodgson does not use tobacco. He loathes it in any form, as I have found out to my dismay!" He smiled ruefully as he recalled his unceremonious ouster from Mr. Dodgson's rooms the night before. "Besides, he insists he was on the bridge, not under it."

Inspector Truscott nodded. "So now we are looking for someone who smokes this particular brand of American cigar, who was under Magdalen Bridge at six o'clock last night. Everett?"

"Yes, sir?"

"Have your men go 'round to the tobacconists and find out who likes this sort of cigar." Truscott turned to Dr. Doyle. "Does that satisfy you, sir?"

Dr. Doyle frowned as he looked at the footprint. He placed himself in the position the smoker must have taken. "Someone stood here and smoked the cheroot. Then he left. Then some undergraduates came back and found Ingram, put him into a bath chair, and carried him off to Christ Church." He looked at Inspector Truscott. "Surely someone must have noticed all this coming and going."

"Someone did," Truscott pointed out. "Your Mr. Dodgson saw the undergraduates."

"And how did they know there was a body under the bridge?" Dr. Doyle pursued the question.

"Because they put it there or saw someone else put it there," Inspector Truscott answered grimly. "If our cheroot smoker didn't do it himself, then he saw who did. Sergeant, start your search at St. Aldgates, at that little shop across from Christ Church, and see if that old body that keeps it knows of an undergraduate who fancies American cheroots."

"Of course, this doesn't tell us much about why Ingram blasted out his challenge in that public way," Truscott complained, as they made their way back to the street.

"He couldn't speak with the person he was addressing directly," Dr. Doyle said slowly. "That eliminates Mr. Dodgson completely. Why shout at the man to meet him in an hour's time, when they were talking right then and there?"

"And anyone might have heard him on the street," Everett reminded them.

"Or even in the college," Dr. Doyle said suddenly. "On such a fine day, all the windows would be open."

Inspector Truscott turned on his tormentor. "You've been no help at all," he scolded Dr. Doyle. "First you narrow things down, then you open them up again!"

"One must consider all the possibilities," Dr. Doyle said cheerfully. "As to motive, there is always that mysterious suitcase of secrets that Ingram kept under the bed."

"There is that," Inspector Truscott admitted. "And I daresay you'll be wanting a peep inside that, too."

Dr. Doyle tried to look modest, and succeeded in looking smug. "I have a good idea what you'll find," he said. "Letters and photographs. Things that were supposed to have been thrown away, but have been carefully preserved by our thrifty friend, Ingram, against a rainy day."

"And who, may I ask, was he supposed to have his hooks into at Christ Church?" Inspector Truscott ask scornfully. "The young gentlemen aren't likely to have the kind of money Ingram was after, and I can't imagine what the dons would be up to that would lay them open to blackmail."

Dr. Doyle frowned. Mr. Dodgson had deliberately refrained from mentioning Miss Cahill and her photograph to Inspector Truscott; but if that photograph was in Ingram's cache of secrets, it would look even worse for him than if the police found it on their own.

"There may be a photograph in that suitcase that was removed from the rooms of one of the dons," Dr. Doyle said slowly. "It was copied by Ingram, with his very expensive camera, and the copy was used to threaten someone. I cannot tell you more than that, Inspector. It is not my secret, and the photograph is quite innocent, I can assure you. It would simply lead to embarrassment on all sides if the object were to be made public."

Inspector Truscott frowned. "By now Chief Inspector Wheeler should have that suitcase open," he said. "If you insist on it, you can come along, and we'll see what little bombshells our friend Ingram had tucked away in it."

"And take the cheroots with you," Dr. Doyle added. Everett obligingly tore a page out of his ever-present notebook, slid it under the offensive cigar ends, and folded the ends of the page.

Back at Blue Boar Lane, Chief Inspector Wheeler was not pleased to see a stranger following Inspector Truscott into his office. The indispensable Constable Effingham had exerted himself, and the suitcase was open for inspection.

Truscott made the necessary introductions. "This is Dr. Doyle, who is acting for Christ Church," he told his chief. "He says there's a photograph in this suitcase that might embarrass someone there."

"There's a good deal more than that!" Chief Inspector Wheeler scowled at the suitcase. "I feel like washing my hands after touching some of this stuff."

Dr. Doyle had no such distaste. He eagerly picked through the debris before him. "My, my, what things people will leave about! Here's a draft of a letter to someone . . . 'My dear, dear boy . . . '?" He scanned the letter, which had folds, as if it had been crumpled and discarded. He pointed to the heading on the stationery. "Whites. Ingram's last place of employment."

"Where he took advantage of the situation to pick up little tidbits like this," Inspector Truscott said. "Here's a packet of promissory notes. Gambling debts, I should think."

"Whose?" Dr. Doyle craned his neck to see.

"Ingram wasn't kind enough to label 'em. I suppose he knew whose they were. Didn't you say something about photographs?"

"Not many of those," Chief Inspector Wheeler said, with some relief. "Just this one, of a pair courting in the park, you might say. And this one." He tapped the photograph that Dr. Doyle had been certain would be there.

"That photograph was taken fifteen years ago," Dr. Doyle stated. "Ingram removed it from the albums of—"

"Mr. Dodgson," Inspector Truscott finished for him.

"I did not say . . ."

Inspector Truscott looked at his chief then handed the photograph to Dr. Doyle. "This being stolen property, I can ask you to return it to its rightful owner," he said solemnly. "And tell your friend to take better care of his belongings."

Dr. Doyle accepted the photograph with a grateful smile. "Mr. Dodgson will be most relieved," he said.

"And the little girl?" Inspector Truscott hinted.

"Is now a young woman," Dr. Doyle told him. "Ingram had given a copy of this photograph to someone, who was using it to threaten her."

"Which might make her a suspect," Truscott reminded him.

"Hardly likely," Chief Inspector Wheeler scoffed. "You can barely see who this little girl is, except for her being stark naked. She could be almost anyone! Truscott, I want this . . . stuff . . . destroyed. Burn the papers; get rid of it all."

"What about the ones who wrote 'em?" Truscott asked.

"What of 'em?" Chief Inspector Wheeler echoed. "Most of this stuff is trash. No names, perhaps a hint here and there, but there's nothing to tell who, if anyone, this was meant for."

"In other words, these would be embarrassing to their original owners but not so much that they would take to murder," Dr. Doyle observed. "Ingram was not a brave man, in my opinion. Most of this is, as you pointed out, open to interpretation. Ingram might have been saving these bits and pieces for future use. I agree, Chief Inspector, burning is the best cure for this sort of disease of the mind."

"So glad to have your medical opinion, Doctor." Chief Inspector Wheeler rose with ponderous dignity. "Now that you've got what you've come for, you may leave. Truscott, show the man out."

Inspector Truscott opened the door, and Dr. Doyle had no choice but to leave with as much aplomb as he could muster.

Truscott shut the door pointedly behind the doctor. "I've had my men out, sir," he reported. "There is a pawnbroker's shop in the lane next to Ingram's lodgings. We found several rather pretty pieces of jewelry, all pawned by Ingram in the last three months."

"So he was a thief as well as a blackmailer." Chief Inspector Wheeler grunted. "You don't throw a man into the river for lifting your watch or your studs."

"And speaking of watches," Truscott continued, "we've got Ingram's. Very nice, that watch. And it was his, not stolen. There's an inscription: 'To James Ingram.' I'd say it was given for services rendered."

"What sort of services?" Wheeler asked suspiciously.

"What indeed?" Truscott's eyebrows were the only things that moved in his immobile face. "The crest is indeed Berwick, sir."

"Berwick? As in Lord Berwick? The one who married the actress?" Wheeler frowned. "What's he to do with anything?"

"His son's at Christ Church now," Everett reminded them.

"Ingram was supposed to have been in private service," Truscott said slowly, thinking aloud. "He was tall enough for a footman. A footman has opportunities that other servants don't to see what's going on in a grand household. Let us suppose this Ingram's got something on Lord Berwick. He gets a watch and a character that gets him into White's. What's he doing here in Oxford, where there's lean pickings for a man of his, um, talents?"

"He's still working for Berwick," Wheeler surmised. "Berwick's one of His Royal Highness's cronies. Marlborough House set, and all that, and a known gambler."

"And that explains what the sergeant-major's business is with Ingram," Truscott said, with a satisfied nod. "Berwick and his friends in London want information on the odds for Eights Week. They send Ingram, and a few more like him, to take up vacant posts in colleges that have likely teams. Then they either nobble the likely winners or fix the odds."

Sergeant Everett looked puzzled. "Why not ask this young Farlow lad? He's likeliest to know what's what, being a Blue himself."

Inspector Truscott considered the problem, then shook his head. "That would never do," he said. "A gentleman don't ask his son to be a spy. They save that sort of thing for the servants."

Chief Inspector Wheeler scowled in disgust. "Call themselves noble sportsmen, do they?" he snorted.

"They don't. The newspapers do," Truscott pointed out. "But what does all this have to do with Ingram's being bashed on the head and shoved into the river?"

"I don't know," Chief Inspector Wheeler said, "but I want you to go and find out."

Dr. Doyle, listening at the door, nodded to himself, and stepped out of the way as inspector Truscott marched out of Chief Inspector Wheeler's office. He was beginning to get an idea of what had happened under Magdalen Bridge. He felt the photograph in his pocket, and smiled under his mustache. Mr. Dodgson would be very pleased to know that his photograph was safely out of the hands of the police, as would Miss Cahill.

Dr. Doyle strode jauntily into the afternoon sunlight of St. Aldgates. He had the photograph. He had proven that Mr. Dodgson was innocent of the crime of murder, and that he was in no way responsible for what had happened to the wretched scout. The only thing left to do was to find the author of that infamous text, and he could go on to his mother's cottage secure in the knowledge that he had fulfilled his obligations to his host.

There was still the question of who had sent Ingram into the river and why. Dr. Doyle had a few thoughts on that matter, but he would consult with Mr. Dodgson before he went ahead.

He glanced up at Great Tom, which was sounding the hour of three, and wondered how Touie was doing at Lady Margaret Hall. If he was right, the answer to part of the question lay there.

Dr. Doyle shouldered his way through a crowd of undergraduates and looked about Tom Quad for Mr. Dodgson. He had news to impart, and there was no time to lose.

CHAPTER 22

Touie had followed the bath chair around the Broad Walk and up the same path that her husband was to take a little later. The chair, a cumbersome object that teetered dangerously on three wheels, was pushed laboriously by the chairman, a skinny specimen who wheezed mightily as he trundled Miss Cahill along Longwall Steet. Had Dr. Doyle been there, he would have informed Touie that the street was named for the remnant of the old walled town of Oxford, which made the street so narrow. Touie was more concerned about avoiding the large horses that seemed to fill the street, making pedestrian traffic nearly impossible.

"How much longer is it?" Touie asked, skirting a malodorous heap left by one of the cart horses.

"We come to the end of Longwall, then continue on St. Cross Road," Dianna said, from the depths of the chair. "I wish you hadn't cut my corsets. Then I could walk, instead of being pushed like a baby."

"I am sorry about the corsets, but you couldn't breathe with them so tight," Touie said severely. "Arthur says that tight lacing is responsible for more female ailments than anything else," she pronounced, with the fervor of one quoting Holy Writ.

The chairman stopped to take a breath as Longwall Street gave way to St. Cross Road. Touie peered into the bath chair to see that Dianna was properly covered.

"How much longer?" she asked again. Her feet were beginning to ache. She had taken the precaution of wearing walking shoes, but even the most sensible of footwear would pinch after a while. Touie had been standing for most of the day, and the stone walls that hemmed in the narrow street seemed to radiate warmth. The air that had seemed so fresh had somehow become still and sultry, and there was an ominous pile of clouds starting to build up in the east.

Once the chairman filled his lungs again, they pressed forward. They crossed the road in front of a tiny church, where Touie caught a glimpse of lawns behind one of the venerable colleges. Beyond that there was the Holywell Mill Stream and two figures in a punt, struggling against the current.

"There are Gertrude and Mary!" Dianna leaned out of the chair. "I could have told you they'd get back before we do. Gertrude is a dab hand at sports."

"Where did you learn that bit of slang?" Touie giggled.

"From Gertrude, of course." Dianna giggled. "She's always the one to know the latest slang. My mother would not approve of my using common talk."

"Your parents seem to have brought you up very carefully," Touie commented.

"Oh, yes," Dianna replied. "Whitby was a very small place, and most of the people there were not the sort Mother wished me to associate with."

"Not even village children?" Touie asked.

"Especially not them," Dianna said. "I used to run away sometimes to play with the fishermen's children on the beaches, but Mother said that I was not to do so because I would get into bad habits."

Touie thought that over as she trudged after the chair. Her own mother had not objected to any of her playmates, but she had had her brother, Jack, to guard her from unwanted roughness.

They had reached the end of St. Cross Road. "Wot now?" the chairman wheezed.

Dianna leaned forward and pointed to the iron gate. "Let's take the shortcut through the park," she ordered. "Otherwise, we'd just have to go around, and that's a bore. I do wish you hadn't cut my laces." She tried to get out of the bath chair.

Touie bent solicitously over the girl. "You really shouldn't walk," she said. "You took in quite a bit of water, and your skirt is very wet."

Dianna sighed again and sank back into the bath chair. "I suppose I must be pushed," she said pettishly. "I really do prefer to do things for myself. I had hoped to be out of cotton wool here at Oxford. Aunt Roswell isn't quite so forbidding as Mother, but she does get upset easily."

"Does your aunt live in Oxford?" Touie asked.

"Oh yes, Uncle Roswell took one of the first houses built in North Oxford," Dianna said. "Of course, as as soon as professors were allowed to marry, they snapped up most of the nicest houses; but Uncle Roswell got the grandest because he had invested in them. Most of the glass in the new houses built in North Oxford comes from the Roswell Glassworks," she added proudly.

The College Parks were a series of lawns and plantings in the natural style favored by such designers as the American, Olmstead. Formal flower beds had been abandoned for the most part, leaving the trees to spread their branches over the grass. The path went along the banks of the Holywell Mill Stream, so that Touie could revel in this unexpectedly bucolic landscape. A family of ducks paddled along, with Papa showing his gleaming green head in the lead, Mama hustling behind, and four fluffy ducklings striving to keep up between their parents. Blackbirds called from the branches of flowering pear and apple trees.

Dianna leaned out of her chair and waved at her friends, still struggling with their punt.

"Halloo!" she called out.

Gertrude stopped poling long enough to wave back. Mary was too busy guiding the punt with the forward paddle to acknowledge the greeting.

"We'll get home before you!" Dianna taunted them.

"Will they be all right?" Touie fussed, shading her eyes with her hand against the glare of the sun on the water.

"Of course they will. Gertrude always comes out on top," Dianna said carelessly. "She's a stunning athlete. She plays rugger and cricket, too."

The College Parks were not especially populous for such a fine afternoon. It was too late for luncheon, too early for a predinner stroll. A few children were bowling hoops along the gravel paths, with their nannies watching from a bench. There were no students' gowns to be seen here, but one elderly don sat alone, contemplating the river instead of his book.

By now they had reached the northernmost end of the path, and the chairman gave one last lunge to get his burden to its destination.

"Norham Gardens," he announced.

"You can leave me here," Dianna said, indicating a small, undistinguished house at the end of the street. "Mrs. Doyle . . . ?"

Touie doled out coins, and the chairman accepted them. He looked up and down the street to find a fare to pay his way back to the center of town, but the only person visible was the boy in charge of the donkey cart full of vegetables, making his afternoon deliveries. The chairman grimaced and began the long trek back to High Street and another possible fare, while Dianna scampered into Lady Margaret Hall, to the consternation of her schoolmates, who crowded about her exclaiming over the state of her dress.

"You're all wet!"

"Look at your hair!"

"What happened to Gertrude and Mary?"

"Miss Cahill had a small accident," Touie explained, as Dianna was escorted up the winding stair to her room to repair the damage the river and Dr. Doyle had wrought on her clothing and hair. "Miss Bell and Miss Talbot will be along shortly."

218

As if to answer the last question, Gertrude and Mary arrived, red-faced from their exertions, but ready to expound on the ferocity of the male of the species in general and the undergraduates of Christ Church in particular.

"We got attacked!" Gertrude declared.

"It was not our fault," Mary said, over the chatter, "but we did get in the way of the rowers."

"And Dianna nearly drowned!" Gertrude added dramatically. "Only this lady's husband is a doctor, and he saved her life."

"This is Mrs. Doyle." Mary performed the introductions. "How is Dianna?"

"She went upstairs," Edith Rix said. "Whatever happened to her shirtwaist?"

Touie smiled ruefully. "We had to cut her laces," she explained, "so that she could breathe. And then she had to come back in a chair, and I came with her to see that she was all right, you see. And to bring the tablecloth back to Christ Church, where it belongs."

Miss Wordsworth and Miss Laurel now made their appearance, deposited at the door by their cab.

Miss Wordsworth regarded Gertrude and Mary with a censorious frown. "Go and change your dress at once," she ordered. "You both look like hoydens." She turned to Touie. "Mr. Dodgson explained your situation," she said.

"My situation?" Touie looked puzzled.

"That you and your husband are only here for the day," Miss Wordsworth said, leading Touie into the Common Room, the luxurious sitting room where several of the students were occupied in reading and needlework. "It seems that Mr. Dodgson was most put out because your dinner last night was inedible; and since Dean Liddell has forbidden him to leave University grounds, and since he feels obliged to provide some sort of hospitality, he has invited Dr. Doyle to partake of the Christ Church dinner in the Hall. However, since no women may dine in the Hall at Christ Church, you must fend for yourself!" She removed her bonnet, displaying a lace cap trimmed with artificial flowers. "Men are quite impossible sometimes, Mrs. Doyle. If you wish, you may take tea and dinner with us here at Lady Margaret Hall, and I can call a cab to take you back to your lodgings."

Touie smiled sweetly. "That is most kind of you, Miss Wordsworth. Dear me, I had no idea how many young ladies wished to study at Oxford!" She looked around the room, which seemed to be full of young women, dressed in simple frocks of pale spring hues. Two girls had daringly opted for Liberty dresses, in the most modern style, with long, tight sleeves and puffed shoulders, smocked over the bosom and loose everywhere else. Miss Laurel's dark green velveteen bodice and skirt stood out among the linens and cottons of the rest of the students.

"Tea!" Miss Wordsworth ordered. She turned to Touie, indicating that she should sit down. "Oh yes, Mrs. Doyle, we are expanding every year. When I began Lady Margaret Hall, we only had seven students, and no teaching Fellows at all. We now have thirty students, and before long I expect to have women well enough educated to become Fellows of the University."

"My!" Touie regarded the female students with awe. "How clever you must all be! I would never have considered going to University."

Miss Wordsworth gazed at her charges with a proprietary air. "We may not be quite as scholarly as our friends at Somerville, but we are, in our own way, as intellectually sound as any other women's college."

"Where do all of you come from?" Touie asked. "I know that Miss Cahill's father is a clergyman."

"Oh, we're all sorts," Miss Rix said carelessly. "Gertrude's family made a fortune in trade, I think, and Dianna's got her rich uncle in glass."

"Most of my girls are gentry," Miss Wordsworth amended. "And then there is Miss Laurel, who came here as a referral from the Women's Educational Alliance."

"Miss Laurel?" Touie looked across the room, where Miss Laurel had stationed herself at the tea urn and was helping the scouts pour out cups for the rest of the girls.

"An interesting case, Miss Laurel," Miss Wordsworth said, dropping her voice. "A governess, you see, is not always as well-educated as one might hope. Mrs. Toynbee, one of our committee women, recommended her to us. Miss Laurel is reading modern literature and languages, with an eye to bettering herself. In fact, I am seriously considering keeping her on as a tutor to some of the young women who come here woefully unprepared to deal with the exigencies of writing essays."

Touie accepted a biscuit from the dish offered to her by one of the scouts and settled into an empty chair with a sigh of relief. "Thank you, Miss Wordsworth," she said. "I must admit, I had never heard of Lady Margaret Hall until I met your students yesterday. One hears such odd things about women in colleges, and there are many who believe that women should not be over-educated."

Miss Wordsworth's plump cheeks grew pink with indignation. "That is sheer foolishness," she retorted. "Men may think they prefer empty-headed ninnies, but the truth is that educated women make far better wives than ignorant ones."

"Then you expect your students to marry?" Touie sipped her tea.

"Certainly," Miss Wordsworth said, with a nod of her head that sent the flowers on her cap fluttering. "I should hope that all my girls make good marriages and lead happy and productive lives. Scholarship is all very well, Mrs. Doyle, but a woman's true vocation should be marriage."

"In that case . . . ," Touie began.

"Why come to Oxford?" Miss Wordsworth smiled graciously. "Because, Mrs. Doyle, an educated woman is one who will further her husband's career as well as her own. My girls may not be belles, Mrs. Doyle, but they will make their marks in the world."

By this time Dianna, Gertrude, and Mary had changed into afternoon dresses and rearranged their hair. They were now ready to present themselves in the sitting room.

"I must thank you again, Mrs. Doyle, for seeing me back to college," Dianna said. "What shall we do with the tablecloth?"

"I shall have it laundered, and it can be sent to Christ Church," Miss Wordsworth decided. "Mrs. Doyle will stay for dinner."

"How jolly!" Gertrude exclaimed. "We don't get that many guests for dinner, especially on a weekday."

"Not unless you count Mr. Dodgson," Mary said. "He sometimes takes Edith out."

"But he doesn't stay to dinner," Edith protested.

"Poor Mr. Dodgson," Touie giggled. "He truly wanted to give us a good dinner, and then the scout who was supposed to serve us forgot all about it; and when we finally got our dinner, it was cold, and Arthur would make jokes; but Mr. Dodgson took it all in bad part. And then Arthur took out his cigar, and Mr. Dodgson told us to leave!" She looked about for a response. None of the girls had been in a social situation quite like that, and there were a few nervous giggles; but Miss Wordsworth's severe frown showed Touie that she might have crossed an invisible line between what was funny and what was cruel mockery.

"I heard that one of the Christ Church scouts was found in the river," Miss Laurel said. "If he was the one who was to serve your dinner, that would explain his absence."

"Well, yes, it would," Touie said. "And one does feel sorry for the man's family, if he had any. But it was very trying, nonetheless; and now that Mr. Dodgson feels he must make it up to Arthur, I am very grateful to you for taking me in, so to speak, at such short notice."

She smiled at Miss Wordsworth, who decided to be gracious and smiled back.

"You have had a long walk from Christ Church, Mrs. Doyle. I shall leave you to rest until dinner." Miss Wordsworth rose majestically from her chair. "Girls, you may walk in the gardens but do not forget your hats and gloves. Miss Laurel, will you see to the clearing up?"

Miss Laurel nodded to the scouts, who began to pick up discarded teacups and biscuits. The girls straggled out, dividing into groups, to walk in the garden until the supper bell called them indoors again.

Touie sipped her tea, while Miss Laurel fussed about with the cups and cake plates.

"Are you quite finished, Mrs. Doyle?" Miss Laurel asked, waiting for the empty teacup.

"I think I will have another cup of tea, Miss Laurel," Touie said. "Do sit down. You have been running about all day, chasing those naughty girls in their punt and now helping with the tea."

"It is very kind of you to think of me, Mrs. Doyle, but I am used to hard work," Miss Laurel said.

"Of course. Miss Wordsworth said you had been a governess," Touie recalled. "And now you want to become a college Fellow. I admire you tremendously, Miss Laurel. I never had a governess, you see, since the Church school was quite good, and my mother thought I should attend there. Were your charges difficult?"

Miss Laurel's severe expression softened slightly. "There were one or two who were a handful," she admitted. "Throwing their toys about, never wanting to go to bed when told, tearing their clothes."

"But there must be some satisfaction in knowing that the children under your care will someday achieve great things," Touie hinted.

"Perhaps." Miss Laurel seemed to mentally review her former charges. "Of course, the boys go off to school when they're six, so it's hard to say what they'll become. Girls are different, but I didn't have girls."

"Of course, once it is known that you have had an Oxford education, you will be very much in demand," Touie said, handing over the teacup.

"I would prefer to remain here. Miss Wordsworth has offered me a position when I finish my exhibitions." Miss Laurel accepted the teacup and followed the scouts into the kitchens.

Touie stared out the sitting room window into the college garden. The girls were strolling up and down the paths, chattering gaily. Gertrude, Mary, and Dianna were apparently demonstrating their accident, with appropriate gestures.

Touie considered what she had learned. She was certain that she had another piece of Mr. Dodgson's puzzle, but she did not know how to proceed. I do wish I could talk with Arthur, she thought. He would tell me what to do.

She scrabbled in her reticule and came up with her card case. She had not thought of paying calls, but one never knew when one might need cards, and now was as good a time as any to use one. She looked about for some kind of writing tool, Aha! There was a desk in the corner, with a pen and inkwell.

Touie wrote a quick note on the back of her visiting card. Now, she thought, how can I send it to Mr. Dodgson and Arthur?

She looked about her then ducked quickly back into the street. The chairman was gone, but the lad with the donkey cart had finished his rounds and was about to move on.

"Hello!" Touie called out. "Young man!"

The greengrocer's boy looked about him. "Me, mum?"

"Yes, you!" Touie darted down the few steps and into the street. "Can you take this to Christ Church for me? It's very important that this note go to Mr. Dodgson of Christ Church."

"I've me rounds to make . . ." the boy protested.

Touie found a penny, the last of her coins. "If you take this message, here's a penny for you, and Mr. Dodgson will give you more," she promised. She looked behind her. It would never do for her to be seen passing the note!

"Please!" She pleaded.

The boy looked at the penny, then at the card. He accepted the first, and tucked the second into the pocket of his waistcoat. "I've me rounds to make," he warned her, "but I've deliveries down St. Aldgates. I'll take your message, mum."

"Thank you!" Touie bestowed a dazzling smile on the boy and darted back into the house.

The donkey and its master ambled along, and Touie was left to hope that Mr. Dodgson would get her message before dinner. In the meantime she would walk in the gardens with the young ladies and enjoy what was left of the afternoon. She only hoped that Arthur had been able to find what he was looking for, and that Mr. Dodgson could put the two halves of the puzzle together before they had to be on their way.

CHAPTER 23

It was nearly teatime when Dr. Doyle made his way back to Christ Church. He stopped at the Porter's Lodge just inside Tom Gate and asked for Mr. Dodgson.

"If you will wait here, sir," the porter told him, with a lofty glance at his tweed suit and deerstalker cap, "I shall see if Mr. Dodgson will receive you."

Dr. Doyle was left to contemplate Tom Quad. The May sunshine was beginning to dim. A threatening bank of clouds was building in the west, and a stiff breeze had begun to send students' gowns fluttering and mortarboards tumbling across the lawn.

The porter arrived with Telling, both frowning their disapproval of the disturbance of college etiquette.

"Mr. Dodgson is conferring with Dean Liddell," Telling announced. "He will join you in the Senior Common Room as soon as he has completed his discussion. I am to escort you there."

"Lead on," Dr. Doyle replied, with a theatrical gesture. It was lost on Telling, who led the guest around the quad, through the Hall, and down the winding medieval staircase to the paneled room at the bottom. Here, in a room full of leather-upholstered furniture reminiscent of the gentlemen's clubs of London, Dr. Doyle was left to the scrutiny of what seemed like an army of men, ranging in age from a pink-cheeked youngster of his own age to venerable white-haired or balding gentlemen, all dressed formally in black suits, most with reversed collars, some bearded and some clean-shaven, all draped in black fustian gowns, and all with expressions of astonishment at this intrusion into their private realm. The only one in the room Dr. Doyle recognized was Dr. Kitchin, the pathologist who had conducted the autopsy that morning.

"Dr. Doyle," Telling announced, and left Dr. Doyle to cope with the dons, while he saw to the tea urns, muffins, and bread and butter.

The chatter in the room ceased as the dons of Christ Church examined the young man with the air of those who have just found a strange insect in their salads. Then the elderly gentleman nearest Dr. Doyle presented himself.

"You are the young man Charles met in Brighton last year, are you not? I am Mr. Duckworth."

Dr. Doyle shook the hand that was offered and bowed slightly. "I am very pleased to make your acquaintance, sir."

"You are a physician, I believe?" Mr. Duckworth accepted the cup of tea handed to him by the nearest scout.

"Yes. I practice in Southsea." Dr. Doyle wondered whether Mr. Dodgson was going to be very long with Dean Liddell. There were things he had to discuss with him, and he could hardly bring up matters like blackmail and murder in front of this gathering of scholars.

"A practicing physician?" Mr. Duckworth's voice was tremulous but shrill. It attracted more attention than Dr. Doyle preferred.

"I also write," Dr. Doyle said defensively. "Mr. Dodgson has gone so far as to recommend my stories to some of his literary friends."

"Then you must be a very good writer, sir, for Charles never reads fiction."

"So he has told me." Dr. Doyle smiled and was offered a cup of tea, which he could not refuse.

Another scholar, stout and bearded, joined Duckworth. "And what are you writing now, young man?" He beamed at Dr. Doyle with the air of one who questions a favorite nephew just back from school.

"I have completed one novel," Dr. Doyle retorted. "And I have seen several of my stories in print."

"And what is your subject matter?" A third don, an ascetic-looking scholar with a straggling white beard, had joined the inquisition. Dr. Doyle was forcibly reminded of his school days, where he was constantly under the supervision of priests who managed to find something wrong in everything he said or did.

As always, when Dr. Doyle's temper rose, so did his Scottish accent. "I have written of my travels in the Arctic Sea," he said. "And I wrote a fictional account of the *Mary Celeste* . . ."

"So that was you!" Mr. Duckworth exclaimed. He turned to the others. "This is the author, not J. Habakkuk Jepson!"

"We debated the issue," the white-bearded Mr. Vere Bayne said. "The argument was well-presented, but we were puzzled as to the feasibility of the explanation of the disappearance of the entire crew."

"The supernatural occurrences seemed to be somewhat exaggerated." A tall, spare don peered over his pince-nez at Dr. Doyle, who took a step backward. The questioner stepped forward, pressing his point.

"It was fiction," Dr. Doyle protested.

"But written as fact," Mr. Duckworth pointed out.

"And not signed," Mr. Vere Bayne added.

"Leaving the reader with the impression that the tale was factual." Dr. Kitchin, the only don in the room not wearing a clerical collar, clinched the matter.

"Which does not preclude there being a supernatural explanation of the case," Dr. Doyle said stubbornly.

"Are you one of those who believes in spiritualist poppycock?" Dr. Kitchin asked, with the air of one who has already made up his mind.

Dr. Doyle had not made up his mind and said so. "I am willing to be convinced," he said. "I am a member of the Portsmouth Literary and Scientific Society, and we have conducted several experiments with mixed success."

Before the discussion veered off into the merits of spiritualism, Mr. Duckworth peered at Dr. Doyle with a puzzled frown and said, "I do not recall your being up at the House."

"I was trained in Edinburgh," Dr. Doyle said curtly.

"Oh, a Scotch school." Dr. Kitchin dismissed anything north of the Border with a wave of his hand and a shrug.

"Might I remind you, sir," Dr. Doyle said, rising to defend his alma mater, "that both Glasgow and Edinburgh were sending scholars out into England when Oxford was just a cattle crossing!"

"I find it odd that Mr. Dodgson should take up with a physician from Edinburgh," Mr. Duckworth complained.

"He rarely takes up anyone over the age of ten, particularly those of the male sex," Mr. Barclay Thompson, a stout man with mutton-chop whiskers sniggered.

Dr. Doyle swallowed hard and explained, "Mr. Dodgson is acquainted with a member of my family—my uncle, in fact—the artist, Dicky Doyle, of *Punch*."

"Oh, well, in that case, Dr. Doyle, it is understandable that Mr. Dodgson would wish to further your career," Mr. Barclay Thompson said, with a knowing smile. "Dodgson fancies himself an artist, if photography may be termed an art."

"Photography is a chemical process," Mr. Duckworth admitted. "However, in the correct hands, such as my friend Dodgson's, photography may be raised to an art. Are you a photographer, young man?"

Before Dr. Doyle could formulate a suitable reply, Mr. Dodgson made his appearance, followed by Dean Liddell, both wearing expressions indicating great internal agony.

Dean Liddell called the group to order. "Gentlemen," he said gravely, "Mr. Dodgson has brought certain matters to my attention that I believe should be addressed by all of us."

Mr. Dodgson swallowed a gulp of tea, looking much like the Mad Hatter at the trial. "I regret to tell you that some of our undergraduates have been behaving disgracefully," he began.

"You needn't interrupt our tea to tell us that," Mr. Barclay Thompson said, with his characteristic laugh.

"Undergraduates will always behave disgracefully," Dr. Kitchin agreed, with a shake of his head.

"In this case the behavior has crossed the line of what is acceptable," Dean Liddell cut across the babble of agreement. "Did any of you witness the regrettable accident on the river this afternoon?"

Another hubbub informed him that several of the dons had, indeed, seen the ladies in the punt and the gentlemen in the scull, and the unfortunate collision. Opinion seemed to be mixed as to whether the rowers should have ducked the ladies or whether the ladies should have known better than to go beyond Magdalen Bridge.

Once again Dean Liddell's voice overrode the babble. "There might have been a tragedy had not this young man"—he indicated Dr. Doyle—"acted promptly and efficiently to save a young lady's life."

"Hear, hear!" There was general applause. Dr. Doyle smiled modestly and did not quite bow.

"Ahem!" Dean Liddell brought the group back to attention. "Mr. Dodgson informs me that the young lady in question has been the subject of scurrilous attacks upon her reputation and that of her college."

"What!" There was another general murmur, this time of disbelief.

"Our lads have nothing to do with the women undergraduates," Dr. Kitchin protested. "Most of the women's colleges are at the other end of town. They come here only for the Cathedral services, if then."

"I regret to tell you that the young lady in question has received a communication, and a . . . a piece of verse. I shall not describe it as a poem. The best that can be said about it is that it rhymes."

Mr. Dodgson produced the typeset sheet. "I have information that this was p-perpetrated by one of our undergraduates. I would like to know if any of you recognize the style."

Various lenses were affixed to noses or screwed into eye sockets as the dons huddled about the page and viewed it through monocles, pince-nez, or spectacles. The reactions were gratifyingly horrific.

"Good Lord!" Dr. Kitchin exclaimed. " 'Lusting after little babies, licking their vulva labies'? I suppose what is meant is labia majora, or possibly pudenda, but that would not rhyme, would it?"

"Neither does this," Mr. Barclay Thompson said, with a grimace. " 'Female scholars having half o' / Pennyworth of sense will worship Sappho.' Quite impossible!"

"If this is what they call undergraduate humor these days, then heaven help us!" Mr. Duckworth frowned. "The tag line is, 'Such is the be and end all / Of instruction at Lady Margaret Hall.' It does not scan. I cannot believe any of our students would commit such an atrocity to paper."

"It is unutterably offensive," Dr. Doyle said. "I would have thought better of your young men than to imply that female students were perverse and bent on evil."

"Oh, that is a matter of opinion," Mr. Vere Bayne said. "What is far more important is that this . . . this travesty should be published, and that the name of Christ Church should be attached to such a dreadful piece of trash. It is badly written, sir! That is far worse than the, er, content!"

Dr. Doyle began to understand how Alice felt at the Mad Tea Party. "Do you mean to say," he argued, "that it is acceptable to compare the ladies of today, serious scholars I am sure, to the young persons who clustered about the poetess Sappho . . . ?"

"Did you say 'Sappho'?" Mr. Duckworth interrupted them. "Dear me. How odd. I would never think it of him."

"Of whom?" Mr. Dodgson asked eagerly.

"Of young Mr. Martin. He was reading the latest translation and questioning some of the actual wording of the text."

"Do you mean that very bold young man who rescued Miss Cahill from the river?" Dean Liddell asked.

Mr. Duckworth shrugged. "I do not know about his heroics. I do know that he is a most conscientious scholar, a linguist of sorts, collecting odd words and forms of speech. I believe he is almost looking forward to using the vulgar tongue on his prospective parishioners." Mr. Duckworth chuckled to himself. "He even took it upon himself to compile a list of Americanisms from his friend, Chatsworth, and brought it to my attention."

"Isn't Mr. Martin the young chap who accosted us last night?" Dr. Doyle asked his mentor. "He said that he believed that Ingram was the thief who was preying on the rooms in Tom Quad," he explained to the assembled dons.

Dean Liddell frowned. "Mr. Martin has rooms on the south side of Tom Quad," he said, "with Mr. Chatsworth and Mr. Farlow. They are the only undergraduates on that side, as far as I am aware. Most of the undergraduates prefer Peckwater Quad," he told Dr. Doyle. "The sound of the bell is less disturbing to younger ears."

"One does get used to it," Mr. Duckworth said, with a shrug.

"Chatsworth, Farlow, and Martin . . . They were in the boat that attacked the girls in the punt and pushed them into the river."

"They were indeed," Dean Liddell said. "And I have been conferring with Mr. Dodgson and Mr. Seward, as proctors, as to the appropriate punishment for their actions."

"What did they do, precisely?" Mr. Duckworth asked.

"I saw it all. They deliberately attacked that girl," Dr. Doyle said. "Someone used an oar to tip her out of the punt and then tried to drown her in the weeds. If Mr. Martin had not taken the action he did, I would never have had the chance to revive her."

"Who was the girl?" Mr. Vere Bayle wanted to know.

"A Miss Dianna Cahill," Mr. Dodgson answered. "Her father has one of the parishes connected with the Cathedral."

Mr. Barclay Thompson frowned down at the pages. "Is she the person referred to in the opening phrase, 'Observe Miss Dye, the little honey. . . .' Where is the illustration?"

"I beg your pardon?" Mr. Dodgson choked over his tea.

"The text clearly indicates an illustration," Mr. Barclay Thompson said, tapping it for emphasis. He leered at Mr. Dodgson. "One of your old photographs gone astray, Dodgson?"

"That will do!" Dean Liddell rescued the offensive verses and returned them to Mr. Dodgson, who handed the paper back to Dr. Doyle, as if the mere touch of it polluted him. Dr. Doyle, made of sterner stuff than the shrinking scholar, merely folded the paper and put it into his breast pocket.

"The illustration is immaterial," Mr. Dodgson said. "What is important is that we find the p-perp-petrator of this outrage and rep-primand him. And then, Dean, I strongly suggest that we remove him from this college."

"As to that, Mr. Dodgson, I shall have to consider the appropriate measure to take," Dean Liddell said.

"I think a word with young Mr. Martin might be advisable," Dr. Doyle suggested.

"Perhaps we can speak with his friends, Mr. Chatsworth and Mr. Farlow as well," Mr. Dodgson added.

"Chatsworth and Farlow?" Dr. Doyle touched his cheek. "I've had more than a few words with those two. Is one of them very tall and fair, the other short and dark and slender?"

A babble of agreement filled the room.

"I shall send for them at once," Dean Liddell announced. "Telling, find those three young gentlemen and bring them to my study."

Mr. Dodgson cleared his throat diffidently. "Ahem. If I may make a suggestion, Dean, perhaps my rooms would be more appropriate for the interview. Your study is, if I may say so, somewhat overpowering for undergraduates, and they may feel constrained in your presence."

Dean Liddell nodded. "In this case, Mr. Dodgson, you may be right. I shall have Seward bring the lads to your rooms, where we may interview them. Of course, I shall notify the police of any pertinent information we discover, should it be necessary."

"Of course, Dean."

Dean Liddell strode out. Mr. Dodgson bit into a muffin.

"I have found . . . ," Dr. Doyle began eagerly. Mr. Dodgson held up a hand for silence.

"We will hear what those undergraduates have to say," Mr. Dodgson said. "And then we shall proceed from there." He finished his muffin, swallowed the last of his tea, and followed Dean Liddell back through Tom Quad to his rooms.

CHAPTER 24

By the time they arrived at Mr. Dodgson's rooms, Chatsworth, Farlow, and Martin had changed out of their muddied rowing clothes and were now properly dressed in the garments each considered suitable for the impending interview. Mr. Martin's tweeds were embellished by a sleeveless pullover, hand knit by his mother. Mr. Farlow had donned his blue blazer, with the Oxford crest on the breast pocket, as a symbol of his preeminence on the field of sport. Mr. Chatsworth's pale cream linen suit was the best Saville Row tailoring. Each young man was properly gowned; each maintained a blank expression, as if to say, "What have I done?" as they stood in a row in Mr. Dodgson's sitting room.

The furniture had been rearranged to accommodate the influx of people. Mr. Dodgson stood in his favorite place by the fireplace while Dean Liddell sat in the large armchair, as befitted his dignity. Dr. Doyle had taken a position near the door, with Mr. Seward, in his role as proctor, keeping a careful eye on the miscreants.

Mr. Dodgson examined the three undergraduates carefully. "Do you know why you are here?" he asked.

"No idea at all," Farlow said carelessly. "Unless it's about that silly cow who tried to run us down in her punt."

"That silly cow, as you so blithely express it, very nearly drowned," Mr. Dodgson said severely.

Mr. Martin burst out, "Is she all right?"

"My wife has taken Miss Cahill back to her college. I can only hope that she has recovered from her shock," Doyle told him.

"It was only a rag," Chatsworth protested.

"And last night's little adventure?" Mr. Dodgson's expression was grim. "Was that also a rag? Moving a body is a very serious offense, young man."

Chatsworth tried to smile, but it turned into a smirk. "We were a little squiffy," he began.

"Drunkenness is no excuse," Mr. Dodgson said. "Particularly if you purchased the wine through the late Ingram. He was removing the bottles laid aside for the Senior Common Room and selling them to a dishonest clerk, who then sold them back to you young fools at an exorbitant rate."

"I told you so," Chatsworth said, with a smug glance at Farlow.

"Minnie, will you be quiet!" Farlow hissed.

"Mr. Farlow." Mr. Dodgson carefully removed a piece of paper from his inside pocket and scanned it, then laid it down on the desk, apparently unaware of three pairs of eyes following his every move. "I am given to understand that you are the leader of our oars this year."

"I am." Farlow bit off the words.

"Then you are supposed to set the moral example," Mr. Dodgson said. "And yet you deliberately attacked the young women in that punt before the eyes of the entire college. I might add, there were persons present on Christ Church Commons this afternoon whose sole introduction to college sport may well be your disgraceful exhibition of temper!"

A dull flush stained Farlow's cheeks. He bit his lip to keep from shouting. "The young women had no right to be out in our way," he said evenly. "Everyone knows that sculls take precedence over punts on the river."

"That may be so, but the young ladies were pulled by the current," Dr. Doyle explained.

"Then they ought not to have been out at all!" Farlow shot back.

"The incident was deplorable on all sides, but most of all on yours," Mr. Dodgson interrupted the spat. "Gentlemen of Christ Church are supposed to set the standard for the rest of the University."

"They really shouldn't have got in our way," Chatsworth backed up his friend. "And two of them just got wet and were quite all right once they dried off. How were we supposed to know that fat one couldn't swim and wore tight corsets?"

"She is not fat!" Martin exclaimed. "She is well-rounded."

"I might add," Dr. Doyle said quietly, "that I discovered marks on Miss Cahill's neck that indicated to me that she was struck, several times, with the oars. If the purpose of the attack was to embarrass the young ladies, why strike Miss Cahill?"

The three young men were silent. Chatsworth automatically reached into his breast pocket and withdrew a cigar case.

"I do not allow tobacco in these rooms," Mr. Dodgson snapped, as Chatsworth took out one of his long cheroots.

"Where did you get this cigar?" Dr. Doyle asked, stepping forward and taking the cheroot out of the young man's fingers.

"I have relations in America," Chatsworth said. "One of my mother's brothers has a cattle ranch. They sent me out last year for the Long Vac. Grand place, Wyoming! You should have come with me, Nev, you'd have liked it."

Dr. Doyle was examining Chatsworth's cheroot. "Most interesting," he commented. "The police found something very much like this under Magdalen Bridge this afternoon."

Chatsworth flushed angrily. "That means nothing. Anyone can smoke a cigar."

"These are American-made cheroots," Dr. Doyle said.

"What of it? A man may buy his cigars in London or have them sent to him direct," Chatsworth pointed out.

"So he may," Mr. Dodgson said. "And just because a man smoked a cigar under a bridge does not necessarily mean that he was involved in murder. However, if you three were responsible for moving that body, you had best own up to it now. Dean Liddell can inform Inspector Truscott. I assume that you three were the undergraduates I saw last night?"

Farlow glanced at Martin and Chatsworth then nodded briefly. "It was as Minnie said, a rag, that's all. We were going to put him in with the anatomy subjects for the next day's lecture at the mortuary."

"How did you come to find him?" Mr. Dodgson asked.

Farlow passed his tongue over suddenly dry lips. "I was passing by, as it were . . ."

"Passing by Magdalen Bridge?" Mr. Dodgson's tone was icy. "Mr. Farlow, I was present when the late Ingram shouted out a challenge to meet him under that bridge at six o'clock. As I understand it, your rooms overlook St. Aldgates. It was a warm day, and your windows must have been open. You heard Ingram's shouted challenge; you went to meet him and found . . . what?"

"Why should I wish to speak to Ingram under Magdalen Bridge? He was my scout. I could talk to him right here in my own rooms," Farlow sneered. "You are building a case out of thin air, Mr. Dodgson. You've had that Scotch swine following me about all day and what have you to show for it? A filthy cigar end and a squib. I'll admit to moving Ingram, nothing more."

"Ah yes," Mr. Dodgson fairly purred, "a squib. A set of verses, which cannot be deemed poetry except by the most vulgar of minds, defaming not only the young lady but her school and its purpose as well. How do you come to know of it, Lord Farlow?"

"Why . . ." Farlow looked to Chatsworth for guidance.

"It's in your hand," Chatsworth said. "That piece of paper . . ."

"This?" Mr. Dodgson looked at the paper on the desk. "This is a list of objects found by the police, which Ingram had stolen from the rooms on his staircase, and which were pawned at a shop on Pembroke Lane."

"I thought he was pinching things," Chatsworth said, with a smug look at his roommates. "Your studs, Greg. See if there are a set of pearl studs on that list, sir. Greg here missed his yesterday. Ingram was a thief and a liar and . . ."

237

"And a blackmailer," Mr. Dodgson added. "The police have found a cache of objects in his rooms that lead them to suspect that he collected half-written letters for use at a later date."

Dodgson turned his eyes to Martin, who had remained silent throughout the interview. "Mr. Martin, I understand you have an interest in the Greek poetess Sappho."

"Eh?" Martin jerked out of a troubled reverie. "Oh, yes. I have the newest translation, but there is so little of her work available that it is difficult to assess her place in the pantheon of ancient literature. I have been working on a new translation . . ." His voice trailed off.

"You have rooms with Lord Farlow and Mr. Chatsworth on the west side of Tom Quad, is that not so?" Mr. Dodgson asked, almost casually.

"That's right," Martin said. "Nev and Minnie and I . . . well, we're old Etonians, and the rooms were available, and Peckwater's too full of Rugby and Westminster boys and . . ."

Mr. Dodgson held up his hand for silence. "And you are all school chums. You are in and out of one another's rooms all day. It would be quite simple for one of the others, Farlow or Chatsworth, to pick up your new translation of Madame Sappho's poems and read it."

"I suppose so, but I don't see what this has to do with . . ." Martin looked at Mr. Dodgson then at his two friends with growing horror. "Minnie! Didn't you have a go at my translation? You and Nev, reading it out loud . . ." He fairly choked with indignation.

Mr. Dodgson turned his attention to the other two men. "Dr. Doyle has a copy of the item in question," he told them. "Now, Lord Farlow, Mr. Chatsworth, I think you had better explain yourselves to Dean Liddell. Sending items of this sort to young ladies is a very serious matter, and threatening to publish them unless the young lady leaves Oxford is even worse."

"It's blackmail," Dr. Doyle elucidated.

Farlow turned on the interloper. "What are you doing here anyway, you Scotch upstart?" he snarled.

"I am here as *amicus curiae*," Dr. Doyle said, with a bland smile and a twitch of his mustache.

"No friend of this court!" Farlow shouted. He swung wildly at Dr. Doyle, who evaded the younger man's attempt at fisticuffs.

"I thought we'd finished with all that!" Dr. Doyle said disgustedly. "Mine is only one copy. Ingram had more. Mr. Farlow, you have admitted to moving a body, which is already a matter for the police. It is also obvious that you are behind this ludicrous attempt to suborn Miss Cahill and drive her away from Oxford. Be a man, sir, and take what is coming to you!"

Dr. Doyle's words only seemed to enrage the younger man. Farlow lunged for the door. Dr. Doyle grabbed at his gown to stop him. Farlow twisted around, trying to get away. The two men teetered back and forth, until Farlow broke out of Doyle's grip and headed for the door, evading the portly proctor, Seward.

"Where do you think you are going?" Mr. Dodgson shouted after him. Seward and Doyle ran after Farlow, as the young man looked wildly about him for a means of escape. The stairs were blocked by two substantial dons on their way up to their rooms. The only exit was the corridor that led to the clock tower.

"Don't go that way!" Mr. Dodgson shouted from his place at the door. "He must not go into the tower!" he gasped out to Dr. Doyle. "The clock is about to strike!"

"The bell!" Dr. Doyle ran after the younger man.

"He must be trying to get to the stairs below the tower!" Seward wheezed.

Dr. Doyle saw Farlow at the end of the corridor, where an ancient wooden door led to the famous tower where Great Tom, the college clock, had its works.

Seward tottered along the corridor. "Get him out," he gasped.

Dr. Doyle loped after Farlow, grabbing at the younger man's flying gown. The cloth slid through his fingers as Farlow opened the door and dashed into the tower room, making for the spiral staircase that led to the roof. Dr. Doyle threw himself on the student before he could reach the stairs. The two of them went down, rolling on the bare boards of the clock tower.

Farlow scrambled to his feet and started to climb up the winding stair, his only possible escape route.

"Don't be stupid, boy!" Dr. Doyle wheezed. "The clock's going to strike at any moment! We have to get out of here!"

As if in response, the bell of Great Tom began to toll. Farlow fell down the stairs as if he had been struck. Dr. Doyle could feel the reverberations throughout his whole body. He grabbed Farlow by the shoulders, swung him around, and planted a good punch on his jaw. The young man sagged, and Dr. Doyle hauled him out of the clock chamber.

Only four strokes, and the bell was still. Dr. Doyle leaned against the wall of the corridor, breathing hard. Farlow groaned and tried to move.

"That was a very stupid thing to do," Dr. Doyle chided him, as he helped the fallen student to his feet. "You have as good as admitted your guilt. Now take your medicine like a good fellow."

"I didn't kill Ingram," Farlow said sulkily.

"I never said you did," Dr. Doyle told him. "Of course, the police may think otherwise, unless you come clean and tell us all you know."

Dr. Doyle and Mr. Farlow staggered into Mr. Dodgson's rooms to the great astonishment of Chatsworth and Martin. Dr. Doyle dumped Farlow into one of the armchairs.

"Will he be all right?" Chatsworth bent over his fallen leader.

"That's the second time I've had to knock him down today," Dr. Doyle said, sucking on his knuckles. "For a student, he seems unwilling to learn."

"He's always been that way," Chatsworth said. "Can't blame him, I suppose. My governor would say it's lack of moral fiber. Very knowing one, my father."

Mr. Martin's round face echoed his friend's concern. "I always felt a little sorry for him," he said.

"Sorry? For the heir to a title, lands . . . ," Dr. Doyle began.

Martin blinked through his spectacles. "Oh, that. Well, as to the title, Lord Berwick, his father, came into it almost by accident, when his cousin died without an heir. Otherwise, I suppose he'd never have been allowed to marry the actress."

"Stop talking about me as if I weren't here," Farlow muttered, as he wiped blood off his upper lip. "Everywhere I go, all people ever talk about is how my pater and mater got married in the teeth of everyone's opposition. Regular Romeo and Juliet, you'd think them." He jerked away from Dr. Doyle's probing hands. "When Cousin Edmund died, the Pater got the title and the estate . . ."

"And Berwick Place, which you loathe," Chatsworth said sagely.

"Great empty barracks," Farlow grumbled. "All the servants eating their heads off in the hall and me alone up in the nursery, with just some miserable chit of a governess and the nursemaids. And Nanny, of course, but she was let go when I went to school."

"I have often thought that the children of the great families have a much harder time of it than children in simpler homes," Mr. Dodgson said. "One hears a great deal of Lord Berwick and his cronies, entertaining His Royal Highness lavishly and being entertained in their turn. Of course, such a life must mean a great deal of expenditure."

"Money!" Farlow spat out. "My pater thought he was marrying it, but the old Methodist wouldn't have an actress in the house, even after she got the title. I'll never forget it! Sitting there for hours, decked out in my best suit, nothing to eat, not even a cup of tea or a biscuit, and then that miserable little girl bouncing in, all yellow curls, chattering about what a nice time she'd had with the sweet gentleman, and the jam cakes . . ." Farlow choked on the memory.

"So you did know who Miss Cahill was. I had wondered about that." Mr. Dodgson nodded again. "I am now going to speculate, Mr. Farlow. You may agree or not, as you wish."

"Your parents keep a large establishment. They would have had footmen. Was one of those footmen James Ingram?"

Farlow nodded. "I almost didn't remember him, but he certainly remembered me. I was the one who got him sacked."

"Eh?" Mr. Dodgson's eyebrows rose.

Farlow reddened. "I found him with one of the maids, in flagrante, as it were. Naturally, the two of them were let go at once.

241

No matter what was going on in the upstairs bedrooms, the servants had to uphold certain standards."

"Which meant that Ingram went up to London with a recommendation from Lord Berwick and a distinct chip on his shoulder," Dr. Doyle summed it up. "Whatever happened to the girl?"

Farlow shrugged. "Turned off, of course, with no character. I was left alone most of the time, except for the rest of the servants."

"Not even a nurse?" Dr. Doyle asked.

"Once I was off to school, the Pater didn't see why I had to have one," Farlow said bitterly. "Of course, there was Greg. His father was Vicar at Berwick, and the two of us were of an age, so I went to the vicarage whenever I could. And then Minnie joined the two of us at Eton."

"Three Musketeers," Chatsworth put in. "What with my mother's being a mill heiress, and his being an actress, the other chaps ragged us unmercifully. And Greg, here, stuck by us."

Mr. Dodgson ignored the interruptions and picked up his tale. "I will leave it to the police to follow Ingram's trail in London. During his travels, he seems to have picked up small items that were of no apparent value, but might be used for extortion at a later date." Mr. Dodgson eyed Farlow and Chatsworth. "Mr. Farlow, did you ever inform Ingram of your encounter with Miss Cahill?"

"Me? Tell Ingram?" Farlow looked puzzled. "Why should I do that?"

"You never spoke of your childhood encounter?"

"Why should I? He was there!"

"What?" Mr. Dodgson exclaimed.

"When the Mater dragged me into Oxford to show me off to her brother, Ingram was the footman then so he knew all about the little b . . ."

Mr. Martin growled threateningly. Farlow amended his statement. "Blond," he corrected himself. "Of course, when he turned up here I didn't recognize him at all, but he reminded me of our past associations soon enough."

Mr. Dodgson nodded thoughtfully. "And you decided to employ him in this scheme to apply to your uncle, who had announced that he would settle a large sum on any of his young relations who achieved honors at University," Dr. Doyle said accusingly.

"What right had she to set herself up?" Farlow burst out angrily. "I saw her there, sitting up on the dais at the Balliol lectures, for all the world like a don herself!"

"So you took it upon yourself to remove her," Mr Dodgson said sternly. "You wrote obscene letters directed to her. You threatened to defame her school if she did not leave Oxford. Finally, when that did not deter her, you wrote the verses in question, and Ingram provided the photograph, which he stole from my rooms." Mr. Dodgson sat straight up in his chair. "What have you to say for yourself, sir?"

Gregory Martin bounded out of his chair. "You said it was a rag!" he exploded. "All because the girls were set up on the dais at Balliol lectures! I am ashamed of you, Nevil! I wash my hands of you!"

"You pious fraud!" Farlow was on his feet, glaring at his boyhood friend. "It was you who had that Greek text in the first place, and . . ."

"I was studying it!" Martin retorted. "And I am not the one who went to that gambling room during the Long Vac and signed chits for money I did not have and could not earn!"

Chatsworth tried to worm his way between his taller, broader, stouter friends. "I wanted you to come with me to Wyoming, Nev," he said sorrowfully. "He always gets into trouble if I'm not about to help him," he explained to Mr. Dodgson.

"Which is why you followed him to Magdalen Bridge last night," Mr. Dodgson said. "Gentlemen, I will not allow brawling in my rooms. Particularly not before the Dean!"

Chatsworth, Martin, and Farlow suddenly remembered that they were in the presence of their leader. Dr. Doyle eyed them as if they were a trio of wild animals, ready to fight one another or anyone else at any moment.

Mr. Dodgson took a deep breath to calm himself. "Now, where were we?"

"Under Magdalen Bridge," Chatsworth said airily. "That's

where this all started, didn't it? With my cheroot. And yes, I confess, I was there last night when Nev went to have it out with Ingram."

Farlow swung around to look at his friend. "I didn't see you."

"Of course you didn't! You were too busy trying to look innocent," Chatsworth retorted. "I was on the other side, down by the Botanic Gardens. You came down the stairs and saw Ingram caught in among the boats. Then you left. It was all I could do to leg it to the Hall and get there before you."

"That is not quite true," Dr. Doyle said. "We found two cigars, Mr. Chatsworth. You did not follow Lord Farlow; you were there before him, possibly with the intention of having that word with Ingram yourself."

Chatsworth's amiably imbecilic expression changed to one of wary watchfulness. "And what if I was?"

"Then it is entirely likely that you witnessed the murder," Dr. Doyle said.

Dean Liddell decided to exercise his authority. "Mr. Chatsworth," he intoned, "it is your duty to tell what you observed."

"All right." Chatsworth glanced at his friends. "I heard Ingram yelling in the street, something about meeting him at six o'clock under Magdalen Bridge. I knew he'd been nicking the college wine, and a few other things as well, and I thought he'd got his hooks into you, Nev, somehow, so I beetled on to Magdalen Bridge to have a word, as Mr. Dodgson said. Only when I got there, I heard him arguing with someone down by the boats."

"Could you tell who it was?" Mr. Dodgson leaned forward in his chair.

Chatsworth shook his head. "I was on the other side," he said ruefully. "I heard a splash and a lot of thrashing about, and then I heard footsteps on the stone stairs."

"What did you do?" Martin asked breathlessly.

"What could I do?" Chatsworth replied carelessly. "I was going to see about helping the chap, when along you came, Nev. So there I was, and there you are. Nev didn't do it, and I can swear to it in any court you like." He looked defiantly from Mr. Dodgson to Dr. Doyle.

Mr. Dodgson frowned. "This is more difficult than I thought," he muttered to himself.

"Sir?" Martin asked hesitantly. "May I go, sir? I wanted to finish my prep for viva voce."

"You may all leave these rooms," Mr. Dodgson told them.

Dean Liddell added, "Do not leave the grounds. You are all gated until further notice. I shall have to consider whether your actions toward Miss Cahill merit more stringent punishment."

"We just wanted to get her out of Oxford," Chatsworth offered as an excuse.

"So that Lord Farlow, here, could receive the bounty of the beneficent Mr. Roswell," Mr. Dodgson finished for him. "I must point out to you that Mr. Roswell's fortune is his to do with as he likes, and that your mother was cut out of the family totally when she went on the stage. Your scheme was based on faulty logic, Mr. Farlow, and the result is that it is you who will leave Oxford in disgrace. Good day, gentlemen!"

Dean Liddell rose majestically from his chair. "Gentlemen, you will remain in your rooms until dinner. I strongly suggest that you consider writing letters of apology to Miss Cahill and her friends, and that you send them to Lady Margaret Hall before the day is out. Thank you, Mr. Dodgson. You have cleared this matter up to my satisfaction. I shall inform the police of your discoveries. Gentlemen!"

Mr. Seward herded the trio down the stairs and around the clock tower back to their rooms on the other side of the quad, while Dean Liddell proceeded to his own deanery, where he could compose a suitably worded report for Inspector Truscott that would exonerate Christ Church from any implication of wrong-doing.

Mr. Dodgson and Dr. Doyle were left alone in the tower sitting room.

"So now we know why Miss Cahill was being blackmailed and by whom," Dr. Doyle summed it up. "But we don't know who killed Ingram . . . or why?"

"Oh, I think I know who and why," Mr. Dodgson said. "Of course, at this point there is no proof, only speculation."

Dr. Doyle looked grim. "Then we must get the proof. What next?"

"You must go across the road and change your dress," Mr. Dodgson ordered. "And then we shall dine in Hall. I have to consider our next steps very carefully. There is a very desperate person about, Dr. Doyle, and I cannot allow another tragedy."

CHAPTER 25

The golden afternoon had turned into a blustery evening in Oxford. Tea had been served and ingested, and there was time before dinner to finish the last tasks of the day. Students bent over their final essays and dons scanned the galley proofs of their essays. Farmers packed up their stalls in the Covered Market and led their patient animals back home, where supper awaited them. Shopkeepers rearranged their stock to attract the last customers before closing.

Inspector Truscott sat in the Blue Boar and moodily contemplated the results of the day's activities. "We're no forrader than we were this morning," he complained to Sergeant Everett.

"We know Ingram was a wrong 'un," Everett consoled him.

"We knew that last night," Truscott said glumly.

"And we know that at least one of those lads at Christ Church must have moved that body," Everett added.

"And every time we try to question those same lads, the Dean pokes his long nose in or that Dodgson or the Scottish doctor . . ."

"Doyle." Everett furnished the name.

"Aye. Doyle. He turns up everywhere you look. If it weren't

for knowing that he's never been in Oxford before, I'd have put him at the head of my list."

Constable Effingham approached the pair with a folded note and an expression of suppressed amusement.

"This just come over from Christ Church," he announced.

Inspector Truscott opened the note and snorted in disgust. "Dean Liddell begs to inform me that he's found the three students who moved the body and is dealing with it according to University principles."

"And we know what they are," Sergeant Everett said. "Did any of 'em admit to killing Ingram?"

Truscott folded the note and put it into his breast pocket. "The Dean did not see fit to inform the police of that little bit of news." He took another pull at his beer mug.

Constable Effingham offered another bit of information. "There was near murder done this afternoon in Christ Church Meadows," he told his chief. "Three ladies in a punt got in the way of the rowers, and one of 'em nearly drowned. That Scottish chap got her breathing again though."

"Doyle again?" Inspector Truscott's eyebrows rose and fell.

"He does get about, doesn't he," Everett commented. "Does the Dean say who his undergraduate body snatchers are?"

"He does not," Inspector Truscott snarled. "But I can guess. Farlow, who is Berwick's heir."

"And I'll be bound one of the other two is Chatsworth. Youngest son of Lord Digby," Everett furnished. "Usually seen in company with Farlow."

Inspector Truscott threw coins onto the table. "I am going to have a word with those two, and this time I will not be balked!" He strode out of the pub, determined to complete his investigation before dinnertime.

Mr. Dodgson and Dr. Doyle were at Tom Gate when Inspector Truscott and Sergeant Everett marched down St. Aldgates.

"I want to see Lord Farlow," Truscott demanded.

Before the porter could respond, a major commotion erupted in the street. A small cart, led by a donkey, had cut across the path of the omnibus, with much stamping and snorting on the part of the horses and braying and kicking on the part of the donkey.

"Wot d'yer think yer doin', yer young bletherskite!"

"Get that donkey out o' here!"

"What is going on?" Mr. Dodgson asked fretfully, as the boy in charge of the donkey accosted the porter.

"I've got a card 'ere for a Mr. Dodgson," he announced. "A lady up by Norham Gardens give it me and said I was to deliver it to Mr. Dodgson and 'e would give me a penny." He thrust the card at the astonished porter, who passed it over to Mr. Dodgson, who duly rewarded the boy and examined the offering carefully.

"This seems to be one of your wife's calling cards," Mr. Dodgson said.

"There's something on the back," Dr. Doyle noticed.

" 'Miss Laurel knows something. Come quickly.' " Mr. Dodgson read. "Oh dear. Inspector, you must go to Lady Margaret Hall immediately."

"And why should I do that, sir?" Inspector Truscott asked truculently.

"Because this communication from Mrs. Doyle leads me to suspect that she has found out something that may be of the greatest importance to your investigations!" Mr. Dodgson began to sputter, a sure sign of mental agitation. "It is imp-perative that you t-take a carriage and get t-to Lady M-Margaret Hall as quickly as p-possible!"

Inspector Truscott frowned. "If you have information, sir, you should go through the proper channels . . ."

Dr. Doyle interrupted him. "Mr. Dodgson, I thought you told me that Touie would be in no danger."

Mr. Dodgson looked more and more distressed. "I was mistaken. I did not realize that a certain person could be that desperate."

"If any harm comes to my wife because you are deliberately being obstructive, Inspector . . ." Dr. Doyle ignored the lowering clouds and started loping up St. Aldgates to rescue his lady from whatever was about to attack her at Lady Margaret Hall.

"Very well, sir, if you will have it so. Everett!"

Sergeant Everett saluted. "Yes, sir?"

"Call out the carriage and take it to . . . where is this Lady Margaret Hall?"

"At the north end of the College Park Gardens, in Norham Gardens," Mr. Dodgson told him. "And hurry!"

Hurry was the last thing possible at that hour. St. Aldgates was filled with carts and carriages, bath chairs and walkers, as the wind began to blow in earnest and clouds boiled up over the horizon. Rain was imminent, and the most important thing was to get under cover.

Inspector Truscott hurried after the impetuous Dr. Doyle. "You don't know where you're going, sir," he pointed out.

"Show me the way, then!" Dr. Doyle exclaimed. "And if this town's police allotment does not run to a carriage, I'll take a hack!"

"There's no need to be in such a state, sir," Inspector Truscott said.

Dr. Doyle turned on him fiercely. "My wife is in danger," he repeated. "I can walk, or I can ride; but I will go and get her! Now!"

"Then you'd best come with us, sir," Sergeant Everett said, leading the frantic husband around the lanes to the stable, where the Oxford Constabulary's sole brougham stood, with a stolid-looking horse ready to be harnessed.

Dr. Doyle had to watch as the horse and the carriage were put together, while he imagined the worst that could happen to his beloved. What were they doing in that women's college that could lead Mr. Dodgson to conclude that Touie was risking her life?

"Step up, Doctor," Inspector Truscott announced. There was only room for a police driver on the box. Dr. Doyle and the two policemen had to sit in the malodorous interior, meant for carting obstreperous drunkards or rioting students to the town lockup.

The streets of Oxford were jammed with vehicles, as the rain began in earnest. Umbrellas startled the horses, which made the tangle of carts, carriages, omnibuses, and drays nearly impassable.

A stream of water gushed down High Street, as the horse splashed mud and muck over the passersby. Students of all ages, workingmen and tradesmen, all added to the hubbub by shouting, which agitated the horse even more.

"Can't this thing go any faster?" Dr. Doyle shouted out. "I'd do better on foot!"

"The rain's got the drains backed up," Sergeant Everett reported. "Once we get clear of Turl we should do better."

Dr. Doyle listened to the rain beating on the roof of the carriage and fretted. What did Miss Laurel know that made it so important to speak to her? How did she fit into this Wonderland of blackmail and murder.

Dr. Doyle wished he could contact Touie through the medium of thought projection. Since he could not, he sat in the carriage and worried. He wanted to rush to her side, to protect her from danger, and instead he was cooped up in the carriage with the two policemen, while the rain poured down.

"Take St. Giles!" Truscott ordered. "It's not as direct, but there's no getting through Longwall at this hour."

The driver turned the carriage, and the horse broke into an animated trot up the broad avenue that led toward the newer sector of Oxford. Here were the houses that had been built to accommodate those dons who had chosen to marry and raise families, once they had been given the dispensation to do so. Dr. Doyle peered out the grimy window of the police brougham.

"Is it much farther?"

Inspector Truscott patted his arm. "We'll get there, sir, no fear. What harm can come to your lady in a women's college?"

CHAPTER 26

❦

Once she had sent her note, Touie had joined her new friends in the small garden behind the house. Neat herbaceous borders marked the edges of the lawns. A tall hedge shielded the ladies from the view of rowers on the Holywell Mill Stream.

"What a charming spot!" Touie enthused.

"Yes, isn't it?" Dianna agreed.

"Miss Wordsworth is very strict about our using the gardens," Mary said. "We may walk, but we must always wear our hats and gloves."

"Such a bother," Gertrude declared. "It's not as if we were flaunting ourselves out in the streets."

"Gertrude!" Mary turned to Touie with a smile. "Gertrude is something of a firebrand, Mrs. Doyle. She's always doing something outrageous."

"Like accosting Mr. Dodgson in the Cathedral," Dianna said. "Or punting on the Cherwell instead of the mill stream."

"So that was her idea," Touie said. She looked up at the sky. Gray clouds were racing across the previously clear expanse of blue. "Oh dear, it looks as if it is coming on to rain!"

As if to answer her, the wind picked up Mary's straw hat and sent it wheeling across the lawns.

"We'd better get indoors before we all catch our deaths," Touie said, clutching at her hat. "Oh dear, here comes the rain!"

Sure enough, the first fat drops sent the girls running through the door that led from the gardens to the vestibule behind the stairs to the upper floors of the house. Touie hesitated, as Gertrude, Mary, and Dianna headed for the stairs.

"Come on up, Mrs. Doyle," Gertrude invited her. "We have to change for dinner, and you can talk to us while we do."

Miss Laurel shook her head at them in disapproval as they dashed toward their rooms. "You look like a set of hoydens," she scolded. "What must Mrs. Doyle think of you?"

"Tush!" Gertrude pushed her red-gold hair out of her eyes. Mary's neatly pinned chignon did not seem to be the worse for wear, but the wind had given Dianna's curls the general aspect of Medusa's mop of snakes.

"Come up and talk to us," Gertrude invited, and Touie followed them to the upper reaches of the house, where each girl had her own chamber. The three gravitated to Miss Bell's room, a large corner suite dominated by a four-poster bed. A dressing table with a mirror stood between the two windows that looked out on the gardens, while a wardrobe held Miss Bell's clothing. The room seemed to be cluttered with books, papers, and sporting equipment. A pair of foils and a cricket bat were propped up in one corner, while a tripod and box camera lurked in the niche between the door and the wardrobe. The extreme modernity of the house was demonstrated by the nearby commode and bathtub. Clearly, Lady Margaret Hall was a new addition to the architectural hodgepodge of Oxford.

Touie edged into the bedroom with a smile and perched on Miss Bell's bed. "I hope you do not mind," she said apologetically. "But I would like to dress my own hair, and I wish I had my evening dress. One likes to change for dinner, even if it is only to put on another pair of gloves."

"You'd have to ask Miss Laurel for gloves." Gertrude laughed. "She's got so many pairs!"

253

"It's her hands," Mary explained, in her soothing murmur. "She must have had a dreadful life as a child. Her hands are quite red and chapped."

"Oh, the poor thing," Dianna said with true compassion.

"I notice, you always address her as 'Miss,' whereas you refer to each other by your Christian names," Touie remarked.

The three girls exchanged looks. "It's just that she's so much older than we," Mary said at last. "And she's very shy. She never walks out with the rest of us. I suppose it comes of having been a governess. The governess in a great house is always at a disadvantage."

"It must be quite difficult for them," Touie said sympathetically. "After all, a governess is a lady and cannot associate with the other servants."

Gertrude made a rude noise through a mouthful of hairpins. "It's grossly unfair," she said. "My cousin's tutor always sits at table with company, but my governess was obliged to eat her meals alone in her room or with me in the nursery."

Touie considered the plight of the governess as she took down her hair and began to rearrange it. "It seems quite different in novels," she said. "Of course, writers must make things interesting. My husbands writes stories, you see, and he reads them to me."

"But does he put a governess in them?" Dianna wanted to know.

Touie had to admit that governesses did not appear frequently in Dr. Doyle's adventure tales. She turned to Dianna. "Miss Cahill, a thought has occurred to me. Is it possible that the maidservant who took care of you at Mr. Roswell's house might have gone on, so to speak, to another nursery?"

"I suppose she could have," Dianna said blankly.

"Because, you see, the question still remains: Who knew about the photograph and what became of the one Mr. Dodgson sent to your uncle's house?" Touie went on. "Arthur told me that the man who was found behind Christ Church, the scout, had collected a number of incriminating documents, things that people had thrown away, that could be used for blackmail."

"Do you mean that the person behind the verses that Dianna got was a scout? I don't believe it!" Gertrude said scornfully.

"I don't think he wrote the verses," Touie said. "He probably acted as a courier, coming here with the letters and taking the copy to the printer. But he must have known that there was a photograph, even though he did not have a copy himself, otherwise, why should he remove Mr. Dodgson's copy from his albums?" She looked at the girls, who nodded in agreement.

Touie shoved in one last hairpin and put her hands in her lap. "Now, let's look at this logically, as Mr. Dodgson would say. What are the facts?"

"Only that the photograph was taken when I was six, and no one even knew about it but me and Mr. Dodgson," Dianna quavered.

"And the maid," Gertrude reminded her.

"Can you recall anything about that visit that you haven't told us?" Touie pleaded with the girl. "Anything at all?"

Dianna screwed her face up in an agony of thought. "It was so long ago!" she protested. "Mostly I remember being very cold. My uncle Roswell was very strict about having fires in bedrooms. He thought it was wasteful and led to a weakened constitution."

"Mr. Dodgson's tea party must have been like heaven," Gertrude giggled. "He keeps his rooms very warm. Otherwise you would never have been able to take your clothes off."

"What about the maid? The one who acted as your nurse for the time of your visit?" Touie prompted her. "Think!"

Dianna sighed and closed her eyes again. "Let's see . . . she wasn't all that old, although I suppose she seemed ancient to me. She had some kind of flower name . . ."

"Rose?" Gertrude questioned her. "Lily?"

"Daisy!" Dianna cried out triumphantly. "That was it! Daisy!"

"Well that is something," Touie said, with great satisfaction. "Her name was Daisy, and she worked for Mr. Roswell fifteen years ago."

"Not much to go on." Gertrude sighed.

"It is enough for the police," Touie said. "They can find out what happened to this Daisy person."

"Do you think she might be here in Oxford?" Dianna asked.

"It is certainly possible," Touie said. "If Daisy knew about the photograph, would she have told anyone about it?"

"Servants always gossip," Mary said, with the air of one who is totally familiar with the ways of the downstairs staff.

"So that the servants in Mr. Roswell's house would have also known about the photograph," Gertrude pointed out.

"Perhaps," Touie said. "Daisy would have eaten in the kitchen with the rest of the servants, but as a very young maid, she would hardly have been in a position to speak to them. She might well have kept this adventure to herself."

"Except that the copy of the photograph was sent to Mr. Roswell's house," Gertrude pointed out. "So the servants would have seen it then."

"And what would they have done with it?" Touie asked.

"They couldn't very well give it to Uncle Roswell," Dianna said. "Uncle Roswell is quite strict. He's got prints on his walls, of course, framed chromos of Mr. Wesley and copies of famous paintings, but nothing without clothes. Not even angels," she added.

"And at the same time, they could not destroy it," Touie concluded. "So Daisy must have kept it."

"And she showed it to someone," Gertrude said.

"But who?" Dianna asked.

"Whom." Miss Laurel appeared at the door to Gertrude's room.

"If you insist," Dianna said, with a twist of her lips. "What is it, Miss Laurel?"

"Miss Wordsworth would like Mrs. Doyle to join her in her sitting room before dinner," Miss Laurel stated.

"How very kind of Miss Wordsworth," Touie said, with a smile. She turned back to the girls. "If you can think of anything else, do let me know. Arthur and I must leave in the morning, so we will turn over whatever we find out to Mr. Dodgson. He will inform the police, of course." Touie stepped aside to let Miss Laurel precede her down the winding staircase.

"What have you learned about Miss Cahill's dilemma?" Miss Laurel asked breathlessly.

"Only that the one who wrote the verses must have been one of the students at Christ Church," Touie said. "Since the man found behind the college was one of their servants, I suppose he had been involved as a go-between, a messenger, nothing more than that."

"You think so?" Miss Laurel asked.

"Of course," Touie said carefully, as they reached the bottom of the stairs, "if he was a very wicked person, he might even have taken something written by one of the students as a prank, what they call a rag, and put it together with the photograph himself and threatened someone with it."

"But there would be no point to that, would there?" Miss Laurel's voice had taken on a sharper tone.

"No. I don't suppose there would be," Touie said. "If Miss Cahill was to be removed from Oxford so that someone else could receive Mr. Roswell's money, then the person who benefits from the blackmail would have to be this other heir. Except that Miss Cahill is quite sure that there isn't any."

"Is she?" Miss Laurel dismissed Miss Cahill with a sniff of disdain. "How would she know anything about it? She was only a child."

"Indeed? How would you know that, unless . . ." Touie looked at Miss Laurel with growing concern. "Unless you were the person delegated to care for the child when she visited without her own nurse."

Touie began to chatter, thinking aloud, trying to distract the increasingly agitated woman while she looked around the vestibule for a means of escape. Her thoughts raced frantically. Had Arthur gotten her note? Was he able to act on it? Where was he?

"I wondered at the name 'Daphne Laurel,' " Touie went on, trying to sound like a scatterbrained fool and wishing that she could use the mental powers Arthur was so certain existed so that she could communicate with him on the astral plane. "I am not a classical scholar, but Arthur and I have been reading Mr.

Hawthorne's clever adaptation of the Greek stories. Daphne was a nymph changed into a laurel tree to escape the attentions of Apollo."

"You know a great deal, Mrs. Doyle," Miss Laurel hissed. Her sharp features seemed fiendish in the half-light that filtered in through the doors to the garden. A sudden flash of lightning and a crack of thunder made Touie jump.

Miss Laurel edged closer. "What have you told that interfering husband of yours?"

"I haven't had the chance to tell him anything yet," Touie said, trying to step away from the other woman. "I suspected that you were the maid who took Miss Cahill to Mr. Dodgson's rooms when I had a chance to think it over last night. You said that she was a clever and pretty child, but how could you know that if you had only met her when she and you came to Lady Margaret Hall? And you just mentioned picking up clothes and washing little boys. A governess would never have to do that, but a nursemaid would."

"And what if I have been a maid?" Miss Laurel snapped out. "If a man may better himself, may not a woman do the same?"

"There is no reason to think otherwise," Touie told her, hoping that her calm voice would soothe her adversary until rescue arrived. "But you took on the position of governess under false pretenses. You use a name that is not your own."

"Many people change their names," Miss Laurel countered. "Miss Roswell became Miss Mary Rose on the stage."

"And her brother cast her aside and would not even see her, even after she became Lady Berwick," Touie said. She was now backed up against the garden door.

"Hypocrites! All of them!" Miss Laurel was working herself into a rage. Touie tried to slide away, but Miss Laurel grabbed her by the sleeve and pulled her around. "After the little girl left, I asked if I could find another nursery place, and Mrs. Roswell sent me off to Berwick to tend the little boy."

"Mr. Farlow? The one who tried to push Miss Cahill into the river?" Touie tried to pull away, but Miss Laurel's grip tightened on her arms.

"Master Nevil. A naughty boy, always running off, looking about at things he shouldn't. And the goings-on when my lord and lady were there! But let one of us slip, and we'd be turned off without a character!"

"I see." Touie tried once more to bring Miss Laurel back to reality. "You were a servant at Berwick and so was Ingram."

"Oh, he was a one!" Miss Laurel laughed harshly. "He had all of us under his thumb, but he promised that I was the only one he truly loved."

"And you were caught," Touie said.

"By little Master Nevil."

"And turned off."

"Without a penny to my name!" Miss Laurel's voice throbbed tragically.

"And you decided to seek other employment." Touie tried to slip out of that deathly tight grip on her arm. "But not as a nurse-maid. You decided to become a governess."

"I'd been sitting there when Master Nevil had his lessons. I'd learned as much as he. I could read and write and figure, and I could take Master Nevil's book of questions with me as he went off to school." Miss Laurel shook Touie, as if to make her take notice. "A nursemaid is nothing. A governess is a lady."

"And no one questioned your qualifications?" Touie tried to pull away, but Miss Laurel held tight. They revolved around the little vestibule in a weird sort of dance, until Miss Laurel's back was to the stairs again.

"Why should they?" Miss Laurel sneered. "I was hired to instruct the little boys in their letters and numbers and set them on the road to school. If it weren't for Mrs. Toynbee and the Women's Educational Alliance I'd be doing it still."

"But you passed the examination and found a place here," Touie said. "And your secret was safe."

"And then he came!" Miss Laurel's voice rose to a shriek. "I saw him once when he came with a letter. I knew it was him!"

"Ingram?" Touie looked over Miss Laurel's shoulder. Someone was coming down the stairs. Miss Laurel's grip tightened as she pulled Touie closer.

259

"He didn't know me until he saw me at tea in Mr. Dodgson's rooms," she whispered. "Then he told me to meet him under the bridge."

"And you killed him," Touie said.

"I hit him with the paddle," Miss Laurel admitted. "And now I have to kill you!"

She released Touie's arms and reached for her neck. Touie ducked under the other woman's outstretched arms as a shaft of lightning seemed to pierce the sky. A clap of thunder resounded through the house, covering Touie's cry for help.

Miss Laurel grabbed at Touie again, catching her by the sleeve and turning her around. Touie fended off the other woman's blows, kicking and scratching whatever she could find. They reeled back and forth in the confines of the hall until Miss Laurel forced Touie against the stairs.

Touie kicked the other woman's legs out from under her. They fell on the stairs, unaware of a third pair of shoes on the riser above them.

Miss Laurel's strong hands were around Touie's throat, squeezing. Touie tried to breathe but could not. Suddenly the pressure on her throat was relaxed as Miss Laurel cried out and fell over her.

Gertrude stood on the stairs, triumphantly waving her cricket bat. "I heard the ruckus and ran back for this!" she announced, as the rest of the girls emerged from their rooms to see what the noise was about.

Mary and Dianna rushed to support Touie, while Gertrude stood over Miss Laurel, ready to strike if the other woman should show any more indication of violence.

"What is this disturbance?" Miss Wordsworth had also emerged from her private sitting room.

Before Touie could answer, there was a knock at the door.

"It's Inspector Truscott of the police," the scout on duty announced, as the rescue party tramped in.

"Arthur!" Touie ran for the comfort of her husband's arms.

"Touie! Are you all right?" Dr. Doyle fussed over his wife's bruises.

"Yes, Arthur," Touie managed to rasp out, "I am quite all right, but Miss Bell hit Miss Laurel on the head with her cricket bat."

Dr. Doyle bent over the fallen woman. "A wicked shot," he pronounced. "Miss Laurel should recover her senses soon enough."

As if in answer to his diagnosis, Miss Laurel groaned and tried to pull herself into a sitting position. Gertrude stood ready to defend her new friend, but there was no need. Miss Laurel looked about, saw the horrified expressions on the faces of the women around her, and buried her face in her hands in abject humiliation.

"Whatever is going on?" Miss Wordsworth looked at the male invasion of her feminine domain.

"I am very sorry to tell you that it was Miss Laurel who killed that man, Ingram," Touie said.

"What!" "Why?" "Miss Laurel?" The girls on the stairs burst into startled speech. Miss Wordsworth faced the police with her usual aplomb.

"I think you had better come into the sitting room, gentlemen, and explain yourselves." Miss Wordsworth eyed the disheveled combatants. Touie's hair had come down in the struggle, and she was now attempting to put it right again. Miss Laurel had tucked her bodice into her skirt band and smoothed down her hair.

Miss Wordsworth led the policemen, Dr. and Mrs. Doyle, and Miss Laurel into her private sanctuary. "Now," she said, taking her favorite seat, "will someone please tell me what is going on here?"

CHAPTER 27

❦

Inspector Truscott bowed slightly toward Miss Wordsworth. "Mr. Dodgson of Christ Church sent us. He seemed to think that Mrs. Doyle might be in some danger."

All eyes turned to Touie, who was still trying to put her hair straight after the strenuous activity had tumbled it down. "It was Miss Laurel who sent that man, Ingram, into the river," Touie explained.

"And she tried to kill Mrs. Doyle," Gertrude burst out, from her position at the door. Miss Wordsworth pointedly rose, closed the door in the faces of the eager students, and resumed her seat.

"There is no need to upset the undergraduates," she said firmly. "Now, Miss Laurel, why did you attack Mrs. Doyle?"

Miss Laurel had recovered some of her customary reserve. "I apologize to Mrs. Doyle," she said at last. "I was overwrought."

"Then you did attack my wife!" Dr. Doyle was incensed.

"It was a momentary madness," Miss Laurel protested.

"Momentary madness?" Dr. Doyle echoed.

"I found out she wasn't a governess," Touie said hoarsely.

"That's no reason to try to kill my wife!" Dr. Doyle turned on the other woman fiercely.

Miss Wordsworth put up a hand for silence. "Miss Laurel, have you anything to say in your own defense?"

Inspector Truscott cleared his throat apologetically. "I must warn you, Miss Laurel, that anything you say now may be used against you in a court of law."

"Is she being arrested?" Miss Wordsworth demanded.

"Mrs. Doyle has made an accusation, ma'am. We must question this woman as to her involvement in the death of James Ingram," Truscott stated.

"But must it be in a police station?" Miss Wordsworth asked, her voice rising in disdain.

"Perhaps we could question Miss Laurel in Mr. Dodgson's rooms at Christ Church," Dr. Doyle offered. "Dean Liddell will want to be present and so will Mr. Seward, the proctor, acting for the University."

Miss Wordsworth literally rose to the occasion. "In that case, I shall accompany you to Christ Church, Inspector. Mr. Dodgson is a good friend, and I cannot imagine why he would accuse one of my undergraduates of a heinous crime."

"He hasn't accused her," Dr. Doyle pointed out.

"She told me herself that she hit the man with a punt paddle," Touie added.

Miss Wordsworth was already giving orders. "Miss Johnson, you may take my place at dinner. I am going out."

"Now, ma'am?" Her second-in-command was aghast.

"There is no time to be lost. Since no one else will come to her assistance, it is clearly incumbent upon me to escort Miss Laurel to Mr. Dodgson's rooms and, if necessary, to procure legal aid for her."

"But . . . dinner?" Miss Johnson could not conceive of anyone leaving before dinner.

"I will have a light supper when I return," Miss Wordsworth said grandly. "Inspector, if you do not have room in your carriage, I shall have to call a hack."

"I think we can squeeze you in, ma'am. Sergeant Everett will have to ride on the box, with the driver." Inspector Truscott glanced at Miss Laurel, who refused to acknowledge his presence.

Miss Wordsworth and Miss Laurel were handed into the carriage ceremoniously by Sergeant Everett. Dr. Doyle sat with Touie, glaring at the woman who had dared to choke his wife.

The traffic had thinned out, as the rain turned into a chilly drizzle that penetrated even the carriage. Touie shivered, as much from the sudden cold as from the realization that she had nearly been choked to death.

Telling met the carriage at Tom Gate. He blandly accepted the presence of three women within the all-male preserve of Christ Church at the unheard-of hour of seven-thirty at night.

"Mr. Dodgson's compliments and would you please go directly to his rooms? Dean Liddell and Mr. Seward are waiting for you." Telling's eyes widened as he saw the rotund form of Miss Wordsworth, followed by the tall, lean Miss Laurel.

Inspector Truscott nodded to the driver. "Wilkins, tell Effingham his wife's wanted. Have her come over here as quickly as she can." He turned to Miss Wordsworth. "Mrs. Effingham is a very respectable woman, ma'am. The wife of one of our constables. She can take this, um, lady, in charge."

Telling led the way up to Mr. Dodgson's rooms, maintaining his professional dignity with great difficulty. He opened the door to annouce the late visitors: "Inspector Truscott, Dr. and Mrs. Doyle, Miss Wordsworth, Miss Laurel."

Mr. Dodgson blinked as Miss Wordsworth bustled into the room. "Miss Wordsworth? What are you doing here?"

"I am looking after the welfare of one of my students, Mr. Dodgson," Miss Wordsworth said, with immense dignity. "Miss Laurel has been accused of a crime, and I am here to see justice done." She looked about for a seat and defiantly took the second armchair next to the one in which Dean Liddell was enthroned, beckoning Miss Laurel to stand near her.

"This is rather difficult . . . ," Mr. Dodgson began.

"You summoned me here, before dinner, to tell me that you had solved this problem," Dean Liddell reminded him. "We are expected at the High Table, Mr. Dodgson."

"I am very sorry, but this could not wait." Mr. Dodgson turned to Miss Laurel. "You see, it was to you that Ingram addressed that extraordinary speech yesterday."

"I?" Miss Laurel echoed.

"What was it, precisely, that he said?" Mr. Dodgson turned to Dr. Doyle for elucidation.

"I believe the exact words were, 'I don't take pictures of little girls, and I don't pretend to be what I'm not.' "

"A most unusual accusation," Mr. Dodgson said. "I have not pursued my photographic interests for many years, certainly not while Ingram was in residence, and I have never pretended to be anything other than what I am."

"There's the matter of your pseudonym," Dr. Doyle pointed out.

"That is not a matter of pretense," Mr. Dodgson rebutted. "That is a matter of privacy. It occurred to me that Ingram was not addressing me at all but someone behind me."

"That could have been anyone," Miss Laurel said, with some of her previous aplomb.

Mr. Dodgson ignored the interruption. "But who, precisely, was behind me? None of the three young ladies was anything other than what she was supposed to be. I am acquainted with Miss Talbot's family. Miss Bell's origins are equally well-known. As for Miss Cahill, her parentage is vouched for by none other than our dean." Dean Liddell bowed in acknowledgement. "But what about Miss Laurel? What do we actually know about her?"

Miss Wordsworth bristled. "Miss Laurel was recommended to me by Mrs. Toynbee, who is a personal friend and a benefactor of Lady Margaret Hall. She told me that Miss Laurel had been with Lady Berwick, among others."

"But not as a governess," Touie broke in. "She was the nurse-maid. And her name's not Daphne Laurel either. It's Daisy something."

"I was born Daisy Lowell," Miss Laurel admitted defiantly.

"Is this true?" Miss Wordsworth gazed on her star pupil in growing horror and disbelief. "How could you!"

Miss Laurel's defiance melted under that reproachful look. "I couldn't go on the streets," she pleaded. "I had no other choice."

Touie regarded Miss Laurel with sympathy. "It may sound dreadful, but I must applaud you, Miss Laurel, for your fortitude. You were in a dreadful pickle, and there are so many others who would have become something far worse."

"Quite so," Mr. Dodgson said. "Miss Laurel might have made an excellent tutor had not James Ingram come back into her life."

"Back?" Inspector Truscott looked puzzled. "When did he come into it at all?"

"At Berwick Place, I imagine," Mr. Dodgson said, looking at Miss Laurel. "Is that not so? You were sent on by Mrs. Roswell to her sister-in-law, Lady Berwick."

"And where does she come into it?" Truscott demanded.

"Lady Berwick is the sister of the philanthropic but puritanical Mr. Roswell," Mr. Dodgson explained, "who has offered a generous gift to any of his relations who attain high honors here at Oxford."

Miss Wordsworth was still unsatisfied. "What does this have to do with the wretched man who was found yesterday?"

"James Ingram was a footman at Berwick Place," Mr. Dodgson said. "Inspector Truscott will undoubtedly find evidence to that effect."

"And he was with Lady Berwick, who came to the Roswell house the day that Miss Cahill's parents took her to tea," Touie put it together.

"When she was merely Miss Roswell, Lady Berwick had had the temerity to perform on the stage," Mr. Dodgson reminded them. "The theater is anathema to Mr. Roswell, and he cast her off completely, even after she had attained a title. She was coming to flaunt herself and that title in her brother's face, and Miss Cahill was to be gotten out of the line of fire, to use a military expression."

"But what's all this ancient history got to do with what happened to Ingram?" Truscott asked.

"On that occasion I took a photograph of Miss Cahill, undressed," Mr. Dodgson confessed. "It was not a good photograph, but I made two copies. One I sent, as I always do, to the child. The other I put into my personal albums, and to tell the truth, I forgot that it was there. I was much occupied with other things. I was writing my second *Alice* adventure, and there were college matters to attend to." He turned to Miss Laurel. "Perhaps you can tell us what happened to the copy I sent to Mr. Roswell's house?"

Miss Laurel moistened her lips. "I took it," she whispered. She went on, peering up into Mr. Dodgson's face. "I was on my way out, to go to Berwick Place, when the postman came," she explained. "And he put the post into my hands, and I saw one packet from Christ Church, and I thought that must be the photographs. And I was curious to see how they'd come out, and I saw the one with Miss Dianna, as nature made her, so to speak. And I thought, if Mr. Roswell sees this, he'll do to her like he did to his sister, cast her off, and her parents with her, and it will make poor Mrs. Roswell unhappy. So I took that photograph out of the packet, left the rest, and went on my way."

"No one knew that you had abstracted the print?" Mr. Dodgson pursued the point.

"Not at Mr. Roswell's house," Miss Laurel said. "But later, at Berwick, James and I were talking about some of the goings-on with the grand folk that Lord and Lady Berwick had down; and he called them a pack of liars and hypocrites, who wouldn't let the servants do what they did themselves, and how he was going to make them all pay for it one day. And I agreed and told him about Mr. Dodgson and the pictures. And so he knew that there was a photograph and who had it." Tears welled up in her eyes. "I never thought he'd do what he did with it! When we parted—"

"Ah, yes," Mr. Dodgson interrupted her. "You and Ingram. The footman and the nursemaid. Footmen are not usually allowed into the nursery, but Ingram seems to have been something of a privileged character at Berwick."

"He would be serving in the drawing room when I brought little Master Nevil down to see his parents when they were in residence," Miss Laurel said. "I was not bad looking then, although quite young. Too young to realize the sort of man James Ingram was," she added bitterly.

"He took advantage of you," Touie said sympathetically.

"And when the boy found you out, both of you were dismissed." Mr. Dodgson was not so sympathetic.

"I was turned off without a character and without a penny," Miss Laurel said resentfully. "So I took Master Nevil's books and answered an advertisement for a governess."

"Whereas Ingram got a gold watch and a much better position in London, at White's," Dr. Doyle finished for her, "where he could continue in his career of discovering secrets about noble gentlemen, which he could later exploit."

"Lord Berwick is a notorious gambler," Mr. Dodgson murmured. "I daresay he employed his old servant in many ways, not necessarily to the best interests of the club."

"One of 'em being to find out the likely odds on rowers in Oxford for Eights Week." Inspector Truscott took over. "We can't pin anything on any of 'em, of course. Gentlemen will wager on almost anything, and it's not illegal to get inside information and use it to shift the odds to their advantage."

"However," Dr. Doyle said, with a knowing grin, "I don't think it will do them any good now that the scheme has been unmasked."

"Still, it don't explain why Ingram landed in the river," Truscott said. "Or why this woman is accused of doing it."

"He must have tried to get information from her," Touie said. "Isn't that right, Miss Laurel?"

Miss Laurel nodded. "I met him under Magdalen Bridge at six o'clock," she said. "He was dreadful. He threatened to expose me to Miss Wordsworth as a fraud, a maid pretending to be a lady. He wanted me to find out secrets for him, to read letters and steal drafts of other letters that might otherwise go into the dustbin so that he could use them later."

"That being his *modus operandi*," Dr. Doyle said smugly to Inspector Truscott. "Ingram seems to have been a most enterprising sort. He could lift small objects to pawn, purloin unfinished letters from wastebaskets and dustbins, and steal college wine, all fueled by his hatred and resentment of his position."

Miss Laurel swallowed hard. "I told him I would not do it. I would not spy for him, I would not be his slave or anything else.

Then he said that if I did not do as he asked, he would see that I was denounced as an impostor and read out of college, and that the only thing left for me would be the streets, except that no one would have me!"

"And then you hit him?" Mr. Dodgson asked.

Miss Laurel nodded. Inspector Truscott stepped forward.

"Miss Laurel, or Lowell, I must inform you that if you speak now, anything you say may be taken down and used in evidence against you."

Miss Wordsworth had been listening carefully. Now she said, "Miss Laurel, how could you even think that we would have believed such a story? Or, even if you had been a servant, that we would have read you out of college? It would be against everything that we are trying to do here!" She glared at Inspector Truscott. "You need say nothing more, my dear, until I have spoken to my solicitor."

Miss Laurel shook her head. "No, Miss Wordsworth. It is true. I hit him with the nearest thing I could find, which was the paddle of one of the punts lined up under Magdalen Bridge. He went into the water, and I hit him again and again. Then I threw the paddle into the river and ran back here."

"I see." Miss Wordsworth rose to her feet. "Inspector, take Miss Laurel if you must, but I will see to it that she has the best defense we can find for her. She was clearly trying to defend herself from a bully."

There was a knock at the door. Telling announced, "Sergeant Everett and Mrs. Effingham."

Inspector Truscott stepped forward. "Miss Daisy Lowell, I arrest you in the name of the Queen. I must warn you that anything you say can and will be taken down and used against you in a court of law. Sergeant Everett, you may take the prisoner."

A stout woman in a drab dress and drabber bonnet stepped forward. Miss Laurel raised her chin and prepared to leave with the air of Mary Queen of Scots being led to the block.

Miss Wordsworth asked, "Where is she being taken?"

"Town Hall, ma'am," Inspector Truscott told her.

Miss Wordsworth rose majestically and patted Miss Laurel's

hand. "I shall send for my solicitor," she told the stricken woman. "You were clearly defending yourself against a blackmailer, a thorough rogue." She turned to Mr. Dodgson. "I would have thought better of you, Mr. Dodgson."

"It was not I who struck Ingram," Mr. Dodgson said, with immense dignity. "However, we are not finished yet. Inspector, do not leave. We have one more matter to deal with. Miss Wordsworth, you may not wish to stay. This is an internal matter, pertinent to the House."

Miss Wordsworth sailed out after Miss Laurel. "You shall inform me in the morning," she told Mr. Dodgson.

"And now," Mr. Dodgson said, once the ladies had left, "I can tell you who really killed that wretched man."

CHAPTER 28

Inspector Truscott glowered at Mr. Dodgson. "Do you mean to tell us that the woman didn't do it?"

"Not at all," Mr. Dodgson corrected him. "Miss Laurel, or Lowell, certainly contributed to Ingram's untimely death. She hit him several times with a punt paddle then ran off to leave him to drown in the river."

"But the blows on the head weren't enough to kill him," Dr. Doyle objected. "They might have made him a bit groggy, but . . ."

"Mr. Chatsworth is here, sir." Telling interrupted them.

"Chatsworth?" Dean Liddell frowned. "What has he to do with this?"

Mr. Dodgson held up a hand for silence. "Telling, have Mr. Chatsworth come in."

Minnie Chatsworth had prepared himself for dining in Hall. He was in correct subfusc: dress suit, wingcollar, black gown, and mortarboard cap, with its distinctive tuft, indicating that he was the younger son of a peer. He regarded the assembled dignitaries with a lazy smile that faded as the silence grew.

"Good evening." Chatsworth looked about him and fixed

on Dean Liddell as the senior person present. "Er . . . I don't know what you want with me, sir. I only helped in the business, that's all."

"What business would that be?" Dean Liddell asked.

"Why, the rag about the body. That is why you sent for me, isn't it?" Chatsworth asked anxiously.

"There were some points about your story that I felt needed further explanation," Mr. Dodgson told him.

Chatsworth's hand went toward his breast pocket. "May I smoke, sir?"

"You may not." Mr. Dodgson turned to Inspector Truscott. "I believe you will find cigars in Mr. Chatsworth's pocket that match the ones found under. Magdalen Bridge."

Dr. Doyle stepped forward and took the cigar case from Chatsworth's pocket. He removed one of the distinctive cheroots and handed it to Inspector Truscott.

Chatsworth's smile had turned to a sneer. "What of it? Everyone smokes cigars."

"Not like these," Dr. Doyle said. "American. I noticed them when you and your companions were being interviewed earlier."

"I've had my men out," Inspector Truscott said gravely. "None of the shops near Oxford carry these cigars. Of course, it could be that an American visitor stood under Magdalen Bridge yesterday, but it's not likely."

Mr. Dodgson coughed to gain the floor again. "Ahem! May I see your hands, Mr. Chatsworth?"

"My hands?" Chatsworth looked at his interrogator in total disbelief.

"Your hands. You do not wear gloves, Mr. Chatsworth. You are a Hearty, a sportsman. They make it a point of not wearing gloves, unless the temperature demands it, and sometimes not even then. May I see your hands, sir?"

"This is ridiculous!" Chatsworth exposed the palms of his hands. "Are they clean, sir? Am I to be expected to pass a hygienic examination before being allowed to proceed to Hall?"

"Dr. Doyle, will you note the condition of Mr. Chatsworth's hands?"

Dr. Doyle frowned as he peered into the palms offered for his inspection. His frown deepened, and he produced his magnifying glass. "I note several small blisters and rough spots," he announced at last.

"Well, of course, you dunce! I'm on the rowing team!" Chatsworth clenched his fists.

"But you do not take an oar yourself," Mr. Dodgson pointed out. "You are the coxswain. You do not row; you exhort the others and give them the stroke. That is your specialty, is it not, Mr. Chatsworth? You do not take action yourself but aid and abet those who do. You instigate, you propel, you motivate, but you rarely take part in the physical activities of your friends. Except, of course, this once, when you decided to lend a hand, as it were, and finish what Miss Laurel had started."

"What!" Inspector Truscott gasped.

"Do you know what you are saying, sir?" Dean Liddell was quieter but no less appalled.

"Unfortunately, yes," Mr. Dodgson said. "Miss Laurel hit Ingram several times."

"There were three cuts on the man's scalp," Dr. Doyle confirmed. "None of them deep enough to have caused death."

"But as you told us before, enough to make him, er, groggy." Mr. Dodgson turned back to Chatsworth, who was trying to edge toward the door. The combined bulk of Sergeant Everett and Mr. Seward was enough to deter him.

"You were under Magdalen Bridge," Mr. Dodgson told the undergraduate. "You heard the discussion. You saw Miss Laurel hit Ingram, you saw him fall into the river. You could have pulled him out at that time, but you did not."

"Why should I?" Chatsworth shot back. "He was a filthy thief and a blackmailer."

"Indeed?" Mr. Dodgson's eyebrows rose. "And how would you know that, Mr. Chatsworth? Was Ingram blackmailing you?"

"No, of course not," Chatsworth said quickly. "I heard him threatening Nevil Farlow one day, that's all."

"And he was being employed to carry some very unpleasant messages to a young lady at Lady Margaret Hall," Mr. Dodgson went on. "A set of verses, of which you, Mr. Chatsworth were the instigator, if not the primary author."

"We didn't mean anything by it," Chatsworth said sulkily. "It was a rag, that's all, done for fun. Everybody writes squibs. Most of 'em are forgotten."

"Some are not." Mr. Dodgson quoted, " 'I do not love thee, Doctor Fell. / The reason why I cannot tell; / But this alone I know full well, / I do not love thee, Doctor Fell.' That particular verse is known to every schoolchild in England."

Chatsworth sniggered. Dean Liddell cleared his throat and the snigger died.

Dean Liddell's face grew grim. "Threatening young female students with disgrace is not a source of humor," he stated. "I have seen this attempt at levity; and I may inform you, sir, that whatever your motives, the result is contemptible. The verse is bad; the intention was worse. The matter was compounded when the verses were illustrated with Mr. Dodgson's photograph, which was, I may add, stolen property. What have you to say for yourself, sir?"

"I told Nev that it wouldn't work," Chatsworth pleaded.

"Did you know the purpose to which this piece of literature was to be used?" Mr. Dodgson asked.

"Well . . ." Chatsworth's courage failed under the unnerving glare of so many eyes. "We'd seen the girl in lectures, and Nev was furious because she was going to bag all of old Roswell's coin; and I only said that if she left Oxford, the old boy would be forced to look about and there Nev would be, waiting for him. Nev's a Blue, a triple Blue at that!" Chatsworth's voice took on a pleading whine. "Anyone with any sense would favor him over some fat girl, and I told him so."

"Which would be enough to set him firmly on his course," Mr. Dodgson said. "Let us return to last night's escapade. You saw Ingram fall. You went to observe him. He was in the water but had recovered his senses and was attempting to rise. At which point, you took action.

"You lifted an oar from the oarlock of the nearest rowing boat and used it to hold Ingram's head underwater until he ceased movement. Then you heard more steps and ducked back under the bridge.

"You saw your friend Nevil Farlow approaching the boats. You saw him pull Ingram out of the water. You then ran back to the House to be here before Lord Farlow."

"So you say," Chatsworth sneered. "Where's the proof?"

"Two cigars," Mr. Dodgson said. "You smoked two cigars, one while Miss Laurel had her interview, the second when Farlow approached the boats."

"I'll admit to seeing Nev under the bridge," Chatsworth said. "But you can't prove that I held that man under."

"Oh, but I can," Mr. Dodgson said. "Your hands are blistered and rough, although you do not touch the oars. The legs of your trousers will have weeds on them, which could only have been thrown up by the thrashing of the unfortunate man. Dr. Doyle pointed out that his fingernails showed signs of dirt. He was very much alive when Miss Laurel left him, and he was very dead when Mr. Farlow found him. You, Mr. Chatsworth, were the only one who could have held him under long enough to drown him."

"What? Little me?" Chatsworth cried out.

"According to Sergeant-Major Howard, you are an able gymnast and fencer," Dr. Doyle said. "All you had to do was push on the oar, and your friend would be free of a leech."

Chatsworth looked at the faces of the men in the room. "You still can't prove that I went anywhere near that man," he said.

"There is one piece of evidence that will surely convict you," Mr. Dodgson said. "Inspector Truscott, Dr. Doyle told me that you found a locked suitcase in Ingram's lodgings but no keys."

"That's true," Truscott said slowly.

"Is it logical to assume that the keys must have been removed by the person who killed Ingram?"

"It's certainly possible."

"I strongly suggest that you search Mr. Chatsworth, and if he does not have the key on his person, that you search his rooms, which, Telling informs me, are on the extreme end of the corridor, looking out over the mews and across the lane. Mr. Chatsworth could easily have observed Ingram's activities and come to certain conclusions. I would prefer to think that you were removing what you considered a blight upon society, Mr. Chatsworth, rather than take the uncharitable view that you might have intended to pursue the career of a blackmailer yourself."

Chatsworth's amiable expression had vanished, replaced by a furtive snarl. "And why should I do that?"

"Younger sons rarely inherit fortunes," Mr. Dodgson commented. "Ingram's grudge was understandable. You, on the other hand, I find most despicable."

Dean Liddell regarded the undergraduate as if he were some species of insect. "I shall have to consider whether this man should be held on criminal charges or expelled. Mr. Chatsworth, you will remain in your rooms until such time as I have consulted with the rest of the Senior Students. Your father will have to be informed, of course."

"But that might kill the poor old chap!" Chatsworth exclaimed.

"You should have thought of that before you picked up that oar and struck Ingram down with it," Mr. Dodgson said severely. "It is given to all of us, Mr. Chatsworth, to face our trials in this life. Your moment came when you saw Ingram go into the water. Miss Laurel will stand her trial in public. You, on the other hand, will have to live the rest of your miserable life with the knowledge that you could have assisted Ingram. Instead, you killed him."

"And a jolly good thing, too," Chatsworth burst out. "I could see him, in his digs, with his box of papers, just gloating over whatever he had. I knew what sort of man he was."

"Then it was your duty to go to the police," Dean Liddell said, with a nod toward Inspector Truscott.

Chatsworth lost some of his bravado. "I couldn't do that, sir. I ask you! What business is it of theirs?"

"Blackmail is our business, young man. Catching criminals is what we're here for," Inspector Truscott reminded him. He turned to Dean Liddell. "And now you've put me in a very nasty spot, sir. I've got a woman in charge who thinks she's killed a man when she didn't, and this young sprout did it and we can't touch him."

Dean Liddell's frown deepened. "I must dine in Hall," he

muttered. "Inspector, you must leave now. I shall inform you of the decision taken by the Senior Students tomorrow."

Chatsworth pouted. "Am I to have no dinner then? I can't very well sit in Hall with everyone glowering at me as if I were a common criminal."

"Telling!" Dean Liddell called out.

The ubiquitous scout edged into the sitting room.

"You may serve Mr. Chatsworth dinner in his rooms," Dean Liddell ordered.

"I have dinner ready to serve here, sir," Telling said stolidly. "Since the lady cannot dine in Hall. I shall instruct one of the scouts to make up a plate for Mr. Chatsworth, if that is your wish."

"I must consult with the rest of the Senior Students," Dean Liddell muttered. He hurried out of the room, leaving Seward to take charge of Chatsworth, and Inspector Truscott to stamp down the stairs in frustration.

CHAPTER 29

N ow we shall have our dinner," Mr. Dodgson announced, as
Telling placed a tureen of soup on the table.

"And you must tell us how you put it all together," Touie said,
as her husband seated her ceremoniously.

"I do not speak while I eat. It avoids choking." Mr. Dodgson
took a spoonful of soup and nodded appreciatively at Telling.
"Quite good."

Telling's face remained impassive, but the flush of pleasure betrayed his emotions. "I could do no less, sir. The honor of the
House demanded that your guests be served a proper dinner."

"Of course. You may continue to serve dinner, Telling."

Dr. Doyle leaned over to his wife. "Are you quite sure you are
up to this, Touie? I can see you back to the White Hart . . ."

"Nonsense!" Touie sipped at her soup. "I was a little shaken,
of course. One does not expect to be choked! But Miss Bell had
her trusty cricket bat and the will to use it. She is a most remarkable young woman."

"As are you!" Dr. Doyle gazed fondly at his wife. Mr. Dodgson
looked pointedly down into his soup.

"Surely you can speak between courses," Touie urged him. "However did you light on that young man, Chatsworth?"

"I did not light on him," Mr. Dodgson said testily. "He was there all along. He was Lord Farlow's friend and knew about his debts. He was instrumental in concocting the verses that were sent to Miss Cahill. He has rooms that overlook St. Aldgates and could easily have overheard Ingram's challenge."

"But did he know about the photograph?" Dr. Doyle asked.

"That, I suspect, was Ingram's contribution to the plot. He knew of the existence of the photograph because Miss Laurel had told him of it when they were, er, intimate. When he saw the verses and learned of the use to which they were to be put, he must have spoken to young Farlow; and the two of them conspired to destroy the reputation, not only of the barrier to the Roswell fortune, but the school as well." Mr. Dodgson stopped speaking and devoted himself to consuming his fish.

Dr. Doyle had no problem eating and talking at the same time. "Then Farlow had Ingram copy the photograph as well as the verses," he said. "Farlow sent Ingram up to Lady Margaret Hall to deliver the packet. I'm surprised that Ingram and Miss Laurel never met."

"Why should they?" Touie said suddenly. "Ingram would have taken good care to keep out of sight, and Miss Laurel is a reclusive sort of person, who does not go out in society. Poor woman, how dreadfully she must have suffered! Having to hide her true identity, watching her manners and her speech, and all for nothing!"

"Her actions when she met with Ingram are understandable but cannot be condoned," Mr. Dodgson. "One cannot go about knocking one's former associates on the head with punt paddles."

"Did she mean to kill him, I wonder?" Touie took another bite of whiting. "This is quite good, Mr. Dodgson."

"I don't know about Ingram, but she certainly meant to kill you," Dr. Doyle said fiercely. "And that, my dear, I will not allow!"

The whiting was removed and another course produced.

"Fowl, sir." Telling offered the chicken, properly carved, and set a small gravy boat on the table.

"What led you to suspect Miss Laurel?" Touie asked, as Telling continued to oversee the meal.

"During our first interview with Miss Cahill and her young friends, Miss Laurel said that Miss Cahill was a pretty and intelligent child. It struck me as an odd remark, coming from one who, to my knowledge, was not acquainted with Miss Cahill before coming to Lady Margaret Hall. It was you, Mrs. Doyle, who gave me the information that led me to suspect that Miss Laurel was not all that she appeared to be. I had not considered the child's maid in my calculations."

Touie blushed pink and glanced at her husband. "Arthur was useful to you, too," she reminded their host.

"Of course. Dr. Doyle's contribution was invaluable. You gave me the facts, sir. Your report led to the conclusion that there were two persons connected with Ingram's death, not one." Mr. Dodgson looked fondly at his young guests.

"I wonder why he did it," Touie said, as Telling signaled the scouts to set up the next course.

"Misplaced loyalty, I expect," Dr. Doyle surmised. "These public school chaps tend to stick together."

"Mr. Chatsworth is the youngest of a large family," Mr. Dodgson said, laying aside his fork. "In fact, his father was up before I was. I recall being told of the athletic exploits of Chatsworth. I was tutor to the eldest Chatsworth son, and there were several daughters as well as the young man who retrieved us from our plight in February, Dr. Doyle. I understand that you, too, are the eldest son in a large family."

Dr. Doyle nodded. "Yes, sir. I have a younger brother and three sisters. My father is . . . unwell. They all depend upon me for support."

Mr. Dodgson sighed. "I know how difficult that can be, Dr. Doyle. I, too, am the eldest son of a large family. My brothers and sisters look to me for guidance and some monetary support. Mr. Chatsworth, on the other hand, has always been the cosseted baby of his family, the runt of the litter, as the farmers say. He is small and dark, in a family of large, fair persons. He has, perhaps, felt like the, er, odd man out, to use a sporting term. His friendship with young Farlow means everything to him. I doubt that it has gone so far as, er, some, but Chatsworth may well have thought it worth the effort to remove Ingram from this earth before he could do more damage to his friend Farlow."

"An altruistic murder!" Touie cried out.

"In a sense," Mr. Dodgson said. "But murder all the same. I cannot approve of Dean Liddell's actions in permitting the boy to go free. Once one has killed, one may kill again."

"Perhaps Mr. Martin will be able to convince his friend to come forward and accept his due punishment," Touie said with a sigh. "He seems like a very sincere young man. Miss Cahill could do much worse for herself."

"I only hope that they will not convince him to join them out of some misplaced loyalty," Mr. Dodgson countered. "I would not like to see a young man's career ruined because of evil companions."

Telling appeared with a plate of small cakes. "Meringues," he said. "The specialty of the House."

"How lovely!" Touie tasted the treat.

"Excellent dinner!" Dr. Doyle was enthusiastic in his praise.

"Thank you, sir." Telling bowed. "We could not let Mr. Dodgson's guests leave thinking that the House was deficient in any respect."

"We shall have our tea in the sitting room." Mr. Dodgson ordered. "And then, Dr. Doyle, you must allow your good lady to rest. She has had a long and strenuous day, and you will have to continue your journey tomorrow."

Dr. Doyle's eye fell on the portfolio spread across Mr. Dodgson's desk. "I see you've been reading my new story," he blurted out.

"Ah, yes." Mr. Dodgson cleared his throat. "I must confess, Dr. Doyle, that yesterday's events preyed upon my mind so much that I could not quite bring myself to get past the first page. However, I assure you that I will read it tonight and present the manuscript to you tomorrow morning before you continue your travels."

"In that case, sir, I will take Touie back to the White Hart so that you can finish it," Dr. Doyle told him.

"I will walk with you, while you enjoy your cigar," Mr. Dodgson offered. "And I will join you for breakfast tomorrow before you must be on your way so that I can return this fascinating tale."

With that, Dr. Doyle had to be satisfied. The Doyles and Mr. Dodgson parted at Tom Gate as the great clock was striking nine, the magic hour by which time all students had to be inside or otherwise accounted for.

Mr. Dodgson bowed courteously to Touie and offered his hand to Dr. Doyle.

"This has been a most memorable visit," he said. "I regret that you did not have the opportunity to continue your research into the events of 1685. If you can come back to Oxford, I shall attempt to find some of the relevant documents for you."

Dr. Doyle knew an apology when he heard one and decided that he, too, could be generous. "And when I do," he promised, "I shall make sure to give you ample warning so that you can arrange for me to read the documents under University supervision."

"And I sincerely hope that the next time we come to Oxford there will not be any nasty murders," Touie told her husband, as they crossed the road to the White Hart.

Across Oxford, the day's activities were discussed and rehashed, over tea, coffee, port, and sherry.

In the Senior Common Room at Christ Church, Mr. Dodgson was forced to listen to his colleagues' rambling discourse, while he went over the chain of logic he had built up. Was Dean Liddell right to let Chatsworth escape the gallows he so richly deserved simply because he was the son of a peer? Chatsworth had not planned to murder Ingram, but he had taken advantage of an opportunity given to him by a distraught woman, who would undoubtedly suffer for her crime.

"Ah, Dodgson." Dean Liddell stood before him, sherry in hand. "I trust Dr. and Mrs. Doyle enjoyed their dinner?"

Mr. Dodgson nodded. "I felt that since last night's dinner was quite spoilt by Ingram's defection, I should remedy the situation by offering another dinner in its place. Telling was of the same mind. We cannot allow guests to leave the House with a bad impression of our hospitality."

"Nice young fellow, Doyle." Vere Bayne came up to join the conversation. "A trifle pugnacious, but those Scots are, I believe. Doctor, you said?"

"Yes. And a writer as well," Mr. Dodgson hastened to assure his friends that he had not sunk so low in the social scale as to hobnob with a mere general practitioner. "In fact, I must now leave you and continue reading his latest work. It is a most ingenious piece of fiction."

"Fiction?" Vere Bayne's bushy eyebrows signaled his astonishment at the eminent mathematician slumming, intellectually speaking.

"Of a very unusual order," Mr. Dodgson said. "I suspect we shall be hearing more from Dr. Doyle very shortly. Good evening."

Mr. Dodgson hurried back to his rooms. He had promised to read this story, and he never went back on his word. He sat down at his desk, adjusted the lamp to the most effective angle, and picked up the manuscript from where he had laid it down the previous night.

He was soon engrossed in the story. The doctor had taken rooms with a most peculiar fellow, who did chemistry experiments in the sitting room, shot holes in the walls, took drugs, and had very odd friends. Eventually, the doctor and his friend were requested to attend the scene of a murder.

Mr. Dodgson did not approve of murder as a subject for recreational reading, but this story was no hodgepodge of mysticism and fantasy. Instead, the tale was set in modern London, and the characters were ordinary people. Mr. Dodgson bent over the manuscript, totally wrapped up in this tale of deduction and revenge.

It was only when he heard a series of shouts from the quad that he came out of the enthrallment of the story.

"What is going on?" Mr. Dodgson called out.

"Someone's fallen out a window," came the reply.

"Dear me!" Mr. Dodgson hurried down to the quad, where scouts, students, and dons were clustered around the lane next to the mortuary.

"Let me through!" Mr. Dodgson shouldered his way around the crowd.

There was no need for anyone to call for assistance. The group parted to allow the Dean to march unimpeded to the fallen student.

Minnie Chatsworth lay on the ground, groaning, with Constable Effingham triumphantly standing over him.

"Mr. Chatsworth," Dean Liddell said, in his most awe-inspiring tone, "what are you doing there?"

Gregory Martin leaned out the upper window. "He was, er, doing a bunk," the prospective vicar explained.

"I couldn't wait for you to send me down," Chatsworth said, teeth clenched against the pain. "I thought I could get out. I've done it before. Can't think why I slipped this time."

Mr. Dodgson was examining the thick ivy that covered the ancient wall like a living tapestry. "The rain has left this ivy quite slick and slippery," he said. "Rather like yourself, Mr. Chatsworth. I had thought better of you."

"If undergraduates are using this ivy as a means of exit, I shall have the ivy removed," the Dean decided. He turned to the uniformed constable. "Who are you, and what are you doing here?"

"I saw this-yer chap comin' down the walls," Constable Effingham stated. "Bein' stationed here to watch the premises, I accosted this-yer individual."

"He startled me, and I fell down," Chatsworth said.

Dr. Kitchin pushed through the crowd of chattering students and bent over the fallen undergraduate. "Broken collarbone," he announced, with a twist of his lips that expressed his opinion of undergraduates so clumsy as to fall off the ivy when they were trying to get in or out without being seen.

"Best take him to Radcliffe Infirmary," Dean Liddell ordered. "Constable, you may inform Inspector Truscott that after due consideration, I shall not impede the cause of justice. Mr.

Chatsworth, you may consider yourself under arrest. Telling, what is it?"

The chief scout approached deferentially. "I have taken the liberty of sending to Radcliffe Infirmary, sir. An ambulance wagon should be here momentarily."

The aforesaid ambulance arrived in a few minutes. Two burly orderlies carried off the slender body of the undergraduate, while the college as a whole chattered in wonder.

In the upper rooms, Nevil Farlow and Gregory Martin looked at each other and shook their heads.

"Poor chap." Martin sighed. "I had no idea he was so devoted to you, Nev."

"Devoted?" Farlow snarled. "He clung to me like a leech! Ever since Eton . . . I say, Greg, what can I do about Miss Cahill?"

"I intend to call on Miss Cahill tomorrow at Lady Margaret Hall to see if she is all right. If you like, I can offer your regrets at having put her to so much inconvenience." Martin adjusted his spectacles.

"I mean, about the, er, squib."

"Best forgotten, old chap. The least said about that, the better." With which comforting thought, Mr. Martin left his old playmate and schoolfellow to compose a letter that would at one time exonerate himself from all blame in the matter and suggest that Miss Cahill use her good influence with the wealthy Mr. Roswell so that some of that wealth might find its way into the pockets of Lord Nevil Farlow.

At Lady Margaret Hall, Miss Wordsworth's arrival was greeted with shrill cries for further information.

"Where is Miss Laurel?"

"Did she really attack Mrs. Doyle?"

"Is it true that she was never a governess at all?"

Miss Wordsworth wearily removed her hat and allowed her subordinate to lead her to the dinner table, where some cold chicken and hot tea awaited her.

"Miss Laurel has been arrested," Miss Wordsworth informed

her students. "She has confessed to attacking James Ingram, the man whose body was found behind Christ Church last night."

"But why?" That was Gertrude Bell, in front of the pack.

"It seems they were previously acquainted. Miss Laurel was originally in menial service, and this Ingram person was threatening to expose her as a fraud."

"How dreadful!" Miss Johnson exclaimed, but it was hard to say whether she was more upset about Ingram's threats or Miss Laurel's previous servile status.

"I have sent for my solicitor to find adequate representation for her," Miss Wordsworth said. "We can do no less."

"Of course not!" Gertrude declared.

"And to think I didn't even recognize her!" Dianna wailed.

"The unfortunate woman," Mary added.

"We must stand by her," Gertrude said stoutly.

"Of course we shall," Miss Wordsworth decreed. "But I suggest that you young ladies retire to your own rooms. It is quite late, and it has been a most exhausting day."

Miss Johnson shooed the girls upstairs and returned to find Miss Wordsworth in her sitting room, her head in her hands.

"I blame myself for this," the older woman moaned. "I should have been more careful. I should not have taken Miss Laurel at her word."

"You had no way of knowing," Miss Johnson said, patting Miss Wordsworth's hand. "We all accepted her."

"The question is, how can we keep the name of Lady Margaret Hall out of the gutter press? It was hard enough to get the University to permit our girls to attend lectures and receive tutorials before this happened. Now . . ." Miss Wordsworth let her hands sketch a large question mark in the air.

Miss Johnson frowned. "Perhaps, if you could have a word with the magistrate, we could convince Miss Laurel to plead to a lesser charge, such as assault and battery, rather than murder. She would serve a prison term, I suppose, and there would be less sensational nonsense in the press."

Miss Wordsworth took a deep breath, wiped her eyes, and gave her second-in-command a watery smile. "That is exactly what I shall do, Elizabeth," she said. "And now, I shall have another cup of tea."

Inspector Truscott was almost ready to return to his own family when he got the news that Herman Chatsworth had been caught while trying to escape and had been transported to the Radcliffe Infirmary with a broken collarbone.

"And there he will stay," Truscott said grimly. "Let's see his noble father get his son out of this mess!"

"He'll try," Sergeant Everett said gloomily.

"That he will," Inspector Truscott said. "But the college has clearly washed its hands of the boy by putting him into hospital. Murder's no college prank, and this Chatsworth's gone his length. He'll stand his trial like everyone else."

"And pigs may fly," Everett said quietly, as he watched the Inspector marching out the door.

CHAPTER 30

The rain of the previous night had left Oxford cleansed and ready for another spring day. Dr. Doyle and his wife dealt with the minutiae of leaving the venerable White Hart Inn, while Mr. Dodgson waited for them in the breakfast room, where chafing dishes had been set up on a long table.

He greeted them with a bow and handed Dr. Doyle the precious manuscript, neatly tied in its portfolio.

"Thank you for reading it, sir," Dr. Doyle said, accepting the pasteboard portfolio.

"I was kept up all night," Mr. Dodgson admitted. "A very interesting tale, well-presented, and quite logical. Except for the central portion, which seems to me to be beside the point."

"But that provides the motive for the murder," Dr. Doyle argued.

"A love story set in the past?" Mr. Dodgson looked up as a waiter filled his cup with coffee.

"As we have seen ourselves, sir, events in the past tend to have long-reaching effects," Dr. Doyle reminded him.

"And I cannot entirely approve of the element of taking drugs.

It is a dreadful vice. Some of our more adventurous undergraduates have indulged in it. I, myself, was once accused of experimenting with cannabis, due to the illustration Tenniel put into *Alice's Adventures in Wonderland* showing the Caterpillar and the hookah."

Dr. Doyle explained, "There have been a number of experiments made with cocaine . . ."

"Not upon your person, I sincerely hope!" Mr. Dodgson exclaimed.

Touie had provided her husband with a plate of eggs and toast. Now she sat down and attacked her own breakfast. "What will happen to that poor woman?" she asked, to forestall any more exchanges between the two men that might lead to additional misunderstandings.

"She will go before the magistrate today," Mr. Dodgson explained. "Miss Wordsworth has offered to see to her defense, and I am sure Miss Laurel will be properly represented."

"And that dreadful young man?" Touie had no sympathy for Minnie Chatsworth.

"That is another matter," Mr. Dodgson said. "Last night he attempted to leave the House through the window. He lost his grip on the ivy and fell."

"Not to his death?" Touie gasped.

"Oh, no," Mr. Dodgson assured her. "He merely broke his collarbone, an accident quite common among undergraduates. He was taken to Radcliffe Infirmary, where he is now under police guard."

Dr. Doyle considered the fate of young Chatsworth. "Is he to stand his trial?"

Mr. Dodgson took a deep breath. "That, of course, is difficult to say. His father is, after all, a well-known member of the House of Lords, and his older brother is Undersecretary to the Home Secretary. They may well feel that it would be best if their young son and brother should not air the family linen, as it were. I suspect that Mr. Chatsworth may find himself on a ship to America or Australia quite soon."

Dr. Doyle frowned into his coffee cup. "I don't like it," he pronounced. "Poor Miss Laurel, or Lowell, or whoever she is, will go to prison, while this young sprig goes free."

"I do not think he will ever be quite free," Mr. Dodgson said. "He has lost the respect of his friends and comrades, and there will always be a shadow over his reputation that will be difficult for him to overcome."

"Arthur," Touie reminded her husband, "we shall miss our train!"

Dr. Doyle gathered up his manuscript and offered his hand to Mr. Dodgson, who shook it gravely.

"Good-bye, Dr. Doyle. It has been a most . . . interesting visit."

"I hope I was of some help, sir."

"You were indeed, Dr. Doyle."

"Perhaps you will advise me on some other stories?" Dr. Doyle hinted.

"Oh, no," Mr. Dodgson said. "I think you will do far better on your own, Dr. Doyle."

"I was thinking," Dr. Doyle said, as Touie urged him toward their waiting cab, "that I might sign myself slightly differently. I noted that many of your scholars use two names instead of one, as in Mr. Vere Bayne. Perhaps I should insist on my name appearing as A. Conan Doyle?"

"It would be quite distinctive."

"Arthur! The cab is waiting!"

Once more the two men shook hands and bowed. "I think you should send your story around to several publishers," Mr. Dodgson advised. "It is bound to find a place; and when it does, I venture to say that the tables will be turned, and my old friend will be known as A. Conan Doyle's uncle."

AFTERWORD

M iss Daphne Laurel, born Daisy Lowell, was convicted of aggravated assault upon the person of James Ingram and sentenced to fifteen years at hard labor. She was a model prisoner, assisting in the prison school, and was paroled after only seven years. She continued to teach inmates, becoming known as the Prison Angel, until her death in 1914.

Further investigation into the activities of James Ingram regarding the contents of his suitcase and the attempt to influence the Eights Week boat races was blocked by an influential group of well-connected gentlemen, some of whom were close to His Royal Highness, the Prince of Wales.

Mr. Herman "Minnie" Chatsworth was held at the Radcliffe Infirmary pending his arraignment. Before he could be presented to the magistrate, Lord Digby had his son removed from the hospital, insisting that the boy should be treated at home. He was then put onto the next ship leaving for America to join his maternal uncle in Wyoming. He never got to the ranch, preferring to live by his wits and charm instead. He eluded the police of several major cities, while operating as a jewel thief, card sharp, and swindler, until he learned of the deaths of his older brothers' sons in World War I. Thinking that he could now claim his inheritance as the last of the Digbys, he sailed for England on the *Lusitania*. He is presumed to have been among those drowned when the ship was sunk.

Mr. Nevil Farlow left Oxford in disgrace. However, when he explained the circumstances, his mother was completely sympathetic and thought the verses were very amusing (if a trifle strong). She showed them to one of her old friends, who asked if the young man could come up with more. Nevil Farlow found himself much in demand as a creator of lyrics for music hall ditties. When his father died in 1895, Lord Nevil Berwick shocked London society by marrying the young lady best known for singing his ballads, Miss Cecilia "Cissie" Huntingdon. They produced several theatrical shows and three children, including a daughter who eventually was educated at Lady Margaret Hall.

Mr. Gregory Martin was duly ordained in the autumn of 1886. He and Miss Dianna Cahill were married the following year. They lived a long and happy life together, during which he served as vicar of several different parishes, and she worked cheerfully alongside him.

Mr. Dodgson gave several lectures on logic at Lady Margaret Hall. He also published the facsimile version of the original *Alice's Adventures Underground* in 1886.

Dr. Doyle copied out his story (now titled *A Study in Scarlet*) and sent it to several magazine editors who had previously accepted his writings. They found various flaws in the story and refused to publish it. He did not give up but sent it out again . . . but that is another story.

HISTORICAL NOTES

Henry George Liddell was the dean of Christ Church from 1855 to 1891. Mr. Dodgson's friendship with the dean's children is well-known, especially since it resulted in the two great works of fantasy, *Alice's Adventures in Wonderland* and *Through the Looking-Glass*. However, the two men were often at odds over college policy, and the relationship became even more strained when Mrs. Liddell decided that Mr. Dodgson's attentions to her daughter were becoming too particular.

Alice Liddell married Maj. Reginald Hargreaves in 1880. Mr. Dodgson did not correspond with her until 1885, when he asked if he might transcribe the book he made for her twenty years before through a new photographic process, zinc facsimile. Mrs. Hargreaves loaned the book, which was photographed and then returned to her. Through a long set of circumstances, the book was sold several times and eventually was given to the British Museum, where it is now on display for all to see.

Reginald Fairclough, Dr. Vere Bayne, Mr. Barclay Thompson, and Dr. Kitchin were all senior students in 1886. Telling was the chief steward in charge of the Senior Common Room; Seward was proctor, in charge of keeping the students in order (rowdy teenagers are difficult to handle at the best of times).

Miss Elizabeth Wordsworth was the founder and lady principal of Lady Margaret Hall, one of the first two colleges for women at Oxford, the other being Somerville. St. Hilda's College was added as a residence for less affluent students.

Gertrude Bell became a well-known explorer, archaeologist, and shaper of Middle East policy. Mary Talbot worked in settlement houses until she died at a relatively young age of complications in childbirth.

The Covered Market is one of the major attractions of central Oxford. The statue of Mercury had been removed early in the nineteenth century and was not replaced until after the time of this story. Vincent's is still there, on a side street just north of Christ Church.

Mr. Dodgson and Dr. Doyle never met. The events of this story are meant to be read as fiction.

ACKNOWLEDGMENTS

I consulted several biographies of Charles Lutwidge Dodgson to get the information for this story. In particular, I recommend:

Cohen, Morton. *Lewis Carroll: A biography*. New York: Viking, 1995.

Stoffel, Stephanie Lovett. *Lewis Carroll in Wonderland: The life and times of Alice and her creator*. New York: Abrams Discoveries, 1993.

Jones, Jo Elwyn, and J. Francis Gladstone. *The Alice Companion: A guide to Lewis Carroll's Alice books*. New York: Macmillan Press, 1998.

Information about Miss Elizabeth Wordsworth and Lady Margaret Hall came from: Battiscome, Georgia. *Reluctant Pioneer, a life of Elizabeth Wordsworth*. Constable & Co., 1978.

I am also deeply indebted to Mr. Fred Wharton, chief custodian at Christ Church, who gave me the full "Lewis Carroll" tour; and Ms. Joelle Hoggan of Lady Margaret Hall, who arranged for me to tour the gardens with a stalwart young undergraduate.

And, as always, I must thank three people who are always there for me: my ever-helpful editor, Keith Kahla; my enthusiastic agent, Cherry Weiner; and my husband, Murray Rogow, without whom none of this would have been possible.